A GOLDEN GRAVE

A GOLDEN GRAVE

A ROSE GALLAGHER MYSTERY

ERIN LINDSEY

MINOTAUR BOOKS

NEW YORK

First published in the United States by Minotaur Books, an imprint of St. Martin's Publishing Group

A GOLDEN GRAVE. Copyright © 2019 by Erin Lindsey. All rights reserved. Printed in the United States of America. For information, address St. Martin's Publishing Group, 120 Broadway, New York, N.Y. 10271.

www.minotaurbooks.com

Designed by Omar Chaps

Map by Emily Langmade

The Library of Congress Cataloging-in-Publication Data is available upon request.

ISBN 978-1-250-18067-4 (trade paperback)
ISBN 978-1-250-62092-7 (hardcover)
ISBN 978-1-250-18068-1 (ebook)

Our books may be purchased in bulk for promotional, educational, or business use. Please contact your local bookseller or the Macmillan Corporate and Premium Sales Department at 1-800-221-7945, extension 5442, or by email at MacmillanSpecialMarkets@macmillan.com.

First Edition: September 2019

10 9 8 7 6 5 4 3 2 1

This book is dedicated to the legions of amateur historians who so generously share their passion and knowledge with the rest of us via their blogs, websites, podcasts, and books. Novels like this wouldn't be possible without you.

ACKNOWLEDGMENTS

So much goes into researching a book like this that it would be impossible to individually acknowledge every resource. A few, however, merit particular mention. In addition to those I noted in the acknowledgments of *Murder on Millionaires' Row*, which I continue to draw upon regularly, I'm especially indebted to Edmund Morris's *The Rise of Theodore Roosevelt* and Margaret Cheney's *Tesla: Man Out of Time*. I also drew upon Mark Twain's autobiography, which, like everything he wrote, sparkled with wit.

I'm grateful to Lyndsay Faye, Tasha Alexander, and Mary Robinette Kowal for their kind support, which means the world to me; to everyone at Minotaur, but especially Sarah Schoof and Allison Ziegler, who've been so helpful and dynamic; to my outgoing editor, April Osborn, who provided such a strong steer for *A Golden Grave* and *Murder on Millionaires' Row*, and to my incoming editor, Nettie Finn, for bringing new energy and enthusiasm to the series. And special thanks as always to my hard-working agents, Lisa Rodgers and Joshua Bilmes, and to my husband, Don, for his unwavering support.

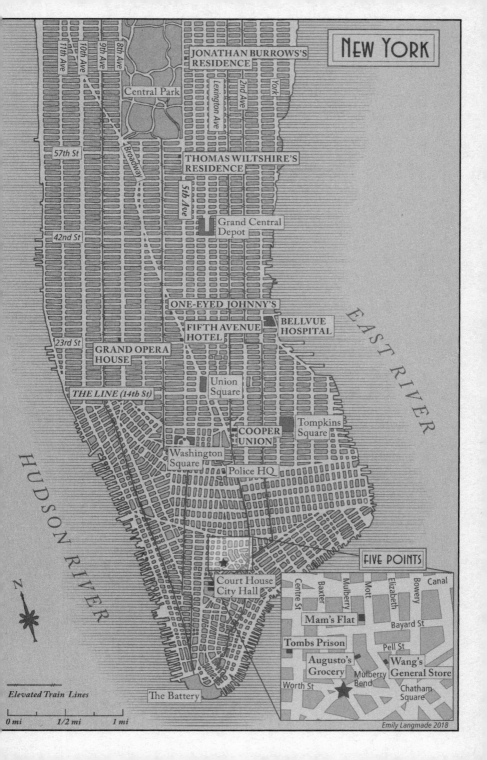

A GOLDEN GRAVE

CHAPTER 1

ROSE GALLAGHER OF THE PINKERTON
DETECTIVE AGENCY—THE ART OF
FALLING—NOVICES OF NEWPORT

The way the yellow-back novels tell it, being a female detective is full of flash and breathless adventure. To look at the covers, you'd be hard pressed to think of a more glamorous vocation: sly, svelte heroines smoking cigarettes and toting Colt revolvers, bursting onto murder scenes with petticoats billowing. Well, trust me, the real thing isn't like that at all. I tried my hand with a Colt .45, but it was much too heavy. I don't smoke, I'm more skinny than svelte, and my skirts are distinctly not of the billowing variety. As for glamour, well . . . it's hard to look glamorous when you're being thrown face-first to the floor.

I should know. By the autumn of 1886, I'd had plenty of practice.

If you'd told me back in January that I would be learning jujitsu, I'd have laughed, mostly because I'd never heard the word *jujitsu.* A humble housemaid from Five Points doesn't have much occasion to acquaint herself with Japanese martial arts, no matter how devotedly she studies *Harper's Weekly*. Of course, she has even less occasion to learn about ghosts, or shades or fae, or half a hundred other things collectively known as *the paranormal*. Your average housemaid, like the vast majority of New Yorkers, goes through her whole life without ever knowing such things exist. As for me, I'd learned about them only recently, and my world had never been the same.

For the most part I was grateful for that, but every now and then I found myself pining for the simple days when I was just Rose the Maid, scrubbing floors and mending linens. Back when Thomas Wiltshire was my employer instead of my partner; before he asked me to join him at the special branch of the Pinkerton National Detective Agency and spend my time chasing after all things paranormal.

Back when it never would have occurred to him to throw me to the floor like a sack of dirty linens.

On the morning in question—the day all the trouble started—he'd done it twice already, and I'd had about enough.

"Don't worry, Miss Gallagher," he said, "it's early days yet." And he offered me a hand, which is as close to being gentlemanly as it's possible to get when you've just tossed a lady onto her face.

Except it wasn't early days, not anymore. After eight solid months of training, I ought to have been able to last more than ten seconds against my sparring partner, even if he was the instructor. Though to be fair, it didn't help that I still couldn't come within five feet of Thomas Wiltshire without feeling a little weak in the knees, which is something of a disadvantage in hand-to-hand combat.

"It's terribly frustrating, I know," he said as he pulled me to my feet, "but don't be discouraged. I spent the better part of my first six months in Japan on my backside. You'll get there."

And without further ado, he grabbed my wrist, swept my ankles, and we both went down. He landed on top of me, pinning me beneath him. His face hovered barely an inch above mine, the press of his body so close that I could practically feel his heartbeat against my own flesh.

"Good," he said brightly.

It took me a moment to find my voice. "H-How is this good?"

"You landed brilliantly. Falling properly is half the battle."

I'd fallen properly, and no mistake.

There was a long pause. Thomas made no move to release me, apparently oblivious to the scandalous disposition of our persons. Then: "Are you going to try to break free?"

"Yes, of course." A furious blush warmed my face. "That is, I should have, but—"

"But the moment's rather passed." He rolled gracefully to his feet. "Next time. In any case, I suppose we ought to adjourn. We'll need you in top shape tonight."

I hauled myself up and set to righting my disheveled clothing. Try as I might, I simply could not get used to trousers, even the white cotton ones we used for training. They were forever becoming twisted up around my legs, and it was impossible to look dignified wearing them. Not that there was anything dignified about me that morning. Even my carefully pinned hair had come undone, leaving wisps of strawberry blond poking out in all directions.

"Shall I fetch us some water?" Thomas headed for the washstand, leaving me alone with the handful of other new recruits gathered around the tumbling mat for the morning lesson. I tried to busy myself with repinning my hair, but I was painfully aware of their gazes. We were few in the special branch—barely more than a dozen in the entire country, nearly half of whom were new recruits like me—but even so, there was always an audience for my humiliation.

"Well done with the falling, Miss Gallagher," Cabot Fisk drawled. "It's important to have a specialty." A ripple of amusement went through the group of gentlemen, though most were too well bred to laugh out loud.

"And here I thought my specialty was fieldwork," I said, and had the satisfaction of watching Fisk's expression curdle. At the moment, I was the only first-year recruit on active field duty, which went a long way to explaining the chilly reception I'd had from my peers. At least, that was what I told myself.

"Here we are." Thomas reappeared with a cup of water. "Now, you gentlemen will get along fine without us?"

Fisk gave a crisp nod. "Admirably, sir, thank you."

"Excellent. Mr. Murray, you'll take over as lead. Please observe the proceedings carefully—I'll want a full account later. Miss Gallagher, shall we?"

I held my head high in retreat, but I could feel their eyes following us out of the hall.

"You're still trying to counter me," Thomas was saying as we walked. "Rather, try to use my momentum against me. That way, strength and weight become irrelevant . . ." And so on, but I wasn't really listening. All I wanted was to get out of that training hall—a repurposed ballroom, actually—away from the whispers and judging eyes, and take a nice long soak in the porcelain tub in my bathroom.

Yes, you read that right. *My own bathroom.* You had to hand it to the special branch: They'd spared no expense when it came to grooming their new crop of agents. The Queen Anne "cottage" they'd leased as a training facility sprawled over a verdant expanse of Ochre Point, one of Newport's most eligibly situated communities. It boasted fifty rooms, including a library, music hall, billiard room, and something called a *conservatory*, which was stuffed with so many potted ferns that it resembled a small outpost of the Amazon. There were tennis courts, stables, a shooting range, and ample gardens. Best of all, each guest chamber was equipped with *its own bathroom*, a luxury I'd taken full advantage of. I'd thought it was a step up trading the communal privies in Mam's tenement for the shared servants' bathroom in Thomas Wiltshire's Fifth Avenue row house. But private guest bathrooms—why, even Mr. Burrows, who was rich as a Rockefeller, was astonished to hear of it.

Of course, none of this opulence was for our benefit. It just provided a convenient disguise for the true nature of the training facility, which, like everything else about the special branch, was a closely guarded secret. Here in Ochre Point, we could hide in plain sight, blending in amongst the Boston Brahmins and New York Knickerbockers at play. Riding, shooting, archery—the silk-stocking pastimes of the East Coast aristocracy provided the perfect cover for all manner of weapons training. To the casual observer, our little band of novice agents would appear to be nothing more than a group of wealthy vacationers. And if we kept to ourselves—well, our blue-blooded neighbors were only too happy to keep their distance from the vulgar nouveaux riches.

Luxurious as it was, though, I'd had my fill of it—the theoretical classes, the etiquette lessons, the infernal jujitsu. Most of all, the inescapable feeling that I was a disappointment to Thomas, who'd vouched for me so staunchly.

"Rose." He touched my arm, drawing me up short. As my partner, Thomas could take such liberties—an intimacy that also allowed him to guess my thoughts. "Try not to be so hard on yourself," he said. "These things don't come easily to anyone."

"Are you sure about that?" I kept my gaze on the parquet floor, unable to meet his eye. "The others seem to manage just fine."

"That's hardly a fair comparison. Those gentlemen are all accomplished athletes. Cabot Fisk was a champion boxer at Yale. Lawrence Murray wrestled for Columbia, and Archibald Rennington gives fencing lessons at the Pewter Club. On top of which, the mere fact that they're—"

"Men?"

"I was going to say *lucky*."

He didn't just mean fortunate, I knew. In the exclusive, highly secretive circles of the paranormal community, *luck* meant something very specific: a breed of extraordinary abilities possessed by a tiny fraction of the population. A tiny fraction of the *general* population, that is; around here, it seemed like every other person was gifted. After all, who better to handle cases involving luck than those who were lucky themselves? Even so . . . "I don't see how extraordinary eyesight or an exceptional mind for numbers is a great advantage at jujitsu."

"So the martial arts are not your forte. You have other gifts, Rose."

"Yes, I'm told that I fall brilliantly."

He smiled. "Mark my words, you will be one of the Agency's most valuable assets. Sharpe has great faith in you."

"Mr. Sharpe?" I hadn't seen the head of the special branch since he'd agreed to hire me back in January. As far as I knew, he'd been in Chicago ever since, doing whatever it is lucky, high-ranking Pinkertons do. "Why should he have faith in me?"

"Because I do."

I glanced up, meeting his gaze at last. Those eyes . . . pale blue and flecked with green, full of warmth and intelligence and curiosity and all the things I loved about Thomas Wiltshire . . . they always threatened to undo me. "I'm grateful," I murmured, distracted by a brief but vivid fantasy of showing him just how grateful.

"No gratitude necessary. We are partners, are we not? Now, we'd better get on if we're to make the city by sunset. Jackson won't thank us for being late."

I groaned inwardly. Another weekend chasing shades all over New York. We'd been at it since January—Thomas and I, along with Mr. Jackson, a senior agent and powerful necromancer—and I'd had about enough. A year ago, the very idea of hunting roaming spirits of the dead would have sent a shiver of dread down my spine. But after so many months, the task threatened to become as monotonous as scrubbing floors. A higher risk of death, certainly, but even that had lost much of its bite. I guess there are only so many times you can worry about the touch of a dead person stopping your heart before the thrill wears off.

Thomas saw it all in my expression. "I know, I've grown weary of it as well. But we're nearly through, and just think of all we've achieved. How many spirits we've helped to find peace, not to mention how many of the living we've kept from harm. Every time we restore one of those spirits to the otherworld—"

"I know. I'm just tired, that's all. Do I have time for a bath?" The thought of sinking into that warm, scented water brought a pang to my aching muscles.

Thomas reached instinctively for his Patek Philippe, only to remember that he was still wearing his jujitsu whites. "Blast. My watch is upstairs. But if we leave in an hour or so, we should have plenty of time."

"That'll do," I said, and started up the staircase.

We parted ways on the landing, Thomas turning left for the men's quarters while I headed right for the women's—which I very nearly had to myself, there being only four women in the special branch. One of those four passed me in the corridor, and her gaze was not friendly.

"Was it you who left the windows open last night?" Viola Fox asked, without so much as a how-do-you-do. I guess she figured that since she was an instructor and I a mere novice, she didn't owe me even the basic pleasantries.

"I-It was, yes, ma'am. My room is right above the kitchens, you see, and—"

"I fairly froze to death. It is *October*, you know."

"I'm sorry," I said instinctively, though I really wasn't. Why should I make any effort to please this woman when she could barely trouble herself to be civil? Whatever I'd done to offend her, she seemed intent on holding it against me forever more, even if that meant inventing silly complaints like open windows.

"Do try to consider others next time, Miss Gallagher," she said, and swept past.

I stayed where I was, drawing one steadying breath after another. *It's almost over*, I told myself. *Just a few more weeks*. After that, the new agents would disperse—to Washington, Boston, San Francisco, every place deemed important by the Pinkerton National Detective Agency. Even Mr. Jackson would head back to Chicago, and then it would just be Thomas and me, the only two agents of the special branch permanently assigned to New York. How I longed for that day.

But in the meantime, there was a job to be done, so with a rueful sigh, I headed back to my room and started packing my trunk for the train ride back to New York. We had shades to catch.

CHAPTER 2

OF HACKS AND HANSOM CABS—PEAS IN A POD—A CONVENTIONAL MURDER

We arrived in the city a few minutes after sunset. A cold gray drizzle drifted down over Grand Central Depot, polishing the paving stones to a high gloss. Gentlemen hunkered under their umbrellas, ladies burrowed deeper into their fur tippets, and horses blew out plumes of steam under the glow of the gaslight. I pulled my own shawl more tightly about my shoulders, casting a despondent look at the hack stand—deserted, of course, it being nigh on impossible to get a cab in the rain in New York—but I needn't have worried. As usual, Thomas had planned ahead.

"That's us, I believe," he said, steering me toward a carriage painted in the distinctive yellow of the New York Cab Company.

"A coach." I shivered with relief at the sight of its snugly enclosed confines. "Thank goodness. I don't think I'd have managed a hansom cab in this weather."

"My dear Rose, when have you ever known me to take a hansom cab? I'd rather walk."

Plenty of New Yorkers felt the same, but I was surprised to hear an Englishman say so. "I thought hansoms were all the rage in London."

"There are few subjects upon which I take the American view of things, but on the matter of two-wheeled carriages, they certainly have the right of it." He opened the door and offered a hand up, and I ducked gratefully inside.

It was a short ride to 726 Fifth Avenue, and we arrived to the wonderful aroma of Clara's cooking. Somehow, in spite of all the extra duties Clara had to contend with since being appointed housekeeper and overall manager of Thomas Wiltshire's household, the quality of the dishes she turned out had only improved. With her typical modesty, she'd put it down to giving herself a more generous budget for ingredients, but I knew the truth: It was a sign that she was happy.

I went down to the kitchen and hugged her in greeting. "What's cooking? It smells incredible."

"Bouillabaisse."

"Bouillabaisse," I echoed wonderingly, peering under the lid of a simmering stockpot. "How exotic!"

"About as exotic as fish soup. It only sounds fancy 'cause it's French."

"Well, it was obviously a lot of work." Scraps littered every surface of the kitchen, and the apron wrapped around her petite form was as spotted as a pinto pony. She even had flour in her braids.

"It'll warm your bones, anyway." Clara went back to kneading dough for her famous biscuits, her fine-boned hands a blur of practiced motion. "Been like this for days. Can't say I'm ready for winter."

"I am," I said with a bit too much feeling.

She eyed me sidelong. "That the Irish in you, or ain't you having much fun out there in champagne country?"

"You know perfectly well which it is. I've done nothing but complain about it for weeks."

"Don't I know it."

"One of the privileges of being my best friend."

Clara gave me a wry look but otherwise let that pass. "If it makes you so miserable, why do you keep going back?"

"It's not as if I have a choice. The Agency has put a lot of resources into this first big expansion of the special branch. They want to make sure we're well trained."

"I don't see where shooting arrows and jumping little fences with your horse is much use. This ain't Camelot."

She had a point. Learning to fire a pistol or throw a punch was one thing, but it was hard to see how horseback riding and dancing the waltz came into it. "The worst of it is, I'm starting to wonder if any of it will be useful. These past few months, what we've been doing . . . what if that's all there is to the job?"

"I thought you liked all this ghost business?"

"Shades."

"Come again?"

"Ghosts are projections of spirits from the otherworld," I said, reflexively reciting from *Pullman's Guide to the Paranormal*, the little handbook we'd been given as a reference. "Whereas shades are still tied to the physical world. They're similar, but not the same."

Clara planted a flour-coated hand on her hip. "Why, thank you. It's a good thing you straightened me out. I might've gone my whole life without knowing the difference, and then where would I be?"

"Sorry," I said with a guilty laugh. "Habit. Between the

training and the shade-hunting, it's hard to remember what it was like before we knew any of these things existed. Back when life was—"

"Normal?" She sprinkled another pinch of flour on her dough. "Ain't hard for me. Tell the truth, I'm half sorry I learned about any of it. All this keeping secrets . . . Feels like I'm keeping part of my life locked away from my family. From Joseph, especially. Ain't right, keeping things from your fiancé. On top of which, the whole business gives me the jimjams. I liked it better when ghosts and magic was nothing but children's stories."

"I know what you mean."

There must have been something in my voice, because Clara paused, dusting flour from her hands. "What's wrong, honey? Something happen out there?"

"Nothing that hasn't happened a hundred times before. I humiliated myself in jujitsu, and the other recruits—"

Clara clucked her tongue impatiently. "Weren't you the one said they was just jealous 'cause you already out there doing the real work?"

"But that's hardly my fault. Thomas only needs me because I can sense shades." I'd been able to do it ever since the incident at Hell Gate, when a fragment of a spirit had become embedded in my body. It had nearly killed me, and when we'd finally found a way to banish it, I discovered that I could still sense it when shades were nearby. Even if they were invisible, a shiver down my spine would always warn me of their presence. Handy if you were in the business of hunting down escaped spirits of the dead, but otherwise . . . "Hardly something to wish for."

"Maybe it ain't what you're doing they're envious of, but who you're doing it with."

"Meaning?"

"Didn't you tell me there was lots of folks lining up to be Mr. Wiltshire's partner, and now here you are stepping in? Maybe you're stepping on some toes while you're at it."

"I don't see how they can blame me for that."

"Rose, Rose." Clara shook her head. "And you a detective and all."

I started to ask what she meant, but just then Thomas appeared on the stairs. "Good evening, Clara. Supper smells wonderful."

"It's ready if you are, unless you're dying for biscuits."

"Excellent. Jackson has just arrived. Shall we, Rose?"

"I'll be right there." I blew out a sigh as I watched him head up the stairs. "Another day, another shade."

"You could always come back to work here," Clara said, gesturing vaguely at the kitchen.

She was joking, of course. Clara knew better than anybody how unhappy I'd been as a housemaid. "Thanks for the offer," I said dryly, "but I'd feel terrible about displacing the new girl. How's she working out, by the way?"

"Who, Miss I Don't Work Weekends?"

"Poor Louise. You're being unfair. That was Thomas's idea, remember? To keep her out from underfoot?" The strategy had largely worked. With Thomas and me away at Newport most of the week, we rarely crossed paths with my replacement.

"If he hadn't asked for it, she would have, believe you me. Thinks about as much of this job as you did."

"Oh, dear." I laughed. "Now I really do feel sorry for her."

Clara eyed me pointedly. "Maybe you oughta remember that next time you're fixing to complain about your new job. Now get on upstairs. Don't wanna keep Mr. Wiltshire waiting."

"And Mr. Jackson."

She made a face. "That one can eat his soup cold for all I care."

I *tsk*ed. "Why do you dislike him so? I thought for sure you'd get along."

"Why, 'cause we're both colored?"

"Of course not!" I felt myself blushing. "It's just . . . he's a very nice man."

"He's a *witch*."

"He prefers warlock."

"I don't give two bits what he prefers. Call it what you like, witchcraft is the devil's business."

I rolled my eyes. "Ye sound like me ma," I said in my thickest Irish accent.

"Off with you," she said, brandishing a spoon at my backside.

The gentlemen stood when I arrived in the dining room, a formality I still hadn't quite got used to. Only a few months ago, my entrance would have earned nothing more than a glance, maybe a distracted smile, and then I'd be left to get on with whatever chore had brought me into the room. *But you're not a housemaid anymore*, I told myself firmly. Thomas pulled out my chair—another gesture I had yet to get used to, resulting in more than one awkward incident—and I lowered myself down with perfect dignity. Hopefully.

"Good evening, Mr. Jackson," I said, inclining my head in the demure nod they'd taught us in etiquette class. "And where are we off to tonight?"

"Harlem." He poured a glass of wine and set it before me. "The shade that eluded us in Central Park last month has been spotted again."

I tried to look delighted.

"We'd best be on our guard this time," he went on, helping himself to a glass. "He's a crafty one. I do believe if you hadn't warned us he was near, he might have got the better of us."

And that, right there, was the only reason I wasn't spending my weekends in Newport along with the rest. I wondered how the others were passing their Friday night. Playing billiards, maybe, or whist, or trading tales over cognac and sherry. Whatever they did, I wasn't a part of it and never would be.

"Come now," Thomas chided, "there will be plenty of time to discuss business after supper."

"Forgive me, you're quite right." Mr. Jackson took a sip of his wine. "Tell me, Miss Gallagher, how is your mother keeping?"

"Better, thanks. She's getting out of the flat a bit more these days. She still gets confused now and then, but she's lucid more often than not."

"I'm glad to hear it. She lives in Five Points, does she not? Troubled times in that part of town, with all these recent break-ins."

"Break-ins?" I cocked my head.

"Haven't you heard? Half a dozen businesses in the past week alone. Some new street gang, according to the papers."

"I'm afraid I've been too busy to read the papers lately."

Mr. Jackson looked slightly taken aback, as though the idea of not reading the papers was very bizarre indeed.

"Understandable," Thomas put in smoothly, "with all the reading materials they've been inundating you with at Newport. Which reminds me, Jackson, did you see Fillimore's essay in the *Journal of Paranormal Studies*?"

"On the lost domains?" Mr. Jackson nodded. "Interesting. Electromagnetism sounds plausible enough, but where's the empirical evidence?"

"Still, the theory is altogether fascinating."

I braced myself for the question I knew was coming.

"And you, Miss Gallagher?" Mr. Jackson turned to me. "What did you think of Fillimore's paper?"

Both men looked at me expectantly. I tried to think of some vague reply, but there was no point in trying to fake it. "To tell the truth, I didn't understand much of it."

"Ah. Well." Mr. Jackson smiled blandly. There was an awkward pause; the clock on the mantel ticked through the silence. "In any case," he said, turning back to Thomas, "I'm sure we haven't heard the last of the idea. In fact . . ."

I didn't even bother trying to follow the rest. Even by the standards of the paranormal community, Thomas and Mr. Jackson were of a scientific bent, and here I was barely an initiate. Deciphering their conversations was like trying to read Shakespeare while you were still learning the alphabet.

Watching the two of them—one full of energy and imagination, the other practical and methodical—it was impossible not to be reminded of Clara and me. They were two peas in a pod, just as Clara and I had once been, back before we barely saw each other. I'd given that up, and for what? To try to make my way in a world that wasn't my own?

Oh, quit blubbering in your bonnet. The voice in my head was Mam's.

After supper, we readied ourselves for another long night on the streets. I'd headed upstairs to fetch my warmest gloves, and that's how I happened to overhear Thomas and Mr. Jackson talking quietly in the foyer.

"I'm not questioning your judgment, Wiltshire. I just wonder if perhaps you're pushing her too hard."

I stopped cold on the stairs.

"Because she had difficulty parsing Fillimore? Be reasonable, Jackson. The man's syntax is impenetrable at the best of times."

"It's not only that. She seems . . ." The next few words were too muffled to make out, as if Mr. Jackson had lowered his voice still further.

She seems . . . A dozen possible conclusions to that sentence ran through my mind, none of them flattering.

". . . a mistake," Mr. Jackson said.

The word hung there, polluting the air like the smoke of a cheap cigar.

I didn't want to hear any more. "Ready!" I called, tromping my way conspicuously down the remaining steps.

They stood in their overcoats and hats, walking sticks in hand. Mr. Jackson wore an oddly grave expression, while Thomas flashed a tense smile that didn't quite reach his eyes. "Jackson and I have been talking it over, and I wonder . . ." He paused, clearing his throat. "That is, we thought perhaps you might fancy taking the evening off."

I stared.

"Such disagreeable weather," he went on. "On top of which, you've been working so hard."

My glance cut between them. "I don't understand. You don't want me to come?"

"We just think you've earned a bit of rest, that's all. Isn't that right, Jackson?"

"But you need me. You said it yourself, that shade is dangerous—"

"You needn't trouble yourself about that," Mr. Jackson put in. "We'll get along just fine without you."

That stung.

"Spend some time with Clara, or curl up with a good book. Jackson and I will take care of this. Enjoy your evening." So saying, Thomas touched his hat and the two of them stepped out into the night.

For a moment, all I could do was stand there staring at the door. Numbly, I replaced my overcoat on the rack, my umbrella in the stand. My hand trembled ever so slightly, and a lump gripped my throat.

Cabot Fisk, Viola Fox, even Mr. Jackson—their disapproval might wound my pride, but it didn't really matter in the end. But Thomas . . . He'd told me only this morning that he had great faith in me, but apparently I'd disappointed him one time too many.

She seems . . . a mistake.

I felt the prick of tears behind my eyes.

"Tea," I whispered. "You need tea."

I headed for the kitchen. Clara had already turned in for the night, having finished the tidying up while the rest of us worked out our plan of attack. I didn't even bother to light the lamp, staring vacantly into the shadows while I waited for the kettle to come to a boil.

It had just started to whistle when a knock sounded at the front door; answering it, I found a familiar grandfatherly face. "Sergeant Chapman! How lovely to see you!" We hadn't crossed paths since last spring, when a greengrocer had been killed by a shade in the Gashouse District. "It's been too long."

"Miss Gallagher." The aging detective doffed his hat.

"Please, come in. I've just put the kettle on, if you'd like some tea."

"What, no coffee?" Mischief crinkled the corners of his watery eyes. He knew well enough how I felt about coffee. "Can't stay long. Your boss around?"

Partner, I started to say, but for some reason the word stuck in my throat. "I'm afraid not, but is there something I can help you with? I'm . . . Well, I'm a full-fledged agent myself now."

More or less.

"That so? Well, good for you. How's the ghost-hunting coming, anyway?"

I didn't bother to correct him. Clara was right: The difference between ghosts and shades only mattered to people like me. "Well enough. We've caught most of the spirits that escaped through the portal, and we're closing in on the two or three that are left."

"Glad to hear it." His gaze did a slow scan of the foyer. "But if you ain't the help no more, what're you still doing living here?"

I felt myself blushing. "Yes, well. Our work is a secret, as you know, and we haven't figured out a cover story just yet. We moved my things down to one of the guest rooms, but that's about as far as we've got."

Chapman grunted. "Anyways, you mind telling Wiltshire I stopped by? We got a real bag of nails down at the Grand Opera House, and I got a feeling it's more your type of work than mine."

"The Grand Opera House?" I'd heard something about that. "The Republican Convention, wasn't it?"

"That's right. Wrapped up a few hours ago, but not before we had six dead delegates on our hands."

"How awful! What happened?"

"Coroner's saying typhoid, but that don't add up, least not in my ledger. I got a greenback dollar says it's foul play. And not the ordinary sort, neither."

"I see. And you think—what? A shade?"

"That's my guess. Either that or we're looking at something new."

A shiver of excitement ran through my bones. (Beastly, I know, but what can I say? After nine straight months of chasing shades, *something new* sounded positively heavenly.) "What makes you think it's supernatural?"

"Twenty-eight years on the job. Every instinct I got tells me that coroner is lying, and his boss, too. Trouble is, I got no way of knowing for sure, seeing how I ain't a doctor."

I paused, an idea already forming in my head. "And if you could know for sure?"

He shrugged. "It'd be a start, anyways."

"In that case, just give me a moment."

Chapman watched me grab my overcoat and hat, one sleepy eye narrowed. "What're you up to, Miss Gallagher?"

"Why, Sergeant, I'd have thought it was obvious. I'm taking your case."

CHAPTER 3

SOMETHING STICKY—THE WORST KIND
OF LUCK—A MORBID REQUEST

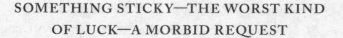

Sergeant Chapman regarded me with a paternal sort of amusement. "Taking my case," he said in his unhurried way. "Is that so?"

"Why not? Have you forgotten that I was the one who found Mr. Wiltshire when he went missing?"

He shook his head. "You was a big help with the Jacob Crowe case, too. I'm not doubting your capabilities, Miss Gallagher."

"Then what?"

"I don't much fancy explaining myself to your boss."

"Thomas is no longer my boss," I said, deliberately using his given name to emphasize the point. "He's my partner. The senior partner, to be sure, but I don't answer to him. I am my own woman. My own agent." I'm not sure which of us I was trying harder to convince.

Chapman sucked on a tooth, a sure sign he was mulling over something he didn't like. "Why do I get the feeling I'm stepping in something sticky?"

"I'm sure I don't know."

He gave me a long, shrewd look. "Well, I guess that's for you two to sort out. If I don't get some answers in the next few hours, I got a feeling I'll never get 'em."

"So I'm hired?"

"Guess so. Best grab yourself a mushroom, though. It's still raining out, and—"

"Right here," I said, plucking my umbrella from the stand, and before he could change his mind, I hustled him out the door. "It's a bit of a walk, but hopefully we'll find a nighthawk."

"No need. That's my cab across the street. Came here straight from HQ." He started across the rain-glazed cobbles, moving with a purposeful stride that belied his age. "So, where we headed? The morgue, or you want a peep at the crime scene first?"

"The morgue, I think, but we need to fetch someone first. He lives just a little way up the Avenue."

Chapman stopped dead in his tracks. "Just a minute. I ain't sure—"

"Not to worry, Sergeant. The man we're going to see is perfectly discreet." In fact, he was the most guarded man I'd ever met, though he did a very good job of hiding it. "Seventy-Third Street," I told the cab driver, and hopped in.

We mounted the smooth steps of an elegant brownstone row house across from Central Park. The bay windows stood dark, shrouded in heavy velvet curtains, but a sliver of golden light between the folds hinted at life within.

"Nice place," Chapman said, scanning its stately facade. "Real nice." He shot me a questioning glance but otherwise held his peace.

A sour-looking butler answered the door. As many times as I'd called here, I'd never seen him wearing any other expression. "Good evening, Bertram," I said sweetly, taking a petty sort of pleasure in the familiar greeting. The first time we'd met, I'd been a mere housemaid, a creature for him to look down upon—and look down upon me he had, with relish. Now the tables had turned, and it seemed only fair to remind him of the fact.

But the old boot wouldn't be conquered so easily. "It's rather more night than evening, madam," he said, drawing out his watch and consulting it with a disdainfully raised eyebrow.

"I suppose that's true, but I know what a night owl Mr. Burrows is. Would you kindly inform him of our visit?"

The butler surrendered, though not what you'd call gracefully. He handled our overcoats and hats as though they were plague-infected, and upon depositing us in the smallest of Mr. Burrows's parlors, suggested that we might warm ourselves by the fire, which is butler for "don't sit on the furniture." Only then did he forge into the inner chambers of the brownstone in search of his master.

Chapman's gaze did a slow tour of the room, taking in the fine gilt furnishings, the marble fireplace, the thick Persian rugs. "And here I thought Wiltshire was rich."

I didn't respond, too busy admiring a sumptuous Gallé vase on the mantelpiece. There was something almost indecent about the way the blown-glass flowers opened in swollen relief, voluptuous and scandalously red, and I felt a touch of heat in my cheeks—which is almost certainly what its owner intended.

"You said his name was Burrows?" Chapman's gruff voice was like sandpaper against the soft opulence of the room. "As in *the* Burrowses?"

"Of the Philadelphia branch. Jonathan Burrows is a close friend of Mr. Wiltshire's."

"And he can help us how?"

Before I could answer, the door opened to admit the gentleman himself. As I'd guessed, he was still in his evening attire, clad in a smart cutaway and sapphire damask waistcoat that brought out the bright blue of his eyes. He held a cigar in one hand and a glass of cognac in the other; the slight flush of his skin suggested it wasn't his first round. "Why, Miss Gallagher," he said with a rakish smile. "This is an indecorous hour for a young lady to come calling. Better you had sent me your card, and I could have come to you." He punctuated this outrageous remark with a wink, in case I wasn't already blushing.

Sergeant Chapman cleared his throat, assuming by Mr. Burrows's fresh behavior that he hadn't noticed the presence of a third person in the room. But I knew better. "I would make the introductions, Sergeant, but I do believe Mr. Burrows has just introduced himself better than I ever could."

"How rude of me." Mr. Burrows stuck out a hand, perfectly unabashed. "Jonathan Burrows. Sergeant—?"

"Chapman." The detective shook hands bemusedly.

"Ah yes, Wiltshire's mentioned you. From the Crowe case, isn't it? Then we're all friends here." By which he meant, *We all know about the things that go bump in the night, so we can speak freely.* "How may I be of service this evening, Sergeant?"

"Beats me."

Mr. Burrows cut me a sidelong glance.

"Nothing to worry about," I assured him. "Not for you, anyway." Though Mr. Burrows had shown no sign of concern at the presence of a copper in his parlor, that didn't mean much. Jonathan Burrows made a habit of keeping his true feelings to himself.

"Not for me," he echoed. "How intriguing. And where is Wiltshire this fine evening?"

"In Harlem," I said offhandedly, "rounding up another shade."

"Yet New York's finest shade hunter stands in my parlor. The plot thickens." He gestured for us to sit, settling himself into a leather armchair. "Very well, then, let's have it."

Sergeant Chapman went over what he'd told me about the deaths at the Grand Opera House, including his suspicion that the coroner was lying. "Miss Gallagher seems to think you can help us out with the investigation," he concluded, his tone making it plain that he didn't see how.

Neither did Mr. Burrows. "I'm not much of a political fellow myself. I know several of the delegates, and I could perhaps be of some assistance in arranging interviews, but other than that . . ."

"I had something else in mind," I said. "You're not going to like it, but I do hope you'll agree."

Mr. Burrows eyed me warily.

"We have our suspicions that the cause of death wasn't really typhoid, but we need to be sure."

"I don't understand. I'm not a doctor, what could I . . . ?" He trailed off, eyes widening in horror. "Dear God, you can't possibly want me to . . . ?" He let out a sharp laugh. "No. Absolutely out of the question. Have you any idea . . . ? Thank you, no." He tossed back the rest of his cognac, wincing.

"It would only take a few minutes of your time."

"That's not the point and you know it! It is quite simply the most revolting idea I've ever heard. You wouldn't put horse manure in your mouth to find out what the animal has been eating, would you?"

"Well, I don't think it's quite the same . . ."

"No, it's worse!" He sprang to his feet and poured himself another dram of cognac. "*Really*, Miss Gallagher."

"Sorry, folks," Chapman interrupted, looking annoyed. "What're we talking about here?"

I looked at Mr. Burrows, silently asking permission to reveal his secret. "Sergeant Chapman knows about our work," I reminded him, "so this isn't going to be much of a stretch for him."

"Oh, well in that case, be my guest."

Pretending to miss the sarcasm, I turned to the detective. "You see, Sergeant, Mr. Burrows has a unique talent. A sort of extra sense, if you like, in addition to smell and taste and the rest. He can sense the composition of things just by touching them."

Chapman's brow creased. "You're gonna have to talk me through that, Miss Gallagher."

"When he touches an object, he can tell exactly what it's made of, down to the elemental level. Not only that, he can sense what it's come into contact with recently. Say he were to pick up your hat, for instance. If you'd just come from a railway station, he would know it, because he would sense traces of smoke. Or if you'd been to the Gashouse District, he would sense the coal gas. He can sense people, too. If you lined up a bunch of identical hats, he could pick out which one was yours, because he's shaken your hand and so he knows . . . well, your body's unique signature, I guess you could call it. Any bit of hair or skin you'd left behind, even if it's too small to see, would tell him whose hat it was."

I'd struggled mightily to understand all this when it had been explained to me, but Sergeant Chapman got it straightaway. "That sounds like a real handy talent for a fella in my line of work."

Mr. Burrows rolled his eyes. "So Wiltshire is constantly telling me. If you ask me, it's a very dull gift indeed."

"How's it done?"

"It's a form of what's called *luck*," I explained, "which is just a broad term for any sort of extraordinary ability we don't really understand. There are lots of different types. For instance, do you remember the bounty hunter who helped us track down Freddie Crowe's killers?"

"The one with the foul mouth. I remember. Said she could smell where the killers had been."

"Ah," said Mr. Burrows, "that must be our dear Annie Harris. They call her the Bloodhound."

Chapman's glance cut between us. "You all got lots of friends with these sorts of talents?"

"Less than one percent of the population is lucky," I said, "but it's hereditary, so families with luck do tend to end up moving in the same circles."

"How come I never heard of it?"

"Because families like mine go to great lengths to see to it that you never do," Mr. Burrows said. "Luck has made many of us here on the Avenue very wealthy, and we have no desire to have it known how we came by our fortunes."

A trump concealed is ten times more powerful than one your opponent knows you're holding was how Mr. Burrows had explained it to me. I understood it, but it still brought a stab of resentment to my breast. Being dealt a trump card was one thing. Concealing it, though—that's called *cheating*.

But we didn't have time to get into any of that. "I think Mr. Burrows can use his luck to determine whether those men really died of typhoid."

The scowl returned to Mr. Burrows's handsome features. "Have you any idea what you're asking? You might as well have me lick a corpse."

I grimaced in spite of myself. "Surely it's not that bad?"

"*It's not far off,*" he said hotly.

"I wouldn't ask if it weren't important. But if Sergeant Chapman is right and the coroner is lying, they'll bury the evidence before we have a chance to prove it."

"Surely the matter proves itself? We've all known people with typhoid. A child could tell you it doesn't work that way. Why, my cousin Agnes was bedridden for nearly a month before she succumbed."

"New strain, is what they're saying." Chapman's tone made it clear what he thought of that explanation. "Kills within a few hours. Coroner claims they must've caught it at the Fifth Avenue Hotel, where they was all gathered before the convention."

"Nonsense."

"Reckon so, but I gotta be sure before I go pointing fingers at the higher-ups. It'll be the end of my career if I'm wrong."

"And if you're right? No one would take my word as evidence, even if I were prepared to disclose my secret. Which, by the way, I am not."

"But you might be able to tell how they really died," Chapman returned doggedly. "That'd be something, at least."

"Surely you have a theory?"

"The beginnings of one, anyhow. Witness saw a man take a couple of the victims by the scruff of the neck. Nothing too rough—like he was greeting an old chum, say—'cept the victims didn't seem to appreciate it. Few minutes later, they keeled over. Witness said one of 'em was clutching at his chest, like maybe he was having a heart attack."

"Killing at a touch? That sounds like a shade."

"That was my first thought. No ice on the bodies, though, like you would expect if a shade got 'em. And the witness didn't mention nothing odd about his appearance. Described him as a tall, gangly fella. Nothing about him resembling a ghost."

"Even so, surely Miss Gallagher—"

I shook my head. "I can only sense them when they're nearby, not after they're gone. But if it was a shade, you might find traces of ice left inside the bodies." *Like a half-thawed side of beef.* I kept that last bit to myself, figuring it wouldn't help my cause.

Mr. Burrows's lips pressed into a thin line. He was wavering.

"Please, Jonathan," I said, greatly daring.

It worked. My use of his given name caught him off guard, and he met my eye. That was his undoing. A gentleman of Mr. Burrows's disposition simply cannot refuse a lady. "I must be mad," he growled. Then he poured himself another drink—this time a good deal more than a dram. "I daresay I'm going to need this," he said, and downed it in a gulp.

CHAPTER 4

MISERY LANE—LA FOLIE FRANÇAISE—
THE INVISIBLE AUTOPSY—HOT WATER

So," Mr. Burrows said as we waited for his carriage to be brought around, "are you going to tell me the real reason you're not with Thomas this evening?"

I avoided his eye, watching Sergeant Chapman's cab fade into the mist. We'd catch up with him at the morgue and go our separate ways afterward. "There's nothing to tell. He gave me the night off."

"And yet here you are."

"Sergeant Chapman called and I decided not to wait. Matters like these are highly time sensitive, you know."

"Indeed. And now you have your first case as an independent agent."

There was something altogether too knowing about his smirk. "Unless you count the time I solved Thomas's kidnapping," I said coolly.

He just laughed and offered me his arm, as though we were stepping out for a pleasant evening at the Astor House instead of heading for the city morgue. Though he clearly didn't look forward to the grim business ahead, having framed his mind to the task, he was back to playing the carefree rounder.

"You really are incorrigible," I muttered, allowing him to escort me down the steps.

It was well after midnight by the time we arrived at Misery Lane, that blighted passage of Twenty-Sixth Street between First Avenue and the river. Bellevue Hospital reared up out of the shadows, its brick facade stained a ghoulish red in the glow of the gas lamps. My gaze roamed involuntarily over the grounds, and I couldn't suppress a shudder, recalling all too vividly the horrific descriptions in *Harper's Weekly* of wasted souls in agonies of disease. At least the beggars and thieves had long since dispersed from Charities Pier, ferried off to their grim fates on Blackwell's Island.

"This way," Chapman said, and we followed him into the morgue, our footfalls echoing along the empty corridor.

"This isn't my first visit to a morgue, you know," Mr. Burrows said conversationally. "I toured one in Paris a few years ago."

"What, for amusement?" I made a face.

"You needn't look so horrified. It's a major attraction, right along with Notre-Dame. Not my cup of tea, I'll grant you, but the French are positively mad about it. Then again, the French are mad on a great many counts."

Chapman cut him a look that suggested he thought Mr. Burrows was a bit touched himself. "Through here."

He led us into a narrow white-tiled room, where a row of marble-topped tables stood under the glare of a single electric light. Upon these tables lay half a dozen corpses, pale and naked but for the towels draped discreetly across their private parts. Their clothes hung from hooks on the wall, as though they were merely guests for the night and might fetch up their coats and hats and depart at any moment. The place reeked of chemicals and a fleshy sort of odor that reminded me of a butcher's shop, and I had to force myself not to bring a handkerchief to my face. It wouldn't be fair to Mr. Burrows, given what I'd asked him here to do.

"They'll be loading 'em into pine boxes anytime now," Chapman said.

I looked at him, startled. "What, no autopsy?"

"Like I said . . . fishy. So we'd better get on with it."

"*I'd* better get on with it, you mean." Mr. Burrows looked ill at the prospect, but he was as good as his word, handing me his hat and stick and tugging off his gloves. Then, with only the slightest hesitation, he reached out and touched the hand of the first victim. His features twisted in disgust, but he soldiered on, pressing his fingertips to the dead man for several minutes before moving on to the next. He repeated the process for all six, and though he flinched a little less each time, I could tell it was a struggle for him.

When he'd done, his skin had taken on a greenish hue, and the look he gave me smoldered with resentment. "That was easily the most repugnant thing I've ever experienced."

"What'd you get?" Chapman asked, looking half awed, half skeptical.

"Besides the fact that this chap had oysters for dinner and that one had a fondness for cheap sherry? Nothing."

"You sensed their *stomach contents*?" My own guts twisted at the thought.

"How else to be thorough, Miss Gallagher?" he asked coldly. "Or did you not consider what you were asking of me? Nor was that the worst of it, I assure you."

I stared at him in dismay. He was right—I hadn't thought through what I was asking of him. I'd been too busy trying to prove something.

"So you didn't sense typhoid?" Chapman asked, sticking to the matter at hand.

Mr. Burrows gave a curt shake of his head. "It's been a long time, but I didn't detect anything that reminded me of the disease my cousin suffered from. Nor did I find any trace of ice or anything else that would suggest a shade—though I'm not entirely sure what I'm looking for."

Thomas would know. I could tell from Mr. Burrows's expression he'd had the same thought.

"What about poison?" Chapman asked.

"I don't think so. There were any number of things I couldn't identify, but none of them were common to all six. Whatever killed these men, it's no longer present in their systems. Not being a physician, that's all I can tell you."

I glanced over at the nearest body. "I suppose someone checked them for wounds?"

Chapman nodded. "Nothing to speak of. This many hours after the fact, even strangling would leave a mark."

"It must be a shade, then. There's no other explanation." At least, none that I could see.

"That's why I came to you all."

"What about your witness? Might we speak with him?"

"Sure, if I had a name. He was hustled outta there before I could even finish my interview."

"What do you mean, hustled out? By whom?"

"Byrnes himself, if you can believe it."

"I'm sorry, who—?"

"Inspector Byrnes. Chief of the Detective Bureau. Haven't

seen him at a crime scene in I dunno how long, and suddenly he's personally escorting a witness down to HQ?" Chapman shook his head. "Fishy."

"No other witnesses?"

"Not so's I've heard."

We stared at each other, at a loss.

"Well, then," Mr. Burrows said, drawing his gloves back on, "it seems we've reached the limits of our collective experience. So if you don't mind, I'd like to repair to my library and get extremely drunk. I presume you'll need a lift, Miss Gallagher?"

"If you're still willing to offer me one." It was a feeble joke, thoroughly deserving the cold silence that greeted it. "We'll speak tomorrow, Sergeant, once I've had a chance to discuss the matter with Mr. Wiltshire." Oh, how it stung my pride to have to say that, but the truth was as stark as the bodies on those tables: I'd been as good as useless. I needed my partner, even if he didn't need me.

We'd just turned to go when Mr. Burrows said, "By the way, Sergeant, how did it come out? The convention, I mean. Whom are they putting forward for mayor?"

"Some Knickerbocker called Roosevelt. Quite the dude, judging from his picture in the papers."

Recognition flickered across Mr. Burrows's features, but he made no reply, turning and heading for the door. All I could do was follow.

"I'm sorry," I said once the coachman had shut the carriage door. "I didn't realize—"

"It's done." He gazed out the fogged window, his profile sketched in shadow. "I'd rather not dwell on it."

"I feel awful."

"That makes two of us." He paused, sighing. "But I'll get over it, as should you."

The remainder of the ride passed in silence, Mr. Burrows staring out the window while I turned Sergeant Chapman's murders over in my mind. I had no idea what to do next. Chapman had been right about the coroner's lies. That, and the strange behavior of the chief of detectives, suggested that whatever had really happened at the Republican County Convention, powerful people wanted it kept hush. But why?

By the time we pulled up at Number 726, I was so lost in thought that I'd already stepped down from the carriage before I noticed Thomas standing on the stoop.

"Oh, dear," said Mr. Burrows, sounding grimly amused. "I do believe you're in hot water." Then, with the faintest of sighs, he descended from the carriage himself, since it would be terribly bad form to drive off without greeting his best friend.

"I'm very glad to see you both," Thomas said, his expression a mixture of relief and irritation. "I was concerned. When I asked after you, Clara said you'd gone out, but she had no idea where. You could have at least left me a note."

"Something came up suddenly." The chill in my voice surprised even me. "Sergeant Chapman came by with a case. I thought I could be useful *there*, at least."

Thomas blinked, taken aback.

"Alas, I was recruited to the cause as well," Mr. Burrows put in, "but I'll let Miss Gallagher fill you in on the details. I've an engagement with a very expensive bottle of armagnac." He touched his hat and alighted in the carriage once more, and with a jingle of harness and clatter of hooves, he was gone.

"I do beg your pardon, Thomas," I said coolly, sweeping past him into the foyer.

"Rose."

I checked my stride. Hurt as I was, his voice still cast a spell on me.

"Why didn't you wait for me?"

I didn't turn around. If I could avoid those pale eyes, maybe I could get through this without losing my composure. "It was late, and Sergeant Chapman was afraid the evidence would be buried."

"You could have left me a message. I'd have come straightaway. We're partners, Rose."

"It seems to me that you're the one who left."

"Left? I merely suggested you take the night off."

"It wasn't a suggestion. You *informed* me that I wasn't to come. Because of what Mr. Jackson said, I suppose."

"I'm sorry?"

I couldn't help it; I whirled to face him. "I heard you. As I was coming down the stairs, I heard Mr. Jackson say that I was"— my voice wavered dangerously—"I heard him say it was a mistake."

"He disagreed with my decision, it's true, but I thought it for the best. You've had so little time to yourself recently."

"Wait." I paused, digesting this. "What decision did he disagree with?"

"To carry on without you. He thought it a mistake. But I know how wearying it's been these past few months, and Jackson said he thought you seemed terribly unhappy, and so it seemed to me that the thing to do—"

I blew out a breath. I'd had it all wrong. Part of me wanted to kiss him, but another part wanted to grab him by the lapels and give him a good shake. "Thomas, the next time you're tempted to presume how I feel, just ask me."

"Yes. Well." He fidgeted with his cufflinks. "I shall certainly do that." An awkward pause. Then he said, "Tea?"

My insides felt warm again, and it wasn't just the tea. Thomas and I sat in the kitchen, just the two of us, his lean frame angled toward me as he listened to my account. He didn't interrupt except to nod every now and then—that is, until I came to the part about enlisting the help of Mr. Burrows, at which point he reeled back with a horrified expression. "*Rose!*"

"I know. I feel awful. I didn't realize what it would involve, not fully."

"Poor devil. What a thoroughly revolting idea. And yet"— his beard twitched as he tried to suppress a smile—"undeniably ingenious."

"Ingenious? It was a beastly thing to ask of him."

"I wouldn't have suggested it, certainly, but mainly because the idea would never have occurred to me. It was terribly clever of you. And to think he actually agreed . . ." Thomas shook his head. "We'll have to make it up to him, of course."

I wasn't sure what sort of flowers said, *I'm sorry for making you sense the stomach contents of a corpse,* but I supposed they must be very expensive.

"And what of the result? No typhoid, I presume."

"That's the worst of it. Poor Mr. Burrows went through it all for nothing. He couldn't find anything unusual—no disease, no poison. No sign of a shade, even."

"A null result is hardly *nothing.* Eliminating hypotheses is always useful. Though as to the shade, that remains the most likely explanation. If the spirit touched its victims only briefly, any trace of ice would long since have melted by the time Burrows got hold of them."

"What about the shade in Harlem? Did you and Mr. Jackson catch it?"

Thomas shook his head. "Not so much as a glimpse. We'll have to wait for another sighting."

"What if it's the same one?"

"That would be quite a coincidence." He paused, slender fingers tapping the table in thought. "You said there was a witness?"

"Yes, but he was spirited away by the chief of detectives. Sergeant Chapman doesn't feel he can press the matter, but maybe if we spoke with the chief ourselves—"

Thomas hummed a skeptical note. "Inspector Byrnes is a formidable figure, and widely rumored to be corrupt. If he's been enlisted to conceal this crime, whether by power or money, I doubt he can be enticed to change his mind. Not without leverage, and we haven't any." Another thoughtful pause. "Tell me more about the victims. Do you have their names?"

I handed him a page torn from Sergeant Chapman's notebook. "Mr. Burrows didn't seem to recognize any of them."

"Why should he?"

"I just thought since they were at the convention . . ."

Thomas smiled. "Not everyone on the Avenue is a Republican. Besides, whatever Burrows's preferences as a voter, men of his stature are rarely involved in politics. They view it as a vulgar sort of business, quite beneath them."

"He seemed to know their candidate for mayor."

"Oh?" Thomas tilted his head with interest. "Who got the nod?"

"Someone named Roosevelt. Sergeant Chapman called him a *dude*."

Thomas's eyebrows flew up. "As well he might! Well, doesn't that give the lie to everything I've just said. The Roosevelts are about as close to royalty as it comes in New York. I'd heard Theodore's name bandied about for some of the less notable positions, but mayor . . . Why, he's only twenty-seven years old!"

"That seems plenty old enough to me."

"Does it?" Thomas cocked a dark eyebrow playfully. "You do realize that makes him only two years older than me?"

Of course I realized it. I was acutely aware of Thomas's age; in particular, the fact that he was five years my senior and getting on in age to still be a bachelor, two things I tried *very hard* not to connect in my mind.

Aloud, I said, "I think you'd make a wonderful mayor," whereupon he suffered a mild shudder.

"We'll want to head down to the venue tomorrow and take a look around. I'll telephone Sergeant Chapman in the morning. And speaking of morning"—he consulted his watch—"it's terribly late. We ought to turn in."

I took an instinctive step toward the servants' staircase before remembering that I didn't sleep in the attic anymore. Louise had taken over my old room, while Clara had moved into the housekeeper's generous quarters. As for me, I lived on the second floor now, so I followed Thomas up the main staircase like a full-fledged member of the household. Already, I could feel my eyelids drooping, and I felt sure I'd sleep better than I had all week. There was something perverse in that, I suppose, but that didn't bother me much. For the first time in a long time, it was just the two of us. No Mr. Jackson. No Viola Fox or Cabot Fisk. Just me and my partner, and a brand-new case.

Murder or not, that was heaven.

CHAPTER 5

PAPERING OVER THE TRUTH—THE GRAND
OPERA HOUSE—FINGERS AND PIES

If the actions of the coroner and the chief of detectives weren't evidence enough of a whitewash, the morning papers made the matter plain. Not a single one mentioned the mysterious deaths at the Republican County Convention.

"How can that be?" I tossed *The New-York Times* aside in disgust, narrowly missing the butter dish. "Column after column about Roosevelt's nomination, and not a word about six dead delegates!"

"I'd have thought to see the incident attributed to typhoid, at least," Thomas agreed, scanning the *Herald*. "To have no mention of it at all, in spite of an auditorium full of reporters . . . I don't think even Byrnes wields that kind of influence."

"Then who?"

He shook his head. "Someone very powerful. More than

likely several *someones,* in fact. I daresay we'll have our work cut out for us today. Speaking of which, we'd better get on. Sergeant Chapman will be waiting."

The cab ride down to the Grand Opera House took almost half an hour, most of which I spent worrying. The events of last night had made it painfully clear just how green I was when it came to investigating murders, and the last thing I wanted was to flaunt my inexperience all over again. *Just follow Thomas's lead,* I told myself. *You have nothing to prove.*

If only I believed that.

Sergeant Chapman met us under the twin stone arches at the front entrance. "Had the place opened up for us," he said as he pulled on the door, "but we're on our own from here. Didn't tell my captain I was headed down here."

"Prudent," Thomas said. "If your suspicions about your superiors are correct, it's best to keep a low profile."

Electric lighting blazed through the lobby, but the auditorium itself was illuminated by gaslight, its soft glow burnishing the edges of a vast cavern of stone and velvet. Row upon row of seats lined the floor and mezzanine levels, the latter fringed by elaborately carved balconies, rather like frosting between the layers of a cake. *This place must hold two thousand people,* I thought. *Where do we even begin?*

If Thomas felt overwhelmed by the size of our crime scene, he hid it well. "How many in attendance last night?"

"About eighteen hundred," said Chapman, "not counting the press boys."

Thomas strolled down one of the aisles, surveying the hall with an unhurried air. Not knowing what else to do, I mimicked his movements down another aisle. Sergeant Chapman, meanwhile, observed from the back row. "Party bigwigs was either up on the platform or in the boxes," he called, gesturing at the scalloped balconies on either side of the stage. "Rank and file here, press mostly there, and random curious types in the back here."

"And the deceased?" Thomas's smooth tenor carried easily under the domed ceiling. "Were they together?"

"Not that we know of. I got some fellas at the station looking into what they might've had in common—besides being delegates, I mean—but so far, it don't look like they came as a group. Only two of 'em was sitting in the same spot, down near where Miss Gallagher's standing. Fifth row, about the middle there."

I scanned the row the sergeant had indicated. "So to reach them, the killer would have had to file past all these seats?"

"That's right."

Thomas and I exchanged a look across a sea of red velvet.

"Hard to do without touching anyone," I said, speaking the substance of that glance aloud for Chapman's benefit. "If it was a shade, it was a very careful one."

"Maybe it was after someone in particular."

"Even so," Thomas said, "one would expect to see multiple victims in the same row, if only accidental. The merest touch of a shade can be fatal, whether the spirit wills it or not."

"And even if you survive, it's painful, not to mention terrifying." I should know. I hadn't even been able to scream when the shade of Matilda Meyer had touched me back in January. It was like being dropped into a freezing river. My muscles had seized, my lungs refused to draw air. Even my eyelashes had ice on them. "I don't see how something like that could go unnoticed."

"Apparently it was a pretty lively affair. People standing most of the time, calling out from the floor and whatnot, which would've distracted from any doings in the seats. And there was plenty of milling about in the lobby n' such. That's where the witness saw two of 'em fall."

"Tell us about that," Thomas said, turning.

"Like I was saying to Miss Gallagher, I only found one fella who noticed anything suspicious. He was out in the lobby most of the time, doing some last-minute vote peddling, so he had a better eye on things than most. Said the victims went down about twenty minutes apart. In both cases, they was approached by the same man a minute or two before they fell, which was what struck the witness as fishy. To be honest, as many people as there was milling about, we was lucky to get that much."

Thomas frowned. "Others noticed someone collapsing in their midst, surely?"

"Noticed, yeah, but they didn't think much of it, least not at first. You see a guy faint, you figure he's sick, 'specially if the event organizers drag him off before you have time to think about it. Far as you know, it's an isolated incident. Took a while for people to catch on that there was more than one sick delegate, by which point the party machine had its story straight."

"Only your witness happened to see two victims fall, both of whom were speaking to the same man a minute or two prior to collapsing." Thomas drummed his fingers on the back of a seat. "Was it closer to one minute, or two?"

"Yeah, the witness wasn't too precise on that point. Said one fella went down quicker than the other. The first victim just keeled over like he fainted, but the second was clutching at his chest."

"No signs of ice? Or shivering, perhaps?"

"Not so as he mentioned."

By this point, I'd wandered up to the stage. Gazing out over the rows of seats, I imagined eighteen hundred faces staring back at me, packed into tight rows like kernels on an ear of corn. A shade making its way through a crowd like that . . . "It sounds awful to say, but it could have been so much worse. If it was a shade, it could have killed dozens, maybe more."

"You keep saying *if*," Chapman said. "What else could it be? Your friend Burrows said it wasn't poison, so . . ." He trailed off, shrugging.

"Burrows isn't a physician," Thomas said, sounding distracted. "But perhaps . . . Sergeant, you said the coroner had already gone home by the time you and Miss Gallagher visited the morgue. Did you speak with him before that?"

"Sure. He peddled the typhoid story."

"Was he the only physician on duty?"

"The only one I was allowed to talk to, but no, now you mention it. There was a couple of others there. Assistants, I guess. But I don't think they was allowed to examine the bodies."

"Even so, one of them might know something."

The sergeant narrowed one sleepy eye. "Even if they did, what makes you think they'd talk to you?"

"The Pinkerton Agency keeps a number of coroner's assistants on the payroll. As you can imagine, it comes in handy from time to time."

The sergeant didn't like that answer one bit. He scowled, muttering something about fingers and pies. "Lemme guess. You'd rather I passed on this next interview."

Thomas at least had the grace to look awkward about it. "To preserve the confidentiality of our sources. I'm sure you understand."

"Oh sure, Wiltshire, I understand. It's not as if corruption is half our problem in the first place."

"I didn't set up the chessboard, Sergeant. I merely play my pieces to best advantage."

Chapman rolled his eyes but otherwise let it go. "Can I at least assume I'll get the benefit of what he says?"

"We'll send word when we've finished," I put in before Thomas had a chance to demur. I didn't know much about chess, but I did know cards, and Thomas liked to keep his pretty well hidden until he was ready to play them. But this was Chapman's case, and it seemed only fair that he be kept in the picture.

Since I was the junior partner, it wasn't really my decision to make, but if Thomas was annoyed, he didn't let on. Instead we spent the long ride crosstown going over what we'd learned at the Grand Opera House. To my way of thinking, that wasn't very much, but as usual, Thomas saw more than I did.

"We can rule out random attacks, at least. Accidental or opportunistic deaths would have been clustered together, not dispersed throughout the auditorium. At least some of the victims were deliberately targeted, which means there was motive." He tapped a finger on the griffin head of his walking stick, gaze abstracted in thought. "Perhaps we'd do well to consult police records, or even newspaper archives, looking for suspicious deaths of local politicians over the past year."

"So you're convinced it was a shade, then?"

"As of now, it remains the most likely explanation, assuming Chapman and Burrows are correct about the lack of wounds and the absence of poison, respectively."

"I didn't see anything on the bodies last night, but I didn't do a thorough check." That felt like an oversight now, but Thomas waved it away.

"Sergeant Chapman would have exhausted all other explanations before referring the matter to us. It's possible that you might have caught something he missed, but not very likely, given his experience."

"But you're hoping one of the coroner's assistants might have noticed something."

"It doesn't hurt to try."

I wasn't too excited about heading back into the morgue for the second time in as many days, but happily I didn't have to; Thomas went in alone. He came out that way, too, directing us to a lunch joint nearby. "Our informant will meet us there. He can't be seen talking to us, obviously."

We sidled up to the counter to wait. The coroner's assistant must have been the paranoid type, because he took his time, and when he finally did appear, he lingered in the doorway throwing such suspicious looks around that he might as well have worn a sign saying *shady character*. He looked to be a year or two older than me, short and thin as a reed, with a complexion not much rosier than the folks he worked on.

"Mr. Walker," Thomas said, and the young man flinched, even though there was nobody else within earshot. "Thank you for coming. May I offer you something to drink?"

He shook his head. "I can only stay for a minute. If anyone saw me . . ."

"Of course. Just a few questions. You were on duty last night, you said?"

"Called in. Thought we would have to do a bunch of autopsies at once, so we needed all hands."

"You *thought* you would," I echoed. "But you didn't?"

He shook his head again, his gaze still darting around the room. "We started on the external, but before we got to the cutting, we were told to stop. The coroner said he would see to it personally, that we should head home." He hitched a shoulder. "So that's what I did."

"How many victims did you examine externally?" Thomas asked.

"Two. Didn't turn anything up on the first one. No sign of injury, unless you count the bruised knees from his fall. Nothing under the fingernails, no pathology I could see. The second one, though, I thought he might've shown signs of sudden cardiac failure."

Thomas narrowed his eyes. "What signs?"

The young man touched the base of his neck. "Swelling in this area. You see that sometimes with sudden cardiac death."

Sudden cardiac death. Such as might be caused by the touch of a shade, for example. I wasn't sure if Mr. Walker was an initiate in the paranormal community, so I kept the thought to myself.

"How confident are you in that diagnosis?" Thomas asked.

Walker gave a high-pitched, nervous laugh. "From an external alone, without a medical history? Not very. More of a hunch, really. No way of knowing without a look inside, and maybe not even then."

"And the official finding of typhoid? What is your opinion of that?"

The young man started to answer—and then his gaze dropped. "Coroner must've had his reasons," he mumbled. "Guess I missed something."

I scoffed quietly, but there was no point in pressing him on it. We already knew the coroner was corrupt; forcing his assistant to admit it wouldn't accomplish anything. "Before he sent you home, did you see him talking to anyone?"

"There was a police detective there. Older fella, balding . . ."

Chapman. "Anyone else?"

"If there was, I didn't see 'em."

"So you have no idea why the coroner sent you home?" Thomas asked. "Whether someone instructed him to, for example?"

The young man shook his head. "It was late. I was just happy to get out of there, so I didn't ask questions."

Thomas sighed. "Very well, Mr. Walker, thank you. We'll be in touch if we need anything else." The assistant didn't look too happy about that prospect, but he nodded and went on his way.

"So," I said when he'd gone, "where does that leave us?"

"Not very far up the pitch, I'm afraid. It looks as though we'll have to arrange to speak with Inspector Byrnes after all, though I'm not hopeful we'll get much from him. I just wish we could work out whether we're dealing with a shade or a man. The answer greatly affects our strategy from here. In the meantime, we'll have to keep operating on the assumption that it is indeed a spirit." With another sigh, he added, "Which means we'll be spending a very dull afternoon looking through those police records. If we do find a likely candidate, perhaps we'll be able to track him."

"Speaking of tracking shades, what will we tell Mr. Jackson?"

"About this evening? Why, that we've another case, of course."

"And Newport? We're not likely to have things wrapped up by Monday."

He shook his head. "We'll have to convey our regrets. Your training is nearly complete, in any case, and Miss Fox can take over jujitsu instruction in my absence."

"But won't they object? After all, if the police are denying a crime even took place, I don't suppose they'll be paying us for our trouble."

"I shouldn't worry about that. If the police refuse to pay, the Agency will simply refer itself to the War Department. There's a discretionary fund for sensitive cases such as these, a holdover from the days of the Agency's services to Lincoln during the war. Besides, given the urgency of the matter, I don't think we can ethically turn away."

I was quiet a moment as the significance of those words settled in. "You think he'll kill again."

"We can only speculate at this point, but the mere prospect of it is too terrible to contemplate. A shade targeting politicians at the height of a mayoral race . . ." He shook his head grimly. "Think of all the events, Rose. The crowds. A shade whose very touch, even accidental, can be fatal, wandering loose among all those people . . ."

"He could kill dozens." I crossed myself instinctively.

"Under the eyes of every newspaperman in the city, no less. We can't let that happen. We have to track this killer down, and quickly. Because if he does kill again, I'll wager it will be soon."

CHAPTER 6

THE CHIEF OF DETECTIVES—MEET THE PRESS—A CASE OF BAD OYSTERS

'm sorry to rush you," Thomas said, handing me my overcoat, "but we'll need to hurry if we're to make our engagement." A look of distaste crossed his features, and I wondered whether it had more to do with the appointment itself or how we would be getting there. A little of both, maybe.

Our engagement—or rather our audience, as I had come to think of it—with Inspector Byrnes had been arranged under false pretenses, and only confirmed by messenger moments ago. To get there in time, we'd have to take the el, something I'd never seen Thomas do before. The Sixth Avenue line was the cleanest of the lot, but even so, a gentleman of Thomas's elegance stood out rather awkwardly amid the courser flesh of New York, and he couldn't have looked forward to the idea of being packed in with the rest of the cattle, choking on black smoke as we shimmied and lurched our way down Sixth Avenue. But good Englishman that he was, he made no complaint—except perhaps a silent protest in the form of an extra-thick pair of gloves.

We arrived at our destination at a little before nine in the morning. Mulberry Street was quiet; aside from a single copper lounging on the steps, police headquarters looked quiet as well. Even so, a small audience had gathered across the street, a flock of reporters roosting like pigeons on the stoop of the newspaper offices opposite. Even on a Sunday morning, the hungriest of them assembled here like clockwork, anxious to be the first to hear the telegraph wires hum. Thomas touched the brim of his hat with his stick, and more than a few nodded in return. I recognized one or two faces myself, our work having brought me here on several occasions.

None of those occasions promised to be as tense as this one, though. "He's going to lie to us, isn't he?" I murmured as we climbed the steps.

"I expect so, though he may inadvertently provide a clue, if we're quick enough to catch it. But we must take care. By all accounts, Byrnes is not a man to be trifled with."

With that warning ringing in my ears, we strode into the lion's den.

Inspector Thomas F. Byrnes, chief detective of the New York City Police Department, received us in his office. He stood when we entered, revealing an imposing figure with close-set eyes and receding hair, brass buttons and badge gleaming against the deep blue of his uniform. "Well," he declared upon seeing me, "I was going to say *gentlemen*, but here's a surprise. I was told to expect a pair of Pinkertons. Or does that include you, darlin'?" He spoke in a Dublin accent worn smooth with time, his words filtered through a mustache of such magnificent proportions that his mouth was all but obscured. Even so, I could see the amused quirk at its corners, and that rankled me.

"Rose Gallagher of the Pinkerton Detective Agency," I said coolly.

"And a compatriot in the bargain. Or are you American-born?"

"From Cork. We left when I was a baby."

"And you, sir?" Byrnes extended a hand to Thomas.

"Thomas Wiltshire, Inspector. Thank you for seeing us on such short notice. I thoroughly enjoyed your book, by the way."

"You're very kind." Byrnes gestured for us to sit and arranged himself behind his polished rosewood desk. An expensive cigar burned in an ashtray between us, throwing up a thin veil of smoke. "We ought to be in church, the lot of us, but my people tell me you've some important information regarding the unfortunate business the other night."

"Oh?" Thomas feigned confusion. "There must be some mistake. We were rather hoping to be on the receiving end of that information."

Byrnes's expression didn't change, but his eyes went cold. "I have the note right here." He picked it up off the desk, Thomas's card still attached. "*Relevant facts to bring to the attention of the Department*, it says. Clear as day."

"I do apologize, Inspector. It would appear that my errand boy misunderstood."

Byrnes's mustache crooked wryly. He didn't believe a word of it. Not that we needed him to. We'd got our foot in the door, and that gave us a chance to ask our questions.

Or so we thought, but Byrnes was too much of a detective

himself to let us take the initiative. "And how is it that the Pinkertons came to hear of Friday's troubles? There was no mention of it in the papers."

"Yes, we noticed that. Rather curious, is it not?" Thomas smiled blandly, crossing one impeccably tailored trouser leg over the other.

Byrnes, for his part, took up his cigar and leaned back until his chair creaked. "Nothing curious about it. I saw to it myself, on the advice of the president of the Board of Health. We'd an eye to avoiding panic."

So the Board of Health is in on it, too. Somehow I wasn't surprised. "You're still claiming it was typhoid, then?"

"It's not a claim, miss, it's a fact. We've a new strain on our hands. But until we know more, it's best to keep it out of the papers. Wouldn't want to alarm people unnecessarily."

"And if this mysterious strain of typhoid strikes again? Shouldn't people be prepared?"

"Hard to prepare for what we don't understand, miss. The first step is to work out what we're dealing with. So I'm letting the Board of Health do its job. You should do the same."

Thomas adopted a thoughtful expression. "Medicine is fascinating, isn't it? We know so little of bacilli and other parasites. Where they come from, what they do. This one, for example, seems to have a particular taste for Republicans. Quite unusual."

Byrnes gave Thomas a long, appraising look. A detective's look, taking in every detail—the elaborately carved walking stick, the emerald cufflinks, the pale gaze sparkling with intelligence. The end of his cigar glowed as he took a long, meditative puff. He seemed to come to a decision then, because his next words struck me as highly deliberate. "You're right, sir. This parasite has made its preferences clear. But as I said, the first step is to work out what we're dealing with, and in the meantime to avoid panic. So unless you can help us on either count, I'll bid you good morning."

"It's difficult to help without the facts," I said. "The real cause of death, for instance."

"On that score, you have all the facts at my disposal."

Maybe it was the grim look in his eye, or the sudden weariness in his voice, but I believed him. Whatever else he was keeping from us, Inspector Byrnes had no idea what had killed those men. Which meant the situation was out of his control—and yet he was covering it up anyway.

That got my back up. "We know it wasn't typhoid," I said rashly, "and we can prove it. Then there's the small matter of the witness, who saw a tall man grab the victims by the scruff of the neck."

The inspector's gaze hardened, and he leaned forward ominously. "I don't know anything about a witness, but I do recall a fellow being packed off to the insane asylum at Blackwell's Island sometime early in the morning. He'd been nattering the sort of nonsense that gets people all stirred up, so we had to shut him away. For the public good."

I stiffened, and even Thomas paled.

"Such a shame, isn't it, when madness takes over good sense? Have you ever seen the inside of an asylum, miss?"

"You've made your point, Inspector," Thomas said coldly, "and I see that you deserve every bit of your reputation."

Byrnes's lip curled. "Just another Irish thug, eh, Englishman?"

Thomas snorted and donned his hat. "I think you've insulted my partner enough for one day. Miss Gallagher?"

By the time we reached the street, my whole body was shaking, and I had to lean against the rail to steady myself. Thomas put a hand on my arm. "Are you all right?"

"Do you think he'd really do it?" My voice was barely above a whisper.

"Have us thrown in the asylum? I daresay he might. He's known for being ruthless." When I didn't respond, he squeezed my arm again. "Rose, what is it?"

I hardly knew how to answer him. The force of my reaction surprised even me. Though Blackwell's Island had been a source of nightmares for years, it wasn't until that moment that I understood how deeply my dread of that place ran. I didn't think I could explain it, but I tried anyway.

"I almost sent her there. My mother." I clamped my eyes shut, trying to banish the images I'd seen in *Frank Leslie's*: wild-eyed lunatics frolicking with dogs, or being dragged away by stone-faced guards, or grasping pitifully at visitors, like some Renaissance painting of souls trapped in hell. "I didn't know what else to do. I had to earn a living, but her dementia . . . She could barely even cook a meal for herself. If I hadn't found a boarder to stay with her . . . If it hadn't been for Pietro, I would have . . ." I was shaking so badly that I couldn't even finish a sentence.

"But you didn't," Thomas said gently. "And even if you had, no one could fault you for it. There are no easy answers with illness of the mind."

I drew a deep, shuddering breath. "I'm sorry. It's just . . . that place, the very thought of it . . . The *evil* of the man, to even threaten such a thing! All to cover up a crime he barely understands!"

"What do you mean?"

"Byrnes has no idea what killed those men."

"Oh?" Thomas cocked his head. "What makes you say so?"

"It's hard to put into words. Something about his demeanor, I suppose. And the way he looked at you . . . I could have sworn he recognized your cane."

Thomas glanced down at his walking stick. It was a striking piece, fashioned from ash wood and topped with a griffin head. Anyone would admire it for being handsome, but members of the paranormal community would recognize it as something more: a sign that its bearer was one of their own. Ash wood had important spiritual properties that made it handy for fighting off ghosts and shades, so most of us carried some of it on our persons at all times. Mine came in the form of a hairpin; Thomas's, a stick. Like a masonic ring, it marked him as a member of a secret tribe. If Byrnes had recognized it, it meant he was a member, too.

"Interesting," Thomas said. "It would make sense that a man in Byrnes's position would know the truth about the paranormal world. Perhaps he's even lucky himself. Well spotted, Rose. As to the rest . . ."

"I think he was trying to tell us something, right before I lost my head and provoked him." Sighing, I added, "I'm sorry about that. You warned me, but my temper ran away with me."

"Never mind. What I'd like to work out is, if he doesn't know what he's dealing with, why go to such lengths to cover it up?"

"Maybe it's like he said. To avoid panic."

Thomas hummed thoughtfully. "*The parasite has made its preferences clear.* Wasn't that what he said?"

"Near enough."

An idea sparked in his eyes. "Come with me," he said, and started across the street. "Good morning, gentlemen," he called to the flock of reporters on the stoop. Then, in an undertone: "Re-

member, these men don't know what we do for a living. They think
I'm an attorney."

I nodded my understanding. The fewer people who knew we
were detectives, the easier it was for us to do our jobs, and that
meant having a cover identity. Thomas's had been in place for years,
but we hadn't yet worked out one for me—an oversight I would rue
shortly.

"What's the word, Wiltshire?" one of the reporters said in
greeting. "Got a client in there, I s'pose?"

"Something like that. Miss Gallagher, may I present Phillip
Greeves of the *World*. Tell me, Greeves, who handles the political beat for your paper these days?"

"That'd be William Foote. You wanna talk to 'im?" Before
Thomas could reply, Greeves twisted around and hollered up at
the windows above. *"BILL! HEY, BILL, OPEN THE WIN-
DOW!"*

A scrape sounded as a window was raised on the third floor,
and a straw-colored head poked out. "Christ, Greeves. Whaddya
want?"

"Come down here, will ya?"

A few moments later, William Foote arrived on the stoop
wearing a thin overcoat and a scowl. "What?"

"Bill, this here's Thomas Wiltshire. He's an attorney we
come across now and then on the job. And Miss Gallagher here is
his . . . well, his secretary, I s'pose?"

Partner, I nearly blurted, but of course that wouldn't do.
Only a few months ago, Kate Stoneman had made the papers for
becoming the first woman admitted to the New York Bar Asso-
ciation. I could hardly claim to be the second without arousing
curiosity—the opposite of what a good cover is supposed to do. I
didn't have much choice but to smile and say, "That's right."

"Is there somewhere we can talk, Mr. Foote?" Thomas asked.

The reporter glanced up at the third-story window, but seemed to think better of it. "There's an oyster saloon around the corner. Usually pretty quiet in there."

"Lead on."

We followed the reporter to a little dive under a hock shop. Sunlight slanted through the windows in grainy beams, glinting off a well-polished bar lined with trays of iced oysters. Already, a few patrons were downing their tipple of choice, and Foote had only to wave at the barman to order his own. Clearly, this wasn't the first time he'd used the joint as his informal office.

"All right," the reporter said, sliding into a booth. "What's doing?"

Thomas eyed the bench warily, and though it got a pass, the table did not: He dropped a handkerchief over a little puddle of vinegar, so as not to stain his shirtsleeves. "I'm a great admirer of your paper," he began.

"It's a fish-wrapper," Foote said flatly.

"Yes. Well." Thomas pushed aside an ashtray bristling with cigar nubs. "In any case, it does have a reputation for following local politics very closely."

"Yeah, at least one of us does his job. So how can I help you?"

"Were you by chance present at the Republican Convention on Friday night?"

Foote's eyes narrowed. Abruptly, he yanked the curtain across the booth, plunging us into shadow—and shielding us from prying eyes. "You bet I was. And before you ask, it wasn't my choice to leave all that business out of the morning edition. That came straight from Pulitzer himself."

"You're referring to the deaths?" Discreetly, Thomas produced a second handkerchief and laid it over a stray droplet of hot sauce.

"What else? Not every day half a dozen men are poisoned on the floor of a major political convention."

"Poisoned?" I exchanged a look with Thomas. "We were told it was typhoid."

Foote snorted. "You believe that, you're as easy a mark as the rest of 'em."

"Rest of whom?" I asked.

"The delegates. Not a one of them took any notice of what was going on."

"But you did?"

"Not right away. I heard a couple of guys collapsed, but I didn't think much of it at first. Crowds, you know." He shrugged. "Then word goes around that it was food poisoning. Bad oysters or some such. They'll be fine, we're told. I still don't pay it much mind. Then the rumor changes. Typhoid, they're saying now, only that makes no sense at all. Well, now I start asking questions. Like, who's ever heard of instant typhoid? On top of which, it's a hell of a coincidence that all six dead men happened to vote the same way."

Thomas leaned forward eagerly, the peril to his shirtsleeves forgotten. "And what way is that?"

"Every one of 'em for Roosevelt. Now you tell me, what're the odds?"

That confused me. "Weren't the majority for Roosevelt? He was nominated, after all."

"I mean *real* Roosevelt supporters, not just those who were bribed or bullied. He'd never have got the nod on his own, not without the machine cracking the whip. Ol' Uncle Isaac said he reckoned not half a dozen in the room were truly in Roosevelt's camp. And whaddya know—six dead, all of 'em dyed-in-the-wool reformers. Hell of a coincidence," he said again, tossing a draft of gin down his throat.

"Uncle Isaac," Thomas echoed. "I don't believe I'm familiar with that fellow."

"Isaac Dayton. An old party hand."

"Do you know where I might find him?"

"Up at the Fifth Avenue Hotel, often as not. Can't spit without hitting a Republican in that joint."

"Thank you very much for your time, Mr. Foote," Thomas said, rising. "You've been very helpful. Perhaps one day I can return the favor, should you ever find yourself in legal difficulties. In the meantime, please have another round on me. Miss Gallagher?"

Thomas paid the barman, and we climbed the steps into the morning sun.

"You've got that look," I told him.

"What look is that?"

"Like a hound with a scent in his nose. I've never been hunting, but I imagine that's just what it looks like."

He smiled. "Not the most flattering analogy, but accurate enough. We're getting somewhere now. Hopefully Uncle Isaac will prove as useful as Mr. Foote. Now, if the reek of vinegar and cigars hasn't put you off entirely, may I invite you to luncheon, Miss Gallagher? The Fifth Avenue Hotel makes a very fine turtle soup."

"Dining with your secretary? What will people say?"

"I'm sorry about that. Are you very much bothered?"

"About being your employee instead of your partner? Not really. It's enough to be . . ." I'd been about to say *with you*, but of course I couldn't. "It's enough to be on a real case again," I finished, smiling.

"Look at us, grinning away over six dead men. What dreadful people we are. Ah, there's a cab . . ."

He flagged it down, and we were off once again.

CHAPTER 7

WHITE FANGS—UNCLE ISAAC—REPTILES AND AMPHIBIANS—THE DREADED DAY ARRIVES

The Fifth Avenue Hotel sprawled over a full block opposite Madison Square, at the epicenter of New York traffic. Horse-car tracks crisscrossed the street in both directions, and a throng of hacks and hansom cabs, pushcarts, and pedestrians vied for space along the cobbles. In the midst of the chaos, the hotel's stately Italian facade looked on disapprovingly, its white marble pillars gleaming like a row of fangs keeping the rabble at bay.

Though I'd passed the building a hundred times, I'd never set foot inside, and I was eager to see what those fangs were guarding. But we needed to settle a few things first. "Are we still attorney and secretary, then?"

"*Hmm,* I don't think so. Mr. Dayton might be less than forth-coming if our inquiries seem too official. On top of which, we don't yet know where this investigation will lead us, so we'd do well to keep our options open. We'll only tell him I'm an attorney if he asks, and as for you, what do you say to using the same story as we gave Louise?"

We'd told the new housemaid that I was a visiting relative, and that explanation had seemed to satisfy her, imperfect as it was. "It's worked well enough so far," I said.

"Good. As to our approach, I think simple curiosity will do the job."

Thus agreed, Thomas nodded to the doorman, and we headed inside.

We stepped into a sea of white marble. The entrance hall sparkled from floor to ceiling, dimmed only by the haze of cigar smoke. All along its length, gentlemen in frock coats and cutaways milled about, their dark forms seeming almost to float against the bleached backdrop. Glossy hats and shoes and fur-collared overcoats rippled like water under moonlight; gold glinted from fingers and cufflinks and watch chains. There was nowhere to rest my eyes from the glare. I felt awfully self-conscious in my plain tweed overcoat and fading hat, but there was nothing for it; head high, I accompanied Thomas to the counter.

"Good morning," said the young man on duty, "how may I assist you?" To his credit, his glance flitted only briefly over my humble attire before settling, with visible relief, on Thomas's expensive tailoring.

"We were hoping to meet a friend of mine," Thomas said. "Mr. Isaac Dayton? Do you know where he might be found?"

The young man directed us to the Reading Room, a compact gentlemen's den of leather and wood that looked more like a fancy restaurant than a library. There, after another discreet inquiry, we found a genteel-looking fellow tucked behind a table, tutting over his copy of *The New-York Times*.

"Mr. Dayton?" I asked sweetly.

He glanced up, visibly surprised to find a lady in the Reading Room. "Madam?"

"There, you see, cousin?" I touched Thomas's arm playfully. "I'm right after all."

"So you are. I do beg your pardon, sir. Miss Gallagher was quite eager to confirm her hypothesis, and I simply couldn't deny her."

"Not at all," Dayton said bemusedly. "Do I know you, sir?"

"We haven't had the pleasure. Thomas Wiltshire, and this is my cousin, Miss Rose Gallagher. We were only just having coffee with an acquaintance who gave your name as a particular expert in matters of local politics, and now here you sit, before our very eyes. I thought it too much of a coincidence to credit, but Miss Gallagher insisted that it must be you. And what do you say to the charge, sir? Are you indeed such an expert?"

Dayton was visibly pleased, though he answered modestly enough. "If I am guilty, half the men in this room are equally so."

"Really?" I glanced at Thomas in delight. "How wonderful! We shall have the full story now, I expect. Mr. Dayton, may I?" Without waiting for a reply, I arranged myself on the chair opposite, having already decided to play the brazen girl. Thomas, for his part, observed this performance with a mildly scandalized look that I think was only half feigned. "Quite a surprise, isn't it, this Mr. Roosevelt earning the nomination."

Dayton harrumphed into his beard. "To some, certainly. I daresay even to the man himself."

"But not to you?"

"Nor to many others in this room. The party has been abuzz with it for days, and the party bosses busy as bees spreading their pollen." There was more than a hint of disapproval in his voice.

"I'd never heard the name until yesterday, but he seems like a wonderful choice. Why, the coverage in the *Times* is positively gushing!"

I'd hoped to provoke him, and it worked: Dayton's brows gathered, and he set his paper aside with a look of mild distaste. "Isn't it, though? You'd think the man walked on water."

"You don't agree?"

Faced with such a direct question from a stranger, he demurred. "Well, I'm not sure that I—"

"I'm quite perplexed by it myself," Thomas put in. "I'd have much preferred Acton. Now there's a man Wall Street can count on."

"Quite right, sir," Dayton said, energized now that he was sure of a sympathetic ear. "A sensible man who understands the needs of industry."

"And Mr. Roosevelt doesn't?" I asked.

"Roosevelt, madam, is a *free trader*." He raised his eyebrows significantly.

"Oh, dear."

"I said as much from the floor last night, not that anyone would listen. Depew had them eating out of his hand, as usual. Though by then, of course, it was mere theater. The party bosses had already done their work."

"I heard about that," Thomas said. "Some say Roosevelt didn't have much genuine support at all."

Dayton leaned forward and stabbed his newspaper with a finger. "Not half a dozen in that hall, mark my words."

"Really," I breathed, wide-eyed with fascination.

"A poor, misguided lot. I tried to talk them out of it, right here in this room, but they were adamant. Reformers, the lot of them, convinced that Roosevelt's the man to put an end to the spoilsmongering."

"There, at least, I am in perfect sympathy," Thomas said.

"Certainly, but at what cost? He'll—"

"Your coffee, sir." A young man in hotel livery appeared, bearing a silver tray with a steaming cup. Dayton frowned at it before taking a tentative sip. "*Hrm*, what was I saying?"

"At what cost," I said, trying not to sound impatient.

"Ah yes, the cost. The trouble with reformers is that they come in all political stripes. Roosevelt will lure them from the left and right. He'll split the Democratic vote and the Labor vote, too, and then where will we be? Adrift in uncertainty, where even a radical like Henry George has a chance. No, it were better Acton."

"Fascinating," Thomas said. "Thank you so much for your insight. By the way, did you hear about the outbreak of food poisoning?"

"*Mmm?*" Dayton glanced up from his coffee.

"At the convention," Thomas said. "Several delegates were afflicted, I believe."

Dayton grunted, seemingly unconcerned. "No, I hadn't heard. Must have happened after I was jeered out of the hall."

"Jeered!" I clucked my tongue. "How rude!"

"It doesn't pay to swim upstream, my dear," Dayton said sagely.

"Well," said Thomas, "we've taken up more than enough of your time, Mr. Dayton. Thank you for indulging us. Cousin?"

We left Uncle Isaac to finish his coffee and made our way to the restaurant. Thomas greeted the maître d'hôtel by name, and ordered our meal without even glancing at the menu. "You've been here before," I said.

"A favorite of Burrows's, not to mention most of the Fifth Avenue set." He spoke as if he weren't one of them—a habit, I'd noticed. I suppose he felt that as a foreigner, he didn't quite belong. Of course, if he'd lived a day of my life, he'd know what not belonging really felt like.

At least I'd eaten at his table enough times to know what each of the half-dozen specialized utensils was for. That, and the etiquette lessons at Newport, meant that I could at least have a meal among these people without making a fool of myself. Even so . . . "Turtle soup? I'm not sure how I feel about eating an amphibian."

"It's a reptile, actually. If you'd like to try an amphibian, the frogs' legs are quite wonderful."

My stomach squirmed. If *fitting in* meant eating turtles and frogs, maybe it was just as well that I didn't. Not for the first time, I wondered why the rich made a delicacy of things your average ragpicker wouldn't touch if he was starving.

"Now, as to the morning's work, what are your thoughts?"

I said what had been on my mind since meeting William Foote. "If this was a shade, it had a very specific agenda."

"To prevent the nomination of Theodore Roosevelt." Thomas nodded. "Very specific indeed, and an unlikely motive for a shade. Spirits of the dead are usually looking to redress grievances from the past, not influence events in the future. Which makes me doubt it's a shade at all. On the face of it, I'm inclined to think our killer is of the living, breathing sort."

"I agree, which brings us right back to the beginning. How was it done? Thanks to Mr. Burrows, we know it wasn't poison, and the coroner's assistant didn't find any sign of injury. Even if he's right about one of them dying of a heart attack, what does that mean?"

"Having eliminated the other possibilities, we can only conclude that it's luck."

"*Luck?*"

Thomas winced, and I realized that I'd blurted it out far too loudly. There were only a handful of places in New York where such a seemingly innocent word would draw any notice at all—but of course we happened to be sitting in one of them.

"Sorry." I resisted the urge to glance around and see if anyone was looking. "It's just . . ."

"A shocking idea, I know. If it is luck, it's the most potent variety I've ever come across."

"*Pullman's Guide to the Paranormal* says that the more powerful forms of luck dwindled out generations ago. How could one this dangerous survive without anyone knowing about it?"

"Quite. Then there's the question of why it would be put to such a purpose. What threat does Roosevelt pose, and to whom?"

"From what Mr. Dayton said, it sounds as though he has plenty of enemies, especially if he really is the reformer he claims to be."

"On that score, his record in Albany leaves little doubt. Machine politicians of all stripes have much to fear from a Roosevelt administration. As do wealthy industrialists, bankers, and most of Wall Street, at least if Dayton is to be believed." He sighed. "Which makes narrowing down a list of suspects devilishly tricky."

"What about Dayton himself? He made his opposition to Roosevelt plain."

Thomas shook his head. "Remember what he said—the convention was pure theater. By then, the party bosses had already lined up the votes. Those murders did nothing to prevent the nomination, and Dayton would have known that. No, whoever did this must have been privy enough to the inner workings of the Republican Party to know about the nomination in advance, but not so well informed that he understood the futility of his actions. A wealthy donor, perhaps, or a politician with a reputation for corruption. In other words"—he smiled ruefully—"a needle in a haystack."

"I guess we'll just have to sort through them one by one."

"Indeed, but it will take time, and that is something we have precious little of. The election is only two weeks away. If the killer is truly intent on preventing a Roosevelt administration, his failure at the convention will only drive him to more desperate measures."

"More desperate than murder?"

"From murder to assassination, perhaps. Roosevelt will be vulnerable during the campaign. Which is why we need to flush out the killer as quickly as possible."

That was easier said than done, of course. "Where do we even start?"

"Among those with the most to lose," Thomas said. "Roosevelt's direct competition."

"Hewitt and George." Two days ago, those names hadn't meant much to me, but I had a feeling I'd be hearing them a lot in the days to come.

"And their most ardent supporters, though we mustn't rule out the Republicans. It's possible the attack came from within the party, in an effort to secure the nomination for someone else."

"We can't just go around interrogating the candidates for mayor," I pointed out. "Byrnes would have us locked up on Blackwell's Island before nightfall."

"Agreed. We'll need to come at them indirectly, through their agents and backers. It will have to be a covert operation. Soirees, banquets, rallies. Wherever our targets gather in numbers. We can make our start tomorrow, in fact, at the reception for Lord Barringsdale. All of society will be there. We'll need introductions to some of the key players, but fortunately, we know just the man for the job."

"Mr. Burrows? I'm not sure he'll be eager to help after what I put him through."

"Arranging an invitation for luncheon is hardly the same as sifting through the gastrointestinal tract of a dead man."

Unfortunately, Thomas happened to speak these words at the precise moment our soup arrived. If I live to be a hundred, I expect I'll never see a fine luncheon arranged with such haste, and in such perfectly appalled silence. Silver flashed and bone china clinked, and with a perfunctory offer of peppercorns, our waiter fled.

"Please forgive my manners, Rose," Thomas murmured. "Entirely inappropriate luncheon conversation."

"I'm the one who brought it up," I said, gazing unhappily at the contents of my bowl. I needn't have worried, though; bringing a tentative spoonful to my mouth, I discovered that turtle tastes a lot like chicken.

"One more thing we ought to address, which is the matter of your living accommodations."

My spoon froze halfway to my mouth.

"No need to panic. We've bought ourselves a little time with our new cover story. No one will think it inappropriate for a visiting relative to reside with me for a time, particularly if they assume you have a chaperone. But that excuse will not serve indefinitely. We'll need to find you a new home."

"You're right, of course." I forced myself to carry on eating. I'd known this dreaded day would come. But the idea of leaving, of no longer seeing Thomas first thing in the morning and late in the evening, of being just a colleague like any other . . . it hurt in the very center of my being. And where would I go?

"I don't suppose you'll want to return to Five Points, especially if this new street gang Jackson mentioned is as troublesome as all that. But perhaps somewhere within easy distance, so you can visit your mother. There are some very respectable options near Washington Square."

"I could never afford that neighborhood."

"You might be surprised," he said breezily, reaching for a roll. "Prices are not what they once were now that fashion has moved north. With your salary, you ought to be able to find something comfortable."

"Thomas." I set my spoon down, looking at him incredulously. "I earn a good deal more than I used to, it's true, but I also had room and board included. Now I'll have to pay for my own room and board, on top of Mam's, with only a little contribution from Pietro. Either that, or have Mam move in with me and hire someone to look after her. How much of my twenty dollars a week do you suppose will be left after that?"

Thomas's hand faltered as he reached for his wine. "I beg your pardon?"

"Mam's rent isn't too costly, but I also need to keep a little aside, in case something unexpected happens."

His hand remained frozen mid-reach. "I see," he said, and for a fleeting moment, something like anger passed through his eyes. "Forgive me, Rose, I didn't realize." He grabbed his wine and took a hasty sip. "That is, I had forgotten about your mother's expenses."

"Please don't misunderstand. I'm not complaining. I'm sure I'll be able to find something suitable. Just not in Washington

Square." It was all I could do not to smile, in spite of myself. Wealthy as he was, Thomas probably paid no attention to things like salaries and rent. I took some comfort in knowing that there were some subjects, at least, on which he was the novice.

Of course, they were few and far between, as his next words made plain. "You'll have access to the expense account for your toilet, at least."

"Expense account?"

"Certainly. The Pinkerton Agency will be responsible for all costs associated with the performance of your duties. You must look the part, after all."

Confusion gave way to horror as I realized what he meant. I'd thought multitudes of tiny forks were intimidating, but *this* . . . Helplessly I glanced down at my dress, and my fevered imagination took over. Layer upon layer of fabric seemed to materialize before my eyes: chemises and petticoats, bustles and bodices, underskirts and overskirts and stifling corsets, all of it enveloping me in an ever-tightening cocoon. Already it felt as if I were struggling to draw air.

"I trust you paid careful attention during your dancing lessons," Thomas said. "You're going to need them."

CHAPTER 8

LORD AND TAILOR—LOOKING
THE PART—OFF TO BATTLE

Rose, honey, I don't even know what this is." Clara held up a set of cotton stays, buttoned at the front and laced at the back.

"An underbodice?" I hazarded. "Or maybe a corset cover?"

"Is there a difference?"

"I have no idea. I have no idea about any of this!" I gestured helplessly at the mountain of parcels gathered on the floor around us.

They'd been arriving all afternoon: box after box of silk and satin, tulle and lace, summoned by Thomas from the grandest cast-iron palaces along Ladies' Mile. I'd only ever glimpsed such treasures from the el as it rattled past the brightly lit showrooms on Sixth Avenue. I'd never thought to have them arrayed at my feet like this, and now that they were, they terrified me. One box contained reams of satin that glided like water between my fingers, so fine that I was sure my rough housemaid hands would snag it to ribbons. Another was labeled PASSEMENTERIE, which sounded like some sort of pastry but proved to be fringes and braids and sundry other trimmings. There were beaded slippers and suede gloves, miraculously all in my size, as well as a full complement of undergarments. *Also in my size,* I realized with dawning horror as I drew yet another lacy thing from its box. My cheeks grew hot.

"Before you go imagining things, it was me gave that lady from Altman's your size. Mr. Wiltshire passed the 'phone to me, looking even more red-faced than you are right now. Though why you didn't just go down there yourself is beyond me. Least then we'd know what this is supposed to be." She held up a braided wire contraption attached to a leather belt.

"They're not open on Sundays. Frankly, I don't even know how Thomas made this happen."

"Rich folks can make anything happen. But if it was me, I'd've waited till morning and done it myself."

"It wouldn't leave the seamstress enough time, no matter how many assistants she has." That had been my thinking, at any rate, but I almost regretted the decision now. On the one hand, I was grateful to have been spared the daunting marble labyrinth of A. T. Stewart's. Then again, I would never have chosen the alarming shade of yellow that someone at Arnold Constable had seen fit to select. Either way, I was at their mercy, being even less enlightened than Thomas on the subject of elegant women's fashions. All we could do was inform the sages of Ladies' Mile of our upcoming social calendar and leave the rest to their judgment.

Which apparently included a bustle the size of a spotted hog. "Sweet Mary and Joseph," I said, taking the wire contraption from Clara. "How on earth are you supposed to sit with one of these strapped to your caboose?"

She shook her head, eying the thing distrustfully. "And what about jewelry? You can't very well wear *that*."

My hand went to the little wooden crucifix at my throat. "I suppose not. We wouldn't want people to know I'm a *papist*, would we?"

"They might faint clean away."

We shared a wry look.

"When does the seamstress get here?"

"Soon, I hope." Thomas's tailor had already arrived; the two of them were shut away in his rooms, composing yet another impeccable ensemble. It was a measure of the importance of tomorrow night's event that even Thomas, always finely dressed, felt the need for something new. I guess it wasn't every day that a genuine English lord came to town. Presumably, Thomas wanted to make a good impression on his countryman.

"I'll tell you one thing," Clara said, "ain't nobody getting into these stays by herself. I suppose I'm the one strapping you into this costume tomorrow night?"

"If you're willing."

"I've done worse for you."

Now that was the God's honest truth.

"All of society will be there, Thomas says, including Mr. Roosevelt. That means there's a chance our killer will be, too."

"How will you know him?"

"Good question. The only description we have is of a tall, gangly fellow, and we're not even sure he was the killer. All we can do is keep a careful eye on the guests and try to coax some information out of them."

"While you're all togged up like a princess, sippin' champagne at a fancy party. Tough work." Clara held up another length of satin, this one a rich ruby red. "Well, now. *This* is fit for a lord, and no mistake."

"I beg your pardon, ladies." Thomas appeared in the doorway, his tailor in tow. A dapper-looking Englishman, Mr. Jennings was lately of someplace called Savile Row, a name Thomas pronounced with great reverence. "We wondered if Miss Gallagher had selected a fabric, that Mr. Jennings might coordinate various of my accouterments."

I scrambled to my feet and dusted off the seat of my skirt, embarrassed. Aside from the indignity of being caught sitting on the floor, I'd made a thorough mess of Thomas's parlor. Even my generous guest bedroom couldn't accommodate all the parcels, so we'd been obliged to receive them here. Between the boxes and paper and little embossed cards, it looked like a small tornado had passed through.

"I'm not sure what to say, Mr. Jennings," I told the tailor apologetically. "The seamstress hasn't arrived yet."

"May I inquire as to the name of the *couturière*?" Mr. Jennings asked in an accent nearly as posh as Thomas's.

"I beg your pardon?"

"The, er . . . *seamstress*. Whom are you using?"

"Madam Calvary," Thomas informed him, "on your recommendation."

"Very good, sir. In that case, I shall be in touch with her directly, once madam has had the opportunity to make her selection."

I wasn't sure which *madam* he meant—the seamstress or myself—but I could guess.

Thomas showed the tailor out, returning a moment later to find Clara and me struggling to put the parlor right. "Rose, may

I distract you for a moment before the *couturière* arrives? I have a few names to add to our list of potential suspects following my discussion with Mr. Jennings."

"You consulted your tailor about a murder investigation?"

He met my skeptical eyebrow with a challenging one of his own. "Tailors hear a great deal, as do barbers, barkeeps, and bootblacks. A bit of idle chitchat can extract all manner of useful information."

I followed him to his study, where he took up the list we'd been working on and penned a few more names. "I'll copy this out and send it to Sergeant Chapman. He'll be wondering how we're getting on. In the meantime, here are the gentlemen we can expect to find at the reception tomorrow evening." He handed me the list, each name inked out in his precise handwriting, as tidy as a tin plate.

The names, too, were the stuff of newsprint. The cream of New York society, not to mention an assortment of foreign dignitaries, and of course a genuine English lord. My heart started beating faster.

I looked up to find Thomas's eyes on me. "No need to be nervous. It's only supper and dancing."

Only supper and dancing? Clearly, he didn't understand. "This isn't my world, Thomas."

"But it is." He took me gently by the shoulders, turning me about. "Look around you. This room, this house . . . You've lived here as an equal for the better part of a year."

"But a society event . . ."

"There's nothing new in that. You've dined at Burrows's a dozen times."

"Only with the two of you. And the dancing . . . You said it yourself, I'll need to remember my lessons, but—"

"I was only teasing, Rose. I've watched you dance. You'll do splendidly."

That drew me up short. I'd never seen Thomas at our dancing lessons. Aside from jujitsu, he'd always had other business to attend to while the recruits were put through their paces. "You've . . . watched me?"

"Of course." His hands were still on my shoulders, his pale gaze holding me just as warmly.

My insides melted.

The ensuing silence was the most exquisite torture. He was so close that I could hear the Patek Philippe ticking softly in his pocket. I wanted so badly to take that extra step, to force the issue, to have it all out in the open one way or the other. I felt my breath coming faster, my pulse thudding in my ears. "Yes?" he murmured, and it sounded like an invitation.

The door swung open; I nearly leapt out of my skin. The thudding hadn't been my heartbeat after all, but Clara knocking. Her eyes shifted from me to Thomas and back, narrowing. "Seamstress is here," she said, her tone tinder dry.

"Coming," I said weakly.

"Before you go." Opening a drawer in his desk, Thomas produced a small parcel tied with ribbon. "I hope it will be to your liking."

Inside, I found a brooch of pearls and tiny diamonds in an intricate lace pattern, with a single cushion-cut emerald at the center. At which point I very nearly fainted.

"You must look the part, after all."

For a moment, I couldn't find my voice. It was the most breathtaking thing I'd ever seen. Dazzling, yes, but not the vulgar sort of extravagance I'd seen illustrated in the pages of *Frank Leslie's*. The design was elegant and restrained, speaking of a refined sensibility. Speaking, in other words, of the sensibilities of Thomas Wiltshire, leaving me little doubt he'd chosen the piece himself.

"It's incredible," I breathed. "New clothing I understand, but *this* . . . The Agency must be doing very well indeed."

"Actually . . ." He cleared his throat. "This came from my personal funds."

My head snapped up. "*Thomas.*"

"A necessary measure. Every lady in the room will be wearing her best jewels, and we can't very well allow your cover to be compromised by such a glaring oversight. The gentlemen at Dreicer were good enough to open the store for me, but I would require special permission from the Agency for a purchase of this significance, and we haven't time to obtain it. This seemed the only practical solution."

"Yes, of course." My gaze fell back to the glittering treasure in the box. "Practical."

"I hope Madam Calvary will approve the combination of emerald and ruby, should you opt for the red satin."

"It will match your cufflinks," I said dazedly.

"Yes." There was a stretch of silence. Thomas cleared his throat again. "Well, then, you'd best not keep Madam Calvary waiting." Seating himself behind his desk, he took up his pen once more.

"Thomas."

The pen wavered.

"It's incredible. Thank you."

"You're most welcome, Rose." He didn't look up.

"Well, I suppose that's it." Clara folded her arms, surveying her handiwork. "I think everything's on there right, and if it ain't, it's so far buried under heaps of silk and satin nobody'll know the difference."

"Let's hope so," I said, staring at my reflection in the mirror. It was a strange sensation, seeing myself all togged up like a proper society lady. I'd never felt so pretty—or so self-conscious.

I'd never been so uncomfortable either. I could hardly believe that my waist had been trussed up into the narrow confines of my bodice, and as for my bosom, well . . . I actually had one, for a novelty. Neither of these bothered me so much as the bustle, though. I still couldn't see how a person could reasonably sit down. I supposed I would find out soon enough.

"Quit worrying," Clara said. "That Madam Calvary was as high-and-mighty as they come, but she knows her business. Why, just look at you." She led me through a pirouette. In the mirror, I saw a young society lady in a sumptuous red dress trimmed with lace. The overskirt had been fashioned of the ruby satin Clara had admired, while an underskirt of deep garnet peeked out between extravagant gathers down the back. "That color is mighty fine on you. Brings out the hints of red in your hair. And that brooch . . ." She whistled, and my gaze dropped instinctively to the galaxy of diamonds and pearls fastened at the low neck of my bodice. "Do you get to keep it, or will the Agency make you take it back when this is all over?"

I avoided her eye. I hadn't told her that Thomas had paid for the brooch. Clara knew how I felt about him, and she didn't much like it, figuring that those feelings had only ever landed me in trouble. Which, to be fair, wasn't entirely off the mark. If I'd told her about the brooch, she'd probably have warned me not to read anything into it—or to give it back straightaway. Neither prospect appealed.

"I just hope it's over soon," I said evasively, "though we're not exactly off to a brisk start." I'd spent the entire day sipping tea and browsing through newspapers in the Reading Room of the Fifth

Avenue Hotel, and all I had to show for it was an unholy amount of newsprint on my new white gloves. Hours of eavesdropping and small talk had yielded nothing of use, and I hadn't spotted anyone answering to the description of the suspect. Thomas had fared no better at the Madison Club, though in the plus column, he'd come away with "several viable market tips," and as for me, I could safely consider myself abreast of current events, having consumed every column inch of New York's legion of newspapers.

None of which brought us any closer to finding our killer.

"Oops, that sounds like your carriage." Clara pulled the curtain aside and peered out the window. "A brougham and all. My, my."

All right, Rose. You can do this. I gave myself a final pat-down, making sure everything was securely in place.

"Gloves," Clara said, handing them to me. "Cape. Hat. Bag." And then, with a sigh, "Gun."

"Thanks," I said, tucking the little derringer into my evening bag. "Really, Clara, thank you for everything. I don't know what I'd have done without you. I wish you could come with me."

She gave a hollow laugh. "Then they really would faint clean away. It'd almost be worth it just to watch."

"Almost, but not quite?"

"No disrespect, honey, but you couldn't pay me enough to do your job."

Glancing at myself in the mirror a final time, I took a deep breath. "Wish me luck. I'm going to need it."

I picked my way down the stairs, gathering my multitude of skirts about me as best I could. Awkward as it was, it still felt like a dream. Except that even in my wildest fantasies, I'd never dared to imagine *this*. The little girl in me, the one who never let go of visions of herself as a princess, was leaping with excitement. But she felt very small and alone down there in the pit of my stomach. And she was making me nauseous.

I found Thomas in the parlor. He stood gazing into the fire, a glass of cognac in his hand. I didn't think I'd ever seen him drink cognac before. I'd dusted that crystal decanter for the better part of two years without ever seeing its level drop, but it was noticeably lower now. He'd poured himself a stiff drink, though it didn't look like he'd actually downed any of it. Instead he just swirled the amber liquid around restlessly. *He's nervous,* I thought. *Why should he be nervous?* He wasn't the one living out a fantasy. Feeling suddenly like a voyeur, I cleared my throat.

He turned. For a moment he seemed not to know what to say, as if the awkwardness from before still lingered. Maybe he'd sipped some of the cognac after all, because there was a glassy look in his eye, and when he smiled, it had an almost wistful quality to it. "Good evening, Rose. You look lovely. Very lovely indeed."

"Thank you. And you look very fine as well."

Fine was not the word I wanted to use.

I'd seen Thomas in a swallowtail coat more times than I could count, and he always looked immaculate—whites gleaming, kid gloves fresh as new, silk hat brushed to a high gloss. But the sight never failed to send embers swirling through my insides, and though we were to spend the evening as cousins, I was already entertaining some extremely un-cousinly thoughts.

"These are for you," he said, taking a bouquet of lilies from the banquette at the window. He himself wore a small rose in his buttonhole, of the same brilliant red as my dress. "Not very practical for our purposes this evening, I admit, but I didn't want to overlook the gesture entirely. We can have Louise put them in your room."

I brought the lilies to my nose, inhaling deeply. Though their scent relaxed me a little, it still felt like a dream. "They're beautiful, thank you."

"Sherry?" Then, with a wisp of a smile: "Or perhaps something stronger?"

"I don't dare."

"Very well, then." Setting his own glass aside, he grabbed his hat. "To battle."

CHAPTER 9

A CATHEDRAL IN MARBLE— OYERLAND—A DASHING RESCUE

The carriage trundled up to the Hendriks mansion at precisely ten-thirty. Liveried footmen waited to receive us, and no sooner had my head emerged from the brougham than an umbrella was opened over it, even though we were protected under the porte cochere. Between the drizzle and the moonless night, I couldn't make out much of the grounds, but I'd passed the house plenty of times on my errands, and I knew it for one of the handsomest palaces on the Avenue. I could hardly believe I was actually mounting its steps, still less that I was doing so on the arm of Thomas Wiltshire, even if it was under false pretenses.

"Are you ready, cousin?" he murmured.

"As I'll ever be, cousin."

It was like stepping into a cathedral, or so it seemed to me.

The entrance hall yawned before us, its twenty-foot ceilings supported by pillars of blue-veined marble and fluted Roman arches. The walls, too, were marble, a stark white canvas for massive oil paintings and heavy velvet curtains. A magnificent staircase branched down from the mezzanine level in twin cascades, its iron lace balustrades entwined with ivy and yellow orchids. Clouds of lilies and jasmine graced every available surface, even the risers of the stairs; their spicy fragrance perfumed the air. Above it all, gas lamps hung in gilded pendants, bathing the hall in a golden glow.

"*Sweet Mary and Joseph.*"

"In the French château style," Thomas informed me. Then, lowering his voice: "Rather too baroque for my tastes."

Passing between the embracing arms of the stairs, we came to a wide corridor lined with palms and ferns, where we met the tail end of the receiving line.

"The ladies' dressing room is on the second floor. That will be an excellent place to pick up interesting gossip. If you lose sight of me, it's most likely because I've put myself to the same purpose among the men in the games room."

"You've been here before, I take it?"

"Twice. Mrs. Hendriks's annual February ball is one of the most prestigious events of the social season. This will be a much more subdued affair, I should think."

"Visibly."

"Sarcasm is unbecoming, Miss Gallagher."

And then there was no more time for advice. We'd arrived at the head of the receiving line, where an elegant matriarch in green satin awaited us. Mrs. Hendriks was the very picture of civility, as were her daughters, but our time with royalty was brief; Thomas introduced me, I murmured a few polite banalities, and we were off, but not before a small box had been pressed into my hand.

Inside, I found a dainty silver bracelet with a dangling charm. For a moment I just stared at it, incredulous. "Thomas, they've given me jewelry."

"A favor." He showed me his own gift, a silver scarf pin adorned with a single black pearl. "From Tiffany's, or so says the ribbon."

"Should I wear it?"

"If you like. It's yours to do with as you please."

I glanced around; the other young ladies were indeed putting theirs on, with great shows of interest and admiration, so I did the same. It dangled prettily from my wrist, a welcome flash of interest against my white satin gloves.

Continuing on, we made our way through a procession of parlors separated by heavy damask curtains. Everywhere, tasteful signs of wealth were on display: rosewood furnishings, silver bric-a-brac, painted porcelain. And the flowers. Sweet Lord, the flowers. On mantels and tables, chiffoniers and chandeliers, in such multitudes that I had to tuck my fingers under my nose to keep from sneezing. Thomas offered me his handkerchief, but snuffling into a gentleman's fine linens was hardly the first impression I wanted to make. "I'll be all right," I said. "I only need a moment to get used to it."

Just then, a familiar laugh rang out in the next parlor; pushing aside the portiere, we found Mr. Burrows, sherry in hand, surrounded by a gaggle of admiring young ladies. He looked even more handsome than usual, a fact of which he was most evidently aware, and I almost felt sorry for the Knickerbocker princesses vying for his attention. If there was a more inveterate rounder in all of New York, I hadn't met him.

He spied Thomas first. "There you are, old man. And can this be Miss Gallagher? Why, I hardly recognized you."

"Mr. Burrows." I inclined my head demurely, as was appropriate.

Which of course he was having none of. He took my hand and kissed it, a playful smile teasing his lips. "You are a vision."

Thomas, for his part, greeted the assembled ladies with a courtly nod. Then, before we could be drawn into conversation: "I say, Burrows, we've just passed the most extraordinary picture. Have you taken a look?" He gestured at a distant painting and raised an eyebrow pointedly.

Excusing himself from his admirers, Mr. Burrows followed us to a discreet remove. "Admiring a picture is a poor cover, Thomas," he said once we were safely out of earshot. "Anyone who knows me is not likely to be fooled by it."

"My dear Burrows, I am merely burnishing your reputation as a man of culture." Thomas gestured at the painting as if he were pointing out something of interest.

Mr. Burrows duly observed the canvas, but the rakish smile had returned. "I must say, Miss Gallagher, it is a shock to the system to see you like this."

"For us both."

"Simply radiant. I especially admire that brooch. Draws the eye to the *décolletage*."

"Jonathan," Thomas murmured disapprovingly.

"All right, let us be serious." Mr. Burrows made a half-hearted gesture at the painting. "Why am I pretending to admire this ghastly thing?"

"I hadn't time to telephone, but Rose and I are meant to be cousins. She's visiting from Boston, so you haven't known her for long, understood?"

"In that case, my kissing her hand was terribly fresh."

"It was terribly fresh anyway," I said, "as you perfectly well know."

He shrugged. "Perching at the edge of shocking is just about the only amusement to be had at such events."

"A luxury we do not have," Thomas said. "We're trying to catch a killer, a task with which your assistance would be most appreciated."

Mr. Burrows's expression darkened.

"Come now, you needn't look at me like that. I ask only for an introduction here and there, and perhaps another set of eyes."

Mr. Burrows took a long pull of his sherry, as though to banish a bad memory. "And what am I looking for?"

I took my own turn to admire the painting, a gloomy depiction of some revolutionary battle or another. "Do you remember the description Sergeant Chapman gave us of a tall, gangly fellow?"

"That's awfully vague."

"Indeed," Thomas said, "and there's our difficulty. The only other clue we have is that it appears the killer sought to prevent the nomination of Theodore Roosevelt for mayor."

As before, the name registered on Mr. Burrows's features. "Do you know him?" I asked.

"We were at Harvard together. He was ahead of me, but we saw each other now and then at the Porcellian Club. Is he in some kind of danger?"

"Possibly," Thomas said. "We've only the shadow of a theory at this point."

"He's supposed to be here tonight," I said. "If he does come, it would be a great help if you could introduce us."

Mr. Burrows's gaze grew abstracted with memory. "I watched

him get the tar beat out of him once. In the ring, my freshman year at Harvard. He was completely outclassed, staggering about and gushing blood, but he wouldn't give up." He shook his head. "I'll say this, if someone is out to get Roosevelt, he'll have his work cut out for him. The man is a bull."

My glance did a tour of the room, taking in the fine specimens in their bright plumage and glossy coats. It was hard to imagine a killer among them, still less an assassin.

"Don't let those refined facades fool you," Mr. Burrows said, guessing my thoughts. "A good share of these people are lucky, and they won't hesitate to use that to their advantage."

"A timely reminder," Thomas agreed. "We must remain on our guard—especially you, Rose. These people are new to you, and you don't know what they might be capable of. Burrows and I will do our best to warn you where we can, but not all of their powers are known to us. Many have chosen to keep their talents hidden, and those are the most dangerous of all."

I nodded, feeling a little queasy.

"All right, then," Thomas said, "let's be about it. I'll introduce you to as many of our potential suspects as I can, and then we'll have to split up."

Taking our leave of Mr. Burrows, we made our way through the enfilade of parlors and drawing rooms, leaving a trail of handshakes and *pleased to make your acquaintance*s behind us. We saved the ballroom for last, and by the time we got there, the dancing was well underway. Several of the ladies were already resting, collecting in small clusters to sip wine and converse, and it was to one of these gatherings that Thomas guided me next. "This is as good a place as any to begin your inquiries," he said in an undertone. "The lady in silver is Mrs. Gilbert Walsh. You recall, the banker?

He was a key force pushing for Acton to earn the nomination. See if you can determine his whereabouts the night of the convention."

But before we reached our target, we were hailed by royalty. Ava Hendriks called Thomas's name, and we had no choice but to answer the summons of our hostess.

"Miss Hendriks," Thomas said with an elegant little bow. "What a perfectly lovely evening. You remember my cousin, Miss Gallagher, from the receiving line?"

"Of course." She extended a gloved hand, and we shook. Or rather, I shook; Miss Hendriks permitted her hand to be grasped while she surveyed me with a cool-eyed gaze, subtly but unmistakably sizing me up. "We are in your debt, Miss Gallagher. We see Mr. Wiltshire so rarely. With his cousin in town, he will surely feel obliged to favor us with his presence more often." She bestowed a radiant smile on Thomas.

"I do believe Miss Hendriks intends to marry you off, Mr. Wiltshire," put in one of her companions, a pretty brunette with a mischievous cast to her features. "She's lined up several eligible candidates."

"*Honestly,* Miss Islington." Miss Hendriks tutted theatrically. It was clear from her smile, though, that she wasn't the least bit put out by this remark; on the contrary, she seemed to await Thomas's response.

He fended her off masterfully. "By all means, Miss Hendriks, send me your list. With your reputation for matchmaking, it promises to be intriguing."

"A worthy reply," said the mischievous brunette, saluting Thomas with her glass.

"It is ever my aim to please, Miss Islington." Then he spotted one of our targets nearby. Turning to me, he said, "Cousin, may

I bring you some champagne?" And before I could reply, he'd abandoned me to the mercy of Miss Hendriks and her court.

Five pairs of eyes fixed on me. Nobody said a word. The ladies sipped their champagne, studying me as if I were some queer little creature in the Central Park menagerie.

It was the princess herself who broke the silence. "Your dance card, Miss Gallagher." She gestured at the blank piece of paper in my hand. "You haven't any names at all?"

Don't blush. Don't you dare blush. "Oh," I said, turning it over as though I'd forgotten all about it. "I've been so preoccupied learning all the new faces and names. It's been a whirlwind." Smiling demurely, I added, "But I'm having a wonderful time. Thank you so much for your hospitality."

Her smile didn't quite reach her eyes. "And you're from Boston, is that right? Do you know the Halversons?"

"I can't say I'm acquainted with them, no."

"Oh, really?" A tiny crease marred Miss Hendriks's perfect brow. "The Philippses? No? The Huntington-Smiths, surely." With each shake of my head, her expression grew colder.

"Gallagher," said another of her companions, a fragile-looking thing in blue satin. "That's Irish, isn't it?"

This pronouncement hit the floor like a lead weight.

The matter was plain, of course, Gallagher being as Irish as a jig, but so far no one had been tactless enough to mention it. Now it was *out there*, forcing everyone to openly face the distressing notion that an Irishwoman had been set loose in the ballroom.

But of course I'd been prepared for that. "My grandmother— Mr. Wiltshire's great-aunt—married an English landowner in Ireland, and my mother married an Irishman. I was actually born there myself, though I've no memory of it." This was pure hocus-pocus, of course; I was no more a member of the Ascendency class than I was the Queen of England. It would have hurt Mam terribly to hear me spin such tales, as though I were ashamed of my heritage, but I didn't have much choice.

Or so I thought, but as it turned out, I needn't have bothered.

"That explains the accent," Miss Hendriks said. "The way you say *Oyerland* is just sweet."

I stiffened. My *R*s were a touch hard-edged, maybe—in spite of my best efforts, growing up in an Irish household had left its mark—but it took a keen ear to hear it. A keen ear—or a spiteful one. The message was clear: As far as Ava Hendriks was concerned, Irish was Irish. In her eyes, I was no more worthy than a potato farmer. Or a housemaid.

The next few seconds were very delicate indeed. Mortification twisted my insides, and fury, too, but I didn't dare show it. Did she even realize she'd insulted me?

I gazed into her cold blue eyes and decided that she did.

I might have said something very unfortunate then, but thankfully, I didn't have the chance.

"Miss Gallagher." Jonathan Burrows appeared, an indolent little smile hitching his mouth. "I can hardly believe my good fortune. They're starting a waltz, and here you are unoccupied. Would you do me the honor?" He extended a gloved hand.

"Certainly, Mr. Burrows." Mustering every scrap of dignity I had left, I allowed myself to be escorted to the dance floor. For a moment I feared I'd leapt from the frying pan into the fire, but when he clasped my waist and drew me in, my lessons took over, and I fell into step naturally enough. Even so, I waited until he'd led me through a few gentle spins before I felt confident enough to speak. "Thank you for that."

"Not at all. What did she say to you, anyway? You looked fit to explode."

"Nothing. I'm fine."

His glance went over my shoulder, lingering on Ava Hendriks and her coterie. "The little viper. She's been spiteful since she was a child." Gathering me in closer, he said, "Laugh, Rose. I've just said something terribly witty."

"Pardon?"

He tucked his face into my neck, so close that his breath was warm against my skin, his voice purring just below my ear. "Laugh. Go on." I did as I was told, awkwardly at first, until he murmured, "You sound like a strangled cat," at which point I really did laugh. "That's better." He drew back, his gaze going over my shoulder once more. "What was Wiltshire thinking, throwing you to the wolves like that?"

"He thought I could manage it, and I should have. It just caught me off guard, that's all. I expected them to be cold, but not so uncivil as that."

"It's the only thing they're truly good at, I'm afraid. None of them has a thing to say for herself, except Edith Islington."

"The brunette?" I cast a discreet glance in her direction as we spun past. "She seemed a touch arch to me."

"Well, I'm hardly one to criticize on that score. These sorts of functions are difficult enough for a sensible man to endure. For a clever woman, they must be torture. My mother used to say that society doesn't know what to do with a clever woman, so she makes her amusements where she can. I daresay that for Edith Islington, that means stirring things up. And for Ava Hendriks, it means tormenting anyone she deems beneath her. Which is just about everyone."

"Never mind." I meant the words at least as much for me as for him. "I'm a professional, and I have a job to do."

"That's the spirit. Though if Miss Hendriks should happen

to take a tumble by way of some mysterious Japanese wrestling technique, I promise not to tell a soul."

This time, my laugh was perfectly genuine.

I left the dance floor feeling lighter, if a little foolish that I'd let myself be distracted by such trifles. I was only glad Thomas hadn't been there to see it. I'd spotted him out of the corner of my eye while I danced with Mr. Burrows. He'd returned with my champagne, but finding me otherwise occupied, headed off to pursue his investigations. I needed to do the same.

I spied my target across the ballroom floor. Mrs. Gilbert Walsh was making her way to the dining room, and fortunately, she was alone. It was time for my first interview.

CHAPTER 10

THOROUGHBRED—CHASING THE WHITE
RABBIT—DEE-LIGHTED—A SOLEMN VOW

Mrs. Gilbert Walsh was a bore.

That sounds unkind, I suppose, but really—how else to describe a woman whose conversation revolves entirely around other people's frocks? Listening to her was like reading the society pages of *The New-York Times*, without the benefit of tea. She offered a running commentary on each costume that passed her by, except she insisted on calling them *confections*. She had a silk-stocking name like that for everything. Nobody wore just yellow or blue; instead their dresses were *jonquil* or *cerulean*. (Mine, if you want to know, was *vermilion*.) I was educated as to the fine distinctions between Brussels and Valenciennes lace, and between pompadour and Catherine de' Medici necklines. There are only so many ways one can fake an interest in this sort of thing, even if one is a professional liar. And when I finally managed to herd her toward the subject of the Republican Convention, she just shrugged and said, "I've no idea if my husband was there, but I doubt it. Fridays are for the mistress, you know."

By this point, it was after one o'clock, and my stomach was growling audibly. Figuring I wouldn't be much use if I fainted from hunger, I headed for the supper table.

I never made it.

"He thinks he was being terribly chivalrous, I suppose."

I turned to find Edith Islington wearing her arch little smile, a fresh glass of champagne in each hand.

"I beg your pardon?"

"Jonathan Burrows. Earlier, when he swooped in to rescue you." She handed me a glass. "One has to admire his loyalty to your cousin, but he's just sealed your fate."

"I had the impression my fate was sealed upon being born Irish," I said coolly.

She made a dismissive gesture. "That was a test. Ava wanted to see how you'd react. Whether you'd be a meek little thing, or venture a riposte."

"Well then, I suppose I failed."

"You didn't have the chance. Mr. Burrows whisked you away and then made a great show of flirting with you. Which makes you the enemy."

"The enemy of whom?"

"Why, of every unmarried woman in New York. You do realize Mr. Burrows is one of society's most eligible bachelors?"

"I could hardly fail to notice his crowd of admiring females."

"Those poor besotted creatures are not the ones you need to worry about. It's the Ava Hendrikses and the Betty Sanfords. They're far more calculating, and they're not after his money or his charm. It's his pedigree they want."

"His pedigree?"

She smiled wryly. "Jonathan Burrows is a thoroughbred, darling. The competition to put him in harness is fierce."

"I can assure you I'm not a competitor."

"I believe you." She considered me with a curious tilt of her head. "Which makes you very interesting."

The remark brought to mind what Mr. Burrows had said about a clever woman making her amusements where she could. Well, I had no desire to be this woman's entertainment. Taking a page from Thomas's book, I said, "I'm pleased to be of service, Miss Islington."

She sighed. "You think I'm one of them, I suppose. Well, I can't blame you. I should have said something to distract Ava from her prey, only I was curious to see how you'd respond. It's a poor excuse, I know. So . . . a peace offering."

Thinking she meant the champagne, I took a polite sip. "Thank you."

"You're welcome, but that's not what I was referring to." Lowering her voice, she said, "I noticed your hairpin. It's very beautiful. That bit of white peeking through—is it ash, by any chance?"

Instinctively, I reached up to touch the hairpin holding my chignon in place. A gift from Thomas, it was fashioned from ash wood and jade. Terribly handy for fighting off shades—and for telegraphing my membership in the paranormal community. Edith Islington was telling me that she'd received the message.

"Good eye," I said warily.

"A *gift* of mine. I notice things, and I never forget them." Then, meeting my gaze deliberately: "It runs in the family."

I blinked in surprise. No one, not even my fellow Pinkerton recruits, had ever divulged their luck to me so bluntly. "That's . . . a lot of trust to place in someone you've just met."

"It is, and I hope I haven't misjudged you. But I really do feel awful about letting Ava get away with that nonsense. And besides, I trust your cousin, so why shouldn't I trust you?"

That didn't make much sense to me, but it wouldn't do to say so. Instead, it seemed only right to return the gesture. "As for me, I haven't any gifts." It wasn't quite a fair trade. There's nothing special about admitting you're nothing special.

"The same cannot be said of Ava. Be careful, Miss Gallagher. After that business with Mr. Burrows, she'll make a point of trying to put you in your place."

"Thank you for the warning, but . . ." I trailed off, my gaze snagging on something in the ballroom. A lanky fellow in an ill-fitting jacket had appeared among the dancers, milling about the dance floor as though searching for someone. *Searching for Theodore Roosevelt, perhaps?*

"Miss Islington, do you know that gentleman?" Before she could turn around, he'd disappeared into the crowd. "I'm terribly sorry," I said, thrusting my champagne at her, "could you excuse me?" And with greater haste than was strictly dignified, I gathered up the hem of my dress and hurried into the ballroom.

I paused on the threshold, my gaze raking the crowd. The man in the ill-fitting jacket had been nearly a head taller than anyone else; if he had been among the dancers, he would have been easy to spot. I headed for the nearest drawing room and was just in time to see him slip past the portiere. I hastened my steps, muttering *excuse me*s and *I do beg your pardon*s as I side-slipped my way through the bodies.

I lost sight of him in the next room, caught a glimpse in the one after that, only to lose him again—on and on through the endless enfilade of drawing rooms. It was maddening, and I felt more than a little like Alice chasing the White Rabbit through a labyrinth of silk and velvet.

Eventually the maze disgorged me into the entrance hall. The room took my breath away all over again, and I couldn't help letting my gaze climb the magnificent staircase. That's how I happened to be looking to the second floor when the tall man rounded a corner of the hallway and disappeared.

I paused, allowing myself a quiet sound of dismay as I contemplated trying to climb the stairs at speed while draped in several pounds of satin. *There's a reason the Bloodhound wears men's trousers,* I thought sourly, thinking back to Annie Harris's bounty hunter garb. But there was nothing for it, so I hitched my hem to the scandalous height of my calves and began the climb.

Reaching the top, I found a pair of carved wooden doors standing ajar. Cigar smoke and masculine laughter tumbled out through the gap, and I hesitated. This was clearly no place for a woman, but what else could I do? Squaring my shoulders, I went inside.

The room was thick with gentlemen, most of them gathered on the far side of a pair of billiard tables. None of them so much as glanced in my direction, too absorbed in conversation to notice an interloper in red satin. A strange current of energy crackled among them. They all faced inward, fixed upon the same subject, clustered like iron filings drawn by a magnet. The crowd was so dense that I couldn't see who stood at its center, but a high, hoarse voice carried over the laughter.

"Come, gentlemen, let us be serious. This is most unbecoming."

Through a gap between the bodies, I spied a young man holding court. Finely dressed though he was, in a trim cutaway with satin lapels and tails that nearly reached the tops of his shoes, he made an unlikely-looking king. Brown hair, sturdy build, middling height . . . there was nothing remarkable about him, yet his companions gathered around him like elderly men around a hearth, basking in his glow. I recognized the figure that had them all so transfixed, having seen his likeness in the papers. Not a king holding court after all, but a mayoral candidate campaigning.

"I tell you this, Roosevelt, and take no offense, but your odds are longer than your person."

The candidate's teeth flashed in a smile. "You venture little there, sir, for I have never been accused of towering."

A ripple of laughter. "Longer than your years, then."

"And here you venture still less! Though as to the charge that I am a boy, they said the same in Albany, though I daresay they've forgotten it by now."

Motion at the edge of my vision. The tall man in the ill-fitting jacket stepped out from a shadowed corner of the room. He paused for a moment, looking anxious; then resolve hardened his features, and he started making his way toward the cluster of gentlemen. *Making his way toward Roosevelt.*

He was too far away. I'd never reach him in time.

"Excuse me! Mr. Roosevelt!" I waved a white-gloved hand, frantic to get his attention.

The tall man pushed his way through the others. He slipped a hand inside the breast pocket of his jacket, then reached for the candidate—

"*Mr. Roosevelt, you're in danger!*"

Everyone froze.

Theodore Roosevelt blinked at me from behind a pair of pince-nez. "Madam?"

Silence. I looked around me. Twenty gentlemen were staring

at me as if I were a madwoman—including the tall man, who stood motionless beside the candidate, an envelope bearing the name *Roosevelt* in his hand.

A message. He'd been delivering a message.

Rose Gallagher, you ridiculous nit.

The candidate took the envelope distractedly, his eyes never leaving mine. "Danger, madam?"

"Y-yes. Er, that is, you are in danger of . . ." *Think, damn it!* ". . . of usurping Lord Barringsdale's place as guest of honor!" Having finally spat out this masterful bit of buffoonery, I smiled for all I was worth.

Mr. Roosevelt's brow puckered fleetingly; then he smiled the indulging smile of the politician. "You're very kind, madam, but I rather doubt that. All the truly glamorous persons are downstairs, isn't that right, gentlemen?"

"Well," I said, still scrambling to smooth over my blunder, "as for me, I couldn't help but come up here to meet you. I've been reading all about you in the papers, Mr. Roosevelt, and I just had to tell you that if I were allowed to vote, you'd certainly be my choice."

"Why, thank you. I've always been in favor of women having the vote, and now I see that I was entirely correct." More laughter from his appreciative audience.

"Sir," said a familiar voice, and Thomas separated himself from the others. I'd been so busy preventing assassination by envelope that I hadn't even noticed him. "May I present my cousin, Miss Rose Gallagher?"

"Dee-lighted!" Blue eyes crinkled behind the pince-nez, and he offered me a hand, not in the manner of a gentleman, but of a politician greeting a constituent.

I took it—and nearly jumped out of my skin as a sharp tingle ran up my arm. It was as if his very flesh were charged with energy. Even through two pairs of gloves, it made my skin buzz all the way up to the elbow. I didn't need Thomas to tell me what that meant, and when I glanced over at him, he gave an almost imperceptible nod. He'd felt it, too.

Theodore Roosevelt was lucky.

Of course he was.

"Sir," the tall man interrupted, "forgive me, but I think you'll find that note is rather urgent."

The candidate scanned the letter with a frown. "*Hmph*. Well, I suppose there's no getting around it. Gentlemen, it seems I am called away. Please accept my regrets."

Thomas and I exchanged a look of dismay. If we didn't catch him now, there might not be another chance.

"I do beg your pardon, sir," I said, "but before you go, I wonder if we might . . . that is, I would be so grateful . . ." I flailed about for a reason to speak with him in private, but couldn't think of a single decent excuse. And then:

"Roosevelt! I thought I heard you in here."

For the second time that evening, Mr. Burrows had come to my rescue.

"Burrows, my dear fellow, how are you keeping?" The candidate seized his hand and pumped it so vigorously that Mr. Burrows was in danger of spilling his cognac.

"Oh, passing well. Delighted to hear of your nomination, of course. You'll make a wonderful mayor. Which, by the way, would you mind . . . ?" Mr. Burrows motioned the candidate aside.

"Certainly."

Thomas and I followed, and the four of us withdrew to a discreet remove.

"Now then." Mr. Roosevelt turned to me. "This young lady

was about to tell me why I'm in danger." Seeing my surprise, he added, "Not to disparage your skill in subterfuge, madam, but I know genuine fear when I see it."

I blushed. "I'm sorry if I alarmed you. As it turns out, it was nothing."

"You do yourself a disservice, Miss Gallagher," Thomas said. "If you hadn't intervened, I certainly would have." Reaching into his pocket, he produced a silver card and presented it to the candidate. "We're with the Pinkerton Detective Agency."

Mr. Roosevelt peered at the card and grunted. "Special branch, is it?"

Thomas blinked in surprise. The card bore no lettering of any kind, just the single staring eye that was the symbol of the Agency. Even members of the paranormal community would be hard pressed to identify it, yet the candidate had known it at a glance.

Aren't you just full of surprises, Mr. Roosevelt?

"I see you've encountered our kind before," Thomas said. "In that case, I'll come straight to the point."

Mr. Roosevelt gripped Thomas's shoulder and drew close, bowing his head with a studious frown. "Tell me."

"You may be aware that there was an unfortunate incident at the convention the other night."

"I heard. A number of my supporters were taken ill."

Clearing my throat delicately, I said, "In fact, they died."

"Died?" He looked up, aghast. "Why, surely not all of them?"

"I'm afraid so."

His astonishment quickly hardened into a grim expression. "Suspiciously, I take it?"

"Murdered," Thomas said, "and though we aren't certain of the killer's motives, there's a chance you will be his next target."

"I see." Mr. Roosevelt straightened. "And what would you have me do?"

His matter-of-factness took me aback. I glanced at Mr. Burrows, but he just shrugged, as if to say, *What did I tell you?*

"For the moment, nothing," Thomas said. "We merely thought it prudent to warn you. We believe the murderer may be capable of killing at a touch."

"Good heavens. And the police? Where are they in all this?"

Where indeed? Aloud, I said, "They're claiming the delegates died of typhoid. We tried to persuade them to help our investigation, but . . ."

"But they have stressed the need for discretion," Thomas said, in what was certainly the understatement of the evening.

Mr. Roosevelt sighed, looking suddenly older than his twenty-seven years. "It seems I have some condolence calls to make."

"I'm sorry," I said. "I suppose you knew some of them."

"Good men, every one." His eyes grew cold then, and he seemed to take up a little more space in the room. "I trust the Pinkerton Detective Agency will find the man responsible."

Though I couldn't say why, I felt the weight of those words like a physical burden, as though a charge had been laid upon me by the highest authority. "We will, sir. You have my word."

"Very well, then. Thank you for informing me, and I wish you the best of luck in your investigation. Now if you will excuse me, I'm late for another engagement. Burrows." Shaking hands once again, Mr. Roosevelt withdrew.

Thomas consulted his watch. "Perhaps we ought to call it an evening. We'll want to start bright and early tomorrow."

"Yes, you had better." Mr. Burrows's eyes twinkled with amusement. "Rose has made a promise, after all. When thou vowest unto God, defer not to pay it."

I scowled. "It wasn't as worshipful as all that."

He just laughed. "It's nothing to be ashamed of. He has that effect on people, especially the first time they meet him."

"Yes, he packs quite the voltage, doesn't he?" Thomas glanced over his shoulder to where the candidate was still making his farewells. "I suppose everyone knows about it?"

"Everyone who recognizes the signs. Some are more sensitive to it than others, but I doubt anyone has ever met Theodore Roosevelt without feeling that pull to some degree or another. Most simply put it down to charisma, but some of us know better."

"Which variety, do you think?"

Mr. Burrows stifled a bored yawn. "I haven't the faintest. Whatever the species of luck, I daresay it will carry him far in life."

If he survives. No one had to say it aloud.

It was nearing a quarter to three by the time our carriage pulled up, and I was stifling some yawns of my own. "All that work, and for what? We didn't accomplish anything."

"Except to warn Mr. Roosevelt," Thomas said, tapping on the roof of the brougham to set it on its way. "Still, you're right. I only managed to eliminate a handful of names from our list. There are simply too many potential suspects. We need to go about this in another way."

"Maybe we should stay close to the candidate. Wait for the killer to make his move."

"Risky. We don't know for certain that Roosevelt is a target, and even if he is, there's no guarantee we'd spot the killer in time. Unless . . ." He frowned, staring off into the distance.

"What is it?"

"I've just had an idea. An inventor friend of mine is working on a few devices that may be of some use to us. Perhaps we ought to pay him a visit tomorrow."

"I didn't know you had an inventor friend. Anyone I've heard of?"

Thomas smiled. "Not likely, but if there is any justice in the world, his will soon be a household name. He's a genius to rival Edison. Perhaps even greater."

"That's quite a claim."

"A fair one, I assure you. But you can make your own determination tomorrow. We'll visit his lab. Though"—he looked over at me, suddenly grave—"I must warn you, Rose, don't touch *anything*."

I drew back in alarm. "Why, is it dangerous?"

"The most dangerous place you've ever been."

CHAPTER 11

TAMMANY HELL—THE WIZARD OF
CHATHAM SQUARE—AWESTRUCK

I went down to breakfast feeling as if I were half naked. Compared to the heavy gown I'd worn last night, my simple dress seemed like little more than underthings. Liberating as it was, I was sorry to be without at least one part of my costume. The brooch Thomas had given me was much too extravagant for everyday wear, but oh, how I hated to tuck it away. It reminded me of how I'd felt when I returned his watch back in January, after days of keeping it in my breast pocket. The Patek Philippe had been a piece of him to carry with me; giving it back was like having something torn out by the roots. As for the brooch, though I'd had it barely two days, I treasured it more than anything in the world, and not because of diamonds and pearls.

I'd just reached the bottom of the stairs when the doorbell rang. Answering it, I found a bedraggled Sergeant Chapman. His normally smooth jaw bristled with stubble, and his eyes were threaded with blood. "Long night?" I asked, inviting him in.

"You could say that. Is Wiltshire here? He oughta hear this."

We gathered in the parlor. Chapman dropped onto a chair, rubbing his balding pate restlessly. I didn't think I'd ever seen him so preoccupied.

"Are you all right? Can I bring you some tea?"

"Can't stay. Fact is, I probably shouldn't be here at all. Ain't gonna do any of us a lick of good if I'm spotted."

Thomas arched an eyebrow. "I think perhaps you'd better expand on that remark, Sergeant."

"Got a summons from Chief Byrnes yesterday. He was none too pleased with me. Tore into my hide about involving the Pinkertons in police business."

"Oh, dear." I sank onto the sofa, feeling anxious myself now. "How did he know it was you?"

"He's no fool. I was the investigating officer on the scene. And I was sniffing around that witness, which he didn't appreciate none."

"He discouraged you from making further inquiries," Thomas said.

"That's one way of putting it. Threatened to have my badge if I kept it up. 'Cept it wasn't my badge so much as my hindquarters, and that wasn't the word he used, begging the lady's pardon."

"He threatened us, too," I said, shuddering at the memory. "He's an evil man."

Chapman hitched a shoulder. "I wouldn't go that far. When it comes to ethics, he don't sweat the small stuff, but he's still a copper, and he gets the job done. However he's mixed up in this, I'd guess it has more to do with cleaning up a mess than making one. But that don't mean he ain't dangerous, which is why it's probably plain stupid for me to be here. Byrnes finds out, I'll be eating this badge for breakfast. I'm gonna have to take a step back for now, lay low for a couple of days."

Thomas nodded. "Eminently sensible."

"You might consider doing the same. Byrnes has a lot of power in this town, and from what I can tell, there's even more powerful folks cracking the whip. Tammany's been all over him since this thing started. Every time I look up, there's some Democratic bigwig or another chewing his ear off, and boy, is he in a sweat about it. Which explains the mood. Up till yesterday, I thought he liked me well enough. Then Croker and his boys show up and it's all fire and brimstone."

"Wait." Thomas straightened in his chair. "Richard Croker was at the police station?"

"Down at HQ, in Byrnes's office. Him and a bunch of other Tammany types. HQ's been hell ever since."

I'd read about Croker in the papers. What was the boss of the Democratic Party doing at police headquarters? "You think it has something to do with the murders?"

He shrugged. "Tammany fellas come around now and then, but the boss himself? That's new."

Thomas's eyes narrowed, and he trailed a thumb along the neatly trimmed line of his beard. "If the Democratic machine is involved at the highest levels, it would certainly explain why Byrnes is under pressure. And I can well imagine that the party would wish to keep the whole thing quiet. An assassination attempt could create a major sympathy vote for Roosevelt."

"Maybe," I said, "but it was the Republicans' convention. They must have an interest in keeping it hushed up, too, or it would have got out whether the Democrats liked it or not."

"True enough. It's all very interesting, isn't it?"

"I'll leave the politics to you folks," Chapman said. "I just wanted to warn you what's doing down at HQ."

"Thank you," I said, and I meant it. With all the distractions of the past two days, the threat of Inspector Byrnes had faded from view. It was helpful to have the reminder that our killer wasn't the only menace lurking out there.

"Now, that being said . . . You all know a fella called Andrew Price?"

I'd heard the name. "He's wealthy, isn't he?"

"Extremely," said Thomas. "His father made a fortune on real estate speculation, though he himself has since rolled the profits into other, less savory endeavors. Which is why he wasn't among the guests at last night's reception, incidentally. Mrs. Hendriks would consider a man of his reputation quite beneath her."

The apple doesn't fall far from the tree, I thought sourly. "What's wrong with his reputation?"

"Rumor has it he owns half the cathouses in New York," Chapman said with his characteristic bluntness.

Well, I could hardly fault Mrs. Hendriks for *that*. "But what does a brothel owner have to do with any of this?"

"He was there. At HQ, I mean, with Croker. They was gabbing about the election."

"*Hmm,*" said Thomas, "there may not be anything in that. Price is a major Democratic donor, and the party boss would have little else on his mind these days."

"Sure, but listen to this. Croker said something like *Someone will have to answer for it,* and Price said sure, of course, he'd give him up when it was done."

Thomas leaned forward sharply. "Repeat that, please. Do you recall his exact words?"

Chapman squinted, thinking back. *"When it's done, you'll have him.* Or, *I'll give him to you.* Near enough, anyways."

I turned the words over slowly. "You'll have him . . . when it's done. Have who when what is done?"

"Exactly. Sounds to me like they got themselves a gull."

Thomas cocked his head. "I beg your pardon?"

"A dupe," I translated. "You see it a lot in my neighborhood. Men like Augusto trick someone into doing their dirty work, so that if things go bad, the gull takes the blame. It's how people like Pietro get into trouble." Pietro and a hundred others like him, desperate immigrants indebted to an unscrupulous benefactor. So far my mother's boarder had avoided getting drawn into any of his *padrone*'s shadier endeavors, but I feared the day would come. Augusto wasn't the sort of man you said no to lightly. Neither, I'd wager, was this Andrew Price fellow. "He must have found someone to carry out the killings, and he means to turn the assassin over when it's done."

"Slow down," Chapman said with a cautious gesture. "That's one explanation, sure."

I clucked my tongue impatiently. "What else would they be talking about?"

"Any number of things. I got the same feeling as you, but I been on the job long enough to know that these sorta things got a way of sounding how you need 'em to. Best to keep an open mind, is all I'm saying."

"Sound advice," Thomas said. "But it's an excellent lead all the same."

"Well, in that case, good luck to you." Chapman picked up his hat and stood.

"Thank you, Sergeant. Miss Gallagher and I were feeling somewhat adrift. You've helped us immensely."

"Glad to hear it."

"I thought you said we should step back?" I said, taking the liberty of dusting a splatter of mud from his badge with my handkerchief. It didn't help with the stubble or the bloodshot eyes, but at least his uniform could look tidy.

"Yeah, well." He put his hat on. "We all know that wasn't gonna happen. Just keep outta Byrnes's sights, or we're all gonna regret it."

Thomas showed the detective out. I expected him to come back to the parlor, but a moment later, I heard footsteps thumping up the stairs, and when I went out into the foyer, I found him taking the steps two at a time. "Where are you going?" I called after him.

"To write a note to Burrows. We'll need his help to arrange an engagement with Price. I'll only be a moment."

"And then what?"

He peered over the balustrade, looking embarrassed. "Please, Rose, it's terribly undignified to call after each other like this. Besides, I thought we'd agreed on our destination this morning. We're for Chatham Square."

For the life of me, I couldn't recall any discussion of heading down to Five Points. "What's in Chatham Square?"

"Tesla," he said, and disappeared.

"Out with it, then," Thomas said half an hour later as our carriage tumbled along the Bowery. "You haven't said a word since we left the house. What's bothering you?"

I squirmed. He was right; I did have something on my mind, but it made me terribly uncomfortable. "It's . . . an indelicate question."

"We're partners. You needn't worry about being delicate."

I glanced out the window, avoiding his eye. "The note you sent. I'm just surprised . . . That is, I suppose I couldn't help wondering . . ." Dear Lord, this was mortifying. "How does Mr. Burrows know a cadet?"

"A what?"

"Someone who traffics in prostitutes," I mumbled, blushing all over.

"Ah, I see! Thank you, Rose. You are slowly educating me in the local vernacular. As to your question, there's nothing unusual in it. For the most part, society is content to feign ignorance as to the nature of Price's business. It makes it less awkward for all concerned. Besides, with due respect to Sergeant Chapman, I wouldn't call Price's establishments *cathouses,* precisely. They cater to a more exclusive clientele. I believe the correct euphemism is *parlor house,* and it's not unusual for society gentlemen to patronize them."

I gave him a sharp look. "Are you implying what I think you are?"

"Not at all. Burrows has never mentioned any such thing to me, though it wouldn't surprise me."

By this point my skin was so hot that I half wished we were in a hansom cab, in spite of the weather. It amazed me that Thomas could speak so offhandedly on the subject—to a woman, no less. It was undignified to call down from the second floor of his own home, but the notion that his best friend might patronize prostitutes didn't faze him in the slightest.

Then, a new thought formed in my head. If the previous one made me uncomfortable, this one made me positively sick. I glanced at Thomas out of the corner of my eye.

"No," he said quietly. "Never."

"I didn't . . ." I looked away, blushing all over again. But there was no point denying it; he could read me too well. "It's none of my business," I concluded miserably.

Now it *was* awkward.

Fortunately, we didn't have to endure it for long. The hack came to a halt in front of an old factory, one of several wired into the cat's cradle of electric cables crisscrossing the street above our heads. "Now remember my warning," Thomas said. "The man is a wizard, but he is not always cautious with his inventions. Many of the devices he leaves lying about are deadly or worse. If you're not careful, you could find yourself transported to another dimension." And with that bit of everyday advice, he rang the bell.

A moment later the door opened a crack, and a raven-haired young man stuck his head out. "Ah, Mr. Viltshire! Come in, come in." He extended a hand for Thomas to shake.

Thomas hesitated and I didn't blame him. The proffered hand was clean and manicured and surprisingly soft-looking, and it also happened to glow like the business end of a firefly. "Er, is that quite safe?"

"Perfectly safe. It will wear off in a moment."

Thomas didn't look very reassured, but he was too much of a gentleman to refuse a handshake, even if it did look extremely flammable. "May I present Miss Rose Gallagher."

The inventor gave a little bow. "Delighted, madam. Nikola Tesla, at your service." He was a pleasant-looking fellow, tall and reedy, with prominent cheekbones and a tidy mustache. Yet there was something a little too piercing about his gaze; I had the uncomfortable notion of standing before a physician, awaiting diagnosis. "Forgive the gloomy entryway," he said, gesturing for us to follow. "I use electric lighting now and then, but I need as much power as possible for the machinery . . ." He spoke animatedly, in an unfamiliar accent, visibly pleased to have visitors in his lab.

Pushing aside a heavy curtain, he led us into a vast, brightly lit space full of unfathomable contraptions. Hulking shapes of glass and metal dotted the expanse like a herd of mechanical beasts grazing in a jungle of iron. They peeked from behind riveted columns, hunkered beneath a canopy of ductwork. Materials were piled neatly in groupings of three: wires and cylinders and coils, pistons and rods and gears, beakers and vials and vats. Valve wheels the size of supper plates jutted out from a network of pipes that climbed the walls like thick vines to branch out across the ceiling, where they traced an elaborate maze, feeding radiators and engines and little dangling spigots. Of the latter there were a great many, suspended at regular intervals above the machinery.

"Water sprinklers," the inventor explained, following my gaze.

"Why, Mr. Tesla, are you expecting a fire?"

I'd been trying to make light, but he just looked at me gravely and said, "Always." Except he pronounced it *alvays*, which somehow made it sound even more ominous.

We followed him to the far corner of the room, where a desk and a few filing cabinets made up a little office. The scent of cigar smoke pricked my nose, and I realized we weren't the only visitors. A figure lounged behind the desk, his feet arranged over its surface as comfortably as if it were his own. So bright was the glare from the electric lamp that I couldn't make out the face behind it, but Thomas obviously recognized him, and he let out a barely audible groan.

"Thomas Wiltshire." The man rose, revealing a patrician figure with a thick mustache and a luxuriant head of dark, wavy hair—much like Thomas's, in fact, though longer in cut and streaked generously with silver. "I had a feeling it would be you," he said in a playful drawl. Then he stepped out of the glare of the lamp, and I gasped.

"Mental telegraphy, no doubt," Thomas said dryly. "Miss Gallagher, may I present—"

But this man needed no introduction. I'd seen his likeness a dozen times and carried his words close to my heart. "Mr. Clemens." I thrust my hand at him, etiquette lessons quite forgotten. "I am such a great admirer."

"Charmed, madam."

"It's an absolute honor to meet you, sir. I have a very well-worn copy of *The Innocents Abroad* at home. I must have read it a dozen times. I wanted to be a travel and adventure writer, you see, and your letters were such an inspiration. They helped me through a very difficult time, and I really ought to thank you . . ." Lord help me, I was babbling, but could anyone blame me? *Mark Twain.* Here, in the flesh!

His eyes crinkled with amusement. "It's for me to thank you, madam. My hand has been in want of a good throttling all day, and now here you are to perform the service."

"Oh!" I released his hand, which I'd been energetically shaking this entire time. "I do beg your pardon. I'm just a bit . . ." *Awestruck? Moon-eyed?* ". . . excited."

"You flatter me."

"Miss Gallagher is my partner," Thomas said, though just now he was looking at me as though I were a complete stranger.

"And Mr. Clemens is mine, at least in this endeavor," said Mr. Tesla, gesturing about the lab.

"Now you flatter me, Tesla. I am merely an interested investor."

Thomas gave a thin smile. "Mr. Clemens has enlisted Mr.

Tesla's talents in pursuit of a device to enhance thought transfer-ence. That is, communication between minds—what Mr. Clemens terms *mental telegraphy*. They have been about it for several months now."

"At the expense of more worthy endeavors, is what Mr. Wilt-shire means," Mr. Clemens said casually, sticking his cigar back in his mouth.

I glanced between them—Thomas stiff and irritable, Mr. Clemens smiling like a Cheshire cat—and decided I wanted no part of *that* discussion. "Well," I said, "it sounds as though great minds think alike, because Mr. Wiltshire and I are also in pursuit of a device of some kind, to help us with a murder investigation."

I have found that there is nothing quite like the mention of murder to bring a conversation back on point.

This time proved no exception. Thomas nodded gravely, and Mr. Clemens's Cheshire smile vanished. As for Mr. Tesla, he tilted his head with interest. "Murder, is it? And which device are you interested in? The biograph? The teleresonance, perhaps? Or are you looking for another sort of machine altogether?"

"The biograph in particular," Thomas said, "but they are all of interest insofar as they can shed any light on our investigation. Why don't you tell us what you're working on, and we can take it from there?"

Mr. Tesla smiled like a small boy who'd just been handed the keys to the candy shop. "In that case," he said, pulling out a chair, "take a seat."

CHAPTER 12

THE ONLY CLUB THAT COUNTS—MARX TWAIN—SCARLETT—LUCK²

And by such means," Mr. Tesla concluded, "the device detects whether the subject is lying or telling the truth."

Thomas knelt for a closer look at the machine, a box of coils and tubes that was currently connected to Mr. Clemens by means of some wires and an armband. "Assuming your theory about electrodermal activity is correct, that is."

"And what if the subject believes he's telling the truth," Mr. Clemens put in, "but his recollection is flawed? Such as may happen to a man in his declining years?"

Mr. Tesla sighed in the long-suffering manner of a genius surrounded by lesser intellects. "It is a *lie detector*, Mr. Clemens, not a *truth detector*. As for electrodermal activity, the theory is sound."

"Fascinating," Thomas said. "We will certainly keep it in mind once we have a suspect in hand."

"But it is not what you're looking for." The inventor nodded. "Very well, what about the teleresonance?"

"The mechanical medium?" Thomas hummed thoughtfully. "I'm not convinced communing with the dead would do us much good. We already have a description of the suspect, and it doesn't sound as though his victims knew him personally."

"Victims, plural?" Mr. Clemens arched a thick eyebrow.

"An awful business," I said. "Six people dead already." Thomas shot me a warning look, but I stood my ground. "Discretion is well and good, Mr. Wiltshire, but how is Mr. Tesla to help if we don't tell him what we're about?"

"That is true," the inventor said. "The more I know, the more useful I will be. I promise to keep anything you tell me in strictest confidence."

"As do I," Mr. Clemens added. "You know better than most, Mr. Wiltshire, that we Masons are not in the habit of being loose about the lips."

"You're a Freemason?"

There must have been something in the way I said it, because Mr. Clemens chuckled. "I hope that will not tarnish me too much in your estimation, Miss Gallagher. I do so hate to disappoint my readers."

"Not at all," I said, which was not strictly true. I'd nurtured a lifelong distrust of Freemasonry, and even my friendship with Mr. Burrows, himself a Mason, wasn't enough to dispel it.

As for Thomas, he looked momentarily undecided, but then he sighed. "I suppose we haven't the luxury of discretion. But be warned, gentlemen: Certain powerful figures are working diligently to cover up this crime. If they suspect you know about it, it could put you in difficulty."

"How exciting," Mr. Clemens drawled, relighting his cigar.

Thomas outlined our investigation so far, such as it was. "The chief difficulty is that we've too many suspects. There are any number of people with an interest in preventing a Roosevelt administration."

Mr. Clemens grunted. "I can well believe it. He certainly would not have my vote."

For reasons I can't fully explain, the remark rankled. "Personally, I found him quite amiable."

"I'm sure you did, young lady. Theodore Roosevelt is one of the most likable fellows of my acquaintance. Forthright and earnest, full of vim and vigor. But that does not mean he would make a good mayor. A runaway locomotive such as he is bound to jump the tracks sooner or later. In addition to which, he has the grim distinction of being a Freemason, which ought to disqualify him from too much admiration." He winked.

He was teasing, I knew, but his words affected me. *They're all connected, aren't they, these glittering creatures?* Mr. Burrows. Mr. Roosevelt. Even Mark Twain. They went to the same colleges, dined at the same restaurants, danced at the same balls. They had their clubs—the Porcellian, the Madison Club, the Freemasons. But there was only one club that really counted, and it controlled the city, maybe even the country. Was Mr. Clemens a full-fledged member of the Luck Society, or just an honorary one like Thomas? I wondered if I'd ever find out.

"And here I thought Masons weren't loose about the lips," Thomas said dryly.

"Oh, dear, I've discredited myself entirely, haven't I?" The Cheshire smile returned.

"So you are looking for a way to eliminate suspects more efficiently," Mr. Tesla said, focusing on the problem at hand.

Thomas nodded. "I admit I had high hopes for the biograph, but having seen it work, I'm afraid it's not practical for our purposes. It's much too large, and the fact that it has to be wired directly to the subject means that one could use it only in direct interrogation."

"*Hmm.*" The inventor's eyes narrowed. "There may be another option . . ." His gaze grew abstracted, and he drifted away, hands folded behind his back.

"I do hope he solves it," Mr. Clemens said as he watched the inventor pace. "I would not wish any misfortune on Mr. Roosevelt. Outside of the polls, that is. There, I can only hope he receives a comprehensive drubbing. Even another mandate for the thieves of Tammany Hall must be preferred to a Roosevelt administration."

"Why are you so dead set against him?" My question earned me a look from Thomas that plainly said, *Don't encourage him.*

"Because, my dear, the Republicans are the party of bankers and robber barons. And now, to add insult to injury, they've put forward a boy of such blue blood, such glaringly obvious luck, as to be unprecedented in the history of municipal government. People of Roosevelt's stock used to have the good sense to stay out of the grubby business of politics. They had more than enough power, and were content to leave the table scraps for lesser men. Now it seems they've grown too rapacious even for that. It's simply grotesque." He paused to take a long draw of his cigar. "That being said, it promises to be a cracking good contest. Labor versus Capital, with Henry George in one corner and Theodore Roosevelt in the other."

"You seem to have forgotten the Democratic Party," Thomas said.

"My dear fellow, have you not read the papers? All of New York has forgotten it! Poor Hewitt toils in the shadow of grander passions. The working class is all aflutter over this upstart new labor party, and the wealthy in pure terror of its rise. The landlords and monopolists have tightened the yoke one too many times, and if I may be permitted a flight of optimism uncharacteristic in a man of my age, I hope and believe they will finally pay for it at the polls."

"And I hope you're wrong in that," Thomas said. "George's concern for the poor is admirable, but his solutions are dangerous. His brand of populism will bring nothing but trouble, especially for the workingman . . ."

By this point, I'd stopped paying attention. Listening to a pair of rich men hold forth on the plight of the working class was not my idea of stimulating conversation. Instead, I found my interest piqued by something sitting on a corner of Mr. Tesla's desk. It was about the size of a melon, perfectly spherical, and dark as a shadow. In fact, it looked almost as if it were *made* of shadow, but of course that was impossible.

Curious, I approached the desk.

"Mark my words, Wiltshire, this contest is the very incarnation of Labor versus Capital."

"Look, we've all read Karl Marx . . ."

Even up close, the sphere on the desk remained dark, as if it were not so much a thing as the absence of a thing, like a hole in its surroundings. *It's just the glare of the lamp,* I thought. I switched it off, plunging the desk into darkness, but the sphere remained just as visible as before, an even deeper shadow against the gloom.

Don't touch anything, Thomas had warned, but surely Mr. Tesla wouldn't keep something truly dangerous right there on his desk?

Yes, I know. All I can say in my defense is that if you'd seen that ball of shadow sitting there, you wouldn't have been able to resist either.

I touched it.

A burst of flames sent me reeling back with a cry. The sphere sprang from the table, no longer a shadow but a writhing ball of crimson fire. It hovered there for a moment, suspended in mid-air, blazing like an angry red sun. Then it charged at me, swooping straight for my face. I shrieked, throwing my arms up to shield myself—

"Scarlett! *Prestani!* Can't you see you're frightening her?"

The ball of red flame stopped where it was. Mr. Tesla rushed up and grabbed it—*with his bare hands*—and scowled as if it were a misbehaving toddler.

"Rose," Thomas sighed.

I leveled a trembling finger at the fireball. "W-what is that?"

"Scarlett," said the inventor. "At least, that's what I call her."

"*Her?*"

"Her. Him. It." He shrugged. "Impossible to say."

Mr. Clemens grinned. "Isn't it wonderful? Mr. Tesla transported it here from the otherworld."

"Possibly," the inventor said. "I cannot say for certain. I was trying to create a conduit to the otherworld, and the apparatus overheated. There was a *slight* explosion." He held his thumb and forefinger an inch apart. "I lost consciousness, and when I awoke, she was just . . . here." He tapped the flame ball with a finger, and it floated away like a soap bubble. "I have run every test I can think of, and I still cannot determine what she is composed of or where she came from. I don't know what else to do with her, so she stays here in the lab."

Even Thomas was in raptures over the thing. "Fascinating, isn't it?" He reached for the flame ball. It nestled comfortably between his hands, bathing his face in a red glow.

"Is it . . . does it understand us?"

"Who knows?" He held it out to me. "Don't be afraid. It's not hot."

Reluctantly, I reached out, and after a few tentative taps, I relaxed enough to take it into my hands. It felt a little like water between my fingers and emitted the soft hiss of a gas lamp. "It's amazing." I dropped my hands and it floated away, settling on the inventor's desk once more.

"Now then," Mr. Tesla said, "I've had an idea. This way, if you please." He showed us to a humble-looking device on a nearby table. Slightly larger than a loaf of bread, it resembled a tin box connected to the earpiece of a telephone. It bore two dials, the first showing numbers from 0 to 10, while the second looked a little like a compass, except instead of north, south, and so on, it was marked with air, water, earth, and fire, as well as a series of question marks.

Thomas peered at it with interest. "What is it? Something to do with luck, obviously."

"It is designed to help determine what variety of luck a person possesses."

That confused me. "Doesn't a person with luck already know what kind he has?"

"Not always," Thomas said. "The origins of some talents are obvious. The ability to detect oil underground, for example, clearly comes from the earth domain. But what about the abilities of some of your fellow Agency recruits? Where does exceptional eyesight belong, or a brilliant mind for numbers? They don't fall obviously into any of the four classical categories, suggesting that there are additional domains in the otherworld we know nothing about."

"The lost domains," I murmured, remembering Fillimore's essay in the *Journal of Paranormal Studies*. "Dr. Fillimore believes electromagnetism is one."

Mr. Tesla dismissed that with a wave. "Electromagnetism is the conveyance, not the source. That is what the machine detects— electromagnetic radiation."

"Does it work?" Thomas asked.

"Not as it should. But." The inventor raised a long finger. "It does detect when luck is in use. Allow me to demonstrate." He handed me the bit that looked like a telephone earpiece. "Please, Miss Gallagher, point the probe at me."

I did as he instructed, holding the elongated bell shape near his chest.

"Now, I activate this switch and . . ." He closed his eyes, as if listening. There was a pause. Then: "Mr. Wiltshire's watch ticking in his pocket. Miss Gallagher's heart beating at approximately sixty-eight beats per minute. The tobacco burning in Mr. Clemens's cigar."

The box began to produce a series of soft clicks.

"Are the dials moving?"

I glanced down. "A little, maybe, but what—?"

"Farther away, then." His brow furrowed—not in concentration, it seemed to me, but in discomfort. Then he pointed at the door. "A carriage on Doyers Street, just now turning onto the Bowery. We will hear it in fifteen seconds . . . ten . . . five . . ."

A clip-clop of hooves sounded outside the door of the factory. Meanwhile, the clicking sound from the box grew louder and more erratic.

"Keep the probe raised, Miss Gallagher, if you please."

In my amazement, I'd let the bell-shaped tube droop in my hand. I hadn't even realized it, yet somehow the inventor had known, in spite of his eyes being closed. "You heard a carriage from a block away?"

"And I felt it." He tapped his forehead. "Here."

That was impossible, of course, unless . . . "You're lucky." I shouldn't have been surprised. I was starting to think that all of Thomas's friends were lucky—except me.

"Yes, yes, but the needles—where do they land?" He opened his eyes.

As soon as he stopped concentrating, both needles dropped, and the clicking fell silent. "Here," I said, recovering from my astonishment. "This one went straight to ten, while this one hovered back and forth between water and air."

He sighed, visibly disappointed. "The same every time. That dial is useless."

Mr. Clemens laughed. "What did you expect? You have two kinds of luck!"

Two kinds? My mouth fell open. "But *Pullman's Guide to the Paranormal* said that was impossible! Even if several forms of luck are in the bloodline, only one is ever expressed."

"Tesla's is the only known case," Thomas said with a wistful smile. "His cup runneth over."

Mr. Tesla didn't seem especially gratified about the contents of his cup. He scowled, absently sorting little mechanical parts into piles of three. "That is half the trouble, you see. How can I calibrate it on myself? I need test subjects. I don't suppose you are lucky, Miss Gallagher?" I shook my head, and he sighed again. "I thought not," he said, and I tried not to be offended.

"It's brilliant, Tesla." Thomas hovered eagerly over the machine, his eyes gleaming with boyish enthusiasm. "How does it work?"

"Through the application of electrical current to helium gas. In the presence of sufficient electromagnetic radiation, the gas becomes conductive, which is then amplified through the tube to produce a pulse—"

"Excuse me, gentlemen." I softened my interruption with a smile. "I don't mean to be rude, but it sounds as though this could be a rather *long* explanation, and while I'm sure it's very interesting, time is short."

Thomas gave a faint sigh of regret. "You're right, of course. As to the application of this device to our investigation, while it might warn us of an imminent attack, I'm not sure how it would help us eliminate suspects."

Mr. Tesla gestured at the first dial, the one with numbers on it. "Notice that the needle has not fallen entirely to zero. Here, Miss Gallagher, please take the probe again and point it at me. Now, observe." Turning on his heel, he headed for the door, and as he drew away, the needle began to drop. Three, two, one . . . He passed through the curtain separating the entryway from the main part of the lab, and a moment later, we heard the door.

"Well, well," said Mr. Clemens, leaning over the device. "How do you like that? Zero, now that it is only we mortals in the room."

So the great Mark Twain was just an ordinary person like me. I felt a little better after that.

When Mr. Tesla returned, the needle crept back up to three. "There, you see? The apparatus can be used to detect the presence of a person with luck, even if he is not using his gift. Electromagnetic radiation remains present in sufficient quantities to—"

"That's wonderful," I said, "but I'm afraid I still see a few problems."

"As do I, alas," said Thomas. "There are two difficulties. First, that it requires an electrical charge, and second, that it's too large to be hidden on our persons."

"On top of which, we can't very well go around waving a telephone earpiece in people's faces."

Thomas sighed. "Three problems."

Mr. Tesla made an impatient gesture. "There are always problems until there are solutions. Give me a few days."

"I'm afraid we haven't got a few days," I said.

He *tsk*ed, muttering something in an unfamiliar language. "I will do what I can, my friends, but I am not a magician."

"You certainly are," Thomas said, "and we are in your debt, truly. The Agency will of course compensate you for your expenses and labor. And now I'm afraid we must be off. Mr. Clemens, always a pleasure."

"Oh, indeed." Mr. Clemens shook hands, his eyes twinkling.

"And for me," I said. "It was a great honor to meet you both."

"If I may beg a favor," Mr. Clemens said. "I'd be grateful if you didn't mention my half of that great honor to anyone. I promised my dear Olivia that I would refrain from further investments of this kind, at least for a little while. But some vices"—he waggled his cigar—"are just too difficult to give up. I'd hate to disappoint her."

"Mum's the word," I assured him. "And speaking of mums . . ." I turned to Thomas with a guilty smile. "Would you mind if I took the opportunity to visit mine? I feel terrible about missing church yesterday, and since we're just a few blocks away . . ."

"Certainly. Will an hour give you enough time?"

"Perfect," I said, and headed for the door.

CHAPTER 13

SUNDAY DRESS, TUESDAY TROUBLES—
PIETRO FINDS A NEW JOB—FELONIOUS
INTENT

It was nearly ten-thirty by the time I arrived at my mother's flat, and I was surprised to find it quiet. Mam should have been up hours ago, but the curtains were still drawn and the kettle was cold. I busied myself for a few minutes, pulling laundry down from the line in the kitchen and tidying up the newspapers in the tiny sitting room, but when there was still no sign, I started to worry. "Mam?" I knocked gently on her bedroom door. "Mam, are you awake?"

I heard her stirring, and a moment later, the door opened. Mam peered up at me with bleary eyes, her hair sticking out every which way. "Rose? Have I overslept? What time is it?"

"It's going on eleven."

She gasped in dismay. Rushing to her cupboard, she flung open a drawer and pulled out her best dress. "How could this have happened? We'll never make it in time! Oh, why didn't you wake me sooner?"

"Make what in time? Mam, what's the matter?" As far as I knew, she never had anyplace to be except—

"Mass, you silly thing! Hurry up and help me!"

"Mam." Gently, I took her Sunday dress from her hands. "It's Tuesday."

"Tuesday?" She frowned. "Are you sure? I don't remember going to church the day before yesterday." Then, slowly, her brow cleared. "Ah yes, that's right. Peter took me."

A blade of guilt twisted in my belly. "I'm glad Pietro could help. I'm sorry I couldn't come myself, but I had work."

"You used to have Sundays off."

"I know, but I have new responsibilities now." I hadn't told Mam or anyone else about joining the Agency. It would only have worried her, and besides, it would have meant explaining all sorts of other things, like luck and magic and fae. Mam believed in ghosts—she said she communed with my dead granny, and I believed her—but that didn't mean she'd have an easy time accepting the rest of it. Even if she did, she'd put it down to devilry, and I didn't fancy arguing with her about the state of my immortal soul. It was easier on both of us to keep things simple.

"We always went together," she said. "Every Sunday. Now, when you don't come . . ."

It confuses you. "I'm sorry, Mam," I said, swallowing a lump in my throat. "Really. I'll try harder to get away."

"Well, never mind. Put the kettle on, will you?"

I made tea and helped Mam tidy the flat. It didn't take long, its three tiny rooms together being smaller than the foyer of Thomas's townhouse. As usual, there was no food in the cupboard, but the lingering smell of garlic told me that Pietro had been cooking for them. "Do you want me to go out for some things? Bread and some eggs? Maybe a little cheese?"

"I'm not very hungry."

I scanned her tiny frame worriedly. She looked as frail as ever, pale and thin, her skin like parchment over the sharp angles of her bones. At least she was lucid. Things had undeniably gotten better since we'd started following Thomas's advice about the ghost. Visitations from Granny's ghost had done terrible things to my mother's health, both mental and physical, but Thomas had helped us put a stop to that with a few simple measures. "You're taking your mineral water?" I asked her. "Every day, like Mr. Wiltshire said?"

"I'm not a child, Rose."

"I'll take that for a yes. But you still need to eat." Grabbing my coat from the rack, I said, "I'm going to Augusto's. What kind of cheese would you like?"

"Really, you don't need to—"

"What kind, Mam?"

Grudgingly, she said, "I don't mind about the cheese, but if he has any of that salami . . ."

"Good. I'll see you in a few minutes."

It was drizzling again when I stepped outside. I could have shortened my journey by slipping through one of the alleyways connecting Mott Street with Mulberry, but I'd learned long ago to avoid them. You never knew what you might step in, or what might come raining down from one of the tenement windows above. Walking the extra half block was worth it. It also gave me time to work out what I'd say to Augusto if he happened to be in the shop. That, too, was a precaution I'd learned from experience.

Augusto was a shrewd man, and the very last person I wanted accidentally finding out what I did for a living. He'd think of a way to exploit it. He had a knack for such things, which was how a penniless immigrant from Bologna found himself the owner of a successful business in New York. (That a good deal of that business wasn't strictly legal was neither here nor there.) If he learned my secret, it would give him leverage over me. That was assuming he didn't just kill me outright. Pinkertons were even more despised than coppers in my neighborhood, and that went double for men like Augusto, who didn't need detectives sniffing around their business.

Approaching the grocery, I found a familiar figure sheltering beneath the red-and-green awning, his lanky form huddled against the chill. "Good morning, Pietro."

He didn't look all that happy to see me, a suspicion that was confirmed when he said, "Hello, Rose." Pietro rarely called me Rose unless something was wrong.

"Thank you for taking Mam to church on Sunday."

"Somebody had to." There was more than a hint of accusation in his dark eyes, not that I blamed him.

"I'm sorry. I had to work."

"On Sundays now, too. What a wonderful boss you have."

I *tsk*ed. Pietro never missed an opportunity to criticize Thomas, whom he'd disliked from the first. "It wasn't his fault."

"Ah, *sì*. The silver probably needed polishing very badly." He shifted from foot to foot, his hands jammed deep in his pockets.

I scowled. "What's got into you? It's not enough to mock Mr. Wiltshire, you have to insult me, too?"

He sighed and looked away. "Sorry. It's just not a very good day. Are you here for shopping?"

"Just to pick up a few things for Mam. Why is it not a good day?"

"No reason. You should hurry inside, it's cold."

In the nearly three years since he'd been my mother's boarder, Pietro had never been this terse with me. He was one of the most reliably pleasant people I'd ever known, warm and kind and quick with a joke. Whatever this was, it wasn't just about my missing church. "What's going on?"

"Please, Fiora, go away." He cut a nervous glance up the street. "I don't want anybody to see us talking. I'll explain later. Just . . . buy your groceries and go."

"What do you mean? Why—"

He gripped my shoulders, gazing firmly into my eyes. "Go. Away."

The last time somebody had grabbed me like that was in ju-jitsu training; Pietro was lucky he didn't find himself thrown to the pavement. Instinct very nearly took over, but I was distracted by a flash of metal in the depths of his pocket. "Is that . . . Pietro, are you carrying a pistol?"

"*Cristo.*" He grimaced and looked away. "If you shout a little more, maybe they hear you in the Tombs, eh?"

I lowered my voice to an angry whisper. "When did you start carrying a gun? Do you bring that into the flat?"

"Rose, I am begging you . . ." He pressed his hands together as if in prayer and shook them at me. "Go home. We'll talk later."

I stood there a moment, frozen with indecision. I didn't want to leave him, but instinct told me that I was making things worse by staying put. "Promise me you're all right and I'll go."

"I promise."

What choice did I have? I walked away, turning the corner as if I meant to head to Constantino's Grocery—and promptly circling back through the alley until I had a clear view of Augusto's from the north. Keeping out of sight, I watched Pietro loitering under the awning, stirring like a restless animal and casting furtive looks across the street at Mulberry Bend. Both of us, it seemed, were waiting.

We didn't wait long.

A trio of roughs emerged from Bandit's Roost. The alleys of Mulberry Bend regularly coughed up specimens like these, and I might not have taken any notice of them were it not for the effect their appearance had on Pietro. His whole body tensed, and though he smiled, it was taut as a fiddle string. The men started toward the grocery, and I got a good look at them as they passed. Brutish and swaggering, they were the sort that would send you scurrying across the street if you saw them heading your way. When they converged under the awning, Pietro looked scrawny and boyish in comparison, especially when one of them threw an arm around him and jerked him close, laughing like a boorish uncle who'd had one too many.

The thug pointed down Mulberry and made a gesture to take in the rest of the block. Pietro nodded, and they headed out together, all four of them, Pietro walking with his right hand jammed so far down into his pocket that it looked fit to burst through. It was a gesture I knew from experience. *Gripping his gun for reassurance,* I thought grimly. I didn't know what to make of it, but one thing was clear.

Pietro was in trouble.

"You sure that's what you saw?" Clara asked, knife flashing as she peeled potatoes with mechanical efficiency. I'd run straight down to the kitchen after I got home, anxious to relate what had happened on Mulberry Street. I couldn't tell Mam, of course, and I didn't want to confide in Thomas either. He'd feel obliged to help me, and he had more important matters to attend to. That left Clara. She'd never met Pietro, but she'd heard enough about him to know how much he mattered to me. Which was why her next words were: "Whatever it is, you oughta stay out of it."

"Well, this sounds familiar."

"Don't it just. And in case you've forgotten, the last time I gave you that advice, you didn't take it, and you wound up nearly getting yourself killed."

After I saved Thomas's life. I kept that remark to myself; it would only have irritated her. "I remember perfectly well what happened."

It's hard to forget being clubbed over the head with a revolver, or having your heart nearly stopped by a shade, or being stabbed in the chest by your best friend at your own request.

"I'm not about to rush to anyone's rescue. For one thing, I'm too busy trying to catch a killer, and whatever is going on with Pietro, it doesn't seem to be an emergency. But I can't just ignore it either. I owe him more than that, for Mam's sake if nothing else. He's been like a son to her these past few years. If it weren't for him . . ."

"I know. He does for your mama what Joseph does for mine, and that makes him family. I understand you wanting to help, but are you even sure he needs it? Sounds to me like you're making a whole lotta assumptions."

"Maybe I am, but the way he was acting . . . He wasn't himself, and now he's carrying a gun? On top of which, I know the *padrone* he works for. If I'm making assumptions, they're more about Augusto than Pietro."

Clara tossed a naked potato aside and grabbed another. "How about instead of jumping to conclusions, you sit down and talk to the man?"

"I tried. He ran me off."

"He lives with your mama, Rose. I'm sure you can find a way, you being a detective and all."

"Very funny."

"Just promise me you won't go off half-cocked."

"I promise. I did learn a thing or two from last time, believe it or not."

She gave me a wry look but otherwise held her peace.

"I'd better head upstairs. Thomas is expecting me. Thank you for listening, Clara."

"You can thank me by being careful with yourself for a change. I don't need to be stitching anybody up again. Got enough needlework needs doing around here, thanks to Miss I Don't Work Weekends . . ."

I left Clara to her grumbling and headed up to Thomas's study. Voices murmured on the far side of the door; entering, I was only half surprised to find Mr. Burrows occupying the sofa across from Thomas, a crude drawing spread out on the table between them.

"Ah, here she is, our felon of the hour." Mr. Burrows saluted me with a glass of sherry.

"I beg your pardon?"

"Please," Thomas said, gesturing for me to sit. "Burrows and I were just going over the floor plan of Andrew Price's home."

"What I know of it, at any rate," Mr. Burrows said. "I've never set foot on the fourth floor, and I imagine that's where all the fun is had." He flashed a wicked smile.

I ignored him, sinking onto the sofa beside Thomas. "I'm sorry, you'll have to catch me up. Do I take it you have an engagement at Price's?"

"Not quite. That would have been terribly difficult to arrange at short notice without arousing suspicion."

"Even I am not so presumptuous as to invite myself over to someone's home," Mr. Burrows said. "But I did manage to arrange a supper at Delmonico's tonight. Price is meeting us at eight o'clock."

"But why the floor plan, if you'll be dining out?"

Thomas sighed. "I am sorry to put you in this position, Rose, but I don't see another option. I'll get what I can from Price, but I doubt he'd be careless enough to implicate himself. And even if he did, we'd still need proof."

I glanced between the two of them, feeling suddenly wary. "And how do we get that?"

"Larceny," Mr. Burrows said brightly. "Or is it robbery? I can never tell the difference."

It took me a moment to understand; when I did, I blanched. "You want me to break into the man's *home*?"

"It's not my first choice, certainly," Thomas said. "One prefers a more delicate touch where possible, but as I said, I don't see any alternative. We need to look through his study, or wherever he keeps his papers, to see if there is anything that points to his involvement in the murders."

"Such as? Even if he hired the killer, I doubt he got a receipt."

"Most likely not," Thomas said dryly, "but you may find other documents that point to his involvement. Correspondence, ledgers, a journal. Details about his investments. A calendar if he keeps one. Even a train ticket could be useful."

It wouldn't be the first time I'd sneaked into a building without permission, but still. "If I'm caught, I'll be sent up the river."

"You won't be caught," Thomas said, "and besides, it's only a felony if you actually steal something of value. Making off with a bundle of papers would most likely earn you a charge of mischief. Petit larceny at the outside."

Mr. Burrows laughed. "You've been posing as an attorney for so long that you're starting to sound like one."

I scowled at both of them. "It's all very well being glib about this when you're not the one doing the breaking in."

"Apologies, Rose." Thomas inclined his head gravely. "I don't wish to sound cavalier. Sometimes, however, in our line of work, we are called upon to . . ."

"Break the law," Mr. Burrows supplied.

". . . operate at the margins of the penal code. This is one such occasion."

I wondered what Sergeant Chapman would make of that. "So you want me to break in, search the study, and get out before Price comes back from supper."

"Exactly. Burrows and I will try to stretch the evening out as long as possible, but you'll want to be in and out within half an hour. I'd suggest sometime between eleven and twelve o'clock. The streets will be quieter, and hopefully the servants will have gone to bed."

I groaned. Of course there would be servants. "Are there many of them?"

"Oh, about the same number as I have." Mr. Burrows began ticking them off on his fingers. "Butler, housekeeper, two footmen, cook, two housemaids, coachman . . ."

"Yes, all right, that's very helpful." I massaged my temples, feeling a headache coming on. "Please tell me he's a bachelor."

"No," Thomas said, "but his wife and daughter are still in Newport, so you won't have to worry about them."

"Mistress?" I asked sarcastically.

"Obviously," said Mr. Burrows, "but not in the house."

My gaze fell to the sketch they'd drawn up. Five full floors of drawing rooms and libraries and conservatories and God knew what else, every one of them potentially concealing a pair of eyes. I'd have to memorize the layout, and even then, I'd be relying on

Mr. Burrows's memory to guide me. "Thomas . . ." I swallowed hard. "I don't know if I can do this."

"Of course you can. You're the most resourceful person I've ever met." He smiled reassuringly at me. "Now, do you remember how to pick a lock?"

CHAPTER 14

EBONY AND IVORY—THE WASHINGTON
GAMBIT—A VERY LONG WAY DOWN

Picking locks, I soon realized, was the least of my worries. The row house I'd come to burgle sat across from Central Park, at the heart of Millionaires' Row. Though the new social season had yet to begin, there were bound to be any number of soirees planned for this evening, which meant there would be regular traffic along the Avenue. In the few minutes I'd been watching from the edge of the park, four carriages had rattled past, and just now an elegant couple out for an evening stroll was admiring the glass walls of the conservatory through which I'd meant to enter.

All right, then. Plan B.

The lower floor sat below street level, and the short wall around the perimeter gave some cover. Harder to get in, but safer from prying eyes. I waited for a break in traffic, then darted across the Avenue. It was a bit of a jump down from the wall, but I'd worn sensible shoes, and I landed quietly.

I pressed my ear to the door at the bottom of the stairs. No sound, and the familiar smell of Ivory soap told me this was most likely the laundry. *As good a place as any,* I thought, and drew out my tools. Lockpicking was one area of my training where I'd excelled straightaway, and I made quick work of it. I put my ear to the door once more, but all I could hear was my own nervous heartbeat. The back of my neck prickled, and I imagined eyes in every dark windowpane.

Heavenly Father, I know it's awfully fresh to ask this of you under the circumstances, but please don't let them send me to Sing Sing.

I plunged inside.

It was black as pitch in there, and I had to make my way carefully, feeling around corners and bumping softly into unseen obstacles until I found the door leading out to the hall. This too was dark; a good sign, since it meant the servants had most likely gone to bed. I found the stairs and scampered up as quickly as I dared. Reaching the first floor, I quit the shadows of the servants' domain for the brightly lit foyer, where I paused to scan my surroundings.

No sign of life from the hallways above. I took the main stairs two at a time, my footfalls muffled by the thick carpeting. I made it to the third floor without pausing for breath (could it be that my training in Newport was worth something after all?) and quickly found the door I sought. It wasn't locked, which in hindsight ought to have given me pause. In my anxiety, I just celebrated my good fortune and ducked inside, whereupon I found myself in the narrow confines of a perfectly lovely bathroom.

Jonathan. Bloody. Burrows.

The guest rooms were supposed to be on the second floor. Which meant his recollection was off. *Way* off.

A little too much cognac last time you were here, Mr. Thorough-bred?

With nothing reliable to go by, I had little choice but to check each room one by one. So that's what I did, cursing inwardly the entire time, saving the choicest bits of Five Points vernacular for a certain pretty face who couldn't tell a study from a privy. Nor did Thomas escape my wrath. *Not to worry, Rose, you'll most likely be charged with mischief. Petit larceny at the outside. I'm sure it won't matter at all that you're Irish and poor as a church mouse, we're all the same in the eyes of the law . . .*

At last, one of the doorknobs refused to budge. Whatever was behind that walnut paneling was important. I took out my lockpicking tools, and after a moment's prodding, the door swung open to reveal a low-lit room smelling of leather and parchment. I'd found the study. Now all I had to do was look through Price's papers and see if there was anything incriminating. That, and get out of the house without being seen.

One step at a time, Rose.

As my eyes adjusted to the gloom, I let out a whimper of dismay. The study was huge—nearly the size of Thomas's dining room—and positively bursting with paper. Shelves lined with books from floor to ceiling. Mahogany filing cabinets so overstuffed that their glass doors wouldn't close. Every table, every chair, every pigeonhole crowded with page after page. It might as well have been a library, if the librarian had gone on extended holiday. I couldn't get through it if I had all night, let alone twenty minutes.

Deep breath. Start with the desk.

It was a handsome piece, ebony with intricate brass inlay, polished to such a high shine that I could see my own anxious features reflected on its surface. I began with the correspondence, but found nothing useful. Next came Price's diary. On the night in question, he'd apparently dined with someone named Reynolds at the Park Avenue Hotel. A dead end, most likely, but I tucked the diary into my satchel just in case.

The stack of papers at my elbow proved to be a manuscript of some kind, and the little box of calling cards didn't contain a single name I knew. Tension gnawed at me. *This is a fool's errand,* I thought, yanking on the drawer at my left hand.

It wouldn't budge.

Well, now, what have we here?

The brass escutcheon was shaped like a bat, and well scarred from use. For the third time that evening, I reached for my lock-picking tools. This time, though, things didn't go quite to plan. The tension wrench slid into the bottom of the keyhole easily enough, but when I inserted the pick, it felt suddenly warm in my hand. I tried to pull it out, but it was stuck, growing hotter and hotter. Just when I was about to let go, it *vanished.*

My mouth fell open, a strangled sound escaping my lips.

Magic. It had to be. Which meant this lock must guard something important, but how could I get to it?

I expect that if it had been Thomas, he would have found some elegant and arcane solution. As for me, I did what any good Five Pointer would have done: I decided to break something.

First, I pulled the other drawers out of the desk. That left the bottom of the magic drawer exposed, with a good-size gap underneath. Next, I looked for something in the way of tools. That proved a bit more difficult, but I found what I needed among some bric-a-brac on the mantelpiece, in the form of a bust of George Washington and a bit of scrimshaw carved from the tip of an elephant's tusk.

I eyed the bottom of the drawer appraisingly. It didn't look anywhere near as strong as the outer part of the desk, but even so, there was no doubt I'd be making a lot of noise. The servants' wing was two floors down and clear across the house, but just to be safe, I relocked the door of the study.

Whatever is in that drawer, it must be worth the risk. And so, biting my lip in anticipation, I put the tip of the tusk to the bottom of the drawer, grasped President Washington by the face, and struck a mighty blow. The drawer bucked, and a chip flew out of the wood. I froze, listening.

Silence.

I repeated the process twice, each time pausing to listen; when nothing stirred, I set to the task in earnest.

Each fall of my makeshift hammer sounded like a gunshot to my ears, but it was working: The wood began to splinter, then to crack. After about half a dozen blows, the tip of the tusk broke through; another half a dozen and the thing was done, punching enough of a hole in the bottom of the drawer that I could fit a fire iron through and use it as a pry bar. At last I had my reward: a heavy leather-bound book tumbled free, landing on the carpet with a satisfying *thud*.

My triumph was short-lived. When I reached for the book, it refused to open. The pages were sealed together somehow, perhaps by magic or—

Something stirred in the foyer below. Footsteps, followed by voices. *Someone was awake.*

"Did you hear a banging sound, like a hammer?" An older man's voice floated up the stairs.

"I'm not sure what woke me, but I heard something fall a moment ago. Sounded like it broke. I suppose we ought to . . ."

Panic thrummed in my veins. My gaze raked the room, but there was nowhere to hide. The lock on the door might stall them, but not for long. I needed to *get out*.

Scrambling, I fetched up the leather book and jammed it in my satchel. I started to put the drawers back in place, realized I didn't have time, and shoved them under the desk instead, arranging the chair in front of the gaps in the hopes the shadows would conceal the rest. I replaced the scrimshaw on the mantel. President Washington, meanwhile, went headfirst into a pile of kindling, which I scattered across the floor so it would look like the bust had fallen from the mantel and landed in the woodpile. Then I flew to the bay window, opened it, and leaned out.

Cold October air rushed up to meet me. I'd expected to find the Juliet balcony I'd seen from the street, but apparently that was the *other* bay window, because all I saw below me was an eight-inch width of cornice, and below that, about thirty feet of nothing.

Voices in the hallway, and the jingle of keys. It was too late to change my mind. I slipped out the window, gripping the brownstone pillars until my knuckles went white. Below—far, far below—Sixty-First Street was a canyon of shadow. My stomach tumbled, and for a moment I was sure I would fall. I froze, squeezing my eyes shut and clinging to the wall like a spider. But I needed to move away from the window or I'd be seen, darkness or not. And so, inch by terrifying inch, I shuffled along the cornice.

This ledge is wide enough, I told myself. *Plenty of space.* A chill breeze tugged mockingly at the hem of my dress.

The northwest facet of the bay window, on which I was precariously perched, stood at an obtuse angle to the next window over. The gap between them was less than three feet, but to my eye, it might as well have been the Grand Canyon. There was no help for it, though; the recessed window was the only place I could hide from view. Already, I could hear voices in the room. They had only to glance this way . . .

OhGodOhGodOhGod . . .

I jumped.

Funny, isn't it, how heights turn a simple task into a near-impossible one? On the ground, a hop like that would have been child's play, even with a satchel slung over my shoulder. From a third-floor window, it felt like a circus act, and I truly believe that if it hadn't been for my lessons in jujitsu, I wouldn't have made it. As it was, my foot slipped, and I clawed at the brownstone so desperately that I tore the tips of my fingernails clean off. But I made it, and there I clung, bleeding, trying very hard to gasp without making a sound. Inside, I could hear an elderly pair of servants muttering about a careless housemaid, which I suppose meant that my Washington gambit had worked, at least for now. By the light of morning, of course, the matter would be plain, by which point I'd be long gone.

Or so I thought. But the cold October breeze had one more cruel surprise in store. It gusted in through the open window, setting the butterfly windowpanes creaking on their hinges.

Footsteps crossed the room. I flattened myself against the window.

"Look here," said a woman's voice, sounding as if it were right in my ear. "Here's your banging, Steven. She left the window open on top of it, the silly nit. Probably been knocking away in the wind all night long." So saying, the servant shut the window . . . and locked it.

I was trapped. On a window ledge. Thirty feet above the street.

I couldn't tell you how long I stayed there, plastered against the window as I fought off wave after sickening wave of fear. Long enough that my hands were growing cramped with cold, which would make my situation even more precarious. I had two choices: climb or call for help, and I had no desire to spend the rest of the night in the Tombs. Whatever Thomas might say, I had a Five Pointer's instinctive distrust of coppers, and all the blithe assurances in the world weren't enough to change that.

I scanned the wall below. The architectural detail on the building provided plenty of handholds and footholds. So long as I stayed calm and focused, I ought to be able to make it. The windows came in twos, like a close-set pair of eyes, and each one had a ledge at its top and bottom, like swollen eyelids. In between the eyes, another ledge was set a few feet below, like the bridge of a nose; from there, the drop to the next floor was only about five feet. *You can do this,* I told myself.

I slid the satchel off my shoulder and let it drop to the ground, aiming for a row of cedars lining the perimeter wall. Then, whispering a fervent prayer, I started to climb down.

It was a short step from the bottom ledge of the third-story window to the top ledge of the window below, and from there, only another few feet to the bridge of the nose between windows. So far, so good, but the next bit would not be so easy. Pressing myself tight to the wall, I slid down into a crouch. Then I dangled one foot out over the ledge, followed by the other, *slowly, carefully* easing myself down, scraping my upper body along the edge for support, dragging my overcoat and the hem of my dress in the process.

I can only imagine what the view must have looked like from below: a woman oozing bodily over a window ledge, dress hitched up around her armpits, offering a bountiful view of her undergarments. Fortunately, it was well past midnight, and there was no one to see. That I know of, at any rate.

The last few inches were really quite terrifying, but I managed to land on the second-floor ledge. I'd done it. And now I had to do it all over again.

A few scrapes and some trembling muscles later, I found myself on the bottom ledge of the first-floor window, and here my architectural support was at an end. It was at least a ten-foot drop to the servants' entrance below street level. Easy enough to break a leg, but what choice did I have?

I jumped, landing on the balls of my feet and rolling to absorb the impact. I tumbled headfirst into the boughs of a cedar tree, but was otherwise unscathed. (Alas, the same could not be said for the cedar, which now sported a Rose-shaped hole.) I took a moment to thank the Lord—and my training. Maybe falling properly was half the battle after all.

I climbed unsteadily to my feet. My whole body shook, the cold and the aftershock of terror finally taking hold, but my legs were just firm enough to carry me home. Grabbing my satchel, I fled down the Avenue, heading for Number 726.

The lights were still on in the house. I found Thomas and Mr. Burrows in the parlor, sipping port and chatting, looking as though they'd passed a very pleasant evening. I had to fight the urge to grab the bottle and down it at a gulp—either that, or upend it over their heads. "I trust you gentlemen enjoyed your supper?"

"Yes, thank you," Thomas said, oblivious to my tone. "The duck was particularly splendid. As to our work, it was no easy task, I don't mind telling you. In fact . . ." He paused, furrowing his brow. "Rose, what happened to your coat? And your hair. Are those . . . pine needles?"

"I'm going to take a bath. Good night, gentlemen." Tossing the satchel on the floor between them, I marched up the stairs.

CHAPTER 15

THE HIDDEN TIDES OF THOMAS WILTSHIRE—THE PRICE LIST—A FILTHY HABIT

W hat do you mean, you *climbed*? From a third-story window?" Thomas had gone quite pale, butter knife poised above the strawberry preserves. "Good Lord, Rose! You weren't hurt?"

"A few scrapes and bruises. Nothing important."

"Thank God for that! What on earth were you thinking?"

I frowned. "Surely you don't mean to scold me for this? It's not as though I had any choice in the matter."

"You could have called for help."

"And ended up in the Tombs, and maybe Sing Sing after that. No, thank you."

"Rose, listen to me." Thomas put down his knife and gazed firmly into my eyes. "You need never put your life in jeopardy like that. If you had been taken into custody, I would have secured your release, whatever it took. It's well and proper to take your duties seriously, but nothing you found in that house could ever be worth . . ." He squeezed his eyes shut. "Promise me you'll never take a risk like that again."

"I'm fine. It was only—"

His hand shot across the table and seized mine. *"Promise me."*

I paused, taken aback. His eyes burned with raw emotion—determination, fear, and beneath that, an unmistakable shadow of grief. It brought to mind a conversation we'd had last winter.

You lost someone.

It was a long time ago. But it will be with me to the end of my days.

I'd only ever caught glimpses of this side of Thomas—the molten tides beneath the cool, steady surface—and I'd long suspected his well-studied reserve had more than a little to do with his loss. Whatever had happened, he obviously felt responsible. I wanted dearly to take that burden from him, but how could I make a promise I knew I wouldn't be able to keep?

"I'll be more careful," I said quietly. It was the best I could offer.

He said nothing for long moments, his hand still gripping mine. A flush crept into my cheeks. *Where are you, Thomas? Here with me, or somewhere in the past?* There was no way of knowing.

He let go and sat back. "As to the book you found, you're quite right—the seal is most likely magical. I've already summoned Jackson. He should be here soon."

As matter-of-fact as you please, as though whatever had just passed between us had never been.

My cheeks were still warm, from embarrassment now. *Quit projecting your own feelings onto him,* I chided myself. *You have no idea what's going on in his head.*

I cleared my throat. "And what about you and Mr. Burrows? What did you find out?"

"Less than I'd hoped. Andrew Price reads like a man with something to hide, but that's hardly surprising, given the nature of his business. We had a deuce of a time trying to draw him out, but he did mention that he'll be attending the dinner reception for Roosevelt at the Fifth Avenue Hotel tonight."

I'd seen that noted in Price's diary. As for the rest of its pages, Thomas had glanced through but found nothing of use. "Why would he want to watch Roosevelt speak? I thought he supported the Democrats."

"Indeed. His purported aim is to gather intelligence about the opposing platform, but he hardly needs to attend an expensive supper for that. Roosevelt's views are well publicized in the papers. Whatever Price's intentions, Roosevelt will be highly approachable at the event, and therefore vulnerable. We must assume the worst, and be prepared for an attack."

Mr. Jackson arrived shortly thereafter, and a brief examination of the ledger was enough for him to confirm that it was indeed enchanted. "Keyed to the owner's fingerprints, most likely," the warlock said, turning it over in his hand. "Not my specialty, but I'll see what I can do." He started rummaging in his black leather doctor's bag.

"The drawer was magically locked, too," I said. "It ate my favorite lockpick."

"Ah yes, the vanishing lockpick." Mr. Jackson smiled wryly. "A simple spell, but effective. Most likely Price bought one of the ready-made varieties, at Wang's or somewhere like it. Otherwise, he'd presumably have enchanted the drawer itself, if not the entire desk."

"Which means he isn't himself a witch," Thomas said.

"That would be my guess, which gives me hope for this." Mr. Jackson waggled the book. "If the spell were custom-wrought, it would take time, but a stock variety should be quite straightforward."

He placed a series of glass vials on the table. Some were filled with liquid, others with crystals, still others with dried leaves and grasses. One vial, shaped like a perfume bottle, held some sort of slug-like creature, which clung to the inside of the glass, trailing a film of pink ooze. "Any sign of the Harlem shade?" I asked distractedly, unable to tear my gaze away from the implausibly colored slime.

Mr. Jackson shook his head. "Wherever he's got to, he seems to be keeping to himself. In fact, it's been quiet enough that I think it might be time for me to head back to Chicago."

That was the best news I'd heard in weeks, but I tried very hard not to show it. No reflection on Mr. Jackson, but I was anxious to leave our weekend shade-chasing club behind for good.

"Here it is." He selected a vial filled with what looked like black sand. "Wiltshire, can I trouble you for some salt? My stock is running low."

"Certainly." Thomas reached into his jacket and retrieved a little pouch. All of us carried salt on our persons, along with ash wood, since it provided a measure of protection against the dead. Apparently, it helped dispel magic, too, because Mr. Jackson added a few grains to the vial of black sand.

"Now then . . ." He arranged his fingertips over the book. As soon as he touched it, the cover acquired a strange, almost liquid sheen, and an embossed symbol reared up in relief. Honey gold against the black leather of the cover, it arranged itself into the shape of an antique keyhole. Mr. Jackson poured a thimbleful of the black sand into the keyhole, and a moment later, the book flipped open. "*Hmm,*" he said, frowning. "Not quite a stock enchantment after all. The lock has been opened, but not dispelled. I suspect it will reseal the moment the book is closed. Be careful how you handle it or I'll have to start over, and I'm fresh out of onyx dust."

"Duly noted." Thomas started to reach for the book, but a look from me stopped him short. "Apologies, Miss Gallagher. You should certainly do the honors."

I snatched it up and started rifling through the pages. But my eagerness soon turned to confusion, followed by disbelief, then anger. *This can't be all. Please, Lord, tell me I didn't almost get myself killed for* this.

"What is it?" Mr. Jackson asked. "Not what you were expecting, obviously."

"Accounting." I tossed the book aside in disgust. "Nothing more than a series of balance sheets. It's as useless as the diary."

Thomas took it up. "Don't be too hasty," he said, flipping through the pages. "This ledger contains the details of all of Andrew Price's establishments."

"So he's a meticulous brothel owner. Where does that get us?"

"This is not information he would like to have put about, which gives us leverage. And then there's this section." He turned the book around and showed me. The pages bore a list of names, and against each one, a date and an amount.

I shook my head; it meant nothing to me.

"Surely you recognize at least one name on this list," he said, tapping it.

Peering more closely, I drew a sharp breath. "Byrnes. And wait, I know this one, too. He's an alderman, isn't he?"

"Here are two names I know well," said Mr. Jackson, pointing. "New York City coroners, both of them."

Understanding dawned. "This is a list of bribes, isn't it?"

"So it would seem," Thomas said. "And see here, there are two separate entries for Inspector Byrnes this month alone. This one is only two days old, as is this payment." He pointed to one of the names Mr. Jackson had indicated.

There were any number of reasons a man in Price's line of work might bribe the chief of detectives or the coroner, but on the day after the convention murders? That was too much of a coincidence to credit. "Price is paying them off for their silence."

Of his own accord, or on behalf of the Democratic Party? Either way, the evidence was damning.

Thomas smiled. "There, you see? Your efforts were not wasted. We'll need to identify these other names, especially those who received payments within the last few weeks. Our killer might be among them."

"Your Mr. Price has gone to a great deal of trouble with this ledger," Mr. Jackson said. "Surely he'll miss it?"

"Undoubtedly," Thomas said, "but he's unlikely to connect Burrows and me to its disappearance. In his place, I would most likely conclude that someone mentioned in the ledger didn't trust me enough to leave such a potentially damaging bit of evidence lying around, magically sealed or no."

"Someone like Byrnes," I said, my gaze falling to his name in the ledger. "Do you suppose I was wrong about him? Maybe he's doing more than just keeping things quiet. Maybe he knows who the killer is after all."

"Sergeant Chapman didn't think so," Thomas reminded me. "In addition to which, if the chief of detectives wanted Theodore Roosevelt dead, I'm inclined to think the deed would be done by now. Regardless, it will certainly be interesting to hear the good sergeant's views on this book."

"Just remember," Mr. Jackson said, "you'll need to keep it open, at least until you acquire the means to circumvent the enchantment yourselves. I suspect a magical skeleton key will do the trick, but I haven't got one."

"A trip to Wang's ought to sort us out," Thomas said. "We're heading down to Five Points anyway. In fact, we'd better be off. Rose, perhaps you could let Clara know that we'll be dining out this evening, and that you'll require her assistance to don your armor."

"My armor?"

"Once more unto the breach, Miss Gallagher. And this time, I've a hunch we'll see action."

The man who answered the door in Chatham Square was a shadow of the energetic inventor I'd met the day before. Mr. Tesla looked pale and drawn; he'd obviously been up all night working. But he didn't let that slow him down, offering only a cursory greeting before getting down to business. "I'm glad you've come early," he said as he led us across the laboratory. "It will give me time to address any remaining issues before nightfall. I presume you mean to attend the reception at the Fifth Avenue Hotel?" There was no sign of Mr. Clemens, a fact Thomas registered with visible relief.

"I do apologize for the pressure we've put you under," Thomas said. "If we had any choice in the matter . . ."

"I understand, and in any case, I am accustomed to going without sleep. Now, let me show you what I . . . *Scarlett. Get off.*" The otherworldly flame ball sat like an oversize paperweight on the table where Mr. Tesla was working; the inventor shooed it away with a wave. It didn't go far, however, settling onto his shoulder like a stray bit of lint. He hardly seemed to notice, taking an object from the desk. "I must confess, my friends, I am quite proud of my solution. What do you think?" He held out an ivory cylinder slightly longer than a finger.

At first I took it for a piece of jewelry. Slim, elegant, with one end slightly flared like the bell of a clarinet, it was rimmed in silver and inlaid with mother-of-pearl and ebony in the design of a white cherry blossom. "It's lovely," I said, "but what is it?"

"A cigarette holder. Or at least it was. Now it is an electromagnetic radiation probe." Mr. Tesla smiled. "I do not think the fellow who gave it to me would approve of its being put to such use—I'm sure I was meant to woo some elegant lady with it—but it is perfectly suited to the task."

"So small," Thomas said wonderingly. "Are you sure it still works?"

"It does not have the range of the original, but the tube still permits ionization of the gas by an electric field."

"Electric field." I peered more closely at it. "But there are no wires."

"No need. The power is transferred through resonance. The street current passes through an apparatus that transforms it into electrical oscillations of very high frequency, which, when they come into contact with the silver rim of the cigarette holder, set the molecules of the gas into violent commotion."

"I see," I said, though of course I didn't.

He smiled patiently. "It is rather like a tuning fork. If one strikes a tuning fork in close proximity to a crystal glass, it will hum, yes? The vibrations from the fork cause the glass to resonate. The principle here is similar, except that with sufficient power and appropriate manipulation of the magnetic field, proximity need not be an issue. From right here in the lab, I can achieve a radius of several miles."

"This apparatus," Thomas said. "I presume it's the coil you've been working on?"

"The prototype only." The inventor gestured at a hulking contraption on the far side of the room, a tower of copper wire and tubing that looked like a giant metal mushroom. "I have yet to perfect a version that doesn't rely on my luck, but for your purposes, that need not be a concern. I can operate the device from here, and the electromagnetic field will easily reach the hotel."

Thomas looked wary. "Is that entirely safe?"

"Of course. The waves are harmless, and the receiver must be tuned to the proper frequency in order to work. The real difficulty was making sure that the waves would not interfere with the sensitivity of the probe. That took me the better part of the night to resolve, but I have done so. There is just one matter remaining, which is the display." Mr. Tesla nodded toward the tin box I'd operated yesterday, with the two dials. "I have yet to determine how to provide a display that you can carry on your person without drawing attention. The answer is almost certainly to repurpose something, as I have done with the cigarette holder. But what?"

I took the ivory wand from Thomas, examining it with narrowed eyes. It really did resemble jewelry . . . "What about a wristwatch?"

The inventor's eyes lit up, and the flame ball on his shoulder flared a little brighter, as if reacting to his excitement. "An excellent idea, Miss Gallagher! I have never seen one, but so long as I can replace the clockworks inside, it will serve admirably." He started to pace, his willowy frame bent forward in thought. "Now then, how to connect it to the probe? A silver chain, perhaps. Yes, yes. The chain has only to come into contact with the silver band at the base of the cigarette holder, and the natural conductivity of the metal will do the rest. It will be a crude display, but it will serve."

"I have just the thing," I said. "A silver charm bracelet I received the other night as a favor. We can attach part of it to the clasp of the watch. That way, when I hold my arm like so"—I extended it toward the floor—"the charm will dangle over my palm, and I can touch the cigarette holder to it."

"And transmit the pulse." The inventor nodded. "Yes, that will work, provided the silver is pure enough."

"How long will it take to fashion?" Thomas asked.

"Bring me a wristwatch, Mr. Wiltshire, and you shall have it by luncheon."

Thomas wasted no time, grabbing his hat and overcoat. "In that case, it's off to Ladies' Mile. You'll manage on your own at Wang's, Miss Gallagher?"

"Of course." And if that gave me a chance to wander by Augusto's Grocery—well, that was just a happy coincidence.

"Tesla." Thomas gripped his friend's hand. "You really are a wizard. I'll be back as soon as I can."

"Well then," I said after Thomas had gone, "I suppose I'm taking up smoking."

"I would not recommend that, Miss Gallagher, unless you wish to explode."

I blanched.

The inventor laughed shyly into his hand. "I'm sorry, I couldn't resist. Have no fear, helium is not flammable. You may smoke as much as you like."

"Lucky me," I said with a thin smile.

I felt nauseous already.

CHAPTER 16

SPECIAL TEAS AND SKELETON KEYS—A
STROKE OF LUCK—ONE DAY AT A TIME—
THE SHADOW OF A ROSE

hadn't seen the Wangs in months, and as I neared the Chinese
grocery that was so much more than it seemed, I felt a twinge of
guilt. After everything that had happened last January, Wang's
General Store would forever be a bold black star on the map of
my life. The place where I'd first spoken to the spirit of a dead
woman. Where Mr. Burrows and I had planned a rescue mission,
aided by an unlikely team of extraordinary people. Where Mr.
Wiltshire, the man I'd loved from afar for so long, had first asked
me to call him *Thomas.* Above all, the place where the Wangs had
saved my life and offered me their friendship. For which I'd
thanked them by staying away, too preoccupied with my own
business even to stop in and say hello.

It's a poor showing, Rose Gallagher, said Mam's voice in my
head.

The familiar scent of the shop wafted over me as I opened the door, incense and tea and a dozen more exotic things. I found Mei tucked among the rows of tightly packed shelves, explaining to an Italian customer that the mushrooms he was admiring were not for eating. (This she did in the universal language of Five Points pantomime, gesturing at her guts and making a bodily heaving motion.)

"For special tea?" I asked with a smile. Mei's father referred to all his medicinal brews that way, even if they rarely contained actual tea.

"Good for *qi*," she said, putting the basket back on the shelf. "Bad for digestion." She paused, looking me over with interest. "You have a new coat. It's very pretty."

I glanced down at my overcoat, half expecting to see my familiar old tweed; instead I found a stylish dark gray wool trimmed with blue velvet. I'd slipped so easily into my new cover identity that I barely even registered all the outward changes anymore, but of course old friends like Mei would notice—and wonder how I could possibly afford such extravagant things. "Thank you," I said awkwardly.

"How can I help you?"

Straight down to business. It had been so long since I stopped in that Mei just assumed I must be there for work. That would be embarrassing enough if it didn't also happen to be true. "Mr. Wiltshire and I were hoping you might have a magical skeleton key. Something that can open"—I consulted the piece of paper Mr. Jackson had given me—"a latent polarization lock with manually triggered manifestation."

Mei stared at me, baffled. "My English . . ."

"Your English is just fine. It doesn't mean a thing to me either."

"Maybe my father will know." She called to him through the silk curtain that separated the storefront from the much larger complex of back rooms. That was where the *real* business took place, and I don't mean the gambling or the opium. If New York was a vital crossroads of the paranormal world, Wang's was its unofficial saloon—not to mention its post office, quartermaster, recruitment agency, clinic, and town hall.

None of which you could tell by looking, least of all at the man himself. Mr. Wang emerged from behind the curtain wearing his usual modest garb, a long black tunic and wide trousers, completely unadorned except for the braided frog button clasps. He looked me up and down, the way Mam did when she was about to ask if I was eating right. "Miss Gallagher," he said, offering a bow. "Long time."

"Too long, Mr. Wang. It's very good to see you."

"Please tell him what you told me," Mei said.

I repeated the jumble of words, which Mei did her best to translate into Chinese. "I think the important part is the polarization lock," I said. "The rest . . . I suppose it just means that you can't see the lock until you touch it. Mr. Jackson thinks a skeleton key should do the trick."

Mei interpreted for her father, who grunted thoughtfully. "Skeleton key," he echoed in his heavily accented English. "All-lock key?"

"Yes, exactly. For magical locks."

He waved for us to follow, and we trailed him into one of the stock rooms, where he lit a lamp and started rooting around amid the crates and sacks. While we waited, a soft moan sounded from the other side of the wall.

"A man who injured himself at his factory," Mei explained

in answer to my questioning glance. "My father is helping with the pain, and also to heal the wound faster."

Mr. Wang's talents as an apothecary were well known in the neighborhood, and not just among the Chinese community. It was here that Thomas had brought me when the fragment of a dead woman buried in my flesh had almost killed me. I'd probably been in that very room, lying on the same cot as the poor man next door.

A satisfied grunt signaled that Mr. Wang had found what he was looking for: an unassuming brass key, the business end of which was a plain wedge. "All-lock key," he said, adding something in Chinese as he handed it over.

"He says it will open simple magical locks such as those he sells here."

"That would certainly have come in handy last night," I said irritably. "If you ask me, these things ought to be standard issue for agents of the special branch."

Mr. Wang chuckled. "You tell them. Good for business."

"Thank you, Mr. Wang. Please put it on Mr. Wiltshire's account." I turned for the door, but a thought drew me up short. *Tailors hear a great deal,* Thomas had said, *as do barbers, barkeeps, and bootblacks.* If Wang's was the unofficial saloon of the paranormal community, might its saloonkeepers have heard something useful?

"By the way, Mei, have either of you heard of a form of luck that can kill at a touch?"

"Kill?" Mei raised her eyebrows.

"It sounds far-fetched, I know, but this case Mr. Wiltshire and I are on would seem to suggest otherwise." I recounted what the witness had seen, including the description of the tall man. "It has to be luck, unless . . . You don't suppose it could be magic, do you?" Mei's late mother had been a witch, and she dabbled a little herself. I trusted her opinion on such things almost as much as Mr. Jackson's.

"I have never heard of a spell like that, but . . ." She trailed off, looking thoughtful. She asked her father a question in Chinese, and they conversed for a moment. "How does the person die?" she asked.

"All we know for sure is that the victims collapse within moments, and a few minutes later they die. It seems to have something to do with their hearts."

Mei and her father exchanged looks. "We may have seen something like this before. Last year, a man brought his friend to see my father. He was having . . ." She paused, her hand going to her chest. "His heart was not working as it should."

"A heart attack."

"Yes, a heart attack. My father was able to save him, but he was very sick. Even now, he cannot move part of his face."

"That sounds like apoplexy. A stroke, they sometimes call it."

"I don't know, but he had a very bad headache, and then there was no feeling in his face, and he could not see out of his left eye. When we asked what happened, the friend said they had been in a fight in a saloon. One man grabbed the other by the arm, like this." She gripped her own wrist. "The man's heart started to go very fast. He could not catch his breath, and then he fainted. His friend insisted it was witchcraft. My father and I told him this was not possible, that the man probably just had a bad heart. But maybe we were both wrong. Maybe it was luck."

My own heart was beating very fast by this point. "Did they describe the attacker?"

Both Wangs shook their heads. "We didn't ask," Mei said.

"We were too busy with medicine. And we never saw them again after that."

"What about the saloon—did they say which one?"

"No, but it must have been close by, because they came on foot, and the man was very sick."

That narrowed things down, but only a little. If you tried to count all the gin mills, bucket shops, and stale-beer dives within a three-block radius, you'd run out of fingers before you hit Bayard Street.

Still, it was something. "Thank you, Mei. That's a great help. If you remember anything else, please let us know. In the meantime"—I gave her a quick hug—"take care of yourself. And you, Mr. Wang."

My head was spinning as I left the shop. Thomas and I didn't have time to canvass the neighborhood, but maybe Sergeant Chapman? Or we could hire someone. Pietro was always looking for odd jobs . . .

I can't say I believe in Mr. Clemens's mental telegraphy, but somehow I wasn't surprised to see Pietro at the end of the block, as if he'd been conjured by my thoughts. He was taking breakfast at his favorite oyster cart on the corner, the one with the Calabrian chili oil he loved. There was no sign of the roughs I'd seen him with yesterday, so I headed over.

He smiled awkwardly when he saw me. "*Ciao,* Fiora. Oyster?"

"No thank you. Is there somewhere we can talk privately?" After the way he'd acted yesterday, I wasn't too worried about being abrupt.

Pietro sighed, as if he'd been expecting this—which he probably had. "Let's go up to the flat."

"I don't have time—"

"It's half a block." He didn't wait for an answer, wiping his

fingers on his trousers and heading for the flat. All I could do was
follow.

"Peter, is that you? Oh!" Mam drew up short when she saw
me walk in. "This is a surprise. Two days in a row."

"Morning, Mam. Just stopping in for some tea."

"Look what I brought you, Mama." Pietro produced a bright
red tomato from his pocket, the big, juicy kind you almost never
found in the shops. "Last of the season, from Augusto's garden.
Maybe I make you some nice sauce, eh?"

Mam's eyes went round, and she snatched it from his hand.
"Don't you *dare*. This will be beautiful just as it is, with a little
sprinkle of salt. Here, I'll slice it up . . ."

With Mam safely occupied, Pietro drew me into the little sitting room. "I'm sorry for yesterday," he said when we were out of
earshot. "It wasn't—"

"—a good time. Yes, you said. What I want to know is why."
I lowered my voice to a whisper. "Are you in some kind of trouble?"

"No." Seeing my skeptical expression, he added, "Not exactly.
But the men I'm working with right now . . . I don't want you
around them."

"You mean those roughs I saw you with yesterday?"

He frowned. "I thought you left. Were you spying on me?"

"Don't be dramatic. I happened to see them on my way past
the alley, that's all." Not strictly true, but I wasn't about to let him
distract me as easily as he'd distracted Mam. "Who are they?"

"Just some men who work for Augusto. He asked me to help
them for a little while."

"Help them with what?"

"It's better you don't know. Please, Rose, it's my business. I
can take care of myself."

"So can I. I appreciate you wanting to protect me, but—"

"It's not just you I'm protecting." His gaze flicked meaningfully to the kitchen.

I went very still then. "Is my mother in danger?"

"No."

"Pietro—"

"She's not." He lowered his voice still further. "But if something bad happens, I don't want these men, or the police, to go looking for anybody I care about. The less they know about my life, the better."

"If something bad happens? Pietro, you're scaring me. Just what kind of work is this?" I paused, recalling the newspaper stories Mr. Jackson had mentioned. "Does it have anything to do with those break-ins they're writing about in the papers?"

Pietro looked at me grimly.

Click. Like the hammer of a gun being cocked.

"You're one of them?" I couldn't hide the disappointment in my voice.

That hurt him, I could tell. He glanced away. "Don't look at me like that. I'm not one of them. I haven't done any of those things they said in the papers. I just started working with them this week."

"But why?"

He scowled, still avoiding my eye. "You know better than to ask that. Because of Augusto, of course."

I didn't know what to say. Part of me was furious that he'd go along with something like that, however unwillingly. But I'd grown up in Five Points, and he was right, I did know better. Pietro was a survivor. He'd arrived on American shores at the tender age of six, orphaned and indentured, and every day since then had been a struggle. I'd never asked what he had to do to get by— he didn't owe me his story, and if I'm honest, I probably didn't want to know—but somehow he'd managed. Not just to survive, but to be a decent person, always there for Mam and me . . .

Something even more unpleasant occurred to me then. "What's Augusto holding over you? Does it have anything to do with that business last January?" *Dear Lord, please don't let it be that.* Pietro had warned me that asking for Augusto's help would cost him, but I hadn't listened. I'd been too selfish, too wrapped up in looking for Thomas. All I'd cared about was what Augusto could do for me. The *padrone* had come through, helping me track down the men I was looking for, but of course there was a price to pay. "He's called in his favor, hasn't he?"

"It's not just one favor. I owe him for many things. Hiring me for jobs, helping you last winter, lending me money when I couldn't pay the rent . . ."

"The rent? But why didn't you come to me first? I'm earning more these days."

He made a wry face. "I am not borrowing money from a woman, Fiora, especially not a working one like you. Besides, that wouldn't help anything. Augusto pulls on many strings at once, until you dance like a puppet. If it isn't what you owe him, it's what he can take from you."

What could Augusto possibly take from someone who had nothing to begin with? Then I saw the way Pietro was looking at me, and I understood. It wasn't *what* he could take, but *whom*. "He threatened me, didn't he?"

"Not exactly. But he said that if I didn't help protect the neighborhood, people like my sweetheart might get hurt."

"Your sweetheart? He thinks that's me?" I paused, a little taken aback. I'd had sweethearts before—the usual adolescent affairs, accepting flowers and meaningless tokens in exchange for the occasional chaste kiss. As I recall, there'd been a lot of blushing and giggling and dreamy-eyed looks. I'd never behaved like that with Pietro. "What gave him that idea?"

Pietro shrugged. "That day you came by the store, the way you were talking . . ."

"I remember now." I couldn't help blushing a little. "I asked you to come home with me in front of everyone."

"Nobody lets me forget it. They keep asking when I'm going to marry you." He smiled. "I tell them I can't afford it."

That glimpse of the Pietro I knew, the one with the quick smile and easy humor, almost broke my heart. Impulsively, I grabbed his hand. "Don't let him use me against you. I can take care of myself. In fact, I can help you. I've been studying some things, and Mr. Wiltshire—"

His expression curdled, the way it always did at the mention of Thomas's name. "The last thing I need is a Pinkerton poking around."

Pinkerton. He spat the word like it tasted foul on his tongue. What would he say if he knew I was one of them?

"Anyway, it's temporary. I do this, and maybe Augusto doesn't need me for something worse. Besides, I—"

"Here we are!"

I snatched my hand away just as Mam appeared in the doorway with a plateful of sliced tomato.

"I've put the kettle on."

So there we sat, the three of us, having tea and bread and sliced tomato, the air thick with secrets. If Mam noticed, she didn't let on, too happy for the company to let anything ruin it.

Pietro and I parted ways on Mulberry Street, but not before he made one last attempt to reassure me. "These break-ins . . . It's a little bit rough, but it's mostly for show. They're just making sure the local businesses pay some money, for protection."

"*They.* And what about you?"

"Like I said, I only started this week." Ruefully, he added, "But I guess it's only a matter of time. I'm not happy about it, but nobody is going to the hospital."

"Maybe not, but somebody might end up in the Tombs. *You* might end up in Sing Sing."

"It's only for a little while. The merchants are angry, but they know that if they don't pay Augusto, they will just have to pay the police instead, and the coppers are a lot more expensive. They will come to their senses eventually, and then Augusto won't need so many of us anymore."

"Until he finds another job that needs doing."

Pietro sighed from the soles of his shoes. "One day at a time, Fiora. That is the best I can do."

It was the best any of us could do, I supposed. Which was why I couldn't help him, at least not right now. I had too much else on my plate.

Even so, it felt like I was leaving a part of myself behind on that corner with Pietro. As if a ghostly version of me hovered at his side, watching myself walk away from a friend in trouble. Glancing back, I could almost see her standing there, that other, shadow Rose. But try as I might, I couldn't make out her face.

CHAPTER 17

MAKE-BELIEVE—AN UNWELCOME
GUEST—A PREEMPTIVE STRIKE

The reception for Theodore Roosevelt was scheduled to begin at five-thirty. Yet here it was four-thirty already, and I was no-where near ready, struggling into my multitudes of undergar-ments while Clara performed surgery on my silver Tiffany bracelet with a tiny pair of pliers.

"Such a shame," I said, eying the ruins of one of the pretti-est things I'd ever owned. "I only got to wear it once."

"You can console yourself with your new wristwatch."

"It's not a wristwatch anymore. The guts have been replaced. It doesn't even tell time."

"Shucks. I guess now it's just a diamond bracelet."

I frowned. "It's not as though these trinkets are gifts, you know." Well, except the emerald brooch, but that was . . . complicated.

"What do you call it when somebody gives you something for free?"

"It was only a party favor."

"Only." She snorted softly. "It'd spoil the looks of a month's salary, and you got me chopping it up like cabbage."

I paused, petticoats dangling about my hips. "These things don't even belong to me, not really. They're part of a disguise, that's all."

"A damn good one, too. I've known you for years and I barely recognize you."

After what happened with Pietro that morning, that struck a nerve. "What's that supposed to mean?"

She sighed. "Nothing. It's just . . . What're you gonna do when this case is over and you gotta go back to real life?"

"They're only clothes, Clara. It's just make-believe."

"I know that. I just hope you do."

"It's not as though I could forget," I said irritably. "Not if Ava Hendriks and her ilk have anything to say about it. They'll take every opportunity to remind me how far beneath them I am. And that's the make-believe me, mind you—the *real* me is barely fit to polish their silver."

"That ain't so," Clara said severely, pointing her pliers at me, "and don't you go thinking it. Lord Almighty, Rose, we been having this conversation for years. You're always looking up to these rich folks, thinking they're better than the rest of us. You been spending so much time around them lately, I thought for sure you'd finally see that they ain't no different from the rest of us. Instead you're trying even harder to impress them."

"It's part of the job. I need to convince them that I belong. That I'm one of them."

"Convince them or convince yourself?"

As if I ever could. "Look, this is awkward for both of us. I understand if you don't want any part of it."

She gave me a wry look. "You couldn't strap yourself into this getup if you had two extra arms and a week to do it. So unless you're planning to ask Mr. Wiltshire for help, you're stuck with me."

"He wouldn't have a clue."

"Men know more than you think. If they can get 'em off you, they can work out how to get 'em on again."

Which remark threw me into a fit of flushed daydreaming, the general outlines of which you can probably guess.

As soon as I was properly assembled, I headed down to the parlor, where I found Thomas waiting. "Sorry for being late. It took longer than I thought to adjust the watch."

"Not to worry. Burrows is constantly chiding me for my punctuality. Apparently being on time is *not the thing*."

"Speaking of, I wish he were here. We could see if this contraption really works." I brandished the refitted wristwatch, which now resembled a cross between the charm bracelet and a platinum bangle set with tiny diamonds. "It's one thing to make it work in the lab . . ."

". . . and another out in the field." He took my gloved hand, casual as a lover, tilting my wrist to inspect the watch. "At least it looks the part. It's quite lovely on you."

"You have excellent taste, but we knew that already."

He smiled. "Hopefully we can corner Burrows and run a quick test."

"In the meantime, I can make a fool of myself by being the only woman in the room who smokes cigarettes."

"Nonsense, you'll seem very exotic and fashionable."

I doubted that, but there was no help for it now. Thomas grabbed our overcoats, and we were on our way.

The Fifth Avenue Hotel was already bustling by the time we got there, at least a hundred elegant people sipping champagne and milling about the dining room. The space had been completely reconfigured for the event. At one end sat several long tables extravagantly set for supper; at the other, the floor had been cleared save for a few small tables of hors d'oeuvres. Hothouse flowers and potted palms formed an island between the two spaces, like a small park complete with benches.

"I don't see Price yet," Thomas said, "but we have time. Roosevelt probably won't arrive until just before he's due to give his speech."

"Which is when?"

"After supper, when the women retire to the ladies' drawing rooms upstairs."

I gave him a sharp look. "You're not thinking of sending me off with the rest of them, are you?"

"Certainly not. In fact, I doubt you'll be the only woman interested in hearing Roosevelt speak. Believe it or not, suffragists are occasionally found among society circles." He accepted two glasses of champagne from a passing waiter and handed one to me, using the gesture as cover to touch the cigarette holder against my wristwatch. "Look at that," he said in an undertone. "Tesla must have started up his coil."

I glanced down to find the minute hand suspended halfway between one and two. "To think there's electricity running through this room right now. Running through *us*."

"A disconcerting thought," he agreed, handing the probe back to me. "What about the pulses? Can you feel them?"

I let my arm fall to my side so that the dangling charm rested alongside the cigarette holder. The moment the two bits of silver touched, I felt a buzzing sensation against my wrist. "There's a sort of vibration, as if . . ." I paused. "No, wait, I feel it now. And the minute hand has started to—"

"Look at you, Wiltshire." The minute hand jumped to three as Mr. Burrows stepped out of the crowd. "Anyone else in that tailoring would look old-fashioned, but somehow on you it's the very height of style."

"It's called *classic*, Burrows."

"And Miss Gallagher." Then, coolly: "I'm sorry, am I keeping you from something?"

I glanced up sheepishly. "Sorry, I didn't mean to be rude." Lowering my voice, I added, "This isn't really a watch. It's a luck meter."

"I beg your pardon?"

"Here." Thomas handed his champagne to a bewildered Mr. Burrows. "Would you be so good as to tell me where this glass comes from?"

Mr. Burrows's eyes narrowed. "What is this?"

"Humor me. No one will know what we're about, I promise."

"I am not a trained monkey," Mr. Burrows growled, but he did as he was asked, tugging off his chamois glove and turning the glass about in his bare hand. "Tastes like Althaus."

Thomas glanced at me, but I shook my head. "Take your time," I said, pointing the probe directly at Mr. Burrows.

He sighed impatiently. "High lead content. Definitely German. From the Upper Harz region, judging from the undertones of silver . . ." And so on, sounding for all the world like he was describing a fine wine. As he spoke, the minute hand on my watch climbed from three to seven, and the static against my wrist intensified. When I pointed the probe directly at him, the pulses vibrated through my glove like an erratic heartbeat; when I pointed it away, they faded.

"Not very exact," I reported, "but it works. You can definitely tell what direction the power is coming from."

Mr. Burrows regarded my cigarette holder with interest. "Where on earth did you get it?"

"Tesla," Thomas said.

"Ah yes, your favorite prodigy. I'm beginning to see why. Is he looking for investors?"

"Always, but you'd have to share the portfolio with *Mark Twain*." This last in a tone of elegant distaste.

"It's a wonderful trick, but how will it help you? You're not exactly looking for a needle in a haystack here." Mr. Burrows gestured at the crowd.

A needle in a pile of needles was more like it. Though only one percent of the general population was lucky, among the wealthy, the figure was closer to twenty percent. There would be no shortage of specimens here tonight.

"The hope," Thomas said, "is that we can single out the guests we need to keep an eye on, and possibly even be warned of an imminent attack. It's not perfect, but we need all the help we can get."

"And you also need me to stay away so I don't ruin your readings." Mr. Burrows sighed theatrically. "What a shame. I was so looking forward to having Miss Gallagher on my arm, especially when Ava Hendriks is in view."

I groaned inwardly. "She's here?"

"Of course. The hotel is rich hunting grounds tonight. Ava and her fellow Dianas have their bows strung and their quivers full. We stags must be wary, Wiltshire."

Thomas *tsk*ed quietly. "Some respect, please, Jonathan."

"What's disrespectful about it? I for one find it quite refreshing when the roles are reversed. One does tire of always playing the hunter."

"You're an avid hunter, are you?" I asked dryly.

"Oh yes." His ice-blue eyes held mine just long enough to bring a hint of color to my cheeks, and then he was on his way.

"Incorrigible," Thomas and I muttered in unison.

Scanning the crowd, I recognized several guests from the soiree at the Hendrikses'—including Ava herself, whose white satin gown gleamed amid a sea of black swallowtails. Most of the guests were middle-aged men, some of them quite celebrated. I recognized politicians and financiers and newspaper editors, including a certain extravagantly whiskered gentleman I'd give my eyeteeth to be introduced to, and then there was—

I stiffened, sucking in a breath. "Byrnes is here."

Thomas didn't look straightaway. "Where?"

"Near the wall opposite us, under the chandelier."

Slowly, Thomas turned. The chief of detectives stood on the far side of the room in all his uniformed glory, conversing with a handful of older men. His expression was unreadable behind the huge mustache, but he scanned the room every few seconds, as though he were looking for someone.

Thomas swore under his breath. "He could ruin everything, and not just for this case. Fewer than half a dozen people in this room know the truth about me, and only two about you. Byrnes could destroy us at a word."

"What is he even doing here? I thought he was Tammany's man. He's up to no good, surely."

"Not necessarily. It could be a political gesture. To demonstrate the neutrality of the police department, or some such. Or

perhaps he's doing actual police work. There's just no way to know."
Thomas sighed. "I suppose we'll have to talk to him. Try to convince him that we're here on other business."

That sounded like a very tall order to me. With due respect
to Thomas's ingenuity, I didn't see how we could possibly hope to
sell our presence here as a coincidence. There was another option,
though. "I have an idea. It's risky, but . . . Do you trust me?"

He gave me a wary look. "Yes."

"Follow my lead."

Swallowing down a lump of nervousness, I made straight for
Byrnes and his companions.

The chief of detectives didn't notice me until I appeared at
his elbow. "Forgive me for interrupting, gentlemen, but I just had
to say hello. It's so good to see you again, Inspector."

A startled blink was the only hint I'd caught him off guard;
in an instant, his features settled into a perfectly blank expression.
"Madam."

"Rose Gallagher, and I believe you remember my cousin,
Mr. Wiltshire?"

"I remember you both. Very clearly." His gaze shifted between us, as if to say, *What are you up to?*

A question Thomas was almost certainly echoing in his
own head, but he played along, wearing an expression of casual
interest.

"I didn't know you were a Republican," I said, gesturing
playfully at him with my cigarette. I didn't even need to glance at
my watch to read the meter; the weak static against my wrist told
me the inspector wasn't lucky.

"I leave the politics to the politicians, miss. I'm just a copper."

"A sound policy, I'm sure. I imagine it's more than a full-time job, what with the crime in this city. It seems that nowhere is safe anymore, not even Fifth Avenue. Why, did you know that Andrew Price was burgled just last night?"

I thought perhaps I heard a small, strangled sound from Thomas's general direction.

The inspector's eyes narrowed. "I wasn't aware of that, no."

"I understand the thieves made off with a particularly important bit of paperwork. A ledger, wasn't it?" I turned to Thomas, as though for confirmation.

"Yes," he said with a strained smile, "I believe it was."

I shook my head. "Imagine going to all that trouble to meticulously document every financial transaction, who you paid and when, only to have it stolen. Do you suppose the thieves even know what to do with information like that?"

The mix of incredulity and grim amusement on Byrnes's face was quite satisfying. And more than a little terrifying. I was acutely aware of his size in that moment, and the predatory gleam in his close-set eyes. "I don't know, Miss Gallagher. Do they?"

"Well, I suppose that depends on— Oh, look!" I gestured at a gray-haired fellow a few feet away, whose extravagant side-whiskers made him one of the most recognizable people in the room. "Is that who I think it is?"

Everyone looked, and when Thomas turned back to me, his eyes burned with triumph. For a moment I thought he might actually sweep me into his arms and spin me about; alas, he mastered himself almost immediately. "Why, yes, it certainly is. George Curtis," he added, for the benefit of anyone who failed to recognize one of the country's most eminent Republicans—who also happened to be the editor of *Harper's* magazine. "And look, he's chatting with Whitelaw Reid, editor of the *Tribune*. Why, this room is just full of press."

Byrnes smiled at me, and though I couldn't see his teeth behind the mustache, I imagined they were very pointy indeed. "Are you an admirer of *Harper's*, Miss Gallagher? I'd be happy to introduce you. Excuse us, lads." Taking my elbow in a most ungentlemanly grip, he steered me aside.

"Hands off, Inspector," Thomas murmured, close behind me. "I'd hate to make a scene."

Byrnes let me go, but he still loomed over me, leaving barely six inches of space between us. "Now you listen to me, darlin'. I don't know what that performance was all about, but I haven't time to worry about your little variety act tonight. There's too much going on, and I'm too thinly spread. You stay out of my way and I'll stay out of yours. That's a onetime offer, and it expires tomorrow."

"Fine by me, Inspector. Just remember, if you breathe a word about us to Price or anyone else, the press will have that ledger."

He snorted. "I've no loyalty to Price. He's a money purse and nothing more. But I promise you, if you go on making a nuisance of yourself, there's a cell on Blackwell's Island with your name on it."

"I'm glad we understand each other," I said, and I spun on my heel and walked away.

Whereupon my momentary courage fled me, replaced by the same wobbly feeling I'd had after my treacherous climb from a third-story window. As for Thomas, he was flushed and glassy-eyed, as if he'd downed a stiff whiskey. "Rose Gallagher, I could kiss you."

My laugh sounded thin and warbling. "That would be awkward, since we're meant to be cousins."

He glanced back over his shoulder. "So Byrnes is here on

police business after all. In fact, it sounds as though we're pulling in the same direction, however grudgingly."

Grudgingly wasn't the word I'd have chosen. As far as I could tell, Byrnes would just as soon see us at the bottom of the East River. "That man terrifies me."

"And yet you confronted him head-on." Thomas shook his head, smiling. "You know, I think I finally understand why jujitsu feels so foreign to you. It relies on turning your opponent's momentum against him, but that doesn't suit you at all, does it? You prefer a preemptive strike."

"Is that bad?"

He laughed softly, and his hand brushed against mine, a fleeting, forbidden interlacing of fingers. "It's brilliant, Rose. You're brilliant."

The gesture would have been intimate in the privacy of our own home. Here in this crowded place, it was practically a kiss, and it left me nearly as breathless. *If I were struck down this instant, I'd die happy.*

A dangerous thought, that. I should have known better.

CHAPTER 18

OLD-FASHIONED—A RARE BIRD—KICKING
THE HORNET'S NEST—CHAMPAGNE
CHARLIE

By half past six, the reception was in full flight. The champagne flowed, the volume rose, and canapés flew past on flashing silver trays. Andrew Price had arrived at about quarter past and was promptly set upon by his new best friends Thomas Wiltshire and Jonathan Burrows, which left me to mill about the room surreptitiously scanning the rest of the crowd. (Price himself had been my first target, but he proved to be a mere mortal; only his nearness to Mr. Burrows prevented the dial from dropping to zero.) I must have looked positively eccentric wandering about waving my cigarette at unsuspecting party guests, but nobody paid me too much attention. As for my readings, the dial had picked out a handful of lucky people, but so far nobody matching the description of our killer.

It was a dull bit of business, so when a sudden staccato rhythm started hammering against my wrist, it nearly startled me out of my skin. The minute hand on my watch climbed from three to five, and when I veered to my left, it jumped all the way to seven. I was so absorbed in following the signal that I very nearly collided with its source: a stylish brunette wearing a familiar arch expression.

"Cocktail?" Without waiting for an answer, Edith Islington pressed a honey-colored drink into my hand.

"Er, thank you. I'm sorry, what is it?"

"A cocktail," she repeated, as though that told me everything I needed to know. "The old-fashioned kind, with whiskey. I'm not much for these newfangled liqueurs, are you?"

"Not really," I said, which was technically true, since I'd never heard the word *liqueur* in my life. I pretended to examine the drink, letting my eye fall to the dial at my wrist. *Eight. She's using her luck right now.* I supposed that made sense. Some forms of luck were probably never really *off.*

Miss Islington was looking at me expectantly, so I took a sip of the drink—and winced.

"*Hmm,*" she said. "Not a brilliant testimonial."

"Sorry. It's a touch bitter, that's all."

"Never mind, I'll have it." She waved to a passing waiter and grabbed a glass of champagne, swapping me for my cocktail. "There, better?" Now she had a cocktail in each hand. "Well, this should be interesting. Promise you'll rescue me if I do anything too outrageous."

I laughed, despite myself. "I'll do my best."

"Is that a cigarette?" She eyed it with interest. "The holder is a lovely bit of work. Not as lovely as that brooch, mind you. I noticed it the other night. Stunning."

My fingers drifted to the jewels at my neckline. "Thank you. It was a gift."

"Why, Miss Gallagher, are you blushing? From a suitor, then? He must be very fond of you."

If I wasn't blushing before, I certainly was now. "It's a bit extravagant, isn't it?"

"Actually, I was referring to the choice of stone. It speaks volumes."

"How so?"

"An emerald? I suppose it could be a coincidence, but I'll wager he chose it in honor of the Emerald Isle. A sweet sentiment. I do hope he was suitably rewarded." She winked, and I blushed all over again.

"You remind me of someone," I said dryly, glancing across the room at a certain golden-haired swell. Then my eye fell on Thomas, and I found myself wondering if what Miss Islington said was true. Had he chosen an emerald because I was Irish? Or was it to match his cufflinks? Maybe it was just what the jeweler had on hand. I supposed I'd never know.

"Mr. Wiltshire is here too, I see," Miss Islington said, following my gaze. "Ava was right after all. Your arrival has brought him out of hiding."

"I'm sure he hasn't been *hiding*."

"He's certainly been a rare bird. Sightings are few, and enthusiastically reported."

"Enthusiastically reported?" I didn't much like the sound of that.

"Of course. He's played us all masterfully, your cousin. He excited a great deal of interest when he first arrived in New York—mysterious young foreigner and all that—and then he all but disappeared. We see him at three, perhaps four society functions a year. Barely enough to form an impression of him, which of course leaves us all ravenously curious. Not that I imagine it's calculated. I suppose he's just very private?"

"Oh, indeed. Why, I expect you could spend nearly every waking moment with him and still have no idea what's going on in his head." I took a generous pull of my champagne.

"Well, calculated or not, he's made a magnificent success of it. Which is why Ava is so determined to put one of her friends in his path. If she can take credit for helping someone snare the elusive Thomas Wiltshire, her reputation as a matchmaker will be peerless."

As though I needed another reason to dislike Ava Hendriks.

"Speaking of matchmaking." Miss Islington lifted her gaze over my shoulder. "Don't look now, but you're being admired by a walrus."

I nearly blew champagne out of my nose. I didn't need to ask whom she was referring to, and the idea that he was admiring me was almost as funny as hearing him called a walrus. "That's Inspector Byrnes. He's been glaring at me all evening."

"Oh, dear. Why should he do that?"

Think fast, Rose. "Well, he's a Tammany man, you see, and I made my disapproval of their brand of politics quite plain."

That explanation seemed to satisfy her, but I made a mental note to stay on my guard. *I notice things,* she'd told me the other night, *and I never forget them.* The first part, at least, she'd proven several times over, which meant I needed to be careful around her.

"Smokes cigarettes, takes an interest in politics, and speaks frankly enough on the subject to offend high-ranking police officers. Miss Gallagher, you are the most unconventional person I've met in ages."

"Is that a compliment?"

"Dear God, yes," she said with such theatrical vehemence that I couldn't help laughing. "You've single-handedly rescued me from a dull evening. Please say you'll sit with me at supper. We'll have to have a gentleman between us, but your cousin will suit the purpose."

It would have been hard to refuse even if I'd wanted to, but as it happened, I didn't. Quite unexpectedly, I found that I was enjoying Edith Islington's company, and apparently the feeling was mutual. "I'd like that," I said. "Thank you, Miss Islington."

"Edith, please."

"And I'd be very happy if you called me Rose."

"Glad that's settled. More champagne?"

"Er, not just now, thanks." I still had a job to do, and it was high time I got on with it. "In fact, would you excuse me for a moment? There's something I ought to take care of before supper . . ."

"No need to explain. I understand completely." And before I could ask what she meant, she cut a sidelong look at an approaching trio of young ladies. Ava Hendriks, Betty Sanford, and a third woman, whose name I had forgotten, were making their way over to us. "Go ahead," Edith murmured. "I'll make an excuse for you."

Well, I could hardly leave after *that*. I would be damned if I let myself be run off by Ava Hendriks. "Oops, too late," I said, and took a fortifying sip of champagne.

"Good evening, ladies." Miss Hendriks favored me with an anemic smile. "How nice to see you again, Miss Gallagher."

"And you, Miss Hendriks."

"What's that you're holding? A cigarette?" She arched a golden eyebrow. "How very . . . modern."

"Do you think so?" I gave the ivory wand a disinterested look. "It's positively *the thing* in Boston."

"I've spent a good deal of time in Boston," said Betty Sanford, "and I don't believe I've ever seen a *lady* smoke." She put just enough emphasis on the word to make her meaning plain.

"Oh, I shouldn't worry," I said airily. "I'm sure the fashion will make its way to your crowd eventually."

Miss Sanford's smile was an artfully veiled sneer. "I doubt it."

"Did you come with your cousin, then?" Miss Hendriks scanned the room.

"Yes, he's right over there, with Mr. Burrows." Smiling sweetly, I added, "The three of us came together."

Oh, Rose, what are you doing? Kicking the hornet's nest, that was what. I just couldn't seem to help myself.

"How nice for you," Miss Hendriks said. "Well, we won't keep you. They'll be calling us to supper any moment now."

I took the opportunity to consult my wristwatch, discreetly holding the silver charm against the end of the cigarette holder. It didn't occur to me until it was too late that this gave Ava Hendriks a bountiful view of what remained of the Tiffany bracelet her family had given me as a favor, which I'd promptly stripped for parts. Her pale skin flooded with color, and her eyes met mine with a flash of outrage. She didn't say a word, but she didn't need to; I understood perfectly well that war had just been declared.

"That could have gone better," Edith Islington observed as Ava and her retinue flounced off in icy silence.

"Oh, well. Maybe now she'll think twice about trying to marry someone into my family. And speaking of, I ought to let Mr. Wiltshire know about our supper plans. I'll be right back."

I moved off into the crowd, waiting until I was out of sight before I started waving my cigarette at people once more, scanning as many as I could before we were called to supper. As before, nobody took any real notice of me—until I passed the miniature conservatory at the center of the room and heard the sound of my name, at which point I froze in my tracks.

"What do you mean, you didn't see?" Ava Hendriks's voice filtered through the thicket of greenery, piping hot with indignation. She must have been sitting on one of the benches, screened from my view by palm fronds. "The bracelet she was given at my mother's reception. She's cut it up, the little monster. Like a common ragpicker!"

Never mind, the sensible part of me said. *You have work to do.* But I couldn't quite bring myself to walk away. Instead I inched a little closer, relying on the dense shrubbery to conceal me from view.

"Well, what do you expect?" Betty Sanford said. "She's *Irish.*"

"If you can believe anything she says. All that flimflam about her grandfather being an English lord?"

A delighted gasp. "You think she's lying?"

"With that accent? She might hide it passing well, but I promise you, that girl is as working class as they come. If she *is* a relation of Mr. Wiltshire's, it must be very distant. I can't imagine why he would introduce her into society."

"Family loyalty, I suppose," said a third voice, the woman whose name I'd forgotten.

"Charity, is more like it," Miss Hendriks said.

As much as I didn't want to care what these women thought of me, hearing myself dismissed as *charity* was mortifying. Warmth flooded my face, and for a moment I just stood there, ears buzzing.

I was so out of sorts that I didn't even notice the waiter hovering at my side until he spoke. "More champagne, miss?" There was something oddly grim about his tone, and when I looked up, the gaze that met mine was tinged with pity. *He overheard the whole thing.* And thanks to the rush of color in my cheeks, he knew they must be talking about me. As usual, there was an audience for my humiliation.

"N-no, thank you," I stammered, fleeing before Miss Hendriks caught me eavesdropping.

I took a quick turn about the room to compose myself, and by the time I was done, supper had been called. Edith Islington had obviously taken it upon herself to inform Thomas of our seating arrangements, because he stood beside her at one of the long tables, waiting for me. "I hope this is all right," he murmured as he pulled out my chair for me.

"It's fine, thank you."

And so it was—until Ava Hendriks appeared on the other side of the table. My smile wilted. She didn't look any happier about the arrangement, and for a moment I was at a loss to understand it. Why would she choose to sit there, of all places? Then Jonathan Burrows took the seat directly across from me, and I understood.

Rich hunting grounds indeed. Well, I would enjoy watching her stalk her prey. *What was it he called you? A little viper? Good luck to you, darling.*

Meanwhile, Mr. Burrows had guided his own prey to the table, in the person of Andrew Price. Miss Hendriks didn't much fancy that either, greeting Price with a cold nod. And so we were arrayed: Mr. Burrows wedged between Misses Sanford and Hendriks, and Thomas between Edith and me, with Andrew Price, brothel owner and possible murder mastermind, rounding out our merry little group. "I think I'm ready for that second glass of champagne," I announced to no one in particular.

We got off to a rip-roaring start, courtesy of Mr. Price. "How lovely to see you, Miss Hendriks. I hear the event the other night was a smashing success." An event to which he had most pointedly not been invited, as everyone there knew. Ava Hendriks was too well bred not to squirm, which of course was the point.

"I wouldn't call it an *event*," she said. "Just a small gathering, really."

Price started to reply, but then he paused, his glance going over her shoulder. "There you are. I was beginning to think you'd gotten lost."

"I was detained," said a new voice. "May I?"

An unfamiliar gentleman loomed over the empty seat beside Miss Hendriks. He was a dour-faced fellow, tall and gaunt. *Gangly, even.*

My heart skipped a beat. I glanced at Thomas, and the sudden sharpness of his gaze told me he'd had the same thought: The newcomer matched the description of our killer. On its own, that might not mean much, but here at this event, taking a seat across from the man we suspected of hiring the assassin? Too much of a coincidence to credit, surely?

The cigarette holder lay on the table in front of me. Discreetly, I reached for it—

—and promptly spilled champagne all over Thomas.

His chair skittered back, but not in time to spare his trousers. With a squeak of dismay, I righted my glass and grabbed my napkin, but of course I couldn't very well go pawing at his lap, so I turned my anguished attention to the fizzing puddle on the tablecloth. Or at least I tried to, but before you could say *hopeless clod* a mob of waiters had descended on us, fussing and flapping and doing a masterful job of drawing the attention of everyone in the dining room.

"I'm so sorry," I murmured, my face burning. "I don't know what happened."

"Never mind, it's just champagne." A game reply, but I knew only too well the care he and Mr. Jennings had put into that new tailoring. I wanted to die.

"Well, that brings a whole new meaning to *Champagne Charlie*," Mr. Burrows said merrily. I wanted to kill him.

Edith, meanwhile, handed me the ivory wand, sticky with champagne. "I'm afraid that's the end of your cigarette."

I removed the soggy cigarette and wiped the holder down with my napkin, avoiding the glances of my supper companions. "Here you are, miss," said one of the waiters, helpfully depositing an entire stack of fresh napkins in front of me.

"I know a very good laundress," Miss Sanford offered sweetly.

"Thank you," Thomas said, "but I'm quite confident in my own."

Who until recently was me. I swear, I nearly said it aloud. I guess there's only so much humiliation you can take before you become giddy with it.

"Do join us," Edith said to the tall man, doing her best to push past the awkwardness. "I don't believe I caught your name."

"Forgive me," said Price. "Fitz, this is Miss Edith Islington. The lady beside you is Miss Ava Hendriks . . ."

Taking advantage of the distraction, I pointed the cigarette holder in the direction of the man called Fitz. I could feel the pulses, all right, but with Edith so nearby, how could I be sure of the source?

Leaning over, I whispered in Thomas's ear. "Something tells me this is going to be a very long night."

CHAPTER 19

IT'S FANCY 'CAUSE IT'S FRENCH—
SPITEFUL—A VERY BAD WAITER

As though I didn't have enough on my plate, as it were, what was *actually* on the plate proved to be its own kind of challenge. The entire menu was in French, which meant that the first course was not turtle soup but *potage à la tortue*, followed by a series of dishes that I couldn't identify, let alone pronounce. So when the waiter inquired whether madam would prefer the *blanchailles* or the *merlans frits*, I could only give Thomas a helpless look.

"I've had the whitebait before," he said, "and I can recommend it."

"Very well, then, I'll take the whitebait, please." Having determined that whitebait was a fish, I could at least work out which fork to use. Or so I thought, but when it arrived, it proved to be a plateful of artfully displayed minnows. How on earth was one meant to dissect these tiny creatures? Then I observed Mr. Burrows across from me and realized they were meant to be eaten whole, head and tail and all, at which point I felt a little ill.

My awkwardness did not go unnoticed. "Miss Gallagher," said Ava Hendriks, "I'm torn between the *côtelettes d'agneau* and the *vol-au-vent*. Which do you prefer?"

I wasn't going to let her get the better of me so easily. "Oh, I don't know," I said with a dismissive gesture. "One is as good as the other, surely? It's not as though you're choosing a candidate for mayor. There, I don't envy anyone having to decide. What do you think, Miss Hendriks—if you had the vote, whom would you choose and why?"

"Oh yes," Mr. Burrows said with a grin, "do tell."

Miss Hendriks's smile had a razor edge. "I was taught never to discuss politics at the table."

"Ordinarily, perhaps," Edith said, "but tonight? That is why we're here, after all. Some of us, at any rate." She smiled innocently and popped a tiny fish into her mouth.

"I for one am quite looking forward to tonight's speech," Thomas said. "What about you, Mr. Fitz?"

The tall man froze with his fork halfway to his mouth, surprised at being put on the spot. "Just Fitz. And to be quite frank, I'm not overly fond of the fellow . . ."

With the center of conversation safely across the table, I had a chance to try again with the probe. Pointing it directly at Fitz from beneath the cover of the tablecloth, I glanced at the dial on my wrist. *Four.* The reading was too strong to be coming from Edith, two seats to my right. But I couldn't rule out Mr. Burrows, or for that matter, Ava Hendriks. I cursed inwardly.

"Is that a wristwatch?" Andrew Price's voice startled me back to the present. "I'd heard those were becoming quite the fashion in Europe, but I've never actually seen one."

"It is," I said, subtly angling it away so he couldn't see the dial.

"What is it—Cartier? Longines?"

"It's, um, a Tesla."

"Miss Gallagher has all the most interesting accoutrements," Edith declared.

Feeling self-conscious again, I reached for my wine . . . and very nearly knocked it over a second time. Only Thomas's lightning reflexes prevented another disaster, his hand shooting out to settle the glass before it lost more than a few droplets.

For a moment I could only stare. I'd never spilled wine in my life until this evening, and now twice? I started to stammer out another apology, but Mr. Burrows's voice cut across me.

"Oh, dear, does it hurt very badly?" Shaking his head, he explained, "Poor Miss Gallagher had her hand caught in the carriage door on the way over."

Murmurs of sympathy around the table.

"I swear I heard something crack. She was a lioness about it, of course. Barely a peep." He took a casual sip of his wine.

Not for the first time, I marveled at how smoothly Jonathan Burrows lied. Nor did Thomas miss his cue. "I don't think it's broken, but we ought to get you to a doctor in the morning, just to be sure."

I kept my mortified gaze on my lap, which was how I happened to see the minute hand on my wristwatch drop from eight to four. Someone had been using their luck a moment ago . . .

I looked up, and if the smug malice in Ava Hendriks's eyes wasn't evidence enough, the look of fury in Edith's sealed it. *So that's your luck, Miss Hendriks.* Somehow she could trick my body into random fits of clumsiness. She'd been doing it since we sat down. *She's been spiteful since she was a child,* Mr. Burrows had said, and now I could see why. With a talent like that, who wouldn't grow into a bully?

Well, you can imagine how the rest of the supper went after that. Between avoiding the predations of Princess Ava and trying to take sneaky readings of the possible assassin sitting next to her, I barely managed a bite of each course. I didn't dare move too often, lest Miss Hendriks have me stab myself in the eye with a fork, and when I did manage to steal a reading, I couldn't be sure whose luck I was detecting. By the time ice cream was served, my leg was jouncing so impatiently that Thomas actually put a hand on my knee under the table. (It was a measure of my anxiety that I couldn't even enjoy it.)

When the meal was finally over, the guests began to disperse—ladies to the drawing rooms upstairs, gentlemen to the reception side of the room, where the bar was still running. "Who's for port?" Andrew Price asked.

Fitz glanced up from winding his watch. "I'll be along shortly."

At last, I'd have my chance to catch him on his own. "I'll join you in a moment," I told Thomas, "once I've had a chance to freshen up." Discreetly, I tilted my head toward Fitz.

He nodded his understanding. "And you, Miss Islington, will you be staying for the speech?"

"I wouldn't miss it, Mr. Wiltshire."

"Miss Sanford and I are heading upstairs," Miss Hendriks announced, though nobody had asked.

Fitz took his time fussing over his watch, leaving me to loiter nearby. At least Edith stayed with me, so I didn't look completely out of place.

"I'm sorry for what Ava did to you," she murmured. "I should have prepared you better. It's just . . . well, it's terribly bad form, isn't it, to discuss someone else's luck? Especially if they're family."

"Family? Ava Hendriks?"

"Didn't you know? Her mother is an Islington, of the Long Island branch." Edith sighed. "We can't all be as fortunate in our relations as you."

"I'm very fortunate indeed, to hear Miss Hendriks tell it. Why, Mr. Wiltshire's kindness toward me is nothing short of charity."

Her mouth fell open. "She actually said that? *Charity?*"

"Oh, yes. I heard her quite distinctly. And the worst part is, I wasn't the only one. That waiter over there overheard the whole thing."

"Which, the tall, skinny one?"

"Yes. It was completely humiliating, and . . ."

I paused.

The young man who'd offered me champagne stood idle near the potted palms, watching the door with an intent expression. His silver tray was empty, his fingers tapping out an anxious rhythm on its rim.

"Edith . . . that waiter. Would you say he's *gangly?*"

She cocked her head. "I suppose that's a fair description. Why?"

"Have you ever seen him before?"

"Several times. He's worked here for at least a few months. Why, what's the matter? Do you know him?"

"I think I've seen him before, too, in the Reading Room." He'd brought Uncle Isaac's coffee the day we'd interviewed him. "I didn't notice him until now because . . ." *Because he's only a waiter. For shame, Rose Gallagher.*

"I don't understand. What—?"

Her question was drowned out by the arrival, to much commotion, of Theodore Roosevelt.

The waiter tensed like a cat with a bird in its sights. Then he set aside his tray and began tugging off his gloves, his eyes never leaving the candidate.

"Oh, no," I murmured. "*Oh, dear.*"

My gaze raked the room, but there was no sign of Thomas and no time to get him. Meanwhile, Mr. Roosevelt was making his way through a gathering crowd, shaking hands and gripping shoulders.

I hurried toward him, ignoring Edith's voice calling after me. The waiter was on the move now, too, heading for the mob surrounding the candidate. I pointed the probe directly at him, my glance cutting frantically between him and the watch. *Five. Six. Seven. Eight.*

I hiked up my dress and broke into a run.

Mr. Roosevelt saw me first. His gaze met mine, but what he did after that I didn't see; I was too busy making a grab for the waiter. If I could have gotten a solid grip I'd have thrown him down, but he was moving too fast; as it was, I only managed to catch his sleeve. He turned, surprised and angry. "Let go of me!"

Instead I grabbed a fistful of lapel, planting my feet and readying for a throw. "Stay away from him. I know what you mean to do."

The crowd around us continued to press forward, eager to greet the candidate. We were an island of stillness in their midst, anonymous, unnoticed.

"I don't want to hurt you," he said.

"And I can't let you hurt him."

"Let go," he said again, and brushed the bare skin of my arm.

It was a fleeting touch, but it was enough. The moment his skin met mine, my heart lurched in my chest, and my knees buckled. I tightened my grip to keep from falling, and that was my undoing.

"Let go," he said a third time, grimly, and he put his hand on my shoulder.

An electric shock ripped through me. White light flared in my vision, and my heart broke into a galloping, erratic rhythm. Every nerve in my body buzzed. My veins felt like they were on fire. My head swam, I couldn't breathe . . .

The hand released me and I swooned. A galaxy of sparks swam before my eyes. I staggered and would have collapsed had a strong arm not slipped under mine.

"It appears the young lady had a bit too much champagne," said a hoarse voice, and I found myself leaning against the sturdy frame of Theodore Roosevelt. The candidate ushered me to a chair, tutting and shooing away aides and bystanders. "Not to worry, I've got her. No, no, I insist. Give the lady some space, now." And then, in a low murmur: "What's happening? Are you all right?"

I tried to nod, but in truth I wasn't sure. I yanked off my gloves and cradled my head in my hands, letting it fall between my knees while the dizziness passed. Dimly, I registered that my wristwatch wasn't pulsing anymore. *Overloaded,* I thought. Just like me.

"Is Burrows with you?" Mr. Roosevelt straightened, calling over his shoulder. "Has anyone seen Jonathan Burrows?"

"Here."

And then Thomas was kneeling before me, pale and stricken. "Are you all right? Was it him? Did he touch you? *Rose, say something.*"

"I'm not . . . my heart . . ." Still short of breath, I brought a hand to my chest.

Thomas tore off his glove and tucked two fingers under my jaw. "It's racing. We need to find a doctor . . ."

"I think . . . it's passing," I managed. "It's settling down, isn't it?"

He paused, head bowed, concentrating. He gave a short, convulsive nod. "Yes, it's slowing, but—"

I drew a deep breath, then another. My vision was clearing; over Thomas's shoulder, I could see Mr. Burrows and Mr. Roosevelt in whispered conference. Behind them, the New York elite pretended not to gawk at the spectacle of an outrageously inebriated woman accosting their candidate for mayor. Edith Islington was there, too, looking anxious and confused. But there was no sign of the killer. "Thomas, the waiter . . ."

"Waiter?" he echoed blankly.

"He's gone." This from Mr. Roosevelt. "Fled. I saw a policeman giving chase, so I left the business to him. I was quite sure you were going to faint, madam."

"I almost did. Thank you."

"I believe it's for me to thank you. Are you all right?"

"I think so. Whatever he did to me, it seems to be passing."

"Even so, it's best to be sure." Squinting behind his pince-nez, he scanned the dining room. "Arthur Gibbons is here somewhere . . ."

"I'll find him." Mr. Burrows vanished into the crowd.

"You're in good hands with Dr. Gibbons," Mr. Roosevelt said. "Now, I think I'd best not draw further attention to the matter. I've a speech to give."

"Forgive me, sir," said Thomas, "but are you sure that's wise? The assassin could still be in the building. Or perhaps he's not acting alone . . ." He trailed off, since the candidate was already shaking his head.

"I appreciate your concern, but I am not the sort of man to flinch. One must get on with the business. So unless there's anything you can tell me about the identity of the fellow who just tried to murder me . . ."

Thomas glanced at me, but I shook my head. "All I know is that he's one of the waiters here. We'll have to make inquiries."

"Well then, I trust you'll keep me informed. And of course, let me know if you need anything from me. I got a good look at him, and I should certainly know him if I saw him again."

"Perhaps you would at least consider hiring some protection," Thomas said. "The Pinkerton Agency has an excellent roster of—"

"No, thank you. I've managed to take care of my own hide until now." He patted his broad chest. "There's more than a few roughnecked fellows in the Badlands can attest to the fact."

"*Zhànshì*," I said with a weary smile. When he arched an eyebrow, I added, "Just something a friend of mine taught me. It's a compliment."

"In that case, I thank you. And now I really had better get on. I have two more speeches after this. Miss Gallagher." He reached for my hand as if to shake it, but then hesitated. "Perhaps not, until we're sure you're well."

"It's all right," I said, taking his hand. I'd already felt the effects of his luck when he put his arm around me, and it had been a mere frisson compared to the thunderbolt I'd experienced a moment before. "It's comforting, actually."

"I'm glad. Rest now, and I'll see you soon. Take good care of her, Mr. Wiltshire." He patted my hand once more and was gone.

Thomas was still kneeling before me. "Rose . . ." It was scarcely a murmur. Even now, he was aware of the eyes on us.

"Don't. This isn't your fault, any more than it's mine. This is my job."

He gave a slow, grave nod. "Yes, it is." I could tell he wanted to say more, but this wasn't the time or place. Instead, he took out his watch and wrapped his fingers around my wrist, taking another measure of my pulse. Satisfied that it was safe for us to move, he led me into the lobby, away from the crowd and the noise.

Edith followed timidly. "Is she all right?"

Thomas tried for a reassuring smile. "Her heart rate is quite elevated, but it seems to be calming down."

"That's a relief. How are you feeling, Rose?"

"Like I've just run the length of Manhattan, but the worst seems to have passed."

"Miss Gallagher has a heart condition," Thomas began, but Edith held up a hand.

"You needn't trouble yourself, Mr. Wiltshire. Perhaps one day you'll feel you can tell me the truth, but for now it's enough to know that she's all right."

Thomas sighed and nodded. "Thank you for alerting me."

"That was quick thinking," I said. "I must have looked awfully strange rushing off like that." And then, because I couldn't help myself, "I don't suppose you saw where the waiter got to?"

Edith shook her head. "He ran off as soon as he realized Mr. Roosevelt had spotted him. Inspector Byrnes went after him, but he was on the other side of the room, so the waiter had a good head start."

How fortunate for him. Somehow, I had a feeling that if Byrnes caught him, he wouldn't see the inside of a jail cell.

Mr. Burrows arrived shortly thereafter with the plump Dr. Gibbons in tow, who examined me and pronounced that I was recovering from something called tachycardia. He recommended laudanum. Meanwhile, we could hear sporadic laughter and smatterings of applause from the dining room as Mr. Roosevelt *got on with the business.*

By this point, fatigue was crashing over me in waves, and I guess it must have shown, because Thomas said, "Time to go."

"But the waiter," I protested. "We should interview the hotel staff—"

"Tomorrow. I'm taking you home, Rose." The look in his eyes brooked no argument.

"I'll have them call your carriage," Mr. Burrows said. As for Edith, she made me promise that she could come by to visit tomorrow.

Thomas helped me to stand. I leaned on him gratefully as we made our way to the door, and by the time the carriage pulled out into the street, it was all I could do to keep my eyes open. Thomas, meanwhile, was silent as the grave, staring grimly out the window. With only the sway of the carriage and the clip-clop of hooves to fill the silence, I soon fell asleep.

I opened my eyes once more that night, and then only for a moment. I was lying in bed, fully clothed. Thomas leaned over the lamp, his profile brushed in amber. I tried to speak, but the sound wouldn't come. I couldn't even keep my eyes open.

As I sank into darkness, I felt something brush across my forehead. And then I knew nothing more.

CHAPTER 20

THE SILENT TREATMENT—SWAPPING
SECRETS—A SKETCHY PLAN

What do you mean, you woke up in bed? He carried you all the way upstairs?" Clara arched an eyebrow. "He's stronger than he looks."

I'd seen Thomas without a shirt, and the subject of exactly how strong he looked would normally have inspired an energetic response, but this morning all I could muster was an uneasy feeling. Something had changed last night, and not for the better. "He was so withdrawn on the way home, and he barely said two words to me at breakfast. I think he's angry with me."

"He's something, that's for sure." Clara paused to blow on her tea. "I had trouble falling back asleep after you all came in, so I went down to the kitchen to warm up some milk. The light was on in his study, and it was still on when I went back up. Must've been two o'clock in the morning."

I picked restlessly at a loose bit of varnish on the kitchen table. "I understand he had a scare last night, but what does he expect? If the situation were reversed, he'd have done exactly the same thing. Only I wouldn't be giving him the silent treatment this morning."

"There you go, being dramatic again. Just talk to him, why don't you?"

"I try, but he's so . . . *English*."

Clara shook her head. "You can't go on like this. One of these days you're gonna have to tell him the truth."

"That would be as good as saying goodbye."

"Maybe."

"There's no maybe about it, Clara. We're partners. He'll say it's inappropriate. On top of which, he's a high society gentleman and I'm . . ." I gestured dismissively at myself.

"What? Don't you dare say *nothing*."

"A former housemaid with no money and no connections. The Irish immigrant daughter of a schoolteacher and a day laborer. He'd never be able to show his face in society again."

"Look, I'm not disagreeing with you on the particulars. I'm just saying that what you got going on between you right now— the silence, the half-truths—you can't keep it up forever. Pot's gonna boil over sooner or later and make a great big mess. In the meantime, it's eating you up inside. Him too, maybe." When I scoffed at that, she frowned. "Rose, the man's not a fool. Did it ever occur to you that he knows exactly how you feel?"

It hadn't, and the idea was terrifying. "Why? Do you think he does?" Then I remembered something. "I think he might have kissed my forehead last night. What do you think that means?"

Clara shook her head and took our teacups to the sink. "*Talk to him*, Rose."

I headed up the stairs half intending to take that advice, but when I reached the study and saw him sitting there—gaze abstracted, slender fingers drumming the desk, intense and brilliant and beautiful—my heart gave a tug of longing, and I knew I couldn't tell him how I felt. Not if it might mean giving him up forever.

He glanced up at my knock. "Please," he said, gesturing for me to sit.

I perched on the sofa opposite him, trying and failing to catch his eye. "The waiter. I remember him from the Reading Room. He brought Dayton's coffee."

Thomas nodded slowly. "That explains a great deal. He would have overheard all manner of Republican business in that room."

"Like the fact that Roosevelt was going to be nominated, and who planned to support him. Dayton himself mentioned that he'd tried to talk the victims out of voting for Roosevelt. *Right here in this room,* he said."

"I remember." Thomas took up a pen and wrote something down.

"I wonder if Inspector Byrnes managed to catch him."

"He didn't. I've just been on the telephone with Sergeant Chapman. Apparently Byrnes lost him on Fifth Avenue, but not before taking a shot at him. The waiter was wounded but he escaped. The police have no idea of his whereabouts."

"What about the hotel?"

He shook his head. "Apparently he gave them a false name."

Damn. Hiding something in his past, or preparing for the future? Both, maybe. There was one piece of good news, at least. "Chapman's back on the case, then?"

"So it would seem. My guess is that after last night's events, Byrnes has decided that we might be of some use after all."

"How magnanimous of him."

Thomas didn't respond. He still hadn't met my eye, apparently dividing his attention between me and the note he was scribbling. Sighing, I said, "Are we going to talk about this?"

"Talk about what?"

"You've been distant all morning. You're angry with me, but I'm not sure what I've done to deserve it."

He wilted a little, closing his eyes with a sigh. "I'm not angry with you, Rose. I'm . . . processing."

"What does that mean?"

"Please, just give me some time."

Time for what? But I sensed it would be a mistake to press him, so I got back to business. "Did you tell Sergeant Chapman what I found out yesterday? About the man Mr. Wang treated?"

He shook his head.

"His symptoms sounded very similar to what happened to our victims. Wouldn't Sergeant Chapman want to hear about that?"

"We still don't know what Byrnes's stake is in all this, and until we do, it's best to be circumspect about what we share with the police."

"That doesn't seem fair. Chapman brought the case to us, remember."

"Our primary objective is to keep Roosevelt safe. With that in mind, I've wired the Agency in Chicago. Hopefully they can convince him to accept a security detail."

"Good luck to them."

"F. Winston Sharpe is extremely persuasive."

I'd learned that for myself following the Hell Gate incident, when the head of the special branch had somehow managed to convince every newspaperman in New York that a magical fire in the sky had been an unusually southerly occurrence of the aurora borealis. Not that I had a great deal of faith in the newspapers anymore. I'd spent this morning's awkward silence perusing the papers for any mention of last night's incident at the hotel, but of course there was none.

"In any case," Thomas went on, "Chapman is headed to the hotel now, and we can only hope he finds something useful. In the meantime, we ought to follow up on your lead from Wang's." Sighing, he passed a hand over his eyes. "I just wish I knew where to start."

"About that," I said, and the doorbell rang.

I'd been about to say *I have an idea*, but as it happened, my idea had just appeared in the foyer. "Miss Edith Islington," Louise announced from the threshold of the study. "Here to call on Miss Gallagher."

Impatience flickered across Thomas's features, and I think he was about to tell the maid to decline on my behalf, but I stayed him with a gesture. "Thank you, Louise. Please tell Miss Islington I'll be right down." When the maid was out of earshot, I added, "Let me speak to her alone for a minute, if you don't mind. I'll fetch you when it's time."

Edith greeted me warmly when I came into the parlor. "Look at you, hale and hearty. I'm so glad." She squeezed my hands. "You gave us all quite a fright."

"Starting with myself. I've never experienced anything quite like that before."

"Even with your heart condition?" She gave me a wry smile.

"Yes, well . . ." I blushed a little, gesturing for her to sit. "I wanted to talk to you about that, actually. I'd very much like to fill you in, but it would need to go both ways. You've been kind enough to share your secret with me, about your luck, but I haven't told Mr. Wiltshire. I'd like to, with your permission. Once I do,

I think he'll agree that it makes sense to . . ." I trailed off awkwardly.

"To share your secret with me? Very well, you have my permission."

"Good. I'll be right back."

Thomas was already on his feet when I returned to the study, jacket on, tie straightened. "Are you going to tell me what this is about?"

"Now that I have Miss Islington's permission. She's lucky, you see, and I think she could be of some help to us."

He tilted his head, curious. "How so?"

"We ought to discuss it together, but that would mean telling her about us."

"I see." He didn't sound very happy about it.

"I trust her, if that matters."

"Of course it does." Sighing, he added, "And if it will help us find our killer, then I don't see that we have much choice."

"I think it will."

He nodded resignedly and we headed downstairs.

"All right," I said once we were all together, "we're agreed. But I should warn you, Miss Islington, what we're about to tell you must remain in strictest confidence, for your safety and ours."

She paled a little, but she nodded. "You have my word."

"Thank you. Er, Mr. Wiltshire, would you care to . . . ?"

Not particularly, his eyes said, but he took his cue anyway, producing a silver calling card and handing it over. "Miss Gallagher and I are detectives, with the Pinkerton Agency. Are you familiar with it?"

Edith couldn't have looked more astonished if he'd slapped her. "The Pinkerton Agency. You?"

"Indeed. Both of us."

"We're with the special branch," I explained, "which means we focus on cases of a paranormal nature. What you witnessed last night was an attempted assassination. Mr. Wiltshire and I were there to prevent it, but we didn't know who the killer was. As you saw, we were very nearly too late."

"I was entirely too late, in point of fact," Thomas said. "Fortunately, Miss Gallagher is a good deal more observant than I."

I didn't much care for his self-recriminating tone, but we didn't have time for *that* conversation. "The waiter is lucky. What he did to me, making my heart race like that . . . it's how he kills. He's already murdered six people that we know of."

"Good God!"

"He gave the hotel a false name when they hired him, which means the police will have trouble tracking him down. But there may be witnesses in Five Points who can identify him, if only we had a likeness. Which is where you come in. Or more precisely, you and I together."

Edith looked half frightened, half fascinated. "How can I help?"

"What you told me about your luck . . . Can you recall the waiter's face? Exactly, I mean?"

"Yes, but I'm afraid I've no talent at drawing."

"I do, a little." I couldn't help blushing as I said it, especially when Thomas threw me a curious look. I'd never shown him any of my sketches. That would have been awkward, considering they were mostly of him. "I'm hoping that between us, we can come up with a sketch that Mr. Wiltshire and I can show around at some of the local saloons. It's a long shot, but . . ."

"It's a cracking idea, actually." There was something oddly rueful about the way Thomas said it. Apparently he was still *processing*, whatever that meant.

As for Edith, she just shrugged and said, "I'm very happy to try. When shall we get started?"

"Right away, if you can."

She took off her gloves, unpinned her hat, and set them on the sofa. "In that case," she said, "is there coffee?"

"A little lighter in the brows, I think," Edith said. "He looks rather more sinister than he did in real life." She sipped her coffee, even though it must have gone cold ages ago.

"Sorry." I grabbed an eraser and took a corner of it to the eyebrows. "I guess I'm letting my feelings influence my memory."

"That's perfectly normal. It even happens to me, if only in dreams. I'll wake up marveling at how thoroughly my imagination has revised reality."

I paused, curiosity getting the better of me. "Do you remember all your dreams?"

"Down to the last detail."

"I can't imagine what that would be like."

"I've grown used to it now, but as a child I found it quite upsetting. My dreams made so little sense, I thought I must be mad. It wasn't until I was much older that I realized that's just how dreams work." She set her cup aside and tilted her head. "Yes, that's better. And they came to a little peak, just here."

Thomas appeared in the doorway. "How is it coming?"

"We're nearly done," I said. "I'm sorry it's taking so long. I've never had to work on a schedule before."

He came over to examine the sketch. "Impressive. I don't recognize the fellow, but he certainly looks like *someone*."

I held it out at arm's length. "He doesn't look like a murderer, though, does he?"

"They rarely do, in my experience."

Edith glanced up at him. "Do you have a lot of experience with murderers, Mr. Wiltshire?"

"More than I would like, Miss Islington," he said gravely. "Well, I'll let you ladies get back to it."

Edith's gaze lingered on the doorway after he'd gone. "I suppose that seals it," she said with a sigh.

"Seals what?"

She gave me a guilty-looking smile. "I've a confession. I'm afraid I've got the most terrible crush on your cousin."

I swallowed. "Oh."

"I've always been a fool for the mysterious type, but now that I know he's a Pinkerton?" She shook her head. "Doomed."

My gaze dropped to the sketch. I started shading along a cheekbone, quite unnecessarily. "Speaking of confessions, Mr. Wiltshire and I aren't actually related. We're just partners." I kept on shading, avoiding Edith's gaze. Observant as she was, I was afraid she'd read more in my eyes than I wanted her to.

"I see," she said, and I wondered if she did. "But you live . . . here? With him?"

"Temporarily. Purely for convenience, of course."

Well, she didn't know what to say to *that*.

I tried to change the subject. "What about the nose? Do you think it's too prominent?"

There was a pause. "You won't tell him, will you?"

"Of course not."

"I hope it's all right. I would hate for it to compromise our friendship."

"It won't," I said, and I hoped that was true. After all, I could hardly fault her taste in men, and it wasn't as though I had any claim on him. "Mr. Wiltshire and I work very closely together, but as far as I know, he's romantically unattached." I brought the sketch up between us like a shield. "What do you think? Is he ready?"

"Nearly. I'd darken up his eyes a little, and then he's perfect."

"Did you notice anything else distinguishing about him? Scars, maybe?"

"Not that I saw. Though," she added with a laugh, "if he's from Five Points, he's probably covered in them, isn't he?"

I winced inwardly, but my pencil didn't falter.

Clara came in a moment later, bearing scones and strawberry preserves. "Mr. Wiltshire thought you all might be hungry," she said, stealing an appraising glance at Edith as she set the tray down.

"Thanks, Clara." I sniffed at the plate appreciatively. "These smell great."

"How's it coming, anyway?"

I showed her the sketch. "You tell me."

"That's him, huh? Mr. Tall 'n' Gangly?" She cocked her head. "Don't look like much, does he?"

"I tried to make him look more sinister, but Miss Islington wasn't having it." I smiled, but Clara didn't seem to be in much of a mood for joking, because she didn't crack even a half smile back at me.

"Anyways," she said coolly, "Mr. Wiltshire's in the study when you and *Miss Islington* are done."

There was most definitely a tone there, though I wasn't sure why.

Edith must have heard it, too, but like a proper high society lady, she pretended not to notice. "These really do smell wonderful," she said, reaching for a scone. "So now that you have the sketch, will you make copies?"

"No time for that, unfortunately. We'll just have to go door to door, starting with the saloons nearest Wang's General Store." I didn't much fancy the idea. It had been years since I'd set foot in any of the fetid caves that passed for watering holes along Mott Street, and I can't say I'd missed it. Dark and grimy, smelling of spilled beer and lamp oil and day-old oysters . . . As a child, they'd seemed like secret places full of adventure, each one a portal to a different world. As an adult, they just made me ill.

"I don't envy you the task," Edith said. "I've only been down there once, myself, on a slumming tour." She shuddered. "Awful. I can't imagine how those poor people get by."

"Sand and pure cussedness," I said with a faint smile, echoing something my da used to say.

She gave me a quizzical look, but otherwise let that pass. "You should eat something before you go."

"Good advice," I said, reaching for a scone. "Something tells me I'm about to lose my appetite."

CHAPTER 21

INTERLOPERS AND INVISIBLES—SAND
AND CUSSEDNESS—THE LANKY LOOKOUT

The task proved even more dismal than I'd expected.

When you live in a place long enough, you stop seeing the things you don't want to see. They become part of the background, like a trash heap or a pothole or the tangle of electric wires overhead. You know they're there, but you don't really *see* them anymore. Well, I guess it's like that with people, too. I'd stopped noticing my neighbors: the stargazers, the drunks, the guttersnipes with their threadbare clothing. The jobless men loitering on street corners, or coming home from work streaked with the grime of their toil, digging ditches or shoveling coal or sweeping chimneys. Mostly they'd stopped noticing me, too. But walking up Mott Street with my oh-so-elegant partner, we *saw* each other all over again, and it was jarring.

"It's difficult, isn't it?" Thomas murmured, gently shooing

away the latest clutch of small boys pressing around us with their palms open. "Winter around the corner, and these little ones forced to fend for themselves. One gives to the orphanages and the benevolent societies, but it's never enough."

A trio of men watched us from the hock shop on the corner; I glanced furtively at them as we passed, feeling guilty for reasons I couldn't fully explain. "The way they're looking at us . . ."

"Like outsiders."

"Like *interlopers*. As if we were to blame for their troubles. The waiter looked at Theodore Roosevelt like that."

"We were certainly off the mark about him, weren't we? Our killer, I mean. With his luck, I'd simply assumed he was wealthy, but it seems he belongs to that far rarer breed, the working-class man with luck. And not just any brand of luck either. With abilities like that, he would make an ideal assassin for hire."

"Maybe that's all he is to Price. A hired thug."

Thomas hummed skeptically. "After last night, I'm inclined to believe that we overestimated the extent of Price's involvement. He didn't react when Miss Islington came to tell me you were in trouble, and as far as I know, he didn't show much interest in the goings-on around Roosevelt. If he was curious as to the fate of his man, he did a very good job of hiding it. He is certainly funding Tammany's efforts to keep the matter quiet, but that seems to be the limit of it."

We'd crossed Pell by this point, and Thomas paused, eying a set of crooked steps leading down to a cave below the hardware store (the grandly named Crown Saloon, according to the hand-painted sign). "Here's another. How many more, do you think?"

"On Mott? Half a dozen or so. It'll be worse when we head down Mulberry. There must be fifty of them, if you count groceries like Augusto's."

Thomas sighed from the soles of his oxfords. "Very well. Shall we?"

It went on like this for an hour: the two of us descending into one dive after another, showing our sketch by the sickly yellow light of papered oil lamps, each time to be told that no, they'd never seen him, an observation accompanied as often as not by a jet of tobacco juice or some other gesture designed to show contempt for the nosy intruders.

"I'm starting to wonder if they'd tell us even if they had seen him," I muttered as we negotiated our way around the colorful mounds of beans and lentils and cornmeal lining the steps of Constantino's Grocery.

Thomas paused at the top of the stairs, gesturing up the street with his walking stick. "Look, it's Pietro."

So it was, in the company of the three roughs I'd seen him with the other day. They were crossing from one side of Mulberry to the other. *Making their rounds,* I thought sourly, *extorting the local businesses for Augusto.*

"Let's stay out of sight," I said, hurrying my step. "I don't want to have to explain what I'm doing down here with you." *And he won't want to explain us to his new friends.* Before Thomas could let his gentlemanly instincts get the better of him, I ducked into yet another saloon, the floor of which was so generously coated with sawdust that it was like walking through a blanket of fresh snow— if the snow smelled of stale beer and tobacco, with just a hint of human urine.

Pausing to let my eyes adjust to the gloom, I took in the long, narrow space. Only two patrons stood at the bar, both of them eying me curiously, ladies being about as common as leprechauns in a place like this. I walked over to the iron stove and pretended to warm my hands.

Thomas, meanwhile, approached the barkeep with the sketch. I couldn't hear the murmured exchange, but the barman shook his head, at which point Thomas turned to the patrons. They shook their heads, too, but not before I saw one of them nudge the other with his boot. Thomas wouldn't have seen it from his vantage, but from where I stood, it was plain as day.

"Excuse me, gentlemen," I said, sidling up to them, "I couldn't help but overhear, and I must say I think you're being very rude. My friend here asked you a direct question and you went and lied to his face."

Thomas glanced at me briefly, but we'd worked together long enough for him to trust me on such things. "Perhaps it's the light in here," he said, grabbing a lamp. "Would you care to have another look? There's a dollar in it for the fellow who knows him."

One of the men snorted into his beer. "Will you look at this Jack Dandy? You can keep your dollar, mister."

"Think we don't know a Pinkerton when we see one?" the barkeep added. "You ain't gonna find a nose around here, so why don't you head on back up them stairs?"

The third man, though, the one who'd done the kicking under the bar, didn't look so sure. "How about you, sir?" I asked him. "A dollar and a bottle of gin?"

"Lady, that sumbitch owes me a lot more 'n that. I give him to you, he ain't never gonna pay it."

"Why don't you shut your rat trap, Wilson?" the barkeep snapped.

Thomas leaned against the bar, placing himself between the barkeep and the man called Wilson. "A debt, is it? Cards, I presume?"

"Ain't no concern of yours, mister."

"Fair enough. And if I offered to purchase the debt outright?"

Wilson blinked; even his companion looked interested now. He hesitated for a moment, eying Thomas cagily. "It's ten dollars," he said.

Thomas raised an eyebrow. "Rather a princely sum for a fellow of your circumstances."

The barman, meanwhile, was slowly turning an ugly shade of purple. "Goddamn it, Wilson, what the hell you doing?"

"Getting my money, is what. I got better things to do than sit around your joint all day waiting for that soda jerker to pay up. If you know what's good for you, you'll shut *your* rat trap and maybe get a bit of this chink I'm about to make."

"Pinkerton money," the barkeep sneered. "You can keep it."

"Damn sure will, and spend it someplace else, you ornery sumbitch." To Thomas, he said, "His name's Jack Foster. Used to come in here all the time."

"Used to," I said. "Not anymore?"

"Not since he started working at that fancy hotel. Too good for us now."

"Still visits his mama now and then, though," his companion put in, apparently feeling helpful now that there was real chink in the offing. "She lives just down the way, corner of Park and Mulberry. That place above the laundry."

"He was s'posed to come by here first thing in the morning to pay up," Wilson said, "but he seems to have overlooked the engagement." He swigged the last dregs of his beer and inclined his head at the bar. "Now about that ten dollars." Thomas produced the funds, at which point the man added, "and another for that bottle of gin the lady promised."

"One really must commend the entrepreneurial spirit," Thomas said dryly as we mounted the steps.

Sand and cussedness, I thought, amused despite myself. "Do

you suppose that's the joint where the incident happened? The
one with the fellow Mr. Wang treated?"

Thomas tapped his walking stick against his once-shiny oxfords, knocking the sawdust free. "It's certainly possible. We're
only just around the corner from Wang's."

"Closer, even, if they cut through the alley by Augusto's."

"And the mother lives just down the street, which suggests
that our Mr. Foster grew up in the area. I wonder how many of
your neighbors he's murdered in his lifetime?"

"No one would ever know, would they, the way his luck works?
On the other hand, who's to say he's killed anyone before now?
He obviously places *some* value on human life."

Thomas tilted his head. "What makes you say so?"

"He could have killed me if he'd wanted to, I'm sure of it.
And then there's this Wilson fellow. Why pay your debts, or even
lie about intending to pay your debts, if you could quietly take care
of your creditors without anyone being the wiser?"

"A good point," said Thomas. "The mere fact that he owes
money at all is interesting. A contract killer with his abilities would
presumably be flush with funds, unless he happened to be afflicted
with one of the more expensive vices."

"Can't afford to settle a ten-dollar debt and hesitates to kill.
He doesn't sound like a professional assassin, does he?"

"Not especially, but we won't know for certain until we catch
him."

I inclined my head in the direction of Mrs. Foster's flat. "I
know the building they're talking about. There'll be at least twenty
apartments, maybe more. Do we knock on every door or just ask
one of the neighbors?"

"Neither. I'd prefer to keep an eye on the comings and goings
for a little while first."

"I thought we were in a hurry."

"There's little point in haste if it comes at the expense of our objective. Knocking on doors risks arousing suspicion. But if we watch the building for a time, one of the residents will eventually emerge, at which point we can ask which apartment is Mrs. Foster's. Much more discreet than canvassing the building."

"Clever," I said as we started down Mulberry.

"We'll be near Tesla's lab. We can take the opportunity to get that watch of yours fixed. Do you still have it with you? You can drop it off and meet me outside Mrs. Foster's building."

"Leave you alone? What if someone comes out while I'm gone?"

"I'll find out which apartment is hers and wait for you to return. Don't worry, you won't miss a thing."

I didn't much like the idea, but I couldn't deny that it made sense. The inventor's lab was only two blocks away, and since we'd lost our suspect, chances were good I'd be needing that luck meter again. So we parted ways at the foot of Mulberry Street, Thomas turning left for the Chinese laundry while I turned right for Chatham Square.

Mr. Tesla lit up when he found me at his door, touching my shoulder in what I sensed was, for him, an unusually intimate gesture. "I'm so glad to see you well, my friend. The fellow who telephoned last night said you were taken very ill."

I couldn't suppress a shudder. "The killer was at the event last night. He attacked me. His luck set my heart racing, and . . ." Sheepishly, I handed over the watch. "Well, it also seems to have overloaded your luck meter."

"Overloaded?" He took it with a puzzled expression.

"When he touched me, it sent a jolt through my whole body,

almost as if it were electricity. After that, the watch stopped working."

The inventor headed for his workbench. "If it was indeed an electric shock of sufficient voltage, that would explain it. The innards were carefully calibrated to receive wireless electricity at a specific frequency." Selecting a tiny screwdriver, he removed the back of the watch. "Now let us . . . yes, I see . . ." He poked around for a minute or two before pronouncing it fixable. "If you have time, I can complete the work in half an hour or so, once I obtain the part I require."

"Mr. Wiltshire and I are engaged in a bit of surveillance just down the street, outside the Chinese laundry. Maybe we could come by later?"

"That will be fine. Allow me to walk you, Miss Gallagher. It's on my way to the Pearl Street electric station."

The inventor fetched a bowler hat and overcoat and we hurried along, although we did have to pause now and then to feed the birds. (Mr. Tesla, it seemed, had the curious habit of carrying seed in his pockets, a fact that was obviously well known to the pigeons of Five Points, who came whirring and flapping down from every telegraph pole and electric wire along the way.)

We found Thomas a little down the block from the mother's building, rubbing his hands together in the chill. "Nothing yet," he reported.

"Hopefully you will not have to stand out here for long," said Mr. Tesla. "It's too cold to be waiting around outside. Best of luck, my friends." He shook hands and went on his way.

"He's right," I said, shifting from foot to foot, "it's miserable out here."

"I'm sure someone will be along directly."

Alas, *directly* turned out to be optimistic. Ten minutes passed, then twenty, then thirty. We were still there when Mr. Tesla reappeared on his way back, and the cold had started to seep into our bones.

"Still nothing?" The inventor glanced at the building in surprise. "Why, it's been over an hour! Shall I bring you some tea?"

"That's very kind of you," I said, "but you needn't go to the trouble. If we get too cold, I can always nip into Muldoon's Grocery and grab a hot pie." I gestured up the street. "Which, by the way, if you don't know the place, it's a neighborhood favorite."

Mr. Tesla smiled, as though the idea of his grabbing a hot pie in a Five Points grocery were gently amusing. "Thank you for this information," he said politely. "It's beside the pharmacy?"

"Yes, you see where that fellow . . ." I trailed off, narrowing my eyes.

Thomas turned. "What is it?"

"That man. The one who just walked out of the pharmacy. I'm almost certain I've seen him before. At the hotel, maybe?"

"He's headed this way," Thomas said.

The man had a parcel tucked under his arm; I recognized the green twine of the pharmacy. "You said Foster was wounded, didn't you?"

"That's right. Byrnes shot him during his escape. Do you suppose—?"

"Why not?" I said, growing excited. "If I'd been hurt and there were no Clara to take care of me, the first place I'd go is Mam's."

Mr. Tesla observed the exchange with interest. "You believe this man is taking medical supplies to your killer?"

We kept our faces averted as he passed, then watched as he

went through the front door of the tenement where Jack Foster's mother lived.

Thomas and I exchanged a look.

"Tesla," Thomas said, "may I prevail upon you to keep watch out here? If our man tries to run, you can point us in the right direction."

"Certainly," the inventor said with a boyish gleam in his eyes. "How exciting!"

Lookout in place, Thomas and I hurried after our quarry, slipping through the front door into the familiar shadows of a Five Points tenement.

CHAPTER 22

THE DEVIL—A SHOCKING TURN OF EVENTS—THE IMPATIENT PATIENT

I felt eerily at home climbing the stairs of the five-story brick building where Jack Foster's mother lived. Like my own mother's building, it had no lighting, leaving Thomas and me to fumble our way through the dark. And like Mam's, its stairs were so steep and crooked that we had to keep one hand on the wall so we didn't fall and break our necks. The air was thick with cooking smoke, and the clamor of everyday life filled the cramped hallways, spilling out of crowded flats through thin, ill-fitted doors. It was almost enough to drown out the footfalls on the steps above us, but we managed to track our quarry to the second floor. A crack of light flared at the end of the corridor, and he disappeared inside.

Thomas drew his derringer from an inner pocket. "Are we steady, Rose?"

"Steady," I said, fingering my own little one-shot pistol.

Thomas knocked.

Silence.

I pressed my ear to the door. There was a scuffling sound and the creak of floorboards.

With the faintest of sighs, Thomas waved me out of the way, adjusted his overcoat, and kicked the door in.

He'd scarcely stepped over the threshold before someone blasted into him from the side, but somehow he kept his feet, twisting low and upending his attacker in a single smooth motion. I charged into the flat just in time to see a figure being helped out the window by a woman.

"*Stop!*"

The man looked up; I recognized the face I'd been sketching all morning. Foster recognized me, too, and with a grimace, he jumped. I lunged for the window, but the woman grabbed hold of me with a shriek, clutching at my hair like some kind of wild animal. I couldn't get her off me, and Foster was escaping . . .

"*Thomas, he's gone out the—*"

Thomas flew past me in a blur, launching himself out the window and hitting the ground in a roll. Breaking free of the woman at last, I made for the door, leaping over the inert form of the man who'd attacked us on the threshold.

I nearly killed myself thundering down those crooked stairs with my skirts swirling around my ankles, and by the time I burst into the street, there was no sign of Thomas. But our lookout had done his job: Mr. Tesla stood in the middle of the road, hopping up and down excitedly as he pointed toward Chatham Square. "That way! The alley behind the church!"

Hiking up my skirts (I really *did* need to consider trousers) I ran after them. The entrance to the alley was choked with peddlers; I cracked my hip on a fruit cart, and a mule laden with charcoal pinned his ears back when I shoved past. By the time I rounded the corner, Thomas was at the far end of the alley—

—sinking to his knees, Jack Foster's hand wrapped around the back of his neck. He tried to grab at his attacker, but his limbs jerked wildly. His gun lay in the dirt, out of reach.

I cried out and raised my gun, but I was too far away to be sure of my little derringer. I fired over their heads, hoping to scare Foster off, but he barely flinched; he kept hold of Thomas, glowering with determination as he held on and on and on.

"Help! Somebody!"

I tore down the alley in a blind panic, screaming Thomas's name, begging Foster to stop. It was like a nightmare, as if I were wading through molasses to get to Thomas, watching as his head snapped back in wave after wave of convulsions while the devil himself stood over him.

Foster did let go eventually, and legged it up the alley, but I didn't care about him anymore. All I saw was Thomas, limp as a rag doll, eyes rolled back beneath fluttering lids.

I fell to my knees beside him, but I had no idea what to do. Dimly, I registered footfalls scrambling behind me, and then Mr. Tesla was at my side, the two of us on our knees in the muck. "His heart," I whispered.

The inventor paused, listening. His eyes widened in horror, and he put his ear to Thomas's chest. "It stopped!"

"Foster shocked him." I spoke the words in a daze, tears spilling down my face. There was nothing I could do. Nothing anyone could do . . .

"I can feel it. The ionization." The inventor's fingers flitted over Thomas's chest. "The shock must have . . . then theoretically, a countershock . . . but the voltage . . ." He went on babbling, but

I was barely listening, smothered in an ever-thickening cocoon of despair. Then his hand seized my shoulder, startling me back to reality. "Quickly! We need to get him to the street! The wires. I need the wires!"

It made no sense to me, but at least it was doing *something*, so we grabbed Thomas under the arms and started dragging him up the alley. It was awkward and heavy, and I shudder to think how long it would have taken had another pair of hands not joined us, and another after that, the fruit peddler and another bystander rushing to help us lift him. We reached the main street in moments, and then Mr. Tesla was climbing up on the fruit cart, stretching the full length of his lanky frame to reach the snarl of electrical wires overhead.

A crowd had started to gather, and a collective gasp went up as we realized what he meant to do.

"Don't! You'll kill yourself!"

"No," Mr. Tesla said, grabbing a fistful of wires, "I won't."

Sparks flew everywhere. The crowd skittered back in alarm. The inventor jumped down, the wire in his hand spitting and hissing like an angry snake. "Open his shirt."

For a split second all I could do was stare. *Two kinds of luck*, Thomas had said. Here, apparently, was the second.

"Hurry!"

I scrabbled at Thomas's clothing, unbuttoning his waistcoat and shirt.

"Now stand back." Mr. Tesla closed his eyes, whispered something that sounded suspiciously like a prayer, and put his free hand on Thomas's chest. I cringed, but nothing much happened. Thomas's body twitched; Mr. Tesla snatched his hand away and paused, listening. "Nothing." He hesitated, swearing softly in his own language. Then he reached out again.

This time, the effect was truly terrible. Thomas's whole body bucked, arching off the ground for an awful instant before going limp. The crowd cried out.

He's killed him, I thought numbly. *It's over . . .*

"There!" The inventor threw the wire aside and put his ear to Thomas's chest. "I can hear it! His heart is beating, but . . ." He shook his head. "The rhythm is still wrong. It . . . *quivers.* I don't think he is out of danger."

"Wang's," I said, lurching to my feet. "We need to get him to Wang's."

"On Mott Street?" Mr. Tesla shot a despairing look over his shoulder. It was only a block, but it might as well have been a mile.

"Take my cart," said the fruit peddler, gesturing at his little wagon of apples and pears.

"Oh, thank you!" I threw my arms around the man. "I'll buy every last piece of fruit, I promise!"

And so it was that Thomas, with the help of a crowd of Five Pointers, was loaded onto a pushcart and rushed up Mulberry Street to the alley behind Wang's General Store. I banged two-fisted on the back door until a bewildered Mei answered; she took one look at Thomas and yelled for her father, and suddenly I wasn't needed anymore.

Whereupon my knees gave way beneath me, and I sagged, sobbing, to the dirt.

Over the course of the next two hours, I had a glimpse of what it must have been like for Thomas last January, when he'd burst through Mr. Wang's front door cradling my limp form in his arms.

All around me was commotion, but I couldn't do a thing to help. I just stood there, powerless, watching as Mei snatched herbs and tree bark and God knew what else down from the shelves,

grinding or pinching or chopping them before handing them to
her father. When the brew was finished, they got Thomas into a
sitting position and helped him to choke some down. No sooner
was that done than Mr. Wang started in on another concoction.

All the while, Thomas drifted in and out of consciousness.
At one point he murmured my name, but he'd slipped under again
before my fingers closed around his. I kept hold of his hand anyway, afraid to let go. In that moment, *he* was comforting *me*, the
warmth of his skin and the flutter of his pulse reassuring me that
he still lived. His heartbeat was still weak and erratic, but his
chest rose and fell steadily, and the color had returned to his lips.
Eventually, they moved him to one of the little rooms in the back.

A little while later, Mei brought me some tea (actual tea, the
green kind). It soothed the ache in my throat enough that I could
finally push words through. "What's happening to him?"

"His *qi* is blocked. There is not enough *yin* in his blood, which
is causing it to stagnate. This is very dangerous if it continues.
My father gave him special tea to help thin the blood. The other
tea, the one made with cinchona bark, will calm the quivering of
the heart and help the *qi* to flow."

"I . . . don't know what that means."

She put a comforting hand on my arm. "What matters is that
my father has treated this before, with the man from the saloon,
and he learned much. It will take time, but Mr. Wiltshire should
recover." She gave me a reassuring smile and withdrew, closing
the door behind her.

I couldn't tell you how long I sat there, clutching Thomas's
hand and stroking the hair back from his temples. Eventually, his
eyelids stirred, and a moment later they fluttered open.

"Thomas, it's Rose. You're safe." I squeezed his hand. "Can
you hear me?"

He tried to speak, but the sound mustn't have come, because he nodded wearily.

"Foster used his luck on you. Your heart"—my throat closed momentarily around the words—"your heart stopped. Mr. Tesla saved your life. You're at Wang's now, being treated for . . . er, blocked *qi*."

Thomas brought a hand to his neck, feeling for his pulse. "Fast," he whispered, "but most definitely there."

Tears pricked behind my eyes, but I blinked them away. "Most definitely there, and steadier by the hour. How do you feel?"

"Light-headed, a little short of breath." He started to sit up, but thankfully thought better of it. "And weak as a kitten," he finished ruefully.

"But no pain? Headache?"

He shook his head. "Wang. I need to thank him."

"It can wait."

He stitched his brow, as though processing something belatedly. "And . . . Tesla?"

"Yes, he . . . Well, to be honest, I'm not sure exactly what he did. He grabbed some electrical wires and shocked you."

"Shocked me?" Thomas stared up at me, looking very shocked indeed. "With high-voltage wires?"

"With his bare hands, actually." I couldn't help shaking my head at the memory. "He just *grabbed* them. Tore one right down from the pole without so much as flinching. He's repairing them right now, so nobody gets hurt."

"Tesla can manipulate electricity at will. That's down to his luck, but an ordinary person like me . . . How did he know it wouldn't kill me?"

"I'm not sure he did. It took him a couple of attempts to get it right." At this point, Thomas was looking very pale again, so I decided to change the subject. "Foster escaped. I telephoned Sergeant Chapman, but I'm sure everyone was long gone from that apartment before the police got there. I'm sorry, Thomas."

"No, I'm sorry. I should have anticipated he would be lying in wait like that. Instead I rushed ahead like a fool." He sighed, closing his eyes. "And now he's in the wind."

"Not for long. I'll be heading for One-Eyed Johnny's as soon as possible."

"The Bloodhound?" Thomas grunted. "She could be of help, if we're able to find her."

"There's no *we* about it. You're not going anywhere until Mr. Wang says it's all right."

"Rose—"

"Shall we ask him?" I stuck my head out the door. "Excuse me, Mr. Wang . . ."

He appeared a moment later, Mei in tow, whereupon I proceeded to tattle shamelessly. "Mr. Wiltshire is under the impression that he's fit for duty."

Mr. Wang gave his patient a flat look.

"I said no such thing. I merely suggested that in a few hours I might—"

Mr. Wang was already shaking his head. He said something in Chinese, accompanied by a finger-wag that needed no translation.

Thomas listened with growing dismay. "A week? Nonsense, Wang, I can't possibly—"

"You're no good to anyone in the state you're in," I interjected, "and if you push yourself too hard, it will only take longer for you to get well. Besides, I'm perfectly capable of hiring the Bloodhound on my own."

"I've no doubt, but One-Eyed Johnny's is a rough place. It's best to have someone watching your back, and besides—"

"Thomas," I said gently, "I don't need you."

That was a lie in just about every way that mattered, but I couldn't have him worrying about me while he was trying to rest.

I knew we'd won by the way Thomas faded, as though he'd suddenly used up his shallow reserves. "Very well," he said, sinking back onto the cot. "I'll rest, but it cannot be for a week, or anything near it." Mr. Wang said something in a tone of finality, and Thomas nodded. "One night. Then I'm back in my own home, even if I'm confined to bed. Agreed?"

Mr. Wang grunted.

"Glad that's settled," I said. "Now then, I'd fancy a cup of tea, wouldn't you, Mr. Wiltshire?" Mei and her father followed me out of the room, and as soon as we were out of earshot, I added, "Perhaps with a drop of something to help him sleep?"

Mr. Wang answered in Chinese, which Mei translated with a smile. "His thoughts exactly."

It was nearing eight o'clock by the time I left the grocery, too late for a trip to One-Eyed Johnny's. The Tenderloin was no place for a woman on her own after dark, especially if she was too exhausted to be properly alert. I didn't fancy spending the night on Mam's floor either, so I headed for the Franklin Street station, already fantasizing about the hot bath I'd take when I got home. My route took me past Augusto's, and I wasn't surprised to find Pietro loitering outside, along with his new friends from Bandit's Roost. I had every intention of walking right past, but to my surprise, he called out to me.

"Fiora, thanks God." He sprang out from under the awning and grasped me by the shoulders. In the glow of the gas lamp, I saw worry in his eyes.

Two days ago, he'd chased me off this very spot so his companions wouldn't see us talking, and now here he was using pet names and practically hugging me? "What are you doing?" I whispered, but before he could answer, he'd been joined by the big man, who was obviously the leader of the gang.

"We heard there was trouble," Pietro said. "The whole neighborhood is talking about it."

"A rich man was attacked in the alley," his companion added in heavily accented English.

"I heard he died," said another of the roughs from his perch under the awning. He yawned.

"They say he was asking questions in the saloons," Pietro went on. "An Englishman, they said. It sounded like your boss. I was afraid you might have been with him."

Touched as I was by Pietro's concern, it left his tongue dangerously unguarded. "It was nothing," I said, hoping he read the warning in my eyes. "An accident."

"That is not what we hear," said the big man. He was watching me carefully. "An attack, people say."

Damn.

"I . . . suppose it was, yes."

The thug's eyes narrowed. "Then why you say accident?"

"I just . . ." My glance slid to Pietro. "I didn't want to worry you, that's all. Mr. Wiltshire will be fine, and I wasn't hurt."

Pietro started to say something, but the big man cut him off. "Who was it? Who attack you and why?"

"Just some street thugs. It was our own fault, really. A wealthy gentleman like that in this part of town . . . We were just asking for trouble."

A dark look crossed the big man's face. "This street belongs to Augusto. Nobody touches nobody without permission." He added something in Italian over his shoulder, and his fellow roughs rumbled their agreement. Pietro, meanwhile, studied his shoes.

"You see these men again, you tell Marco, *si*?" He pointed at his meaty chest. "I remind them who is in charge."

I had a pretty good idea of what that reminder would consist of, and for a moment I actually considered showing him the sketch, but there was no way to explain how I came to have a drawing of a supposedly random street rough.

I offered Marco some vague assurances and hurried on my way, but not before trading a final grim glance with Pietro. I had a sinking feeling that I'd just made things worse for him.

Again.

CHAPTER 23

THE BLOODHOUND—FUGITIVES—AN IMPROBABLE MUSE

One-Eyed Johnny's didn't open until ten o'clock in the morning, which left me plenty of time to peruse the morning newspapers. I was half afraid of finding accounts of Mr. Tesla's miraculous feat splashed across every morning edition, but only the *New York World* made any mention of it, and in such sensational language as to practically guarantee that no one would take it very seriously. (Witness reports of a foreign wizard electrocuting a man back to life were dismissed by the Edison Illuminating Company as simultaneously "preposterous" and "further proof of the dangers of alternating current." I guess Mr. Edison wanted to hedge his bets.)

Theodore Roosevelt, meanwhile, seemed to be everywhere. Not just in the papers but literally, with an exhausting schedule of campaign appearances all over the city, not to mention a barrage of interviews and editorials. *A runaway locomotive,* Mr. Clemens had called him, and I could see why. He was also, without doubt, the most famous man in New York, which made my job even harder.

"I just wish we knew how deep this conspiracy runs," I complained to Clara while she tidied up breakfast. "Even if we find Foster, there's no guarantee that will stop whatever he's put in motion."

"*Mmm,*" she said, barely audible over the clink of china.

"We were already outnumbered before Thomas was put out of play."

"Even with *Miss Islington*'s help?"

I glanced up from my paper. "There's that tone again. You don't even know her."

"No, I don't. We wasn't properly introduced. All I know is her name is Miss Islington, and as for me, I'm just plain Clara. Not that you made a point of saying so."

"It didn't come up, that's all. I didn't make proper introductions because—"

"'Cause I'm just the help."

I stiffened. "That's not true."

"No? You telling me that if I was one of them high society types, a Miss So-and-So, you wouldn't've handled it different?"

"You're being unfair," I said, my cheeks burning. "I was preoccupied, that's all. I needed her help with the investigation."

"Oh, I know. She's part of the circle now, ain't she? Let her in on your secret, and Mr. Wiltshire's, too. But I bet you didn't tell her everything." Clara looked me straight in the eye, so hard that I squirmed. "Did you mention how you used to be the help, too? Or did you leave that part out?" She didn't wait for an answer. She didn't have to. "Uh-huh," she said, and headed for the kitchen.

I stared after her, angry and confused and ashamed all at once. It was true, I hadn't introduced Clara properly, but I hadn't meant anything by it. It hadn't occurred to me, that's all. I certainly didn't think Edith was *better* than Clara.

"You don't have time for this," I growled to myself, springing up from my chair and grabbing the satchel I'd packed for Thomas. Whatever was eating Clara, I'd have to deal with it later. I had a bounty hunter to recruit.

I caught a stage down to Twenty-Eighth and hiked over to Broadway, at the easternmost fringes of the Tenderloin tenement district. After yesterday, the last thing I wanted was to crawl into yet another hole under a fleabag hotel, but One-Eyed Johnny's was the favorite watering joint of one Annie Harris, also known as the Bloodhound, and about the only place you stood a level chance of finding her. So I took a deep, lingering breath of "fresh" Tenderloin air and plunged into the pit.

First I paid court to the master of the house. Johnny stood behind the bar as always, fiddling with a leaking barrel of flat beer while he readied for the day's business. Already, a few regulars stood at the bar, though it was too dark to tell if the Bloodhound was among them. I greeted Johnny with a nod and a smile, which he returned with a flash of white teeth that was disconcerting beneath the angry scar and eye patch.

"I don't know if you remember me," I began.

"Sure," he answered in his rich baritone. "You with Sir Thomas, ain't you?"

"That's right." I couldn't help smiling, imagining Thomas's irritation at the nickname he couldn't seem to shed. "I was hoping I'd find Miss Harris here today."

"Today and every day she ain't too drunk to stand. Couldn't tell you what I done to earn the distinction, but she pays better 'n

most." He cocked his head at the far end of the bar, where a familiar wreck of a woman hunched over a glass of gin. "Hey, Annie.
Lady here to see you."

The Bloodhound raised her head and peered at me through
a thicket of tangled hair. "That so? And who's she?"

Johnny clucked his tongue impatiently. "Sir Thomas's friend.
She was here when he hired you last winter, remember?"

The Bloodhound leaned back on her stool and stuck a cigar
in her mouth. "I got hundreds of business associates," she pro-
claimed. "Can't be 'spected to remember 'em all."

"Damn sure can't, with that gin-pickled egg you call a brain.
Why don't you get your sodden ass on over here?"

"I don't need no uppish gin-slinger tellin' me how to handle
my business," the Bloodhound grumbled, but she shoved herself
away from the bar and started toward us.

Johnny shook his head and resumed fiddling with his barrel. "And where's Sir Thomas at today?"

"He's not well, I'm afraid."

"Sorry to hear." He paused to dab a handkerchief under his
eye patch; for a terrible moment I thought he meant to lift it, but
mercifully he didn't. He caught me staring and smiled. "Lost it
in the riots of sixty-three. Still weeps now and then, all these
years later."

"I'm sorry."

He shrugged. "Coulda been worse. I'm still breathin', ain't I?"

"Breathin' stale beer and straw," Annie Harris put in, sidling
up beside me. She rapped the bar, the jeweled rings on her fingers glittering in the lamplight. "Another gin, my good fellow."
Eying me up and down, she said, "I remember you now. You was
with that sour old copper at the Tub of Blood."

"That's right. I'm with the Pinkerton Agency now, and we'd like to engage your services."

"Figured that much. What's the rub?"

"We're tracking a murderer. He's killed six already, and has another in his sights, a prominent man."

The Bloodhound snorted. "'Course he's prominent. Pinkertons wouldn't give a dead rat otherwise."

I left that alone. "He was last seen down in Five Points, at his mother's flat. Will you come and take a look?"

"Take a sniff, you mean?" She narrowed one shrewd eye. "You're a Pink now, too, eh? You can cover my fee?"

Your king's ransom, you mean? With what she charged to bring in a bounty, Annie Harris ought to be drinking cognac with the robber barons at the Fifth Avenue Hotel, but you'd never know it. She dressed like a ragpicker and swore like a sailor, and if she'd ever brushed a tooth in her head, it hadn't done the job. I'd seen Bottle Alley bums with better personal hygiene. Only the jewels on her fingers offered any hint of the exorbitant fee she commanded. "The Agency will take care of it as always," I said coolly.

Johnny poured out a dram of gin, and the Bloodhound toasted me with it. "Lady Pink," she said. "I like it." She downed it in a gulp, slammed the glass on the bar, and smoothed her rumpled men's clothing. "All right then, let's get to it. Keep my spot warm, Johnny. With any luck, I'll be back before dark."

We arrived at the scene of yesterday's excitement to find coppers everywhere. They studded Park Row from Baxter to Mott, stopping passersby to talk briefly before sending them on their way. Canvassing the neighbors, I supposed, for all the good it would do them.

"Well, whaddya know," said the Bloodhound, her nostrils flaring slightly. "Your copper friend is around here somewhere."

"Where, in the flat?"

Another sniff, and the narrowed eyes that proved she was seeing, as much as smelling, the scents in the air. "Second floor, I reckon. And something else." She paused, frowning. "Your partner had some trouble yesterday. Bad trouble."

"You can smell that?"

"Sure. Human body puts out ten kinds of stink when it thinks it's about to kick it. No different than a skunk or a squid, 'cept most people can't smell it."

I eyed her uneasily. I'd hired her for this very reason, of course, but that didn't make her abilities any less unsettling. Not for the first time, I wondered how a working-class specimen like Annie Harris could be born with such a potent brand of luck. Bloodlines with a talent like that almost always ended up in high places. Then again, what did I really know about her background? She could be the black sheep of some prominent family.

"Lingers worse 'n a bad fart," she declared.

A *very* black sheep.

We found Sergeant Chapman inside Mrs. Foster's flat, along with another copper I didn't recognize. Chapman didn't introduce him, shooing the younger man out the moment I arrived, but not before the officer gave me a long, penetrating look.

"Tried telephoning you this morning," Chapman said. "Where you been?"

"The housemaid was out this morning, and Clara and I were probably in the dining room when you called." Belatedly, I noticed his grim expression. "What's the matter?"

He didn't answer straightaway, glancing at the Bloodhound.

"Reckon you're here to start the search, so why don't you get on with whatever it is you do?"

Annie's lip curled. "Mornin' to you too, copper."

"Maybe start by that window," I said, pointing. "He escaped through there, and he was bleeding." She nodded and headed off to the little sitting room.

When she was out of earshot, Chapman said, "You got trouble, Miss Gallagher. Byrnes is mad as a hornet, and he's put a target on you and Wiltshire. There's a warrant out for your arrest."

I blanched. "What for?"

"Obstructing police work or some such, but he don't need a real reason. And if he gets his hands on you, might be the Tombs is the least of your worries."

Blackwell's Island. For a terrible instant, those images came flooding back: wild-eyed lunatics frolicking with dogs, or being dragged away by stone-faced guards . . .

"I thought we were on the same side. We had an understanding."

"Whatever understanding you think you had, it's over. Byrnes holds you responsible for letting Foster get away."

"That's absurd! Why, if it weren't for us, the police wouldn't even know who Foster was!"

"I said as much, and he near bit my head off. Said if I knew what was good for me, I'd haul you in right after I got my hands on Foster. Which, by the way, I got no idea how I'm supposed to do, 'less *she* finds something." He hooked a thumb at the Bloodhound, who was presently sniffing around the windowsill. "Byrnes figures he would've had the information on his own if you'd stayed outta the way. He's got a couple of waiters from the Fifth Avenue Hotel in custody. Been interrogating them personally, in the old-fashioned way, if you take my meaning. *Giving 'em the third degree,* he calls it. Reckons they'll sing soon enough, only now the bird has flown the coop."

I wrapped my arms tightly around myself, feeling suddenly small and fragile. "What are you going to do?"

He frowned. "What's that s'posed to mean? You don't really think I'd take you in for something like that?"

"But your orders . . ."

"I ain't been a clean copper this long to start shoveling shit now, not even for the chief of detectives. I'll play along, though, if it keeps me on the case. Meantime, you 'n' Wiltshire better lay low. Police'll be looking for you at the house, if they ain't been there already."

"Mr. Wiltshire isn't there. He's resting at—"

Chapman stopped me with a gesture. "The less I know, the better." Softening, he added, "How is he, anyway? You sounded pretty shook up on the telephone last night."

"He's lucky to be alive. What Foster did to him . . ." I shuddered, still hugging myself tightly. "It wasn't the same as what he did to me. He didn't seem to want to kill me, but Thomas . . . that was different. The look on his face. The *hate*. How can you hate someone you don't even know?"

The sergeant shook his head. "One thing's for sure, he's got an agenda, and he's serious about it. We're still looking into it, but so far the only Jack Foster we've turned up is nobody special. Former printer's apprentice, used to work at some small paper I never heard of. Nothing shady in his background. No reason I can see to give his employers a false name, 'less he was already planning something. My guess is he took the job at the hotel to get close to the Republicans."

That made sense. Everybody knew the Fifth Avenue Hotel was the party's informal headquarters. "Even if he did have a plan, he's obviously improvising now. He started working there months ago, but he couldn't have known back then that Roosevelt would be the nominee."

"S'pose that's true. Are we even sure Roosevelt is the target?"

"If you'd seen what happened at the hotel, Sergeant, you wouldn't need to ask. He's the target, all right—or at least *a* target. I suppose there might be others." The thought hadn't occurred to me until now.

Chapman glanced over at the Bloodhound. "Anyways, he's gone to ground now, so unless your bounty hunter comes up with something, we're stuck."

The Bloodhound overheard that, and she flashed us a rotten-toothed smile. "Don't you fret none, copper. Got me a scent. These boys reek to hell and back, and there's blood on top of it. It'll take some time, but it'll get done."

Sergeant Chapman looked half relieved, half wary. Which made two of us.

"You find something, you let me know," he said, handing her his card.

"At the discretion of my client," she slurred.

Chapman cut me a wry look.

"Let's be on our way," I said, "and let the police get on with their work." The Bloodhound headed for the door, muttering something unflattering about *police work* as she passed. When she'd gone, I added, "Thank you for warning me about Inspector Byrnes."

"Take it serious," he said, fixing me with his watery gaze. "Stay away from the house, and don't be making eye contact with any of them uniforms you see on the street out there."

"Understood." I thanked him again and quit the flat, careful to keep my head low as I walked past the young copper who'd been eying me earlier. The Bloodhound was waiting for me on the street, impatient to get started. We conferred briefly and parted ways, and I headed for Wang's General Store.

Thomas was still in the little room in the back, but at least he was sitting upright, and the color had returned to his cheeks. Even so, he looked the worse for wear, his clothing rumpled and his normally tidy beard in need of a trim. I hadn't seen him this disheveled since his kidnapping last winter, when he'd been so anxious to clean up that he'd actually let me shave him. Even now, the memory sent a delicious little shiver down my spine. "You're looking much better," I said. "How do you feel?"

"Weak. A little like recovering from flu, actually. Wang says I'm coming along nicely, though he insists on keeping it frightfully cold in here. Something about the flow of my *qi*."

"I brought some fresh clothes and a few other essentials." I set the satchel down beside him.

"Brilliant, thank you. I don't suppose you packed my shaving kit?"

"Of course," I said, unable to suppress a blush.

He saw it and smiled. "Don't worry, I can manage on my own this time."

It was the first genuine smile I'd seen from him in days, and it did my heart good—which made my next words all the more unpleasant. "I'm afraid I have some bad news."

He sighed. "I had a feeling you might say that."

"There's a warrant out for our arrest. It seems our truce with Inspector Byrnes has expired." I related what Sergeant Chapman had told me, unable to keep the bitterness from my voice. Thomas, for his part, received the news with a weary nod.

"We knew the threat of Price's ledger wouldn't hold him for long. He's no doubt taken countermeasures by now, assuming he

even genuinely feared exposure in the first place. I daresay it was
the shock of it more than anything that stayed his hand the other
night. That, and the apparently fleeting notion that we might be
of some use to him."

"The coppers will have been to the house by now. Poor Clara."

"Clara is more than capable of handling them," Thomas said,
sliding gingerly off the cot.

She'd certainly had enough practice, thanks to Thomas
and me.

"Give me a moment to change and then we'll confer. Putting
the Bloodhound in play is a sound measure, but we can't afford to
sit tight and wait for results. Things are moving fast now, and
we're going to need a plan."

"It sounds as if you have one."

"The beginnings of one, at any rate. One advantage of being
out of commission is that it gives one time to think. I've had an
idea, though I should be very reluctant to admit it to the gentleman
who inspired it. He makes an improbable muse, to say the least."

"What gentleman is that?"

"Mark Twain."

CHAPTER 24

LABOR VERSUS CAPITAL—TRULY
PETRIFYING—ROSE GALLAGHER AND
EDITH ISLINGTON, SUFFRAGISTS

keep revisiting something Mr. Clemens had said. About Labor versus Capital."

"Oh." I eyed Thomas over the rim of my teacup. "That's . . . um."

He paused to sip his own tea, humming appreciatively. "It is hard to imagine a more perfect pleasure than proper Chinese tea, don't you think? So much more flavorful than the counterfeit bergamot blend we find in the shops here. Now, where was I?"

"Labor versus Capital."

"Ah, yes. You'll recall Mr. Clemens regaling us with his second-rate Karl Marx? He opined that so far as the mayoral race was concerned, the true contest was between the Republicans—the party of bankers and robber barons, I believe he called them—

and the United Labor Party, with the Democrats of trifling relevance."

"I remember."

"It's certainly true that Henry George and his labor party have captured the working-class imagination. His platform appeals particularly to the sorts of firebrands responsible for the rash of violent strikes we've seen lately. Men of extreme political passions, as it were."

Radicals, the papers were calling them. Personally, I failed to see what was so radical about wanting a fair wage, but I guess I was missing something.

"Men of such convictions might be willing to resort to more serious violence to further their cause."

I frowned. "That's a bit of a stretch, isn't it? Setting a few streetcars on fire is a long way from committing murder."

"I don't mean to imply that all labor men are violent, only that they have violent men among them. Witness the Haymarket Affair this past spring."

"That's hardly unique to labor. Violence and politics go together like peas and carrots."

"Quite. Tammany is known for its brawlers, and the tyranny of the industrial barons could itself be considered a type of violence, especially when it's maintained through force of arms. The police or the military or—"

"Pinkertons."

Thomas cleared his throat delicately. "In any case, without debating the merits of their cause, the fact remains that anarchists and socialists have been baying for capitalist blood for years. *Propaganda of the deed,* they call it. What was it Johann Most said about Vanderbilt and Gould?"

"That they ought to be strung from the nearest lamppost." The papers had gnawed on that bone for weeks.

"Assassinating Theodore Roosevelt would be entirely of a piece with that sort of thinking."

"So you think Foster is an anarchist?"

"I wouldn't go that far. His methods to date strike me as too surgical for a true anarchist. I think it more likely that he's trying to help put Labor in power. Not that the ULP would thank him for it. George himself would doubtless be horrified at the notion that anyone would commit murder in his name."

"Even if you're right, why single out Roosevelt?"

"*Mmm*," Thomas said into his teacup. "I've been thinking about that, too. Do you recall my remarking upon Roosevelt being surprisingly blue-blooded for a mayoral candidate?"

"You said people of his class usually stay out of politics."

"Mr. Clemens mentioned that, too. *Grotesque*, he called it. As though the elite weren't already hoarding enough for themselves, they now grasp at one of the few levers of power accessible to persons of humbler birth. What is more, Roosevelt is also known to be lucky."

Adding insult to injury, Mr. Clemens had said, and I was beginning to see why.

"I can readily imagine that in some circles, it would be taken as an intolerable provocation. Perhaps that was so for Foster. Perhaps his original intent was merely to gather intelligence, but when he heard that an aristocrat like Roosevelt was to be the nominee, it was the last straw."

That certainly fit with my instinct that he was improvising. "I suppose we won't know for sure until we catch him."

"As to that, the Bloodhound remains our best option. But in the meantime, Henry George will be speaking later this afternoon at the Battery, and I thought you might attend. I would of course prefer to go with you, but"—his tone soured—"my physician has forbidden it."

I eyed him doubtfully. "You don't really think Foster will be there?"

"Alas, that is probably too much to hope for. But we know at least one of his colleagues from the Fifth Avenue Hotel is working with him, and there may be others. I thought perhaps between you and Miss Islington, you could scout the crowd for familiar faces."

"Even if we do recognize someone from the hotel, that doesn't prove they're part of the conspiracy."

"True, but they might lead you somewhere interesting." Thomas paused, his gaze turning solemn. "Just promise me, Rose, if you do end up following someone—"

"I'll be careful," I said, anticipating him.

Or so I thought. "That's good to hear, but I was going to say, please leave Miss Islington out of it."

"Oh." I took a hasty sip of my tea.

"She's not one of us, and she mustn't be put in danger on our account. It's difficult enough knowing you're at risk. I simply couldn't bear it if *she* came to harm."

I swallowed, the tea suddenly bitter on my tongue.

"I should be off," I said, avoiding his eye. "I'll come by after the rally to collect you. I suppose we'll go to Mr. Burrows's?"

"Until this nonsense with the police has blown over."

"I'll let you know what I find out."

Thomas caught my hand and gave it a squeeze. "Keep your head about you. There's more to fear than Jack Foster now."

I started to turn away, but his fingers tightened around mine, and he pulled me close. My breath hitched, but I kept my eyes on the floor. His watch ticked through a measure of silence. Gently, he tipped my chin until I was looking up at him. "You are hearing me, Rose?" he murmured.

I was hearing him, all right, and feeling his touch with every nerve of my body. I stared up at him mutely, afraid to break the spell.

Something passed through his eyes that I couldn't place. *He sees you,* I thought irrationally. *He knows.*

"Forgive me," he said, his hand dropping away. "I shouldn't . . . I didn't mean to presume."

"You weren't."

"Yes, I was." He sighed, and now he was the one avoiding my glance. "When this is over, I think perhaps you and I ought to talk."

Sweet Jesus, how those words terrified me. I know, I know—there was an assassin on the loose and every copper in New York was looking for us, and here I was worrying about *we need to talk?* All I can say is that if you've ever been in love, you understand how truly petrifying those words can be.

My mouth had gone dry. Wetting my lips, I took a deep breath, summoned all my courage, and said, "I'd better go."

I fled the room, striking out in search of a telephone and the comforting distraction of mortal peril.

Edith found me on the promenade, gazing out over the bay at the distant spectacle of Mr. Bartholdi's great statue. At this distance, the workmen crawling over her Grecian robes looked like ants, as though they were disassembling the poor lady piece by piece and carting her off to their nest.

"She's quite something, isn't she?" Edith said, shading her eyes. "Though I don't see how they'll manage to have her put together by next week, even with all the king's horses and all the king's men."

"I can hardly believe they've managed this much. Two hundred and fifty tons, the papers say, half of that in copper."

"The dedication will be quite the affair, I suppose. What do you say—shall we come down to view the festivities?"

"Assuming we've caught our killer by then."

Edith blew out a breath. "Well, that's me feeling foolish. I do beg your pardon. I'm not used to all this cloak-and-dagger business. How did it go with the sketch, by the way?"

I hadn't filled her in on yesterday's events. It hardly seemed like the sort of thing one ought to discuss over the telephone, but now that she was here, she had a right to know what she was getting into. I recounted the incident as delicately as I could, emphasizing that Thomas was recovering well. Even so, by the time I was through, she'd gone quite pale, and for a moment I was afraid she'd change her mind about helping me.

I needn't have worried. "This Jack Foster belongs at the end of a rope," she said coldly. "I'll do whatever I can to help see to it he gets there."

"For now, all I need is your eyes and ears. If we do see someone we recognize, I'll take it from there. Mr. Wiltshire was quite insistent that I mustn't put you in any danger."

"That's sweet of him, but he isn't here, is he?" Flashing her arch smile, she looped her arm through mine and started toward the broad square beside the fort, where Henry George was to speak. Already, a large crowd had assembled, many of them carrying banners. The unions were here in force, as were the newspapermen; I recognized William Foote, the reporter Thomas and I had interviewed last Sunday, along with a few other regulars from the stoop. Souvenir boys hawked badges and medals of the Statue of

Liberty, and the hot-corn girls were doing a brisk business. There was even a trio of fiddlers calling themselves the Henry George Boys, though I suspect they were just mud-gutters scenting an opportunity.

"How very festive," Edith remarked. "Rather different from Mr. Roosevelt's speaking engagements, isn't it?"

Festive, and utterly chaotic. How would we ever sift through this throng? "There must be a thousand people here."

"Most of them working-class men. Thank goodness you warned me to dress down. I daresay I'd have stuck out in a sable tippet and pearls."

We stuck out anyway, by simple virtue of our sex. Anxiously, I scanned the square for coppers, but I spied only one, and he seemed more interested in his roasted corn than the crowd.

"Oh, look," Edith said, pointing, "here's the man of the hour."

The assembly erupted in cheers as Henry George stepped up to the platform. He was a serious-looking fellow, bearded and balding, short enough that I had to stand on my toes to get a view over the sea of hats. I confess that until that moment I hadn't taken him very seriously, but all that changed when he began to speak. "*I see in the faces before me a power that is stronger than money,*" he roared, "*something that will smash the political organizations and scatter them like chaff before the wind!*"

"Goodness," Edith said.

Reluctantly, I tore my attention away from the speaker. "We need to find a better spot. We can't see anybody's faces from here."

"What about over there?" She pointed to an elevated pier nearby. "We ought to be able to see the whole square."

We climbed the steps and looked out over the crowd, a thousand faces fixed on the candidate as he thundered on. "*Why should there be such abject poverty in this city? What forces our girls upon the streets and our boys into the grog shops and the penitentiaries?*"

"Do you see anyone familiar?"

Edith shook her head. "To tell the truth, I'm half surprised, but I suppose that's silly. Our little world up on the Avenue is so small, one half forgets just how big this city has become. And how angry, apparently. We really are terribly sheltered, aren't we? Or is it different in Boston?"

"Actually . . ." I hesitated, but she deserved the truth. "I'm not really from Boston. That was just part of the cover story."

"Aha. I didn't think you sounded terribly Bostonian. I'd put it down to a sensitive ear, or perhaps a great deal of travel."

I could have left it there, but Clara's accusation from this morning still rankled. "No travel for me, I'm afraid. My family could never afford to go anywhere."

"*I tell you that a child born in the humblest tenement in the most squalid district of New York comes into life with as good a title to this city as any Astor . . .*"

We kept scanning the crowd, but I could sense Edith's confusion. "Are you from New York, then?"

"I grew up not far from here, actually. In Five Points." In other words, in exactly those blighted districts Henry George was fulminating against at that very moment. And now for the worst part. "Until recently, I was a housemaid. Mr. Wiltshire's housemaid, in point of fact."

Silence fell between us, louder even than the din. I could feel Edith's eyes on me, but I couldn't face her. *There now*, I thought. *She knows you for a fraud.*

Edith burst out laughing.

A furious blush scalded my cheeks, but then she said, "Rose Gallagher, you *will* insist on being the most interesting person I've ever met."

I glanced at her sharply, but there was no hint of irony in her countenance. "I—I'm sorry I lied to you."

"I quite understand. But I do hope you feel you can confide in me now, because I simply cannot wait to hear the tale of how . . ."—she lowered her voice—"how a housemaid becomes a Pinkerton detective."

George was nearing his zenith now, and the crowd was in an uproar. It made it awfully hard to see the faces, what with all the hat-waving and fist-shaking. "Anything?" I asked, raising my voice above the clamor.

"Yes and no. That well turned-out fellow near the back works at A. T. Stewart's. This young man over here picked me up in his cab once, and that one runs a lunch wagon in Union Square. So the city isn't so very big after all." Sighing, she added, "But nobody from the hotel."

Henry George closed his remarks with a plea to his supporters to do their duty at the ballot box, and with a final farewell, he departed, sent off like an ocean liner to a flutter of hats and handkerchiefs. "Oh, well," I said, trying not to sound too crestfallen, "it was worth a try."

We came down from the pier and joined the dispersing crowd. The reporters were interviewing people, and the union men pressing pamphlets into palms, but the place was clearing fast. "I'm sorry I couldn't be of more help," Edith said.

"It was always a long shot."

"Beg your pardon, ladies." A young man in a slouching hat thrust a pamphlet at us. I was about to refuse, but the words printed across the top piqued my curiosity. "Thank you," I said, taking it.

"Good to see some suffragists out here. Could use a few more women in our ranks, if you're interested." He touched his hat and was gone.

"*The Knights of Labor*," Edith read over my shoulder. "How dramatic."

"Thinking of joining?" said a voice, and I turned to find William Foote of the *World*, ledger in hand.

I greeted him with a smile. "Maybe. Have you heard of them?"

"Sure. Biggest labor outfit in the country, or at least they were, before all that Haymarket business. These days they're shedding members left and right. Probably why they're out here trying to drum up new recruits. Bit of a sinking ship. Not sure I'd recommend 'em. So listen—Miss Gallagher, wasn't it? What do you and your friend say to answering a couple of questions? It'd be good to get a few words from some suffragists."

I glanced at Edith, who was biting down on a smile. Apparently she found the idea of being interviewed as a suffragist very amusing indeed.

"I'm sorry, Mr. Foote," I said, "but I don't suppose Mr. Wiltshire would want his clients reading about his secretary at a Henry George rally."

His expression curdled. "Sure, fine."

I paused, something tweaking my memory. "You mentioned Haymarket a moment ago." Thomas had brought it up, too. "You're referring to the riot in Chicago last spring, where the bomb went off? Were the Knights involved in that?"

He shrugged, already scanning the crowd for another mark. "Depends who you ask. They were there, but they swear they had nothing to do with the bombing. Either way, they've never recovered from the accusation. Discord in the ranks, as they say. Local assembly here in New York is a case in point. Factions peeling off every other day. Moderates this way, socialists that way, anarchists over there. Sinking ship, like I said."

"Anarchists, you say? Do you think any of them are here today?"

"S'pose so, but don't expect them to own up to it, at least not in public. It can be downright dangerous being labeled an anarchist these days." He must have spotted new quarry then, because he touched his hat hastily and rushed off.

Edith considered me with a bemused little smile. "You've a keen look in your eye. That was useful, I take it?"

"I'm not sure. Maybe."

"In that case, shall we celebrate with a glass of champagne? We're not far from the Astor House, and I'm famished." Without waiting for an answer, she looped her arm around mine once more and began steering me toward Broadway.

Which was a pity, because I'd felt someone's eyes on me just then, but by the time I turned around, there was nobody there.

CHAPTER 25

THE TALE OF ROSE GALLAGHER—
PROTECTING THE NEIGHBORHOOD—THE
WISDOM OF JANE AUSTEN

After that," I said, "it was clear to both of us that we made a good team, and so Mr. Wiltshire asked if I would like to join the Pinkerton Agency. Of course I said yes straightaway."

Edith stared, her half-forgotten champagne glass cocked at a perilously jaunty angle. (I myself had opted for tea, since I needed to keep a clear head.) "Simply amazing," she said. "The stuff of yellow-back novels."

I laughed. "I don't know about that, but it *is* a very unusual tale."

"And now here you are eating cucumber sandwiches in the Astor House, and no one the wiser. You fit in as easily as if you were born to it. You might have taken up a career in the theater, with your talent for playing a part."

"Now I know you're buttering me up. I don't fit in at all. Ava Hendriks knew me for a counterfeit straightaway."

Edith gave a ladylike little snort. "Ava Hendriks considers the Vanderbilts counterfeit, my dear. As for the rest of us, we were quite convinced."

"That's kind of you to say, but it doesn't feel that way. I'm so terribly clumsy and out of place."

"No one feels at home in a new environment. Why, I was awkward as a goose at that rally this afternoon."

"You weren't."

"I was! You just didn't notice. And if you seemed a little self-conscious at the affair for Lord Barrington, you were hardly alone in that. There is nothing quite like a society event to make a young lady feel inadequate."

I couldn't imagine what could possibly make Edith Islington feel inadequate. She was clever and comely and elegant and self-assured . . . On top of which, she was an Islington, and lucky to boot.

"You needn't waste a thought for fitting in," she went on. "You're made of better stuff than the Ava Hendrikses and the Betty Sanfords, and unlike them, you've actually earned your place."

"That's a nice way of saying I have no pedigree. You can't deny that matters in society circles."

"It does," she admitted, plucking a cucumber sandwich from the plate, "but that's changing. New York is slowly coming around to the idea that success is nearly as admirable as birth."

Unless you're Irish. I kept that thought to myself. "I'll never be a Hendriks, and I'll never be lucky."

"Didn't you just finish telling me that you could sense the presence of shades?"

"That's different."

"How? It's an extraordinary talent nobody else possesses, at least no one I've ever heard of. What is that if not a form of luck? Not inherited, perhaps, but earned, just like the rest of it."

Well now, *that* gave me something to chew on.

We went our separate ways after tea, and I left the Astor House feeling contemplative. Edith hadn't reacted to my confession at all the way I'd expected. She even considered me lucky, after a fashion, which made me an honorary member of the most exclusive club of all. I hope it won't sound too shallow if I admit that meant a lot to me.

Even if she does have an ulterior motive, a cynical part of me whispered. *She wants you to think well of her, because she's spoony for Thomas.*

Thomas. What to make of the exchange we'd had that morning? *I shouldn't presume,* he'd said. What exactly had he been presuming?

I carried on that way for most of the walk back to Five Points—tormenting myself with speculation and grumbling over the reserve of the English—until I was only a couple of blocks from Wang's, at which point I thought about dropping in at Mam's. It wasn't yet dusk, and it would be a while before the Bloodhound came calling. I stopped, undecided, and that's how I happened to hear the scrape of shoes on the pavement behind me.

I turned, but there was nobody there.

You're imagining things. Even so, I changed course, turning up Baxter. A moment later, I heard it again: footsteps behind me, hurrying to catch up.

My heart fluttered unpleasantly. *A copper. It has to be.* I hadn't noticed any as I walked, but I'd been preoccupied. I ducked into Bottle Alley, zigzagging to keep out of sight and pretending not to notice the curious gazes of the loafers idling on stoops or leaning out of tenement windows. I didn't think they'd snitch to the coppers—that's just not how we do things in Five Points—but then again, I didn't look much like a neighborhood girl anymore. *Better not take any chances,* I decided, and when I came across a quiet spot where nobody was looking, I crouched behind a rain barrel and waited.

I listened, straining to hear over the thudding of my heart-beat. Distant chatter in Italian, the cluck of a chicken from one of the rear yards. A moment later, footsteps, fast and purpose-ful. Someone rushed past me, heading north.

It was only then, crouched behind a rain barrel trying to calm my racing pulse, that I remembered the feeling of someone watching me at the rally. I'd noticed only one police officer there, and I was fairly certain he hadn't seen me. But if someone had followed me all the way from the Battery, that meant—

Pain blazed across my scalp as someone grabbed me by the hair, dragging me out from behind the rain barrel. Hands seized the back of my collar and twisted. I shrieked and writhed and wriggled out of my overcoat—and then I remembered that I knew jujitsu. Throwing an elbow into my attacker's ribs, I planted my hip and threw him over my shoulder; he landed flat on his back with a *whuff.* He lay there for a moment, stunned, and I got a good look at him. It was the waiter from the Fifth Avenue Hotel—not Foster but the other one, the man from the pharmacy. He groaned and rolled onto his side, at which point I blasted a kick into his stom-ach, which is not something they teach you in jujitsu but is some-thing they teach you in Five Points, at least if you've seen your share of street brawls.

He folded over himself—and suddenly there was a gun in his hand. I barely had time to duck before the shot went off, punching a hole through the linens drying on a line overhead. I went for my own gun only to realize that it was in the pocket of the overcoat I'd thrown aside. The waiter cocked the hammer again, and all I could do was run.

The bullet slammed into the clapboard siding of a shack, missing me by inches. I fled up the alley, bumping into stoops and stumbling over crooked paving stones until I spilled out onto Mulberry, where I collided with someone and went down. The man I'd blundered into went down, too, sending a pistol clattering across the sidewalk. I scrambled to my feet, but the man was faster, snatching his gun back up and pointing it at me. I didn't recognize him, but he clearly knew me, and the cold purpose in his eyes told me he had every intention of pulling that trigger.

He never got the chance. The *crack* of a gunshot sounded from up the street, and the air hissed. The man turned and fled; moments later, a familiar figure charged past: Marco, the rough from Bandit's Roost, trailed by another of Augusto's men. People scattered, screaming.

"Rose!" Someone grabbed me. I flinched, but it was only Pietro, shoving me toward the sidewalk. "What are you doing? Get out of the street!"

He started after Marco, but I blocked his path. "Not that way! There's another one in the alley—"

The waiter burst into the street, revolver raised. I did the only thing I could think of, tackling Pietro to the ground as the gun went off. Pietro rolled away and fired back—a wide, clumsy shot that sent the waiter scurrying for cover.

"This way!" I helped Pietro to his feet and dragged him into the stairwell below the hardware shop. Somewhere down the block, another gunshot sounded.

Pietro looked me over, breathing hard. "Are you all right?" When I nodded, he cocked his gun and peered over the top of the stairwell.

"Don't." I grabbed his arm. "Just stay out of sight."

"You must be joking! He's *shooting* at us!"

"He's shooting at me. These aren't random street thugs."

"I'm not stupid. I know this is Pinkerton business. Your boss has got you in trouble again, and—*Là!*" Uncoiling from his crouch, he fired. "*Merda!* Missed again!"

"Stop it! I need him alive, Pietro!"

"*What?*"

The waiter leaned out from his hiding place. Before Pietro could react, I wrenched the gun from his hands and shoved him down. The waiter took his shot, ringing it off the pavement, and then it was my turn. I sighted down the barrel, took a breath, and fired.

The waiter went down with a bullet in his thigh. I'd taken a leg shot once before and it had gone terribly wrong, but this time I'd had hours of target practice and I knew just where to aim. There would be no bleeding out and no running away.

I bounded up the stairs, gun raised and ready, but the man writhing on the pavement wasn't going to be any more trouble. He'd dropped his weapon, both hands clamped feebly against his leg. I kicked the gun away and stood over him, trying very hard to keep my hands steady while the rest of me shook. "Where is he? Where's Foster?"

He didn't answer, too busy howling over his leg. I thought about kicking him again, but that didn't seem very Christian, and besides, more pain wasn't likely to help him think clearly. It occurred to me then that of all the lessons we'd had, interrogation wasn't one of them, which felt like something of an oversight. *Inspector Byrnes would know what to do,* I thought sourly.

I was still debating how to get him to talk when I heard someone approach. Pietro, I assumed, and by the time I knew otherwise it was too late. Marco walked right up to my suspect, looked him over, and shot him in the head. "*Cazzo.*"

I dropped to my knees, but there was nothing to be done. Blood spilled from the wound in the waiter's forehead, pooling in the cracks between the paving stones.

You let him die. Our best way to find Foster and you let him be executed right in front of you.

Mistaking my reaction for hysteria, Marco put a hand on my shoulder. "It's all right, *signorina*. You are safe now. We got them all."

I didn't know what to say.

Marco and his partner wasted no time getting rid of the evidence, grabbing the waiter's body and dragging him away. *They're right,* I thought. *This place will be crawling with coppers any minute now.*

A shadow spilled over me; I recognized its lean outline. Wordlessly, I handed the revolver back to Pietro.

"That was a very good shot," he said, his tone strangely flat. "A perfect shot, even, since you needed him alive."

There was no point in denying it. Shakily, I got to my feet. "I needed to ask him something."

"I heard. You were looking for someone named Foster." He gestured at my arm. "You're bleeding."

I looked down; there was a deep gash in my forearm. I hadn't even noticed the pain until now. "Must've caught it on a nail while I was running."

"You're one of them."

The words were all too familiar, a near-perfect echo of what I'd said to him when I found out he was working with Augusto's thugs.

Don't look at me like that, he'd said. Now I understood what it felt like.

"I thought you were just helping your boss, but it's more than that, isn't it? Nobody shoots a gun like that on their first try. Nobody stands over a man who was trying to kill them and doesn't even shake. Especially not a woman."

But I was *shaking,* I thought. *I'm still shaking.* I looked down at my hands, but they were steady, as if they belonged to someone else.

"How long have you been lying to me, Rose? To your mama?"

The hurt in his voice, the disappointment, was more than I could bear. I squeezed my eyes shut, ashamed. "I wanted to tell you."

"But you didn't," Pietro said, and he walked away.

Just like Clara.

My vision swam with tears, but I blinked them back. I had to get away from here before the coppers arrived, but I knew better than to leave without paying my respects to the man who'd saved my life. That was how Augusto would see it, at any rate, and besides, I had some explaining to do. I had no fear of Pietro's revealing my secret, but Augusto was no fool; it was best not to take chances.

I fetched my coat from the alley and headed for the grocery. The aging *padrone* was there, standing under the awning with his arms folded, his wild salt-and-pepper eyebrows drawn into a frown. He'd come out to survey the aftermath—he and every other merchant on Mulberry Street, not to mention half the tenants of the surrounding tenement buildings. I wondered how much he'd seen. "*Signorina*," he said as I approached. "Are you hurt?"

"Just a scratch, though it does seem to be bleeding quite a bit. Do you by chance have a handkerchief I might borrow?"

He called out to one of his underlings, but his keen-eyed gaze never left mine. "You seem to have a lot of trouble, Miss Gallagher. The last time we spoke, you had stitches. It looks like maybe you need some more, eh?"

"Yes, well . . ." I hefted my soiled overcoat. "That's what I get for wearing something this trig. They tore it right off my back."

"Was it the same man who attacked your boss yesterday?"

"No, but they were working together." A young man came out of the store and offered me a handkerchief. Pressing it to my arm, I glanced up the street. "Here come the coppers. Do you suppose I might come inside? I really don't want to talk to them."

"Why not?"

"You see, I might have . . . That is, I'm not entirely blameless in this, and I'm afraid . . ." I trailed off, letting the tears I'd been holding back brim in my eyes.

I know, I know. But I'd learned long ago that Augusto had a soft spot for damsels in distress, and you did what you had to in this line of work.

"What if they arrest me?" I whispered, and this time, the fear in my voice was perfectly genuine.

"They will not dare, not without my permission. They know the rules." Even so, he brought me inside, and the next thing I knew I had a blanket wrapped around my shoulders and a glass of wine in my hands. "Good for the nerves, *sì*? Now"—he waved his minions off—"why don't you tell Augusto what happened?" He said it in a grandfatherly way, but I knew better. I'd have to be very careful here.

I sipped my wine, composing my thoughts. "I'm afraid I started all this business. The men who jumped us yesterday stole Mr. Wiltshire's watch. It was precious to him, and he was terribly upset about it, so I decided to go looking for the thugs myself. I brought a gun." Making sure my hand trembled, I drew the little derringer from my overcoat pocket. "I thought they were just common thieves. I was sure they'd hand it over once they saw that I was armed. It never occurred to me they would have guns of their own . . ."

"Why did you not bring this to me?"

"I can't come running to you every time I get into trouble. Besides, it was my fault the watch got stolen. We should never have been in that alley, only I said it was a shortcut. It was my mistake, so I wanted to be the one to make it right. Mr. Wiltshire is . . ." I faltered, drawing a blank.

"You love him," the *padrone* said with a shrug.

I blinked, taken aback. I had no idea when or how he'd come to that conclusion, but it offered a convenient explanation for my actions. "I do," I said, letting my gaze fall.

Augusto was silent for a moment, giving me a long, calculating look. "This story you tell me, *signorina* . . . I don't know what to make of it. It was a very stupid thing you did." Tilting his head, he added, "You don't seem like a stupid girl."

"We are all fools in love," I said, which was very stupid indeed, since I doubted Augusto was an avid reader of Jane Austen.

"True. Young Pietro is about to learn this, I think."

I bit my lip; I'd forgotten that Pietro and I were meant to be sweethearts. "Will you tell him?"

"It's not for me to interfere. He will find out on his own, eventually. You will break his heart, but that's all right. A young man likes to be crossed in love now and then." He smiled, enjoying the startled look on my face. Apparently even Five Points *pa-droni* can't resist Jane Austen.

"That hasn't been my experience," I said dryly.

Augusto shrugged. "Maybe not. But disappointment builds character, *sì*? It will make him stronger in the end."

He didn't fool me for a second. He wasn't going to tell Pietro because it gave him something to hold over me, or so he thought. I don't think he entirely believed my story, but now that he'd found his leverage, he was satisfied. The fact that it was false leverage meant I was satisfied, too.

"Thank you for the wine," I said, rising. "And the handkerchief. I'll have it cleaned. Now, er . . ." I glanced out the window into the street, where the coppers were gathering. "Do you suppose I might use the back door?"

CHAPTER 26

HEAVENLY HUMOR—CONFESSION IN A CARRIAGE—FACTIONS AT THE FACTORY—ON THE MEND

By the time I got to Wang's, the whole neighborhood was talking about the bag of nails in the street. Which probably explains why Mei didn't look very surprised to find me at her back door. "We heard the shots," she said, ushering me inside. "Are you all right?"

"I am, though I can't say the same for our suspect."

"The neighbors are saying it was the Mulberry Street Gang."

"Sort of. It's complicated."

"We'd better have the details, then." Thomas appeared in the hallway, looking grave.

"It was the waiter from the hotel," I told him. "The one we saw bringing medical supplies to Foster yesterday. He must have tailed me from the rally, waited until I was alone in an alley to jump me."

"You're hurt," Mei said, gesturing at my arm.

"It's nothing."

"I have some poultice for that. To help it heal faster." She headed off to fetch it.

Thomas took my wrist, examining the wound. "This will need more than a poultice." He shook his head. "I'm sorry, Rose. I should have been there."

"It's my own fault. Edith and I climbed up on an elevated pier to get a better view of the crowd. I didn't stop to think about how conspicuous that would make us to unfriendly eyes."

"How did the Mulberry Street Gang come into it?"

"They were making their daily rounds. I'd already kicked the hornet's nest yesterday when I told them you were attacked by bandits. They took that as a slight against Augusto, so when the waiter started shooting . . ."

"They intervened to protect their territory." Thomas nodded. "That was fortunate."

"Was it? They executed our best lead."

"Our best lead wasn't worth your life, Rose."

The words drove home just how close I'd come to being killed, and I shuddered. "The second man, whoever he was, nearly got the drop on me. If Marco hadn't shot at him . . ."

Thomas drew a long breath before responding. "Second man?"

"I didn't recognize him. There may have been more, come to think of it, but I only saw two. Marco and his boys killed them. And . . ." I paused, sighing. "Pietro was there. He . . . well, he knows the truth about me now."

"I'm sorry. Do you think he'll tell anyone?"

"No, but I don't think he'll ever forgive me."

"Give it time." With a faint smile, he added, "You forgave me, didn't you?"

That was different, of course. *We are all fools in love,* I thought wryly. "Either way, I can't worry about it right now. Things are moving too fast, and I have a feeling it's only going to get worse."

"Agreed. It would appear our killer is growing impatient. Even allowing that we caught him by surprise yesterday, he and his accomplices have attempted murder three times in as many days. And they've obviously concluded that you and I are obstacles in their path, which means they'll be looking for us."

"We won't be hard to find."

"No. I imagine every shopkeeper in the neighborhood knows you. Do any of them know where your mother lives?"

The question was like a bucket of ice water in my face. "I don't know," I said, my voice skirling upward in alarm. "Maybe. What should I do?"

"We can't bring her to the house. The police will be looking for us there. A hotel?"

"She can't be on her own. Her dementia . . ."

"With Burrows, then? I'm sure he can accommodate us all."

I shook my head. "The best way to keep her safe is to get her as far away from us as possible." I bit my lip, thinking. "There's Clara, or the Wangs, but they're complete strangers. How would I explain that to her?"

He sighed. "There is one obvious choice."

"Pietro." *Dear Lord, you have a cruel sense of humor.* As if being a Pinkerton weren't bad enough in Pietro's eyes, I'd put my own mother in danger, and now I'd be asking him to take responsibility for protecting her. "He's sure to hate me now."

"He'll look after your mother. That's what's important."

"I can't even ask him in person. The streets are crawling with coppers. I don't dare go back out there. Just ducking into a carriage will be risky enough."

"Miss Wang can deliver a letter, along with the funds to pay for a hotel. It's only for a few days, and there are plenty of excuses he might use to explain it to your mother. A problem in the flat, say. Something that needs to be repaired."

It was hard to imagine what kind of problem would inspire a Five Points landlord to dig into his pockets, but I'd think of something.

"You'll make it up to him, Rose," Thomas said gently. "In any case, it's not as though we have a choice. You're right, things are only going to get worse. We're under attack on two fronts, and meanwhile, Roosevelt is more vulnerable with each passing day. It's a race, and we're falling behind." He consulted his Patek Philippe. "And speaking of time, we'd better get on. I'll telephone Clara while you're working on your letter. She can meet us at Burrows's and take care of that arm."

Yet another favor from a friend who was angry with me. "Is that really necessary?" I asked, glancing away. "Tomorrow's her day off. She'll be heading home soon."

"It won't take long. Besides, it's good practice for nursing school, and I'll certainly compensate her for the work."

"Couldn't we just call a doctor?"

"I thought you preferred to have Clara do it."

"What I prefer and what Clara prefers are two different things. Especially lately."

Thomas gave me a quizzical look but otherwise let that pass. He headed for Mr. Wang's office to use the telephone, while I penned a hasty—and extremely contrite—note to Pietro asking him to check into a hotel with Mam until I gave the all clear. Mei took the note, gave me a jar of foul-smelling poultice, and went out to fetch us a cab. She'd have a long walk, cabs being scarce in this part of town, but we didn't have much choice.

When we were safely shut in the carriage heading uptown, Thomas said, "Have you and Clara had words?"

So much for him letting it go. Sighing, I said, "She's certainly had words with me."

"Would you like to talk about it?"

I shrugged awkwardly. "There's not much to tell. She thinks I'm putting on airs."

"That doesn't sound like you."

"That's just it. She thinks I've changed. That all this"—I hefted my fancy overcoat, soiled but still beautiful—"has gone to my head."

"I suppose a degree of change is inevitable, given how drastically your life has transformed. Must that be a negative?"

"If it pushes my family and friends away."

A pause. "Is that what you believe is happening?"

"I don't know. Maybe. Or maybe it's me who's drifting away from them. I feel . . . caught between two worlds, I guess." It should have been awkward admitting this to Thomas—he'd been the one to set me on this path, after I'd practically begged him to let me be a part of his world—but instead it felt good to confide in him. "I don't know if Clara's right, but she's not entirely wrong either. I don't recognize myself half the time. You once told me that Mr. Burrows never really lets his guard down, and I think maybe I'm learning what that's like. I've been doing so much pretending lately that I sometimes feel as if I don't remember what the real me looks like."

"Give yourself time. If it helps, I went through a similar transition when I joined the Agency. I felt completely unmoored at first. Disconnected and alone, as if I no longer recognized the world around me, and it no longer knew me. But you're not alone, Rose. I hope you know that."

I glanced over at him. His face was half sketched in shadow, but I could still see the spark in his eyes, that quiet intensity that had first drawn me to him. "Sometimes I feel as if we're the only two people in the world, but I know I'm not alone."

He smiled. "I'm glad."

There followed the most perfect silence. We clip-clopped up Broadway, each of us lost in our own thoughts, separate but together. I felt more peaceful, more centered, than I had in months. I guess it's true what they say: Confession really is good for the soul.

"Thomas?"

"*Mmm?*"

"You're a very good listener."

He laughed, a little ruefully. "If I sometimes have trouble saying what's on my mind, at least I can listen to what's on yours."

A short while later, the carriage deposited us in front of Mr. Burrows's house. Clara was already there, her shiny new medical bag at the ready. "Least we got proper catgut this time," she said, examining the cut on my arm with an appraising eye. Then, over her shoulder to Mr. Burrows: "Where do you want us?"

"The kitchen, I think," he said, gesturing in that direction. "At the risk of making a poor host, I'll leave you to it. I've no desire to watch. Do you have everything you need?"

"Got any gin?"

"I'm not much of a gin man, I'm afraid. Can I offer something else?"

"It's for Rose, for the pain. Any grog'll do."

"I don't believe I have any *grog*," Mr. Burrows said dryly, "but I do have a century-old Martell."

"Well, la-di-da."

I took a generous swig of the stuff while Clara cleaned me up, and I can honestly say I prefer good Irish whiskey.

Thomas stayed with me, sipping a glass of brandy while he

watched Clara work. "You're getting better," he observed. "More confident."

"I suppose I oughta thank you for the practice," she said, snipping a knot. "Does this mean you all found your man?"

"We did, but"—I hissed as the needle bit again—"he got away. Now we're back where we started."

"I wouldn't go that far," Thomas said. "A great many red herrings have been thrown in our path, it's true. First the shade, then Price and his friend Fitz. But we have a name, a face, and a motive. And we have the Bloodhound." Sighing, he added, "What we don't have is time. If we could investigate these labor organizations one by one, I'm almost certain we could track him down, but as it is . . ." He tossed the Knights of Labor pamphlet I'd been given at the rally onto the table. "There are just too many of them."

Clara glanced at it and grunted. "These fools again. They're everywhere, ain't they?"

"You've heard of them?" I asked, surprised.

She tugged gently on a thread. "Everybody at the factories knows 'em. Half the workers are members, or used to be. Been after Joseph to join for years. Say they need more coloreds, and women, too."

The young man who'd given me the pamphlet had said something similar. "I heard they're desperate for recruits because their membership is deserting them."

"Can you blame 'em, after that business in Chicago?"

"They claim they had nothing to do with the bombing."

"Maybe, but there was more than a handful cheering in private, or so Joseph says. That's why he never joined. Too many fanatics, he said. Always talking about the Cause this, the Cause that. 'Specially after Haymarket."

Thomas glanced up from his brandy. "What do you mean, especially after Haymarket?"

She shrugged. "It's like Rose said. Lotta folks quit after that. Didn't wanna be associated with that sort of thing. The ones that stayed . . . well, I guess they was the ones who really meant it."

"The most zealous," Thomas said, his eyes sharp with interest.

"I don't know about *that*. From what I heard, the real zealots went their own way. Left in a huff, or got themselves tossed out."

"There was bad blood?"

"Guess you could say that. Everybody got caught up in it, too, even if they never joined. There's fellas Joseph's known for years don't even talk to each other no more. Reckon it's the same at all the factories."

"I heard something similar from William Foote," I told Thomas. "That the anarchists and socialists formed their own splinter groups after Haymarket."

Clara paused, her glance cutting between us. "What're you all fishing for?"

"We believe Jack Foster and his accomplices might be ideologues," Thomas said.

"The sort who might have sympathy with the Haymarket bombers," I added. "Do you think Joseph might know anything that could help us?"

She frowned. "Joseph's no anarchist."

"Of course not," Thomas said in a mollifying tone. "But if he or any of his coworkers were courted by these splinter groups, he might have useful information."

"You wanna question him?"

She didn't look too pleased with the idea, and I can't say I blamed her. "Not question," I said. "We'd like to ask for his help.

For anything he might know that could point us in the right direction. Even the smallest detail might be important. Do you think he'd be willing?"

"What, now?"

Thomas shook his head. "You've already donated enough of your evening, and Rose and I need our rest after everything that's happened. This can wait until morning. I know tomorrow is your day off, but would you be willing to exchange it for Sunday?"

"Guess so, but I can't promise he'll come. No offense, but he's got no love for Pinkertons."

"Fair enough," I said wryly. Pinkertons had been providing muscle for the robber barons for years. The special branch was different, but try telling that to a man who's been clubbed over the head for demanding an eight-hour workday.

"I'll talk to him," Clara said. "Just remember, he don't know about all this paranormal business, and I aim to keep it that way. It'd give him the jimjams, and I don't see the upside."

"Understood," Thomas said. "Would you prefer to bring him here, or shall we come to you?"

She paused. "Now you mention it, I wouldn't mind him getting a glimpse of how I spend my days up here."

"It's settled, then. We'll expect you in the morning." Draining his brandy, he stood. "I'll bid you ladies good evening. Thank you again, Clara, for everything."

"Really," I added when he'd gone, "thank you. I know it's a lot to ask, all of this."

"It's all right." She snipped her final knot. "There. That oughta hold you. We'll bandage that up with the poultice Mei gave you, and you'll be on the mend in no time."

"Clara." I reached for her hand. "I'm sorry about earlier, with Edith. You were right, I should have introduced you properly."

She sighed. "I'm sorry, too. I s'pose I came off as jealous, and maybe I am, a little. But mostly I'm worried about you. I thought all this would make you happy, but it sure don't seem that way."

"I'm just having a little trouble adjusting. I'll find my feet eventually."

"I know you will," she said, squeezing my hand back. "But the first thing you gotta do is relax and just *be*. Quit worrying about what other people think and just accept yourself for who you are. Because, Rose, honey, who you are is amazing."

Tears sprang to my eyes, and I threw my arms around her. "What did I ever do to deserve you?"

She laughed. "We working girls gotta stick together, don't we?"

I turned in early that night, but not before saying a prayer of thanks. God had not only spared my life that day, but reminded me over and over that I was surrounded by the most wonderful friends anyone could ask for. I'd taken so much for granted, let myself be weighed down by my own insecurities, but no more. "That's enough whinging now, Rose Gallagher," I murmured into my folded hands. And then, taking a page from Theodore Roosevelt's book: "Time to get on with the business."

I awoke to the sound of an unfamiliar doorbell. For a moment I couldn't work out where I was, and then I remembered. *Mr. Burrows's. Hiding from the coppers.* Sunlight streamed in through a gap in the curtains. I'd overslept.

Heading downstairs, I found we had a visitor in the front parlor. "Miss Islington. This is a pleasant surprise."

She took my hands in greeting. "I thought I'd stop in and see how Mr. Wiltshire was faring after his terrible ordeal."

Thomas inclined his head in polite acknowledgment. Then he handed me a note. "This came for you this morning."

Opening it, I found the messiest handwriting I'd ever seen. "It's from Pietro," I murmured in relief. "They're at the Bowery Hotel."

"I'm glad. They'll be safe there. Please, take a seat." Thomas gestured at the sofa beside him, while Edith and Mr. Burrows arranged themselves in a matching set of wingback chairs.

"How did you know where to find us?" I asked Edith.

"It wasn't difficult. You told me you needed to keep a low profile, and where else would you stay?"

I didn't much like the sound of that. "I hope it's not that easy for the coppers to figure out."

Mr. Burrows shrugged. "I doubt Inspector Byrnes knows much about your personal lives, but even if he did, he wouldn't dare show up on my doorstep."

"Mustn't offend royalty," Edith said, sipping her coffee.

"I wouldn't go that far, but the family name does carry considerable weight. A wily fellow like Byrnes wouldn't want the bother. Better to take you out in the streets."

"Oh, good," I said, "that makes me feel so much better."

"Why has he got it in for you, anyway?" Edith asked.

"We threatened him. Openly challenged his authority. A bully like him . . . he won't let that stand."

"In addition to which," Thomas said, "Tammany has paid him a handsome fee to take care of the Foster problem quietly. It would be highly embarrassing if the Pinkertons caught him first."

"Well," said Edith, "I'm just relieved to see you so well, Mr. Wiltshire. You seem to be recovering admirably."

"He really is," I said, smiling. "Why, only two days ago, he could hardly sit up in bed. Not that it stopped him from trying to work. If it hadn't been for Mr. Wang, I think he'd have insisted on accompanying us to the Battery." I arched an eyebrow at Thomas, daring him to deny it.

He laughed quietly. "I know better than to trifle with Mr. Wang. If I'd tried to defy him, I daresay he'd have knocked me out for a week."

Edith observed this exchange with a polite smile, her glance cutting back and forth between us. "And what about you, Miss Gallagher? Are you wholly recovered?"

Thomas's gaze shadowed over. "She was, until she was nearly shot last night."

Edith gasped.

"*Nearly,* but I'm fine," I said, mainly for the benefit of Thomas, who was still giving me that look.

I'd just started to explain when we were interrupted by the doorbell. I figured it must be Clara and Joseph, but it was another visitor who appeared in the parlor.

"Sergeant Chapman," Thomas said, rising. "This is a surprise."

The detective eyed us grimly. "I know what you're thinking. My being here could tip off Byrnes. But I didn't have much choice."

Thomas and I exchanged a look of foreboding.

"You might wanna sit," the detective said. "I'm afraid I got some bad news."

CHAPTER 27

BAD NEWS—STEAM ENGINES AND
SLAUGHTERHOUSES—THE STRAW

t's your friend," said Sergeant Chapman. "We found her unconscious last night."

I gripped the arm of the sofa until my knuckles went white.
"Clara?"

"The one you call the Bloodhound."

I heaved a very un-Christian sigh of relief.

"They locked her up around two-thirty this morning. Took
her for a drunk, seeing how she smelled like a gin mill."

"To be fair," Mr. Burrows said, "Annie Harris is most definitely a drunk."

"That may be," said Thomas, "but she's never passed out on
the job before."

"And drunks don't usually have their hearts galloping in

their chests," Chapman said. "Not like this. I took her pulse, and it feels like someone's tapping out a telegram in there."

"Foster." I sighed. "He must have got the drop on her."

"Where was she picked up?" Thomas asked.

"Greenwich, just north of Canal. Still had my card on her, which is why the boys from the Eighth wired me. Figured her for an informant."

"Poor Annie," I murmured. "Will she be all right?"

"I had a doctor take a look. Wasn't much he could do for her. Said she was suffering from . . ." Chapman consulted his ledger, holding it out at arm's length and squinting. "Tacky . . . tacka . . ."

"Tachycardia. The same as what he did to me."

"Though apparently more severe," Thomas said. "And yet he didn't kill her, just as he didn't kill you."

"How chivalrous," Edith observed sourly.

Thomas hummed a thoughtful note. "It's possible that Foster hesitates to kill women, but I wonder if that's the reason. Perhaps it's because he doesn't see Miss Harris or Miss Gallagher as belonging to . . ." He trailed off awkwardly.

"The wrong class," I finished for him. "It's all right, everyone here knows it."

"Everyone here, maybe," Edith said, "but how did Foster know?"

"He overheard Ava Hendriks talking about it." Dryly, I added, "I believe her exact words were 'That girl is as working class as they come.'"

Mr. Burrows *tsk*ed, and Thomas looked at me sharply, a flash of color touching his cheeks. "I'm very sorry she was so uncivil," he said, every syllable crisp with anger.

A strange thought occurred to me then. "If she hadn't been, Foster would never have known I was working class. I might just owe Ava Hendriks my life." I couldn't help laughing at that.

"So you think he held back because Miss Gallagher and the Bloodhound is both working class?" Chapman asked.

"Whatever his reasons," I said, "he's obviously changed his mind." When the sergeant gave me a quizzical look, I filled him in on the doings in Five Points yesterday. "Foster let me go the first time, and I made him regret it. Apparently he's looking to fix his mistake."

"Meanwhile," Thomas said, "taking Miss Harris out of play is a severe blow to our investigation."

"Yeah, about that," Chapman said. "I think maybe she can still help us. Indirectly, like."

"Oh?" Thomas cocked his head.

"I was thinking about what Miss Gallagher explained the other night. About . . ." He looked at Mr. Burrows. Then his glance shifted to Edith, and he fell silent.

Mr. Burrows understood straightaway. "I appreciate your discretion, Sergeant, but you needn't worry. Miss Islington and I have known each other since we were children. She's familiar with my luck."

"Good. Hold that thought." Chapman ducked out of the parlor, returning a moment later with a dusty, gin-soaked bit of clothing. "This here's her jacket. I thought maybe you could do . . . whatever it is you do, and tell us where she's been."

Mr. Burrows made a face. "Why can't it ever be a lady's tippet? Or an apron from Delmonico's?" He took the jacket, hefting it between thumb and forefinger as though he were dangling a dead rat by its tail. "Good Lord, has this ever been washed? I sense a hundred different things."

"Perhaps we ought to make a list," Thomas suggested.

Chapman drew out his ledger and a pencil. "Ready."

"Where to begin? An almost infinite assortment of alcoholic fumes, sawdust, and lamp oil. I recognize the particular blend of One-Eyed Johnny's, but you'll forgive me if I can't place the others. This jacket has spent more than one night sleeping rough recently, at least once in the Gashouse District. And I taste the Hudson River, which is always a delight." Pausing, he gave Thomas a rueful look. "Honestly, we could be about this for a week."

"Can you isolate the more recent elements?"

"How?"

"You tell me. Perhaps they taste more strongly. Or rest closer to the surface, as opposed to being ground into the fabric. Perhaps some of them degrade over time, like food spoiling. Draw on your experience. Think it through."

Mr. Burrows closed his eyes, concentrating. "Chemical fumes. Several different kinds, but I only recognize a few. Turpentine. A variety of paints and varnishes. Glue. They're shallow, as you said. They haven't penetrated the fabric deeply."

Thomas leaned forward. "Go on."

"A butcher. No, wait . . . A slaughterhouse?"

"Magnificent, Jonathan." Thomas was actually grinning now. He'd been after his best friend for ages to cultivate his talents; watching Mr. Burrows push himself seemed to delight him. As for me, I was fighting down a wave of nausea at the idea of "tasting" a slaughterhouse. Or, for that matter, the Hudson River.

I wasn't the only one. "You got an iron stomach, Burrows," Chapman said. "If it were me, I'd shoot the cat."

"You're not helping, Sergeant." Mr. Burrows furrowed his brow, digging deeper. "Tannin. A leatherer?"

"A tannery," I guessed. "You often find those near slaughter-houses."

"Yes, of course, a tannery. And if I'm not mistaken, a soap factory, which I'll warrant is the only soap ever to have touched this jacket." He opened his eyes. "That's all I can be sure of, I'm afraid. That, and the smoke of a steam engine, but I don't suppose that narrows things down much."

Thomas sprang to his feet. "On the contrary, it's extremely helpful. Do you have a map of the city?"

Mr. Burrows fetched one, and they spread it out on the table between us.

"So," Thomas said, "the Bloodhound was picked up on Greenwich, near Canal. Your pencil, Sergeant, if I may? Now, assuming our conspirators didn't go to too much trouble divesting themselves of Miss Harris, we can narrow our search to roughly this area." He drew a circle encompassing the Fifth and Eighth Wards, from the river to Sixth Avenue and from Chambers to West Houston.

"That's an awful big search area, Wiltshire." Chapman tapped a meaty finger on the map. "You got three railroad lines through here, and a dozen slaughterhouses at least."

"Precisely. Slaughtering and meat packing are overwhelmingly concentrated here." Thomas drew a circle.

Chapman grunted. "I see. And the chemical factories is mostly around here." Taking the pencil back, he drew another circle, slightly overlapping Thomas's.

"The Hudson River Railroad and the Sixth and Ninth Avenue els run through." Thomas traced a trio of lines.

"And—may I?" I reached for the pencil. "The Pearl Soap factory is here." I drew an X. "You can see it from the el."

Thomas gazed at the map approvingly. "There, you see, Sergeant? We've narrowed it down quite a lot already."

"It's a start, but working out what neighborhood to look in ain't exactly the same as tracking the man down."

"Agreed. There, we can only hope that our next interview will bear fruit. Speaking of which . . ." Thomas took out his watch. "Clara ought to have been here by now. Do you suppose she's having difficulty convincing Joseph?"

"She'll be here," I said. "We just have to be patient."

Happily, we didn't have to be patient much longer. The doorbell sounded, and a moment later the butler appeared. "Apologies for the interruption," Bertram said, "but there is a young colored couple asking to see you, sir. They're at the *front door.*" He arched an eyebrow significantly.

Mr. Burrows looked suitably taken aback. "What do you mean, at the front door?"

"Quite."

"You just left them on the street? Why the deuce didn't you show them in?"

The butler paled. "Well, I . . . that is . . ."

"Don't stand there stammering, man! Get to it!"

With a mortified bow, the butler retreated. *He and Mrs. Sellers would get along brilliantly,* I thought.

Thomas cast a quick glance about the room. "My, this is a rather intimidating cast, isn't it? Perhaps we ought to—"

Before he could finish, Clara and Joseph appeared at the parlor door, wearing their Sunday best. I'd been hearing about Joseph for years, but I'd never met him, and I couldn't help staring. He was a little older than I thought, maybe thirty, and stood well over six feet, making Clara's petite frame seem even more birdlike alongside. He didn't look too happy to be there, and I didn't blame him, especially with the five of us facing him like some kind of jury.

"Mr. Burrows," Clara said, and I could hear the tension in her voice.

"Good morning, Clara. And this must be Joseph." Mr. Burrows stuck out a hand, and Joseph shook it warily. "I apologize for Bertram. He's very good at what he does, but he can be quite ridiculous."

"Didn't realize there'd be so many of us," Clara said, with an awkward glance at her fiancé.

"That's my fault, I'm afraid," said Edith. "I had the poor manners to drop in unannounced."

"Same here," said Chapman. "And I'm guessing you wasn't expecting a copper, so if you all need me to be scarce . . ."

"It's all right," Joseph said. "I got nothing to say that a copper can't hear. Truth is, I'm not sure how I can help you all."

Thomas introduced himself, and they shook hands. "This must have seemed a very odd request. We're grateful to you and Miss Freeman for indulging us."

I could have kissed him. It was guileless, of course; Thomas had no way of knowing how my referring to her as *just plain Clara* had touched a nerve. To him, it was simply appropriate under the circumstances, since Clara wasn't here as his employee. But I knew how much she'd appreciate it, especially in front of Joseph.

"Shall I make the introductions? Mr. Davis, isn't it?" Thomas did the rounds, finishing up with me.

"It's so lovely to finally meet you," I said. "I'm sorry it has to be under these circumstances."

He seemed to relax a little. "Clara said you all are trying to solve a murder?"

"Several, actually. And to prevent even more." I explained the gist of it, figuring Clara could fill in the details later.

"And you think them union types got something to do with it?" Joseph looked doubtful, and I couldn't blame him.

"Not exactly," said Thomas. "Say rather that they might be a link in the chain."

"We're grasping at straws," I admitted with an apologetic smile. "But at this point, we don't have much choice."

"Never underestimate the power of a straw," Thomas said. "It broke the camel's back, after all, and it can break the back of a case just as easily."

"I can vouch for that," Sergeant Chapman put in. "Sometimes the littlest detail is the one makes it all come clear."

Joseph still didn't look convinced, but he said, "I'll do my best."

"That's all we can ask," Thomas said, gesturing for us to sit. "Now, what can you tell us about the Knights of Labor and their offshoots?"

Joseph shrugged. "Not much. I never joined any of 'em."

"But you encountered them frequently at the ironworks, did you not?"

"I guess. They hang around outside at lunchtime or after the whistle blows. Handing out pamphlets, that sorta thing. Sometimes they make speeches. Bosses chase 'em off whenever they get the chance, but they always come back. Sort of a cat 'n' mouse thing."

"They tried to recruit you?" I asked.

"Every now and then. They make it a point with the colored boys."

Clara had mentioned that, too. "When you say *they*—do you mean the Knights specifically, or were there others?"

"Knights was the only ones approached me special, but there's other groups come around. Competitors, I guess you could call 'em."

Competitors or splinter groups? Aloud, I asked, "I don't suppose you happen to know where any of these competitors hold their meetings?"

"Nothing specific. Community halls, mostly. Churches. Some of 'em meet in some real strange places, though, 'specially if they're trying to keep the coppers off the scent. Gets to where you can make a fair guess as to how extreme they are by the sorta place they use as their meeting hall. If it's a rum shop, say, or a shuttered-up something or other, you know you got some real cranks on your hands."

Chapman was scribbling away in his ledger, but I could tell from his expression he didn't think we were getting anywhere. On the face of it, I was inclined to agree.

Thomas, though, looked thoughtful. He leaned back in his chair, fingertips pressed together, eyes narrowed. "These cranks. They were part of the reason you never joined, Miss Freeman tells us. You didn't want to be associated with fanatics."

"That's right. Fighting for an eight-hour workday is one thing. Fair wage, fair enough. But you start talking 'bout throwing off the yoke and hanging rich folks from lampposts, and that's where I get off the train." He shook his head. "Going on about how we ain't free. Seems to me these boys got no idea what it means to not be free, or what it's like to see a man hanging from a lamp-post."

Chapman glanced up from his ledger and grunted, and the two of them shared a look of understanding.

"Were there many who talked like that?" I asked.

"Not too many, I guess, but they was loud. Got people's backs up. Plenty of us worried they was gonna get us all fired."

"Clara mentioned that yesterday," I said. "That after Haymarket, when the Knights started arguing among themselves, it affected relationships at the factory."

He nodded. "We had some real dusters in the yard."

"Dusters." Thomas cocked his head. "Do you mean fistfights?"

"More like brawls. Everybody jumping in, coming to blows."

"Goodness," I said. "That sounds like a very lively workplace."

"Don't it just." Joseph smiled wryly. "Even when things stayed civil, they made quite a ruckus. Waving their pamphlets, shouting slogans. *Eat the rich. Workers Unite. Forward to Freedom.*"

"Eat the rich?" Mr. Burrows rolled his eyes. "Who comes up with these ridiculous slogans?"

"Jean-Jacques Rousseau," Edith said idly. "*Workers Unite* is paraphrased Marx, and *Forward to Freedom* is the slogan of *The Industrial Reformer.*"

Mr. Burrows glanced over at her. "The what?"

"Oh, I don't know." She made an indifferent gesture. "Some penny paper put out by the labor men. I saw it on a streetcar once."

I cut Joseph a discreet glance, but if he was offended by their casual dismissal of the labor papers, he gave no sign.

"They all got names like that," Clara said. "*The Industrial Reformer, The Radical Worker, The Workingman's Times.* Joseph used to bring 'em around now and then."

Chapman's pencil stopped abruptly. Frowning, he flipped back through his ledger. "How 'bout *The Journeyman's Journal?*"

"I guess maybe that sounds familiar," Joseph said. "Why?"

"Guess which paper our friend Jack Foster used to work at, back when he was a printer's apprentice?"

"*Hmm,*" said Thomas. "That makes sense. A paper like that is a prime place to become radicalized."

"*The Journeyman's Journal*." The name sounded familiar to me, too. "Didn't it close shop a few months ago?"

"That's right," Chapman said. "I was thinking to question some of Foster's former associates, but when I tried to look it up, the boys down at City Hall told me the paper didn't exist no more."

"Not since last spring," Edith said, "when the editor was thrown in jail."

Last spring, I thought, *when the Haymarket bombing happened, and all those splinter groups started going their own way. They'd have been looking for new homes . . .*

"Not his first stint either," Edith went on, "according to *The Sun*. He's been arrested a number of times for inciting violence, most recently in—"

"The streetcar riots," Thomas murmured. "I remember now. William Bright. There was a cartoon of him in *Harper's*, brandishing a flag and a speaking trumpet."

Chapman scowled. "Well, ain't that just grand. Nobody saw fit to mention *that* when I was asking around."

"Yes, the record-keeping of the New York City Police Department is a source of perpetual frustration to many of us," Thomas said dryly. "In any case, now that we've made the connection, do you think we might question Bright?"

"Don't see why not. If we head down there now—"

"Wait."

All eyes turned to me.

"What Mr. Davis said a minute ago, about the cranks meeting in rum shops and shuttered-up something or others. What about shuttered-up newspaper offices? The timing would be right, wouldn't it?"

"It's a thought," Chapman said, "but almost all the newspapers is headquartered down in Printing House Square."

"The major newspapers, perhaps," Thomas said, "but a small press could be housed almost anywhere."

"Not *could be*," Edith interjected excitedly. "*Were*. The cartoon you mentioned, Mr. Wiltshire, the one in *Harper's*—it depicted Bright rabble-rousing from the steps of his newspaper offices. He was jailed for inciting bystanders to blockade the tracks and throw stones at police. *On Grand Street*."

We all glanced instinctively down at the map, even though nobody needed to.

"It can't be a coincidence," Thomas said, watching as Sergeant Chapman put the tip of his pencil to Grand Street.

The sergeant grunted. "Well, I'll be damned."

The soap factory, the railroad lines, the overlapping circles—they all came together near the southern boundary of the Eighth Ward, a scant two blocks west of Grand.

"So we weren't far off at all." Thomas traced a thick, dark line along Grand Street. "Five blocks, give or take. I'd call that a viable search radius, wouldn't you, Sergeant?" He glanced up at Joseph with a smile. "What do you say to that, Mr. Davis? It looks very like a straw, don't you think?"

Joseph laughed and shook his head. "If you say so."

"You have our profound thanks."

"You're welcome, but it seems to me Miss Islington had as much to do with it as I did. That's quite a memory for details you got, ma'am."

Edith just smiled.

"And then there's these other marks," Clara said, gesturing at the map. "How'd you come by those?"

"Luck," I said, "and lots of it." She'd understand what I meant, even if Joseph didn't.

Thomas, Chapman, and I wasted no time after that, bidding

our hasty farewells and fetching our overcoats. Thomas fairly crackled with energy; I hadn't seen him this animated since the first day of the investigation. "It's exhilarating, isn't it, when everyone contributes a piece of the puzzle?"

"That's one word for it," Chapman said. "This luck business sure is something."

"I just hope it proves out," I said. "We don't have time for another dead end."

Thomas shook his head. "Not this time. We're getting close, I can feel it."

That was supposed to be comforting, I suppose, but close to Jack Foster was about the last place on earth I wanted to be. I wasn't sure which of us was the hunter anymore, and which the hunted.

I supposed we were about to find out.

CHAPTER 28

THE PRINTERS' PLOT—MR. TESLA'S
SPECTACULAR SPECTACLES—GOOD
COPPER, BAD COPPER

Sergeant Chapman didn't have an exact address for *The Journey-man's Journal*, but we didn't need one. William Bright's role in the streetcar riots had made his little paper notorious, at least to the neighborhood locals. Passersby were only too eager to point us in the right direction—and regale us with their own versions of events.

"Watched the whole thing from that window," a greengrocer said, shouting to be heard over the unholy screech of the Sixth Avenue el. "Haven't seen the likes of it since the war. Coppers marching in columns, beating back the crowd with sticks . . . I had plenty of rotting vegetables on hand, so I . . ." He trailed off awkwardly, glancing at Sergeant Chapman as if noticing his uniform for the first time.

"Anyways," Chapman said, "which one's the paper?"

Sheepishly, the man pointed. "Far end of the street. Beside the paint place."

We crossed under the looming iron latticework of the el, hurrying to avoid the coal ash drifting down as a train shuddered to a halt above us. "There's the soap factory," I said, indicating the familiar redbrick building. "And look—the paint factory." You could smell it from half a block away, acrid enough to cut through the stench of rotting meat from the slaughterhouses. *These boys reek to hell and back,* the Bloodhound had said, and she hadn't exaggerated. "I hope the rent in this neighborhood is cheap," I muttered, bringing a handkerchief to my face.

Chapman paused, eying the stoop at the far end of the block. "Best be ready for anything," he said, pulling his gun. "Hope you two came better equipped than last time. Them little one-shots ain't gonna do much good."

Thomas opened his coat to reveal a Colt .45. "We've learned from our mistakes, Sergeant."

Chapman nodded approvingly. "What about you, Miss Gallagher?"

"Mr. Wiltshire gave me this," I said, hoisting my own gun.

"Never seen one of them before."

"It's a Webley," Thomas explained. "Smaller and lighter than a Colt, but still packs plenty of firepower."

"All right, then. Let's get this over with."

We approached the building cautiously. The windows were thick with grime, making it impossible to tell what lay within. Sergeant Chapman tried the door, but it was locked, so I went to work with my lockpicking tools. Happily, there was no enchantment, and it gave way without much fuss.

Chapman went in first. Thomas and I fanned out behind him, creeping across the floorboards with our guns raised, but it didn't take long to realize we were alone. I didn't know whether to be disappointed or relieved. A little of both, maybe.

"Musta cleared out already," Chapman said, holstering his weapon.

"Or they were never here." I trailed a finger along the top of the printing press; it came away covered in dust.

"Someone was here." Thomas held up a rumpled copy of *The Radical Worker*. "Dated Thursday the twenty-first."

I found more papers scattered across a nearby desk. "This one's in German. *Freiheit*."

"Freedom," Thomas translated. "It's Johann Most's paper."

"That German anarchist fella?" Chapman's eyebrows flew up. "Ain't he the one put out that pamphlet on how to make bombs?"

"The very same."

"There are dozens of issues here," I said, holding up a thick stack of papers. "Going back at least a year."

Thomas hummed thoughtfully. "It would appear that our Mr. Bright has a mentor."

"And an apprentice," I said, "in Jack Foster."

"So it would seem. How delighted he must have been when he realized what Foster was capable of."

I took a slow turn about the room, absorbing the details. As crime scenes go, it was a lot more manageable than the Grand Opera House, and I felt almost like a real detective. "There were at least three of them," I said, examining the contents of an ashtray, "and it looks like they spent some time here."

Chapman glanced over. "Cigar nubs?"

"Three different brands, and plenty of them."

A heavy freight train rumbled down the nearby West Side line, setting the windows rattling. Something shimmied loose from the printing press and *ping*ed off the floor; investigating, I found several more loose bits beneath the machinery. "Doesn't look like the press has had much attention recently."

"There's a blackboard over here," Thomas called from the far side of the room. "Wiped down, but it's seen use."

"That could be from a ways back," Chapman said.

"I don't think so. There's chalk dust on the back of that chair, where I found the newspapers. I expect you'll find some on the papers as well."

Chapman ruffled through the pages and grunted. "Lucky guess."

Thomas lingered in front of the blackboard, as though if he stared hard enough, he might be able to make out what had once been written there. "They were planning something. I'd bet my estate on it."

The printing press was no help. The typesetting looked random to me, as if someone had been fiddling with it, and there were no scraps of paper left inside. A few copies of the *Journeyman* lay about, but they were months old. I scanned them anyway, just to be thorough, and took a glance through the rest of the newspapers, too. There was chalk dust, all right, and a few smudges of ink, and . . .

"Thomas."

I showed him what had caught my eye, and he paled.

Chapman came over. "Whaddya got?"

"An advertisement in the *Tribune,* circled in pen." I turned the paper around.

He squinted. "*Theodore Roosevelt for Mayor.* So?"

"Keep reading," Thomas said.

"*Grand ratification meeting at Cooper Union, Wednesday evening, October twenty-seventh* . . ." He trailed off. "You think they'll try to take Roosevelt right then and there? A bit public, ain't it?"

"I daresay that's the point," Thomas said. "It would certainly make a statement."

"*Propaganda of the deed*," I murmured.

"Precisely."

Chapman looked skeptical. "How will Foster get close to him in a place like that?"

"He doesn't need to," I said. "They can shoot him down from anywhere."

"That don't sound like his style."

"Not until now, perhaps," Thomas said, "but we've already surmised that he's improvising, and growing more ruthless in the bargain. Besides, if his aim is to make a show of it, gunning Roosevelt down in front of thousands of people serves his purpose far better than his usual method."

"This paper tells Foster exactly where and when to find Roosevelt," I said. "Four days from now, at Cooper Union. A public venue he can study ahead of time, and a huge crowd he can blend into on the night."

"So we tell them to call it off," Chapman said. "Or change the location."

I sighed. "Roosevelt will never agree. What was it he said to me? 'I'm not the sort of man to flinch'?"

"We have little choice but to try," Thomas said. "He'll have Sharpe's warning fresh in his ears. Perhaps that will sway him."

"Sharpe?" Chapman looked blank.

"F. Winston Sharpe. Head of the special branch. Our Inspector Byrnes, if you will. When last we spoke, he was going to try to convince Roosevelt to hire Pinkerton bodyguards. In fact . . ." Thomas consulted his watch. "He meant to take the train from Chicago if it looked as though Roosevelt wouldn't budge."

He wouldn't budge, I was sure of it. "We have to assume the event will go ahead. Which means we need a plan."

"Have you any suggestions?"

"None at all."

For a moment we just stood there, staring at one another in glum silence. But I guess when it came down to it, I wasn't one for flinching either, so I gave myself a little shake and tried to focus on our assets. "We know where William Bright is," I pointed out. "Maybe Foster has been in touch with him in prison."

"Perhaps," said Thomas, "and even if he hasn't, Bright might yet know something of use."

"We also know where and when Foster will strike, and we have four days to prepare."

"I'll take this to Byrnes," Chapman said. When I started to object, he held up a hand. "I know what you think of him, Miss Gallagher, but I promise you, he wants Foster as bad as we do. He'll have that event surrounded with coppers. 'Course"—he sighed—"that don't change the fact that there'll be thousands of people there. Finding Foster is still gonna be a needle in a haystack."

"We have the sketch Edith and I drew, and three days to have more copies made."

"That," said Thomas, "and Tesla's luck detector."

There, I wasn't so sure. "That little cigarette holder isn't nearly powerful enough. I could barely pick out someone across the room, let alone in a massive hall like Cooper Union."

"He's worked a miracle for us once already. Perhaps he has some other tricks up his sleeve." Thomas glanced at his watch again. "Half eleven already. We'll need to split up."

"I'll take our editor friend," Chapman said. "A jailhouse crawling with coppers is the last place you two need to be."

"And I'll pay a visit to Mr. Tesla," I said.

Thomas didn't like the sound of that. "Do you think it's wise for you to head back to Five Points after what happened yesterday?"

"It's not wise for either of us. And with due respect to Mr. Roosevelt and his views on women's suffrage, I expect he'll take your warnings more seriously than he would mine."

Thomas conceded the point with a sigh.

"I'll be fine," I promised. "Foster won't think to look for me in Chatham Square."

I was right about the second part, at least.

I arrived on Park Row to find it crawling with coppers. I'd given Mulberry Street a wide berth, swinging south well before Chatham Square, and that meant I had to walk past Foster's mother's flat. I'd assumed the police would be long gone—their suspect had fled two days ago, after all—but here they were, a pair of them outside the flat and another at each end of the block. Chapman was right about Byrnes: He really *did* want to catch Foster. I was glad of that, even if it meant I had to scurry along Park Row like a rat, head bowed, praying the coppers wouldn't look my way. I managed to run the gauntlet unmolested, but I certainly wouldn't be risking it a second time. I'd have to find another route out of Chatham Square.

I found Mr. Tesla hard at work, and not at all surprised to see me. "How is Mr. Wiltshire today?" he asked, ushering me inside. "He seemed almost himself when I stopped by yesterday."

As he spoke, Scarlett appeared from wherever it—she?—had been hiding, circling me briefly before alighting on the inventor's shoulder. I had the unsettling feeling it was watching me, but that was probably just my imagination. "He's very nearly recovered, thank you. You and Mr. Wang ought to consider opening your own hospital."

"Tesla and Wang's Cardiac Institute." He smiled ruefully. "If my fortunes as an inventor continue as they are, I might just consider it."

"Don't say that. You're a brilliant inventor."

"Alas, it takes more than brilliance to succeed, especially in New York."

Well, I could hardly argue with him there.

"You are here about the luck detector, I suppose? Shall I anticipate your request? You need something more powerful."

I smiled. "How did you know? Mental telegraphy?"

"Common sense. The cigarette holder will only detect your killer from a few feet away, which is too close for comfort, as the events of the past few days have demonstrated. That is why I have been working on something entirely new since Thursday. Here, try this." He handed me a pair of spectacles.

I turned them over in my hand. They didn't look like much, except that the frames were made of what seemed to be . . . "Rubber?"

"Not very elegant, but necessary for insulation. Please, try them on."

Warily, I slipped the arms behind my ears and gazed out over the lab. "What am I looking for?"

"Face me, if you please."

I turned and gasped. The inventor *glowed,* his outline haloed in a warm golden light. If he'd had a beard instead of a tidy mustache, I might have taken him for our Lord and Savior. "What am I looking at?"

"Electromagnetic radiation. Put more simply, you are looking at my luck. Now, watch." He closed his eyes, murmuring under his breath as he drew on his power. The halo began to spread, pulsing outward in waves until he was bathed in such radiance that I could barely make out his features. Even the ball of flame on his shoulder was completely eclipsed by the heavenly glow.

"It's beautiful." Maybe it was the Catholic in me, but my eyes actually misted a little.

"Visible from approximately fifty feet away. I am quite pleased with the results. Though . . ." He sighed, and the glow faded. "I do wish I could find a substitute for the minerals in the glass. The key ingredient is exceedingly rare, and unfortunately, it melts in water."

"It . . . what?" Hastily, I blinked back my tears.

"I'm afraid so. The copper vanadate dissolves into its constituent elements upon contact with water. If the lenses become wet, they will cease to function. I must ask you to be very, very careful with these, Miss Gallagher. I was fortunate to obtain a sample of the material the first time, and I have been extremely hesitant to use it, due to its rarity. If it should be lost, I shall not be able to replace it."

"But it's *October*. It rains every other day!"

"Yes. And there is another problem."

Of course there was.

"Similar to the cigarette holder, it relies on the oscillation of electrons, though in this case it is the minerals in the glass that resonate. The copper vanadate conducts energy and amplifies certain spectra of electromagnetic radiation, permitting the halo effect you see now. Unfortunately, however, the specific frequency at which it operates and the power I require to transmit that frequency over any distance . . . Even with my luck, I cannot extend its reach more than a few blocks beyond the lab."

I made a small, despairing sound. "That's an awfully big

problem, Mr. Tesla." I glanced over at the giant copper mush-room in the corner, the contraption he used to make lightning. "Can it be moved?"

His dark eyebrows flew up. "It weighs many tons, Miss Gal-lagher. It could be disassembled and reassembled, but it would take the better part of a week."

"We have until Wednesday."

He shook his head. "Impossible. I would need two days just to take it apart."

"What about building a new one?"

"From scratch? Not much faster, and we haven't the materi-als. I would need hundreds of pounds of copper wire, not to men-tion zinc . . ." He sighed in frustration. "In any case, the real issue is not generating the power, but transmitting the signal. I have been working on the principles of wireless telegraphy for several years." He tapped his head, which was apparently where the work was taking place. "The theory is sound. The problem is time. If I had just a few weeks to construct an antenna . . . Something tall enough to permit line-of-sight transmission, or even better, to reflect the signal off the atmosphere, using the sky as a sort of mirror. But in three days . . ." He shook his head.

"Can you repurpose something, the way you did the cigarette holder and the watch?"

"I considered that. In fact, would you believe, I even won-dered briefly whether I might use a building. The clock tower of the *Tribune,* for example, or Trinity Church. But of course that would not work."

"Because?"

"Because they are not made of conductive material."

"Like the silver in my bracelet," I said slowly.

"Exactly. Or the copper in my coil." He gestured at the apparatus.

"Copper, you say?" My eyes narrowed. An idea was taking shape in my head, crazy enough to give even the most eccentric inventor pause. "How about a statue?"

"I don't think you understand. The antenna needs to be a hundred feet tall. A statue that size . . . why, it would rival the Colossus of Rhodes! Such a wonder does not exist in America."

"Actually, it does. On Bedloe's Island. And it happens to be made of copper."

Mr. Tesla stared. "*Jebote.*"

"I . . . beg your pardon?"

The flame ball on his shoulder flared and sprang into the air. "Please forgive my crude manners. You mean Mr. Bartholdi's statue, yes? Liberty?" He rushed to his desk and began furiously scribbling. In the time it took me to cross the room, he'd already drawn a rough outline of the great lady's torch, to which he was adding a series of T-shapes and what looked like giant saucers. "I station myself here, with a spark-gap oscillator. The power flows into the parabolic reflectors . . ."

"You'll be able to reach Cooper Union with this?"

He looked up, his blue-gray eyes glinting with excitement. "With a few minor modifications, I can reach anywhere in the city. I just need a few days, a little assistance, and . . ." He paused, wincing. "Permission."

"I'll figure it out," I said with a confidence I didn't feel.

When he'd finished working out the plans, he drew up a list of the materials we would need. "It will be expensive," he warned.

I assured him that wouldn't be an issue either. Probably.

"Excellent." He tore the list in two and handed me the

bottom half. "We need the items on this list by tomorrow morning if I am to have any chance of constructing the transmitter in
time."

Scanning the list brought a fresh pang of worry. "It's going
to be a trick getting all this together by tomorrow."

"Indeed, but if we begin immediately, it ought to be possible. Just."

"In that case, I'd better hurry. I'll start at the hardware store
up the road." I gave back the precious spectacles and stuffed the
list into my overcoat pocket. "See you in a short while," I promised.

I never made it.

I'd scarcely gone a block before a familiar figure strode into
view, flanked by a pair of underlings. He loomed over me, mustache crooked, beady eyes narrowed in triumph.

"Afternoon, Miss Gallagher," said Chief Inspector Byrnes.

CHAPTER 29

THE LAST BOAT RIDE YOU'LL EVER TAKE
—THE UNLIKELY SPY—RECKONING

ell, well," said Thomas Byrnes. "The Good Lord is smiling on me today. I could hardly believe it when the boys wired me to say you'd been spotted on Park Row. She wouldn't have the sand to come back down here, I said to myself. But here you are."

They'd noticed me after all, the coppers outside Mrs. Foster's flat. It was the only explanation.

"Inspector." I looked him square in the eye, trying to project calm. "I think you'll be very interested to hear what we—"

He jabbed a finger into my shoulder, hard. "I had him. At the hotel, dead to rights. Trap nicely laid. Only you spring it before it's ready, and he's away like a shot. Then, before I can finish interrogating his mates, you bungle it again, charging into that flat like George bloody Custer. No preparation. Not a word to the police. And surprise, surprise, he's in the wind again. Next I hear there's been a shoot-out on Mulberry Street, women and children scattering every which way, and a girl answering your description at the heart of it." He leaned in so close that I could smell the cigars on his breath. "That's quite enough out of you, Miss Gallagher."

Strong hands seized me on either side, hoisting me toward a police wagon at the curb. "The ledger!" I cried. "The papers will have it if you don't let me go!"

Byrnes sneered, showing tobacco-stained teeth. "Do what you like with that ledger. Price'll deny everything. It's not written in his hand, so you can't prove it's his."

Even if I could, I'd hardly be the first to accuse Inspector Byrnes of corruption. It had been a feeble threat all along, especially now that he'd had time to think about it.

"Don't do this," I said, hating how high and thin my voice sounded. "You don't have to do this!"

"Did you think I was bluffing, girl? I warned you what would happen if you made a nuisance of yourself. A visit to Blackwell's Island will keep you out from underfoot."

I went limp, as if someone had reached down my throat and dragged out my bones. There was a roaring in my ears so loud that I could barely make out Byrnes's next words.

"Make sure they put her on the boat tonight. And no one breathes a word of this. I'll not have Bill Chapman in my office whinging about his pet Pinkerton."

They threw me into the back of the wagon and barred the door, and before I could even brace myself, we were bouncing uptown toward Misery Lane.

What followed will be with me for the rest of my days. Even

now, when I think back on it, the bile rises in my throat and a tremble sets into my hands. I don't recall the details of those first couple of hours, which is probably a mercy, except that I was dragged to the insane pavilion of Bellevue Hospital by an endless procession of rough hands, each one belonging to a rough voice that promised to be even rougher if I resisted. My first real memory, sharp as a razor, is of being told it was my turn to see the doctor. Yet another pair of brutish hands seized me, and the force of it shocked me out of my stupor.

"I don't need to see a doctor," I told the attendant who'd grabbed me. "I'm not sick."

He ignored me, marching me into a small office and throwing me into a chair across from a middle-aged man. They didn't even bother to close the door for a little privacy. The doctor just looked me up and down and said, "Name."

"Rose Gallagher, and I'm not insane."

He wrote that in a book.

"Stick out your tongue."

"I . . . what?"

The doctor's gaze hardened. "Tongue. Out."

I stuck out my tongue, and he wrote something in his book. "Age?"

"Twenty."

"Are you employed?"

"Yes, by the Pinkerton National Detective Agency. Who will certainly come looking for me," I added loudly, "when they realize I'm being held against my will."

The doctor's mouth pressed into a thin line, and something almost like pity came into his eyes. *He doesn't believe you.* And to think—I hadn't even got to the part about hunting dead people.

"This is all a terrible mistake. I'm only here because the chief of detectives has it in for me, but all I'm trying to do is prevent the assassination of Theodore Roosevelt." Dear Lord, I was only making it worse. I drew a steadying breath. "Please, if you could just contact Mr. Thomas Wiltshire or Mr. Jonathan Burrows or . . ."

The doctor's pen just scratched faster. Then, without looking up, he said, "Good afternoon, Miss Gallagher."

"Wait, is that all? How can you possibly tell whether I'm—" The attendant hauled me up, and I was deposited back on a bench in the long white hallway.

I fought to keep calm as I scanned my surroundings. I could try to make a run for it, but I wouldn't get very far. The entrance was blocked by a pair of coppers, the rear by a heavy iron door fastened with a padlock. In between, an endless row of doors stood closed.

You can handle this, I told myself. *It's just an ordinary hospital.* And when I stole a glance at the other women they'd brought in that afternoon, they looked rational enough. Certainly they bore no resemblance to the wild-eyed creatures I'd seen in *Frank Leslie's.*

Thomas will come for you. All you have to do is stay strong until then.

But until when, exactly? Nobody knew where I was; Byrnes had made sure of that. Thomas wouldn't even realize anything was wrong until this evening, when I failed to turn up at Mr. Burrows's. How long would it take him to work out what had happened? *Not before it's too late,* a poisonous voice inside me whispered. *For Roosevelt, and for you.* Without the items I'd promised, Mr. Tesla wouldn't be able to construct his transmitter in time. Thomas would be frantic looking for me, distracting him from the case. All the while, I'd be shut away in the most horrible place in America, fighting to keep from actually going insane.

Who will take care of Mam? She was safe for now, in a hotel with Pietro, but they only had enough money for a few nights. It would run out eventually, and Pietro wouldn't know where to find Thomas, and . . .

"Stop it," I whispered aloud. "This isn't helping."

"Best not be talking to yourself, dearie," said a kind voice, and I looked up to find an Irishwoman about Mam's age leaning on a mop. "If you want to get out of here, that is."

I tried for a smile. "You're probably right."

She considered me with a tilt of her head. "You don't look mad to me."

"Would you mind telling that to the doctor?"

"Oh, aye, and he'd listen to me." She was still giving me that curious look. "Is it true what you said in there? Are you really a Pinkerton?"

"Yes, I really am. And they really will come for me." *Thomas will come for me.* I clung to that with everything I had.

"Well, they'd best be quick about it, because once you get on that boat, I don't care if Grover Cleveland himself comes looking for you, he won't find you. Not if *they* don't want you to be found."

"What do you mean?"

Glancing up and down the hallway, she lowered her voice. "There's plenty as use Blackwell's Island for their personal lockup. Buy one-way tickets for their wives or mistresses, or the sick or elderly they don't want nothing more to do with."

"The coppers use it that way, too, apparently," I said bitterly.

"And politicians and all."

I felt ill, and not just for myself. I could only imagine how many poor souls had been locked up purely for being inconvenient. "How do they get away with it?"

"There's enough doctors and nurses only too happy for the coin, and the patients . . . Well, nobody listens to a lunatic, do they?"

Voices sounded at the end of the hallway. A phalanx of white-capped nurses was making its way toward us, looking grim and determined.

"Take my advice, dearie," said the maid, with a hasty pretense at mopping, "if you mean to get outta here, do it tonight. 'Cause if they put you on that ferry, it'll be the last boat ride you ever take."

"Can you help me? If you could just get a message to Mr. Thomas—"

But she was already gone, leaving me and the other patients in the care of the army of nurses.

"This way," said a huge woman. She looked to be the head nurse, judging from the bundle of keys dangling from her apron. "Get up, all of you. No talking."

They led us into a corridor so damp and drafty that the cold seemed to reach out from the stone walls in thick, grasping fingers. We were marched to a bathroom and told to undress. The first woman to refuse was clobbered on the ear, so the rest of us did as we were told. Then, one after another, we were thrown into an ice-cold bath, scrubbed raw with a filthy rag, and half drowned under bucketful after bucketful of frigid water. By this point I was gasping and shivering so badly that I could hardly stand, so they dragged me out of the bath and shoved a flannel slip into my hands.

"Put this on."

"But I'm soaking—"

A nurse grabbed my arms, and a second yanked the slip over my head. My eyes fell to the black letters across the bottom: LU-NATIC PAVILION, BELLEVUE HOSPITAL.

I burst into tears.

They took my hairpin, the beautiful jade rose Thomas had given me. I fought like a banshee when they did that, but there were three of them, and I was cuffed into submission. They dragged a comb through my hair and cut my already-torn fingernails down until they bled. Then I was shoved into a tiny cell and left to sink down onto my cot, damp and bleeding, ears ringing with the warning of the Irish maid.

It was hard to tell how much time had passed since I'd got here, but it had to be at least two o'clock. The boat came at five. If I didn't find a way out before then . . .

It'll be the last boat ride you ever take.

They came for us an hour later.

"Here," said a nurse, tossing a pile of stained clothing at my feet. This time I didn't hesitate, only too happy to peel off the still-sodden slip they'd put me in after my "bath." My relief was short-lived, however, for no sooner had they given us lukewarm tea than they propelled us out onto the lawn to *take the air*—by which they might as well have meant *take a shower*, since a steady drizzle fell from the sky. Within minutes, I was damp and shivering all over again. But that was nothing compared to the fear coiling around me like an ever-tightening noose. Time was bleeding away, and with it my chances of escape.

"God help us," a young woman muttered beside me. "Do they mean for us to die of fever? Last time they gave us proper hats, at least."

"You've been here before?" *And survived?* I kept that last part to myself.

"My brothers sent me here last year, when I was suffering from a nervous debility. I came of my own free will, tricked into thinking this was a place for convalescing. It was nothing of the kind, of course, but then I played a trick on *them* by convalescing just the same." She smiled sadly. "But I don't know if I can perform the trick again. And if they put me on the boat, I don't suppose I'll ever get back."

"You don't seem very sick to me, if you don't mind me saying so. In fact, I don't think I've seen a truly insane person since I got here."

"The worst ones get sent to the island straightaway. Too dangerous to mix with the rest of us. They go to the Lodge or get put on the rope."

"On the rope?"

"Chained up around the waist, all of them in a long line. Quite a sight, they say."

I shuddered. "How do you know all this?"

"Spend a few nights here and you learn all sorts of things." Her eyes shifted to me, pale blue and bloodshot. "They'll beat us out there, you know. Everyone says so."

The words sank into me like cold claws. I lowered myself onto a bench, and for a moment I just sat there, staring vacantly across the yard. Then I spied the head nurse, and something hardened in the pit of my stomach. If I could just get those keys off her somehow . . .

I have no idea what my plan would have been, but I never got the chance to find out. A pair of coppers appeared in the yard, making their way toward me in determined strides. My companion beat a hasty retreat. The head nurse, meanwhile, joined the coppers in front of my bench. "It's come to my attention that you've got a case of lice, so we'll be needing to take that hair of yours. All of it."

My stomach dropped. "I don't have lice," I whispered. "And you know it."

She leaned in, hands propped on her thighs, until her face was inches from mine. "What I know is that I've special instructions in your case, just to make sure you learn your lesson." And before I could say another word, the coppers were dragging me across the yard, back to the long hallway and the bathroom. I struggled, kicking and cursing a streak so foul that even Pietro would have blushed, but they just laughed. Their fingers dug painfully into my flesh, and they twisted my arms behind my back until I squawked. "We'll start with these," the head nurse said, brandishing a pair of scissors. "After that, it's the razor."

Then a voice said, "Stop."

Everyone froze. A doctor stood in the doorway.

The nurse frowned, miffed at having her fun interrupted. "We had instructions—"

"Yes, well, now we have new instructions," the doctor said impatiently. "She's to be discharged immediately."

Color flooded the nurse's cheeks, but there wasn't much she could say to that, so she dropped the scissors noisily into the sink and flounced off. The coppers followed, and a moment later I was alone.

I sank to the tiled floor, shaking, and there I stayed for heaven knows how long.

When my legs were steady enough to carry me, I made my way down the hall, head spinning. *Thomas must have found a way. Or Sergeant Chapman.* But the figure waiting at the end of the hallway wasn't either of those. At first I didn't recognize him, but then he turned, and my mouth fell open.

"Ah," said F. Winston Sharpe, "here she is."

At first I was too stunned to speak. I'd sooner have thought to be rescued by St. Patrick himself than the head of the special branch. "H-how did you . . . ?"

"The Agency is everywhere, Miss Gallagher," he said gravely. "Are you hurt?"

"They stole her hairpin," put in a familiar voice, and I noticed the Irish maid leaning on her mop a few feet away.

"We'll have that sorted. Thank you, Mary."

"Don't mention it, boss." She winked at me and shuffled off, waving her mop across the floor as she went.

I gaped in astonishment. "Her?"

"The special branch keeps careful watch on insane asylums," Mr. Sharpe explained, lowering his ponderous girth onto a bench. "We've at least one Mary in every hospital in the country, keeping their ears pricked for reports of ghosts and magic and so on. There's no better way to keep abreast of paranormal phenomena."

"I thought you were on the train from Chicago."

"And so I was. Modern technology is a miracle, isn't it? A few clicks on the wires and word of your predicament travels instantaneously to Chicago, only to be flung straight back to New York, so that by the time I step out of my carriage at Grand Central Depot, *voilà*." He drew his lapel aside to reveal a telegram in his pocket. "You're too young to remember a time when that wasn't possible, but a fellow my age still marvels at it." He paused, peering up at me. "Perhaps you ought to sit, my dear. If you'll forgive me for saying so, you look like you've been hog-tied and dragged behind a stagecoach."

"I just want to get out of here."

"Of course, but I thought perhaps you'd like to depart in your own clothing, rather than . . ." He arched an eyebrow at my dress, with the words *lunatic asylum* stamped on the hem. "You can change just in there," he said, pointing with his walking stick. "I'll have your hairpin sent in as well."

He was as good as his word, and a few minutes later I emerged, bedraggled but more or less myself, my precious hairpin back where it belonged.

"Shall we?" Mr. Sharpe stood—and went rigid as I threw my arms around him.

"Thank you," I whispered, fighting back tears.

He patted my back awkwardly. "There, there."

Just then, the doors banged open to reveal the furious figure of Thomas F. Byrnes. One of the coppers who'd dragged me from the yard pointed in my direction, and Byrnes stormed down the hall toward us. "What's the meaning of this?" he roared at no one in particular. "I left clear instructions that this woman was to be—"

"Calm yourself, Inspector," said F. Winston Sharpe. "You'll burst something."

Byrnes strode right up to him, taking full advantage of his size to loom over Mr. Sharpe. "I don't know who you are, old man—"

"Old? Why, I'm barely sixty. As to who I am . . ." Calmly, he produced a silver card and handed it over. It was identical to the cards we agents carried, save that it actually had his name printed on it.

A name that clearly meant something to Inspector Byrnes. The blood drained from his face, and when he glanced up, there was genuine fear in his eyes.

If I live to be a hundred, I don't think I'll ever behold a more satisfying sight.

"It's fortunate we've run into each other, Inspector," Mr.

Sharpe said. "Now I can tell you in person that if you ever lay a finger on one of my agents again, there will be a reckoning such as even a malignant brute like you cannot conceive. Good day."

As we walked away, the only sound was the *tap-tap-tap* of F. Winston Sharpe's walking stick along the cold stone floor.

CHAPTER 30

THE SPECTACLES AND THE STATUE—
A MACHIAVELLIAN MACHINE—FRESH
EYES—A VERY BAD FEELING

do hope there won't be drama," said Mr. Sharpe as the carriage trundled up Fifth Avenue.

"Drama?"

"I despatched a messenger to the Burrows residence with word of your situation. I was concerned that Wiltshire might have the news from Chicago directly, and I wanted to ensure he'd stay well clear of the hospital. He's an admirably restrained fellow on the whole, but I expect he'll have taken the news rather badly, and even I would have trouble smoothing over the murder of a police inspector."

I gave a strained laugh. "Mr. Wiltshire would never do a thing like that."

"*Hrmm,*" said Mr. Sharpe.

It was already dark by the time we arrived at Mr. Burrows's

house. Thomas rushed into the foyer, but the sight of F. Winston Sharpe drew him up short; he froze, fingers twitching at his sides. "Miss Gallagher," he said stiffly. "Are you all right?"

"Yes, thanks to Mr. Sharpe."

Thomas flinched and glanced away.

"No, I didn't mean—"

"It's over now, and no harm done." Mr. Sharpe handed his overcoat to the butler. "Miss Gallagher had a firsthand view of our operations at Bellevue Hospital, that's all."

That was hardly *all*, but I didn't want to think any more about it, at least not now. So when Mr. Sharpe suggested we get right down to a briefing, I was only too happy to oblige.

"Mr. Burrows has kindly offered the use of his study," Thomas said with a curt gesture toward the stairs. He stood aside for us, and I brushed his hand discreetly as I passed. I wanted him to know that I didn't blame him in the least, and I think he appreciated it, because he relaxed a little after that.

We called for tea, and I poured out cup after gloriously steaming cup while Thomas brought Mr. Sharpe up to date on the latest developments.

"Sergeant Chapman didn't get anything useful from the newspaper editor. He'll keep trying, but my guess is that whatever role Bright might have played in hatching the plot, he has no idea where Foster is now. For my part, I spoke to Roosevelt this afternoon, but as we anticipated, neither he nor the party leaders were the least bit interested in changing their plans. The rally at Cooper Union will go forward."

Mr. Sharpe grunted. "Roosevelt will have an agent beside him whether he likes it or not. I've seen to it."

"Oh?"

"With his schedule, it wasn't difficult to persuade his aides that a new stenographer would lighten their burden. Miss Fox will take up her duties tomorrow."

I nearly groaned aloud. After putting up with Ava Hendriks for the past week, now I had Viola Fox to contend with. As stressful as the past few days had been, at least I'd been free of Miss Fox's sniping, her constant reminders of my inadequacies as an agent. Apparently that reprieve was at an end.

"Has the War Department agreed to cover the fee for an additional agent?" Thomas asked.

"They have. Besides, I'd be willing to throw in Miss Fox for free. Theodore Roosevelt has a bright future in politics. Having him indebted to the Agency could come in quite handy someday."

"Ah," Thomas said, and sipped his tea.

"And what about you, Miss Gallagher?" Mr. Sharpe asked. "How did you get on?"

You mean before I was thrown in the cranky-hutch? Somehow, I managed to keep that to myself. "Mr. Tesla had a wonderful idea, but . . ." I trailed off with a gasp. In all the turmoil, I'd forgotten about the inventor's list. "What'll we do now? We'll never get everything together in time!"

"Slow down," Thomas said gently. "Get what together in time?"

I fetched the list from my overcoat pocket and showed it to him. "I promised to help gather these things by tomorrow morning. Mr. Tesla needs them to build a wireless transmitter, but it will take him at least three days to put it together. Where on earth are we going to find that much copper wire, to say nothing of . . . whatever *this* is?"

Thomas glanced over the list. "We'll find a way."

"How? We can't be in five places at once."

"Not alone, perhaps, but we have friends we may call upon. Jackson will help, and Wang. It won't be easy, but we'll manage."

I nodded, relaxing a little. Though it was sometimes easy to forget, we weren't alone. We had allies, and plenty of them.

"What is this transmitter for?" asked Mr. Sharpe.

I explained about the spectacles. "If it all works as it should, we ought to be able to pick out every lucky person in the place. And with the open design of that hall, there's nowhere for Foster to hide."

"I wouldn't be so sure about that, Miss Gallagher."

"It sounds as though you know something we don't," Thomas said.

"There is what I know, and what I suspect." Mr. Sharpe sank into the depths of his chair, folding his hands over the broad expanse of his waistcoat. "This race is being watched very closely, the more so now that there are whispers of a plot against Roosevelt's life. The young man is well liked, but it was never intended that he should win. His patrons merely thought to have a few thousand votes to trade on election day. As for the Democrats, he makes a convenient foe. Credible, but not quite electable, making Hewitt the logical choice for moderate voters terrified at the prospect of a Labor administration."

Thomas hummed thoughtfully. "An assassination would disrupt that calculus."

"The rumor alone has done that. Now the Democrats fear a sympathy vote for the Republicans—hence Tammany's frantic efforts to keep what happened at the convention quiet."

"Efforts funded by Andrew Price," I put in.

"Indeed. And I'm told he promised Byrnes a considerable bonus for the successful capture of Foster, which might explain the good inspector's irritation with the two of you."

"Miss Gallagher and I had already surmised that the Democrats had no interest in seeing Roosevelt harmed," Thomas said. "The same logic would apply to the Labor party, presumably."

Mr. Sharpe nodded. "The labor movement would certainly be blamed, playing into the hands of those who would brand them dangerous radicals. And here we come to the point. The transition, as it were, between what I *know* and what I merely *suspect*. The Republican machine has no love for Theodore Roosevelt. Their motivations in putting him forward were certainly cynical. The question is, how far would they go?"

I stared at him, aghast. "You think Roosevelt's own party is behind this?"

"Not the party as such, no. But certain powerful figures within it? Why not? Politics is a dirty business, Miss Gallagher."

"Even so . . . do you really think they would be capable of something so awful?"

He shrugged. "Perhaps they merely saw advantage in allowing the plot to unfold, knowing it would undermine support for their rivals."

"Whoever is behind it," Thomas said, "they'll have had no difficulty identifying eager foot soldiers. Men like William Bright and Johann Most who splash their radical views all over their newspapers."

"Anarchists working for the evil capitalists?" I was skeptical, to say the least.

"They might not even be aware of it," Thomas said. "Perhaps Foster is merely—what was it you called it? A gull?"

"In which case they can't control him."

"A rabid dog off the leash, then," Mr. Sharpe said. "Or perhaps I'm the one being cynical, and the conspiracy goes no deeper than Foster and his accomplices. Regardless, they must be stopped."

"Which brings us back to the event at Cooper Union," I said. "Even if we somehow manage to get the spectacles working, there'll be no shortage of lucky people in that hall."

"We'll need as many eyes as we can get," Thomas said. "Sergeant Chapman is having our sketch duplicated, but I doubt the party or the police will be eager to have too many officers inside the hall. It will raise questions in the press, and they don't want that."

"We can't rely on them anyway," I said. "Byrnes is working for Tammany, but who knows about the rank and file?"

"Agreed. We'll need to bring some foot soldiers of our own, people we can trust."

Mr. Sharpe grunted. "Jackson and Miss Fox are the only other agents in the city. Aside from myself, of course."

"Burrows will help," Thomas said.

"And Miss Islington. She's"—I glanced at Mr. Sharpe—"very observant."

"Excellent." Mr. Sharpe started to rise. "That's settled, then."

"Er, not quite." I smiled awkwardly. "There's still the matter of Mr. Tesla's wireless transmitter."

Mr. Sharpe flicked an eyebrow. "Are you asking me to help you build this contraption?"

"Not exactly. You see, the transmitter has to be stationed on something very tall, and . . . well, we agreed that the best thing to do would be to mount it on . . ." I cleared my throat. "The Statue of Liberty."

F. Winston Sharpe blinked. "I beg your pardon?"

"Mr. Bartholdi's statue. On Bedloe's Island."

"My dear child, I know what the Statue of Liberty is. But what the deuce do you need it for?"

A slow smile spread across Thomas's face. "Because it's made of copper." He shook his head, still grinning. "Brilliant. But how will the signal reach Cooper Union?"

"Mr. Tesla plans to use the sky as a mirror."

"Ah," he said, as if this made perfect sense.

"The trouble is, I don't know how we'll get anywhere near it. The statue, I mean. The unveiling ceremony is on Thursday, and I'm sure they're in a desperate rush to have everything ready in time."

"Leave that to me," Mr. Sharpe said with a dismissive gesture.

Just like that. All I can say is that it must be terribly convenient to be in charge of the special branch of the Pinkerton National Detective Agency.

"If there's nothing else . . ." Mr. Sharpe levered himself up with the aid of his walking stick. "You two should head home and get some rest. It sounds as though you have a very busy few days ahead of you."

Thomas saw him out, and when he returned, he closed the door of the study behind him. "What happened to you today," he said quietly. "I'm so sorry, Rose."

"You couldn't have known."

"Your dread of that place . . . It must have been a waking nightmare."

I shivered at the memory. "To think I actually believed they could help people like my mother. And that was just Bellevue! Imagine what it's like once you get to the island."

"Thank God we have assets in the hospital."

The words rekindled a smoldering anger I'd been nursing

since the ride home. "But what good are they? The Agency stepped in to help me, but I'm one of their own. What about ordinary people like Mam? The ones who really do see ghosts or some other supernatural thing? We just leave them to their fates? Report back to the Agency and"—I dusted my hands—"job well done?"

"But what can we do? The Pinkertons can't possibly screen every incoming patient to see whose story might be genuine."

"Maybe not, but we could post a medium at Bellevue. That way, if someone really did have a shade or a ghost attached to them, we'd know it, and we could intervene. It'd be a start, anyway."

"It's an interesting idea, but even if we could find someone to take up such a post . . . It's only one hospital, Rose."

"So because we can't help everyone, we shouldn't help anyone?"

He considered that. "You're right. That's terrible logic, isn't it? You ought to take it up with Sharpe."

"Me?"

"I'll support you, of course, but the idea is yours. You should be the one to put it forward." He paused, the slow smile returning. "The statue was your idea, too, wasn't it?"

I blushed and glanced away.

"I thought so. It has all the hallmarks of Rose Gallagher. It's one of the things I admire most about you."

"Harebrained schemes?"

"Innovation and resourcefulness. You see the world with fresh eyes, Rose. It's . . ." He trailed off, and there was something in his eyes that sent a warm shiver down my spine. "Well, it's quite wonderful." He cleared his throat. "Now then, we'd better get on. It certainly does sound as though we have a whirlwind ahead of us."

That was one word for it. We had less than seventy-two hours to procure hundreds of pounds of materials, build a wireless transmitter, and affix it to a hundred-and-fifty-foot statue.

That, and stop a killer.

If someone had asked me before that Wednesday if I was afraid of heights, I'd have laughed. After all, hadn't I managed to climb down from a third-story window—in the dark, I might add, in a *dress*—without panicking? And yet as I stood on the narrow platform of Liberty's torch on that cold October day, I felt as though my knees were made of pudding. My head was a spinning top, my stomach a jar of moths. Only a narrow rail stood between me and the sky. A hundred and thirty-odd feet below, the electric lights that would illuminate the statue were as small as the diamonds in my brooch.

"Are you all right, Miss Gallagher?" Mr. Tesla regarded me kindly, the wind tousling his hair into little raven feathers. "You look a bit green."

"I'm sorry. I'm trying to help, really, but . . ." I glanced down again and swallowed.

"But you have a very bad feeling. No need to apologize. It is a perfectly natural reaction of the body. It knows that a fall from this height would pulverize it beyond recognition."

With these words of comfort, he went back to work.

Focus on the antenna, Rose. Turning my back on the sickening sight below, I surveyed our progress—which is to say, the progress of Messrs. Tesla, Wiltshire, and Jackson, since I'd been all but immobilized with dread since we got up here. They'd managed to affix two of the saucers already, and were now working on a third. The final one would involve Mr. Tesla standing on that thin copper rail (with a rope tied about his waist, but still) so that he could reach the very top of the torch. I had already made up my mind to wait that part out down below, since I couldn't bear to watch.

"What do you say, Tesla?" Thomas handed him another loop of wire. "Will we finish before dark?"

"I hope so, since I have yet to configure the spark-gap oscillator. We are nearing the wire now, that's for sure." The inventor smiled, pleased with his pun.

After the delay at Bellevue Hospital, we'd needed all hands on deck to gather the materials in time. The Wangs had helped, and Mr. Burrows, and even Sergeant Chapman. Mr. Tesla, meanwhile, had worked day and night to get the various components ready for today's installation. We might finish before dark, but there would be no time to make adjustments. Anything less than perfection and we would fail.

"If this works," Mr. Jackson said, "it will be two major scientific breakthroughs in one." He paused to tighten a screw in the coupling he was working on, giving it an experimental tug to make sure it would hold. "The wireless telegraphy especially . . . Why, the applications are almost limitless."

The inventor made a dismissive gesture. "The theory has been widely discussed for years. Half a dozen inventors of my acquaintance are working on it. The spectacles, however . . . *they* are a true original. They will help you find your killer, I'm certain of it."

Please, Lord, let it be so. Though I couldn't put my finger on it, something had been gnawing at me since the newspaper office yesterday. Was it just nerves? A "perfectly natural reaction" to the fact that I was about to face off against an assassin? Or did some part of me recognize a danger my mind had yet to fully grasp?

Unwittingly, I glanced over my shoulder at the hundred-and-thirty-foot drop to the island below. My stomach flipped all over again, and a shudder ran down my spine.

It was a very bad feeling indeed.

CHAPTER 31

MISS FOX SHOWS HER FANGS—A
GLITTERING ASSEMBLY—COMING
TO A BOIL

The atmosphere at Cooper Union that evening did nothing to soothe my nerves. Bonfires blazed outside the hall, staining the bricks a bloody crimson and throwing furtive, shifting shadows along the archways. Rockets hissed into the sky and exploded in showers of sparks, each one sounding like a gunshot to my ears. Even the sky looked ominous, low and heavy, with a rumble of thunder in the distance.

And the crowds. They just kept coming, in wave after endless wave, drawn by the fireworks and the glow of the bonfires, teeming along the avenues on either side of the hall. They felt oppressive, swarming around our little group as we huddled under a tree in the square.

There were ten of us in all: five Pinkertons, four civilians, and a copper. Mr. Sharpe, Mr. Jackson, and Viola Fox were already inside, searching every nook and cranny for anything suspicious. Sergeant Chapman stood with his fellow officers near the doors. That left Edith and Mr. Burrows, Clara and Joseph, and Thomas and me to keep an eye on things outside. Clara and her fiancé had been a surprise, and I almost refused their help, but that would have been foolish. They weren't likely to be in any real danger, and we needed every pair of eyes we could get. Besides, when Clara had pointed out that she and Joseph had a part in this now, too, I couldn't argue. If it hadn't been for them, we would never have known that Foster and his accomplices planned to strike tonight.

Thomas and I had been here since dusk, blending in among the students while we kept an eye on the comings and goings. But as the hour drew near for Mr. Roosevelt to take the stage, it was time to put the rest of our pieces in play.

"Does everyone have their copy of the sketch?" I asked, raising my voice to be heard over the pop of rockets and the excited babble of the crowd.

Nods all around—except Clara, who was giving me a funny look.

"What?"

"Sorry. Just a little distracted by *those*." She gestured at the spectacles perched on my nose.

"You and me both." I couldn't stop staring at Edith and Mr. Burrows, mesmerized by the glow given off by their luck. Edith, especially, whose luck was never really off, burned so brightly in Mr. Tesla's spectacles that I had to peer over the tops of the lenses just to make out her features.

"We oughta split up," Joseph suggested. "Clara and me can take Fourth Avenue."

"Splendid," Thomas said. "Rose and I will take the rear of the building. Better if we're not too visible, since Foster knows what we look like."

"I'll take Third Avenue," Mr. Burrows said.

Edith flashed a tense smile. "Well, I guess that leaves little old me to watch the front."

"It's probably for the best," I said apologetically. "You're more likely than any of us to pick him out."

"And if I do? Shall we tell the police?" She inclined her head at the row of coppers lining the front entrance. Inspector Byrnes was among them, growling out orders and doing his best to look important. I was fairly certain he'd seen us, but he pretended he hadn't, which suited me just fine.

"I don't think so," Thomas said. "We don't know how deep this conspiracy runs, which means we don't know whom to trust. If you spot Foster or anyone else who looks suspicious, do not on any account attempt to confront him. Find Rose and me at the back of the building, and let us take care of the rest." He took out his watch. "Half six. Let's reconvene by the doors in half an hour."

Our friends headed off to take up their posts. Thomas and I were about to do the same when I spied F. Winston Sharpe heading toward us, Viola Fox in tow.

Wonderful. I'd managed to avoid Miss Fox for the past few days while she posed as Mr. Roosevelt's stenographer, but I guess all good things come to an end.

She was still using her cover, obviously; she wore modest, businesslike attire, and her dark hair was pulled back in a severe chignon. As for Mr. Sharpe, he glowed nearly as brightly as Edith. I knew he was lucky, though what his particular gift might be, I'd never had the courage to ask.

"Miss Fox," Thomas said, inclining his head. "Good to see you as always."

"And you, Mr. Wiltshire." Then she turned to me with a coolly appended "Miss Gallagher."

"Jackson is keeping an eye on things inside," Mr. Sharpe said. "We inspected every office and lecture hall and found nothing amiss. What about you two?"

"Nothing to report," Thomas said. "Miss Gallagher has picked out a handful of lucky individuals, but most of them were known to us. Senior figures in the party and so forth."

Miss Fox gave me a dismissive glance. "I wonder that you would delegate such an important task, Mr. Wiltshire. As the senior agent, shouldn't the use of those remarkable spectacles fall to you?"

"Miss Gallagher has my absolute confidence," Thomas replied. "Moreover, it seems only fitting, given her role in helping Mr. Tesla work out how to power the instrument from afar." He gestured vaguely in the direction of Bedloe's Island, where Mr. Tesla perched atop Liberty's torch with his transmitter, sending wireless energy out into the night. Thinking of the inventor, I felt a pang of guilt, imagining how damp and cold he must be up there.

And speaking of cold, Miss Fox looked me over again and said, "I'm sure you're right. Besides, with Miss Gallagher acting as the scout, that leaves someone capable to do the actual apprehending."

Heat flashed to my cheeks. Thomas started to reply, but Mr. Sharpe interrupted him, nodding at a silver-haired gentleman near the doors. "Look, there's Acton. He'll be chairing the meeting. Come, Wiltshire, the two of you ought to meet."

I don't know if it was my frazzled nerves or the fact that my

training at Newport was almost certainly over with, but in that
moment, I didn't care that Viola Fox was the senior agent. The moment Mr. Sharpe was out of earshot, I confronted her. "What exactly have I done to offend you, Miss Fox?"

"Do you really wish to know, Miss Gallagher?"

The way she was looking at me, I wasn't at all sure that I did,
but I couldn't very well back down now. I lifted my chin defiantly.

"Very well, I'll tell you. That you were offered a position in
the special branch, despite being a complete neophyte in all things
paranormal, is galling enough. But what I find truly intolerable
is that you have usurped the place of better agents as Mr. Wiltshire's partner."

"What do you mean, *usurped*?"

"There were half a dozen seasoned agents who would happily
have stepped into that role. Who *deserved* that role, by virtue of
their competence and experience. None more so than me. Have
you any idea what it was like being the first female agent of the
special branch? I had to work twice as hard just to be taken seriously by my male colleagues. And then you come along and undo
it all with one flutter of your eyelashes."

I stared at her, baffled. "What are you talking about?"

"Even now, there are those in the special branch who dismiss
female agents as mere novelties. They suppose we were hired for
the basest of reasons. And now you've proved them right, swooping into a plum role without any qualifications beyond a pretty face.
I'd have thought Mr. Wiltshire above such things, but apparently
not. Men will be men, after all." And with that, she turned on her
heel and walked away.

I felt sick. *Is that what they're saying? That I seduced my way into
the special branch?* Could they really think so little of me? So little
of Thomas?

It was absurd, of course, but that was no consolation. Whether it was true or not, if my fellow agents thought I hadn't earned my place, that I didn't deserve it . . .

"Enough," I growled. "You have work to do." Drawing a deep breath, I headed for my post at the back of the building. I'd have time to process Viola Fox's accusations later. Right now I had bigger worries.

Thomas joined me a few minutes later, and we spent the next half hour scanning the crowd, for all the good it did us. I didn't spot a single golden halo, and as for the ordinary people, every face looked as suspicious as every other. Then we heard the muted notes of a brass band filtering through the windows and we knew it was time to head inside.

"You don't suppose he could have slipped by us, do you?" I asked as we made our way to the front of the building.

Thomas shook his head. "Not with the spectacles to aid us. But with even a crude disguise, he could easily make it past our friends in this crowd."

The others were already gathered by the doors, looking tense. With less than an hour until the candidate took the stage, we were running out of time, and we all knew it.

Sergeant Chapman separated himself from the other coppers and came over. "Filling up pretty fast in there," he said. "You two better get going."

"Joseph and I will keep an eye on the street," Clara said. "If that's all right with you all," she added, inclining her head at the coppers.

"No objection here," Chapman said. "The more eyes, the better."

I gave Clara a quick hug. "We'll be just inside if you need us."

Jaunty music greeted us in the auditorium, tubas and trumpets bouncing along over the steady murmur of the crowd. Already the hall was filled to bursting. Gentlemen milled about the seats, greeting one another with grins and handshakes and enjoying the festive atmosphere. Banners of red, white, and blue wreathed the walls, and American flags hung over the platform, framing a large gilt eagle. At the center of it all, a huge crayon portrait of Theodore Roosevelt gazed down upon the assembly.

"Subtly patriotic," Edith observed.

"There's Sharpe and Jackson." Thomas pointed to a pair of glowing figures near the front row of seats. They stood amid some of New York's most prominent men: I recognized Astors and Whitneys and Rockefellers and Hendrikses, not to mention the editors of virtually every major newspaper. The golden radiance emanating from their little group of notables was so intense that I had to look away quickly, lest my eyes water and damage Mr. Tesla's delicate spectacles.

"Miss Fox will have joined Roosevelt's aides in the wings," Thomas said.

Leaving the six of us to find Foster somewhere amid the throng. At least there were no balconies or shadowed corners to hide in. If he did mean to take a shot at Mr. Roosevelt, he'd have to do it in the open; the only obstacle would be the Corinthian pillars supporting the ceiling.

"We should focus on the areas where a shooter would have a good line of sight," Thomas said, echoing my thoughts. "But we'll need to keep a close eye on the platform as well, including the band."

"Miss Islington and I can position ourselves on the flanks," Mr. Burrows offered, gesturing toward the stage.

"I'll take up a roving position along the aisles," Thomas said. "Miss Gallagher can point out the lucky individuals from up here, and I'll go in for a closer look."

Thus decided, we dispersed once more.

I stood at the back of the hall, scanning the seats one section at a time. Outside, I'd been worried about not spotting any golden halos; here in the Great Hall, I had the opposite problem. The angelic auras were everywhere, swirling about like sparks from a bonfire. It would have been difficult enough if they'd kept still, but of course they had to hobnob as if it were a cocktail party. It was impossible to keep track of them all. No sooner had Thomas checked the identity of one than I was waving him frantically toward another, even as I tried to keep tabs on those he'd already covered.

All the while, the huge clock above the platform ticked relentlessly on, inching ever closer to the moment when Theodore Roosevelt would take the stage. If we hadn't found Foster by then, I didn't like our chances of stopping whatever came next.

You've got to find him. You've got to. I'd given Mr. Roosevelt my word. I'd promised to keep him safe, to catch the monster responsible for murdering so many . . .

Nearing seven thirty now, and the delegates began to take their seats. Mr. Burrows moved to the front row, taking his place among the bankers and railroad barons and steel magnates. *This race is the very incarnation of Labor versus Capital,* Mr. Clemens had said, and here was the proof. A veritable conglomerate of Capital, right there in the front row.

What Johann Most wouldn't give to get his hands on that lot, I thought darkly, remembering what the anarchist had said about hanging rich men from lampposts. *All handily gathered in one place. Why, there wouldn't be lampposts enough in the entire neighborhood to . . .*

I paused.

The newspaper office Foster and his accomplices had been

using as a hideout was littered with copies of Johann Most's paper, *Freiheit*. A paper in which Most had famously called for the assassination of rich men. In which he had, even more famously, printed out a convenient guide to making bombs—just like the one they'd used at Haymarket.

Propaganda of the deed, they call it. Turning murder into spectacle.

Assassinating Theodore Roosevelt would certainly create a spectacle. But it couldn't hold a candle to wiping out an auditorium full of New York's wealthy, lucky elite.

It would be so easy, I realized with dawning horror. The offices of the *Journeyman* were right next to the Hudson River Railroad freight line; I remembered the trains rattling the windows while we searched. There would be dynamite by the crateful in those warehouses . . .

A cold weight settled in the pit of my stomach. I could feel the certainty taking shape there, nebulous instinct hardening into cast-iron conviction. *He had his chance to take Roosevelt quietly and he failed. Now he's going to kill them all in the showiest way possible.*

Frantic now, I scanned the crowd for Thomas, but I'd lost him in the throng. Mr. Sharpe was down there, and Mr. Jackson, but they weren't looking my way; I'd have to wade through the clogged aisles to get to them. There wasn't time. The delegates were already taking their seats. If there *was* a bomb, Foster might not even bother waiting for Roosevelt. He could set it off right now and accomplish his goal.

Think, Rose. Where would he plant a bomb? He could throw it from back here, but Mr. Tesla's spectacles weren't picking out any lucky people in this part of the auditorium. He might be closer to the stage, but then he'd be in danger of blowing himself up in the bargain.

Someplace he could plant a bomb without being seen . . .

Moving purely on instinct, I quit the hall and raced out into the foyer.

I found a side door and went through to some sort of utility hallway. I'm not sure what I was looking for, especially since I knew Mr. Sharpe and Miss Fox would have searched this corridor already, but I followed it anyway. A door at the far end stood ajar; the boiler room, judging from the soft roar issuing from within. As I headed toward it, a shadow moved along the floor, and a moment later, a flash of gold light flitted past the doorframe. Someone lucky was in there—and it probably wasn't the boilerman.

Swallowing hard, I drew my gun. *Are we steady, Rose?*

I plunged inside, gun raised—and promptly tripped over a body lying near the threshold. My gun clattered to the floor and skittered away, disappearing under a thicket of pipes. I scrambled for it, but a blur of motion in the corner of my eye sent me rolling away instead, narrowly avoiding the boot aimed for my head. Springing to my feet, I crouched, righting my crooked spectacles and bracing for attack.

Jack Foster stood near the door, the golden shimmer of his luck mingling with the angry red glow from the open door of the boiler. He wore the coveralls of a boilerman, just like the unconscious figure at his feet, and he carried a heavy-looking toolbox, clutching it to his chest as though it were worth its weight in gold.

Or dynamite.

A toolbox full of explosives ten feet away from a coal-fired steam boiler. I didn't know if Foster had a gun, but it didn't matter. He held our deaths in his hands—Roosevelt's, Thomas's, mine. And of course his own.

"Would you really do it?" I asked quietly. "Blow yourself up along with the rest?"

"I would," he said. "I will."

I looked into his eyes and knew he meant it. I also knew that all he had to do was touch me, and there would be nothing I could do to stop him.

CHAPTER 32

HATCHET JOB—THE COWBOY OF DAKOTA—AN ENCORE PERFORMANCE

I had my back to the boiler. Already, it was uncomfortably hot against the fabric of my dress. Foster's gaze went past me, measuring the number of steps to the burning coals. He had only to toss that toolbox through the door and we'd all be blown higher than the Statue of Liberty. Steam boiler explosions had been known to level entire buildings on their own. With a toolbox full of dynamite in the bargain . . . Slowly, I backed toward the boiler, cutting off his view.

"That wasn't the plan," he said matter-of-factly. "Blowing myself up, that is. I meant to light the fuse and leave it by the door there. There ought to have been enough time. If not . . ." He shrugged.

"And now?"

I was stalling, of course, trying to give my frantic brain time to come up with a plan. So far, my mind was horribly blank. If I had options, I wasn't seeing them.

"No reason why we can't both leave here intact," Foster said, still eerily composed. I don't know what I'd expected a zealot to look like, but it wasn't this, a young man radiating calm along with the angelic light of his luck. "I'm not afraid to die for what I believe in," he said, as if in answer to my thoughts, "but it wouldn't be my first choice. You don't need to die either, sister. I meant what I said that night at the hotel."

"Oh, really? The men who jumped me in the alley don't seem to have got that message." As I said it, I dared a quick look behind me, hoping to spot something I could use as a weapon.

"That wasn't my doing. I don't want to hurt you."

"You just want to kill hundreds of innocent people." A short-handled shovel stood propped against the boiler. It wasn't much, but it might keep Foster at bay long enough for me to think of something else. Discreetly, I took another step back.

"Innocent?" He tilted his head. "Innocent like the robber barons out there, who grow fat off the blood of the poor? Innocent like the politicians they've bought? Innocent like your friend Inspector Byrnes, who earns five times his annual salary in bribes?"

"Byrnes is no friend of mine." Another small step. "My friends are people like Mr. Burrows and Miss Islington, whose only crime is belonging to a wealthy family. They're out there, too. So is Thomas Wiltshire. A good man, the best I've ever known, and you tried to murder him just because he dared to interfere with your killing spree. How do you justify that to yourself?"

"This is war, sister. There will be casualties."

"I'm not your sister, and you don't fool me for a second. I saw the look on your face when you tried to kill Thomas. The hate. There's nothing righteous in that. You're a murderer, plain and simple. You killed six people in cold blood, and for what? Roosevelt was nominated anyway." I dared another fleeting glance over my shoulder, making sure I knew exactly where the shovel lay.

"Yes, he was, and he's even more dangerous than we imagined. Using his luck and his Knickerbocker name to charm the weak-minded, convince them he's a friend to the workingman. He'll win. All the papers say so."

"And that's worth killing over?"

"Don't you see?" he cried, his composure cracking at last. "For once, we have a chance to be led by one of our own! The first-ever Labor administration! But that won't happen unless we *make* it happen. Roosevelt will win, and then it's back to the trough for every one of those plutes out there." He shook his head darkly. "No more. They'll yield to the people or they'll suffer the consequences. Tonight they learn that the common man will stand idle in the face of injustice for only so long before he takes up arms."

Speaking of taking up arms . . . Whirling, I snatched up the shovel and brandished it. "If you come anywhere near this boiler, I'll open your skull."

Brave words, but I don't think he quite believed them. He stood there for a moment, eying me as if to gauge my resolve. I hoped my knuckles weren't white, that he couldn't see the way my shoulders heaved with every shallow breath. The heat of the boiler was intolerable. A trickle of sweat worked its way down my spine.

Foster sighed and set the toolbox at his feet. "I don't need to come any closer. You must realize that. The dynamite is just the tinder. The real explosive is right behind you. A boiler that size, all that pressure . . . It won't need much encouragement."

I did realize that, which was why I was uttering a silent prayer at that very moment.

"Last chance," Foster said. "Drop the shovel and run, and I

won't try to stop you." He drew a box of matches from the pocket of his coveralls.

I was out of time. I did the only thing I could, charging him and swinging the shovel. But he was ready for me, arresting the swing with one hand while he made a grab for me with the other. I kicked his feet out from under him and we both went down, but I couldn't scramble away fast enough; he brushed the bare skin of my forearm.

It wasn't much—not even as strong as what he'd done to me at the hotel—but it was enough. My heart bucked, sending a dizzying rush of blood to my head. I managed to haul myself up to my hands and knees, but it was too late; I could hear the match being struck, the fuse hissing to life.

"You'll be all right in a moment," Foster said with disturbing gentleness. "I've barely touched you. If you hurry, you might make it out of here."

Pinpricks of light still swirled in my vision, but I grabbed the shovel and swung in the direction of the voice, and I felt it connect. Foster grunted in pain. I staggered to my feet and swung again, aiming for the blurred golden glow of Foster's head. He went down without a sound and didn't move again.

I dropped the shovel and propped my hands on my thighs, taking great gulps of air and blinking furiously to banish the dizziness. I could hear the fuse hissing, but if I didn't give myself a moment to recover, I'd be as good as useless. I tore off Mr. Tesla's spectacles and jammed them in the breast pocket of my dress, freeing myself from the disorienting glow. Even unconscious, Foster shone like an angel.

After a few seconds, my vision cleared, and my breath evened out. Foster had told the truth: He'd only incapacitated me long enough to light the fuse and make his escape. He'd managed the first part, anyway: The bundle of dynamite lay on the floor, spark-ing away. It was a long fuse, but not long enough to take the bomb someplace safe, not here in crowded Lower Manhattan. I had to defuse it, but how?

I grabbed the shovel and tried using its blade to cut the fuse, but it wasn't sharp enough. Swearing, I tossed it aside and glanced desperately around me. It was dark in there, and the back half of the room was a maze of pipes. I stumbled about aimlessly. A roar was building in my skull; whether it was the boiler or the blood in my ears, I couldn't tell.

No time. There's no time . . .

A glint of metal caught my eye. A fire ax hung on the wall. I snatched it down and whirled back to the bomb, but there was barely an inch of fuse left now, and I'd never wielded an ax in my life. If I missed, I might strike the bomb, and the metal blade against the stone floor could easily send up a spark.

Panic gave way to cold, hard dread. The roar in my ears re-ceded, replaced by the hiss of the fuse, the hiss of the steam pipes overhead . . .

Steam.

Water.

Coursing through the intake pipes right in front of me.

Taking the ax two-handed, I swung. The blade rang uselessly off the metal. I swung again, with the same result: a spark and a scratch in the pipe, but nothing close to a crack.

I paused. Drew a breath. *Focus, or you die.*

With a shrieking cry, I swung the ax with everything I had. This time, the blade left a dent. I went at it again and again, my swings wild but powerful, and the more I hacked, the more the metal buckled, until—

The pipe split, sending a hard jet of water over me. Throwing the ax aside, I snatched up the bomb and held it under the spray until every inch of it was soaked. Then, for good measure, I grabbed the toolbox and filled it with enough water to submerge the bundle of dynamite entirely. By the time I was sure the bomb was well and truly defused, I was soaked from hairline to hem.

It was only then that I realized Jack Foster was gone.

I raced back to the Great Hall. When I got there, I reached for Mr. Tesla's spectacles in my breast pocket . . . and gasped in dismay when I saw the state of the lenses, pocked and warped and utterly useless. The inventor had warned me that water would dissolve the rare and delicate minerals coating the glass, but in my panic, it hadn't occurred to me to stash the spectacles someplace dry. Now they were ruined, leaving me no quick way of picking Foster out of the crowd.

My gaze raked the seats. Still no sign of Thomas, or Foster. The silver-haired chairman, Acton, was onstage, addressing the assembly.

"You are called here tonight to ratify the nomination of the youngest man who ever ran as a candidate for the mayor of New York . . ."

Any minute now, Mr. Roosevelt would take the podium. Foster's bomb had failed, but the man himself was dangerous enough.

I spied F. Winston Sharpe near the platform and waved frantically. He saw me and frowned, motioning me to come down to him.

"The Cowboy of Dakota! Make the Cowboy of Dakota the next mayor!"

The crowd erupted in cheers, delegates leaping to their feet. I tried to elbow my way through, but they pressed into the aisles, shaking hands and thumping one another's backs, oblivious to the frantic, soaking-wet woman in their midst. On and on the applause went, so long that the band struck up a tune.

"Mr. Sharpe!" I cried, but it was useless; there was too much noise.

A hand seized the sleeve of my dress. I whirled. Foster loomed over me, eyes blazing, cheeks blotched with fury. There was no hint of human decency left in those eyes. Twice he'd let me live, and twice I'd made him regret it. There would not be a third time. He reached for the bare skin of my neck . . .

. . . and went rigid, eyes wide, before pitching onto his knees. Thomas stood behind him, derringer raised. In the clamor, I hadn't even heard the shot.

Foster slumped to the floor. Thomas hesitated warily before tucking two gloved fingers under the man's jaw. He glanced at me, gave a short shake of his head. Then he tore off his glove and dared a fleeting touch, skin on skin. Satisfied that Foster's luck was no longer a danger, he heaved the body into a sitting position. All the while, the brass band played on.

By this time, some of the delegates had begun to stare, but before anyone could comment, Mr. Jackson appeared beside Thomas, and the two of them slipped their arms under Foster's and started dragging him like a drunkard, smiling apologetically and murmuring excuses as they made their way to the back of the hall. I followed on shaky legs, and by the time we reached the back row, Mr. Sharpe was waiting for us.

He wasn't the only one. Inspector Byrnes stood near the rear doors, watching with a scowl. He must have seen Foster go down, but with F. Winston Sharpe standing between him and Thomas, he didn't dare interfere.

"So this is Jack Foster." Mr. Sharpe looked the dead man over. "Well done, Wiltshire."

"It was Miss Gallagher who found him," Thomas said, his expression a mixture of relief and anger. "Where the devil did you go, Rose? You gave us an awful fright."

"I lost sight of you when I realized what was going on. Foster had . . ." I swallowed a sudden rush of nausea. "There was a bomb."

"What's this? A bomb?" Mr. Sharpe tugged his mustache fretfully. "Where is it now?"

"In the boiler room. Defused." I gave them a hasty version of events, practically shouting to be heard above the band.

"Well, thank God you stopped him," Mr. Sharpe said, clapping my shoulder so hard that I flinched. "Now, we'd better disperse before we draw too much attention to ourselves. Wiltshire, Jackson, get Foster out of here before he bleeds all over the floor and gives us away. I'll return to my seat. Miss Fox will be looking for me there." Without waiting for an answer, he turned and headed back down the aisle.

"We'll be back as soon as we can," Thomas told me, and he and Mr. Jackson dragged Foster's body away.

At last the band fell silent, and Theodore Roosevelt bounded up to the lectern, color high and teeth flashing, clearly enjoying his moment. His speech was brief and apparently very witty, judging from the laughter, but I honestly couldn't give you a word of it. I was too numb with shock to process anything he said. It was like watching a play with cotton stuffed in your ears, everything muted and unreal. I was shaking, and not just because I was soaked through; I couldn't help looking over the crowd again and again, wondering if any of these people would ever know just how close they came to being blown sky-high.

By the time Thomas and Mr. Jackson joined Mr. Sharpe near the stage, the speeches were done, to much cheering and waving of handkerchiefs. Mr. Roosevelt's aides, including Viola Fox, gathered in the wings while the candidate shook hands onstage. I could see Mr. Sharpe and Thomas hovering nearby, waiting impatiently to take Mr. Roosevelt aside and tell him what had happened, but the tide of well-wishers showed no sign of ebbing. I watched them detachedly, my gaze skipping from one to the next like a stone over smooth water.

To this day, I don't know how I picked him out. Something about the fit of his suit, maybe, or the expression on his face. Maybe he moved with a little too much purpose.

Whatever drew my eye, I knew the moment I saw the fat man in the bowler hat that he meant Theodore Roosevelt harm. He reached into his pocket. Metal flashed; I recognized the compact form of a derringer. I cried out and waved my arms—just one among many well-wishers clamoring for the candidate's attention. But somehow Viola Fox saw me, and she moved faster than I would have thought possible, rushing across the stage and flinging herself into Mr. Roosevelt's arms, putting her body between the candidate and the gunman. And then Thomas was there, stealing up behind the assassin and dropping him in one swift, discreet motion. It looked for all the world like the man had simply tripped and was helped to his feet by Thomas and Mr. Jackson. Meanwhile, Viola Fox simpered and blushed like a schoolgirl, doing a masterful job of playing the overenthusiastic aide. It all happened in moments, and no one, not even Mr. Roosevelt, was the wiser. Sergeant Chapman appeared and escorted the fat man out, and that was that.

By the time Mr. Roosevelt had finished shaking hands and patting backs, my dress was nearly dry, and my nerves had settled into a dull buzz. As for the candidate, he beamed with satisfaction. "That went rather well," he said brightly as Mr. Sharpe approached. "I could not have asked for a better birthday gift!" I couldn't help feeling sorry for him, watching how quickly he deflated as Mr. Sharpe discreetly related the events of the evening. "Good God," I heard him murmur, his glance cutting to me.

They exchanged a few more words in private before Mr. Sharpe waved Thomas and me over.

Mr. Roosevelt took my hands in his, sending a familiar tingle up my arms. "The city owes you a great debt, Miss Gallagher, as do I. You have my profound thanks. You all do," he added, his gaze taking in Thomas, Mr. Jackson, and Viola Fox. "I only wish we could recognize your efforts properly."

Mr. Sharpe inclined his head. "No recognition necessary, sir. It is our lot to labor in obscurity. You know our creed."

"'We never sleep,'" Mr. Roosevelt said, quoting the famous motto of the Pinkerton National Detective Agency.

"'And we never tell tales,'" Mr. Sharpe added, the second half being the particular addendum of the special branch.

Thomas cleared his throat. "If there is nothing else, gentlemen, I would like to take Miss Gallagher home. She's had a very trying evening. We all have."

Mr. Sharpe nodded. "We'll conduct a full debriefing in the morning. You'll have a copy on your desk by afternoon, Mr. Roosevelt, as will the governor."

"Good, good." The candidate patted my arm. "Get some rest, Miss Gallagher. Heaven knows you deserve it."

"Our friends are outside," Thomas said as we headed up the aisle, "but we can go out the back if you're too exhausted. They'll understand."

"It's all right. They deserve to know what happened. But after that . . ."

"After that, home."

Thomas helped me into my overcoat, and as his arms came around me, I found myself clutching them. He hesitated for half a heartbeat, then folded me against him, his breath warm against the nape of my neck.

It lasted only a moment. Then, as if by some silent accord, we released each other and stepped out into the night.

CHAPTER 33

SLEEPLESS NIGHTS—THE DEDICATION OF LADY LIBERTY—AMENDS AND AMENS

Exhausted as I was, I doubted I'd sleep a wink that night. Beneath the weariness lay a strong undercurrent of jitters, so when we arrived at Number 726 and Thomas offered me a glass of sherry, I accepted readily.

He'd been quiet on the ride home, and his movements as he poured the sherry were oddly stilted, a manner I'd come to recognize as a sign that he was struggling with something. He handed me my drink and drifted over to the fireplace, avoiding my eye. "Another close call," he said.

"Too many. But what can we do? It's part of the job."

"It is." He took a sip of his sherry.

I did the same, savoring the warmth as it hit the back of my throat.

"It's fortunate Foster didn't attack while you were defusing the bomb. Why do you suppose that is?"

"I imagine the ax in my hands had something to do with it. I was swinging it pell-mell and shrieking like a barbarian. I guess he didn't like his chances of getting close enough to touch me. Figured it would be easier once I'd gotten rid of the weapon." He hadn't been wrong either. If it weren't for Thomas . . . I shuddered and took another sip of sherry.

"What you went through tonight . . ." Thomas shook his head. "And not just tonight. How many brushes with death since all this began?"

"I'm trying not to think about it."

"As for me, I can think of little else these past few days."

I paused, sensing a turn in the conversation. Tentatively, I asked, "Is that what you meant by *processing*?"

He nodded, meeting my gaze at last. I saw hesitation in his eyes, but determination too, as though whatever he had to say couldn't be put off any longer. "I've been asking myself some very difficult questions. Questions I've feared all along I would one day have to confront. That's why I hesitated to involve you in this business in the first place."

"What sort of questions?"

"Watching you develop as an agent has been my singular pleasure. Having you as a partner, my great privilege. I am so very proud of you, Rose. I hope you know that."

I swallowed hard. "But . . . ?"

"But it comes at a cost, as has been made vividly clear to me this week. Having you as my partner means watching you put yourself in harm's way again and again. Because you're perfectly right, it is part of the job." He set down his glass, his pale eyes fixed on me. "And so I must ask myself, is it a cost I can bear? Do I have the strength to fear for you? Or, God forbid, to lose you? If the answer is no, what does that mean for our future as partners?"

My heart was beating fast now, the blood rushing to my face. He'd opened the door. It was time to walk through. "And what about our future as Thomas and Rose?"

I'm not sure what I expected, but I was completely unprepared for the look of quiet torment that flickered through his eyes. "There the dilemma is no less real, as you must know."

"I'm not sure what I know. You keep so much to yourself."

He sighed. "Please believe I take no pleasure in that. I'm only trying to protect you. And, if I am honest, myself. There is little to be gained by airing matters that will only bring us grief."

It took a moment for those words to sink in. "You know how I feel," I said softly. "Don't you?"

Of course he did. What I really wanted to ask was, *How long have you known?*

Thomas hesitated, as though searching for the best way to frame his answer. "I know how *I* feel, Rose."

There was a beat of silence. It felt like falling.

"But it's not that simple. Romantic involvement between us would be complicated enough if we weren't partners. As matters stand . . ." He shook his head. "Whatever my feelings, I can't let them take hold of me. I might never regain control, and the consequences—"

In two swift strides, I closed the distance between us and pulled his head down into a kiss.

He stiffened, but he didn't resist. He stood frozen, his hand suspended over my shoulder as though he wasn't sure whether to draw me in or push me away.

After a moment I drew back, gazing up into those pale eyes searchingly.

"We're partners," he murmured.

"Yes, we are. But for once, right now, can we just be *us*?"

I saw it the moment he broke, his restraint shattering into a thousand splinters, and before I could even take a breath, his mouth was on mine, his arms gathering me close. A wave of heat swept through me, and I let it take me. My fingers twined in his hair, raked at his back, things I'd dreamed of doing for so long that my body moved as if to a familiar dance. I kissed him in a way I'd never kissed anyone before, a way that would have made Mam blush, three years of pent-up desire breaking free at last. And Thomas? He finally showed me what lay behind that gentlemanly veneer, and it was more passionate than I could have imagined.

And then, abruptly, it was over. Thomas broke off, though he didn't pull back right away. He rested his forehead against mine, and for a moment he just stood there, hands framing my face, his breath still fast and shallow. His lips brushed mine once more. He kissed my eyes, first one, then the other. He pressed a soft, lingering kiss to my forehead. "Good night, Rose," he whispered, and then he was gone.

I reached a trembling hand for my sherry. Took a long, deep sip.

No, I wouldn't be sleeping a wink tonight.

The steam yacht *Aphrodite* was not, we were assured, especially large. At a dainty 127 feet, she was the smaller of Mr. Burrows's two yachts (the more impressive *Venetia* being anchored at Newport). Yet humble as she was, she cut a lovely figure, with her long, elegant prow, mahogany deck, and steadying sails. She glided across the water with a grace unrivaled by any mode of transport I'd ever used, so I was willing to overlook the fact that her deck saloon was merely twice the size of Mam's flat.

Her captain cut a lovely figure, too, his golden hair tousled playfully in the wind as he dropped anchor amid the throng of tugs and ferries and pleasure craft gathered off Bedloe's Island to witness the dedication of the Statue of Liberty. On this occasion, Mr. Burrows had decided, somewhat scandalously, to forgo a hat, since the sun was nowhere to be seen and the customary captain's cap looked, in his words, *utterly ridiculous*. It was his boat, after all, and besides, I'd learned long ago that Jonathan Burrows did exactly as he pleased, whatever people might think. One of the many advantages of being rich as a Rockefeller, I suppose.

"Here we are, then," he said, joining the rest of us in the deck saloon. "Who's for champagne?"

I myself would have preferred tea, what with the bone-chilling fog drifting over the water, but I settled for cognac.

We were five in the yacht: Thomas and me, Edith and Mr. Burrows, and the decidedly glum figure of Nikola Tesla, whom Mr. Burrows had fetched from the island early this morning after he'd finished taking down the illicit transmitter. I'd related the unfortunate fate of his spectacles more than an hour ago, but the news still hovered over him like a rain cloud. He'd cocooned himself in a blanket on his wicker chaise, emerging only for the occasional forlorn bite of caviar.

"I really am so sorry, Mr. Tesla," I said for the umpteenth time.

The inventor smiled ruefully. "Please, Miss Gallagher, there is no need. Your actions averted an unthinkable tragedy, and I am happy my spectacles played a part in that. Still . . ." He sighed.

"It is very disappointing. I don't suppose I shall ever get my hands on another sample of copper vanadate."

"I can't pretend to regret that," Mr. Burrows said. "It was a wonderful invention, but having one's luck exposed for all to see . . . Who knows what uses such knowledge might be put to?"

"That is the nature of science," Mr. Tesla said, helping himself to another serving of caviar. "Every advancement brings with it potential dangers."

"Not this one, surely." Edith gestured at the statue looming out of the mist, smoothly changing the subject. "She really is remarkable, isn't she?"

"Well done getting the antenna down in time, Tesla," Thomas said. "You must have been up all night."

"Indeed. In fact . . ." The inventor paused, frowning critically at the little mound of caviar on his toast. Taking up the spoon once more, he removed a single tiny pearl, at which point his brow cleared in visible relief. "In fact, I wasn't able to completely finish the job, but I made sure to remove the noticeable parts. Even then, I would not have managed it had the workmen not offered to help me this morning."

Mr. Burrows laughed. "They had little choice, unless they wanted to explain to the president of the United States why the old girl wasn't ready for the dedication."

"I'm just sorry you had to miss the parade," I said. "It was quite something, in spite of the weather."

The inventor gave a little shiver. "I am not much for crowds."

"Listen." Edith cupped her ear. "The band has stopped playing. It must be nearly time."

As we gazed across the water at Lady Liberty, her face veiled in the tricolor of France, I imagined the grand speeches being made at her feet. The papers would print them tomorrow, no doubt. I'd read them aloud to Mam; the schoolteacher in her took great pleasure in a well-turned phrase. For now, I could feast my eyes on the flags and bunting and gaily colored streamers and think my own suitably patriotic thoughts.

"We'd best be ready," Mr. Burrows said, pouring out five glasses of champagne. "This is a momentous occasion. I daresay that statue will outlast mankind itself."

Thomas handed me a glass, and our eyes met briefly. He'd been quiet all morning, and of course we hadn't discussed what happened last night. We'd have to eventually, but for now, we were both . . . *processing*. In the meantime, a moment's eye contact was enough to bring a flash of heat to my cheeks. I could only hope nobody noticed.

"To Liberty," Mr. Burrows said, hoisting his glass.

"And the future," Edith added.

As we drank, the veil dropped from the statue, and Liberty's green-eyed gaze looked out over the water at last. A chorus of cheers went up from the boats; they rang their bells and blew their horns and fired their cannons, and a moment later the sound was echoed from the riverbanks of Manhattan. Smoke and steam mingled with the fog, rising into the sky and obscuring the great lady's face.

"The future," I murmured, taking another sip of champagne. I wondered what it would look like.

After the ceremony, I paid a visit at Mam's. I'd offered to take her to the parade, but like Mr. Tesla, she had an aversion to crowds, and the morning's foul weather had settled it. She'd stay indoors, thank you very much, where it was peaceful and warm. I couldn't blame her; even after my second cup of tea in her little kitchen, my bones refused to give up their chill.

"Still, Mam, it was quite a sight. You ought to have gone down to the Battery, at least. It was a once-in-a-lifetime moment."

Mam made a dismissive gesture. "That's what they said about the Brooklyn Bridge, and St. Patrick's before that. New York has a once-in-a-lifetime moment every other year."

It was hard to argue with that.

"Besides," Pietro put in, "you couldn't see nothing from the Battery. Too much fog." He leaned against the stove, arms crossed, his expression unreadable. He'd been pleasant enough, but that was for Mam's benefit. He'd wait until she headed off for her nap, I figured, and then he'd let me have it.

"Couldn't see *anything*, Peter," Mam corrected. "Anyway, I can't say I'm all that bothered about some French statue. I'm just happy to be back in my own home." Frowning, she cast an eye about the flat. "Though what was in such dire need of fixing that they had to cast us out in the first place, I couldn't tell you. Why, I can't even see that they've done anything."

"I told you, Mama, there were rats living in the walls." Pietro shrugged. "Probably the hole is behind the stove, that's all."

"There have been rats in this flat since we moved in. Don't see why they'd start caring now." Mam continued muttering as she gathered up the teacups, but she didn't seem genuinely bothered, so I left it alone.

"I'll get out of your hair, Mam, so you can sleep. I'll come by tomorrow, if you like, and we can read the papers."

"Tomorrow? But don't you have work?"

"Mr. Wiltshire's given me a few days off, since I've been putting in so much extra time lately."

"He's such a gentleman," Mam said.

You wouldn't say that if you'd seen the way he kissed me last night, I thought, and tried very hard not to blush.

Cutting an awkward glance at Pietro, I said, "Walk me out?"

"Yes, sure. Let me get my coat."

I waited until we were in the street, just to make sure Mam didn't overhear anything through those thin walls. "Thank you for what you did, taking Mam to the hotel like that. I had no right to ask it of you, but I didn't have much choice. I know you did it for her and not for me, and I promise it won't happen again."

Pietro sighed. "That's not true, Fiora. I mean, the first part is true, but the second part . . . I did it for you also. I might be angry with you, but that doesn't mean I'm not your friend anymore."

Tears pricked behind my eyes, and I had to swallow a lump in my throat. "Thank you. That means more to me than you know."

"Are you all right?" His dark eyes scanned me. "This thing with the men who were shooting at you—it's over now?"

I nodded. "We caught them. The ones who were left, anyway. It's over."

"Thanks God."

"What about you? How are things with . . ." I trailed off, unsure how to finish.

"With Augusto?" He shrugged. "Better, for now. Since the shooting, the merchants have all paid up. Maybe they are more afraid of him now. Or maybe they think he really does protect the neighborhood. Who knows, but Augusto says he doesn't need my help with collections anymore." Smiling faintly, he added, "So maybe I should thank you, too, eh?"

I didn't much want to be thanked for my role in the deaths of two men, but I kept that to myself. The words were a sort of peace

offering, and that was more than I'd expected. More than I deserved, maybe. "I'm sorry I lied to you, Pietro."

He glanced away. "I haven't been telling all the truth either.
I should have told you what was happening with Augusto, but . . ."
He hesitated. "But I was ashamed."

"I know the feeling. I'm not ashamed of my work with the
Pinkerton Agency, but I was so afraid of what you'd think. Not
that I blame you. I felt the same at first."

"What made you change your mind? Was it *him*?"

There was something in the way he asked the question that
made me wonder if Augusto had decided to reveal my supposed
betrayal after all, telling Pietro that his "sweetheart" was in love
with Thomas Wiltshire. But now was not the time for that conversation. We had enough to sort out as it was.

"Mostly, it was the work," I said. "The sorts of cases I'm involved in . . . it's nothing to do with union-busting or anything
like that. It's about helping people, just like it used to be when
the Pinkerton Agency was new."

I'm not sure if he believed me, but he accepted the explanation without comment. "And what about your mama? Will you
tell her the truth?"

"Someday, maybe, if she keeps getting stronger. But right
now . . ."

"It would only upset her, and maybe she gets worse again."
He nodded. "I understand."

I smiled, feeling as if a weight had been lifted from my
shoulders. Sticking out a hand, I said, "Friends?"

"Friends," he said, shaking it. "And please let's promise, Fiora,
no more lies. There are not a lot of people I trust in this place. I
trust you, and I hope you trust me."

"I do, but . . ." I paused, biting my lip. "There are some things you might be better off not knowing." In the back of my mind, I was hearing Thomas's voice from nearly a year ago. *The world is a great deal more complicated than most people realize, Rose. There are things we can't explain, things we're told we shouldn't believe in . . .* "I'll tell you everything if that's what you really want, but be careful what you wish for."

Pietro considered that. "these things I might be better off not knowing . . . they're dangerous?"

"They can be, yes."

He nodded slowly. "On my side, too. Maybe we should think about this some more before we decide."

"That's good enough for me." Then, impulsively, I threw my arms around him.

He laughed. "I told you, Fiora, you can't go around hugging stray Italian boys."

"Oh, you know me. I never do what I'm supposed to."

"Amen to that," he said, and headed back to the flat.

CHAPTER 34

DEFEATS AND VICTORIES—UNSPOKEN—
WESTWARD HO

Honestly, I'm surprised," Thomas said, setting the *Tribune* aside with a sigh. "I truly believed Roosevelt would win."

"You weren't the only one," I said. "The papers made it sound as if it were all but guaranteed." Why, *The New-York Times* had been referring to Mr. Roosevelt as *the future mayor* for days, and the *Tribune* had pronounced his election certain.

Our breakfast guest took a different view. "I'm disappointed," Mr. Burrows said, "but not at all surprised. Nor would you be, Wiltshire, if you'd seen the mood at the club these past few days. Some of the staunchest Republicans of my acquaintance admitted they would be casting their votes for the Democrats this time around. The prospect of a Labor administration was simply too terrifying." He took a sip of his coffee. "Still, I feel awful for the old

boy. Must be deucedly hard to hold your head high after a drubbing like that."

I *tsk*ed. "It was hardly a *drubbing*. Sixty thousand votes is
nothing to sneeze at."

"He came in third in a contest of three," Mr. Burrows said.
"In the world of politics, that's a drubbing."

"Well, I agree with the *Times*," I said irritably. "Mr. Roosevelt was badly used by his party. It's nothing but rank disloyalty,
the way so many Republicans deserted him at the last minute."

To my great annoyance, Mr. Burrows just laughed.

"What's so funny about that?"

"Nothing at all. I'll say this for Roosevelt, he has a bright
future in politics if he can command such admiration from someone like you."

"Someone like me?" I leveled a cool look at him. "A working-
class woman, you mean?"

"A working-class woman of surpassing good sense."

"Good enough to see through you, anyway," I muttered,
which of course just made him laugh harder.

"At least we can be reasonably confident that Roosevelt will be
safe now," Thomas said. "As for the mayoralty, I'm sure Hewitt will
perform admirably. In truth, all three were excellent candidates."

"That is as it should be," Mr. Burrows said. "A city as fair as
New York deserves only the finest suitors. And now if you'll excuse me . . ." Taking a final sip of coffee, he pushed his chair back.
"Shall I expect you at the club later, Wiltshire, or will you be otherwise engaged? It looks as though you have rather a lot of correspondence to get through."

"Indeed," Thomas said, eying the stack of morning mail with
a frown. "I don't know how it piles up so quickly."

I took my time finishing with the newspapers, stealing a

glance across the table every now and then as Thomas went on sorting the mail. We still hadn't talked about what happened the other day, and though things between us weren't strained, exactly, they weren't quite right either.

"This one's for you," he said, handing me an envelope from the Pinkerton Agency.

I took it with a sigh of relief. My paycheck should have come last week, and I'd started to worry about the delay. I opened it and set it aside, barely glancing at the familiar figures . . .

"Wait." I snatched it back up, blinking a few times to make sure I wasn't seeing things. "Thomas."

He glanced up. "Is there a problem?"

"My paycheck. It's . . . they've made a mistake."

"Oh?"

"It's twice what it should be."

Thomas snorted quietly and resumed opening his mail. "No, it's precisely what it ought to have been all along."

"What do you mean?"

"The special branch of the Pinkerton Detective Agency has apparently been operating on the belief that female agents ought to be paid less than half of what their male counterparts earn. That day at the hotel, when you told me your salary . . ." He shook his head. "I do apologize, Rose. If I'd known, I'd have dealt with the matter sooner."

"Dealt with the matter?"

"I spoke to Sharpe. Told him it was old-fashioned and a disgrace. He muttered the usual excuses about standard practice and so forth, but I insisted. Frankly, I'm incredulous that no one has done so before now. I'd have thought Miss Fox, at least, would have made her displeasure known, but perhaps she wasn't aware of the discrepancy. In any case, it's been rectified now, for all of you."

My gaze fell back to the figures stamped on the check. "Thomas, I don't know what to say. It's . . . Thank you."

"No thanks necessary. I merely called attention to an injustice. You fully deserve that salary."

"What salary?" Clara appeared in the dining room, ready to tidy up breakfast. "Rose, did you get a raise?"

"I . . . Well, yes, I suppose I did."

"You'll be able to afford your own lodgings now," Thomas said smoothly, gathering up the rest of his letters. "No hurry, of course."

"No," I said, swallowing. "Of course."

Thomas headed up to his study while Clara started clearing up. As for me, I just sat there, staring at the check. Suddenly, it didn't feel like such a boon.

"You don't look like somebody who just got a raise," Clara said as she stacked her tray. That's just how well she knew me.

"Oh, don't mind me." I forced a smile. "I'm just tired, that's all."

"Rose, honey, for somebody who lies for a living, you sure can be awful at it." Glancing at the door, she lowered her voice. "You two still haven't talked, I take it."

I'd told her about what happened between Thomas and me. Thankfully, she'd resisted the urge to say *I told you so.*

"What gives you that idea?" I asked sarcastically. "The fact that he's desperate to have me out of his house?" Not that I blamed him. There had been plenty of sleepless nights this past week. Both of us under the same roof . . . the temptation was just too great. I had faith enough in Thomas's powers of restraint, but none at all in my own.

"What happened between you two . . . There's married folks don't ever share a moment like that. How're you gonna act like it never was?"

"We can't. We'll have to deal with it eventually. But right now, we both need time to think."

"What's there to think about? You're sweet on him, he's sweet on you."

"It's more complicated than that. We're partners. I'm not even sure it's allowed. It could interfere with our work, and . . . then there's what Viola Fox said. There are already rumors about Thomas and me, that he hired me for all the wrong reasons. If we were involved, it would only prove the rumors true. Or seem to, anyway."

"Why should you care what any of them think?"

"Maybe I shouldn't, but I do. I want them to respect me, and they won't do that if they think I'm just Thomas's paramour."

"Paramour?"

"Well, what else could I be, with the difference in our stations?"

She sighed. "So what're you gonna do?"

I thought about that for a spell. "Get a place of my own, I suppose. Carry on like a professional." Thomas and I worked brilliantly together. I wouldn't let anything get in the way of that, not if I could help it.

"Well then." Clara patted my shoulder. "That sounds like a plan."

I helped her tidy up, and then I fetched my overcoat and hat, intending to head to the bank with my check. I was reaching for my umbrella when the doorbell rang; opening it, I found my favorite copper.

"Miss Gallagher." Sergeant Chapman doffed his hat and stepped inside. "Fixing to brave the weather, I see."

"Awful, isn't it? Barely November, and already I'm tired of the cold."

Thomas came down the stairs to join us. "Good morning, Sergeant."

"Wiltshire. Thought I'd drop in on my way to the station to let you both know that Henry Kelly—that's the fella tried to shoot Roosevelt—he was convicted yesterday afternoon. It'll be a hanging."

"Oh," I said quietly. Foster's accomplice certainly deserved to face justice, but still—knowing you've played a part in a man's execution is not pleasant.

"After that, we'll be closing the case," Chapman went on, "seeing how the rest of Foster's boys is already dead, thanks to the Mulberry Street Gang."

I bit my lip. I hadn't told Sergeant Chapman what I'd seen Marco do, and he hadn't asked. "Did you arrest anyone for those murders?"

He gave me a sour look. "You know better 'n that, Miss Gallagher."

I did know better, and it made me ill. *Poor Chapman,* I thought. It couldn't be easy going to work every morning knowing half your fellow officers were corrupt.

"What about the newspaper editor?" Thomas asked.

"Bright?" Chapman shook his head. "Far as we can tell, the only part he played was to introduce Foster to the others. If he knew the specifics of what they was planning, he ain't saying."

"You said the rest of them are dead, but are we sure about that?" I asked.

Chapman shrugged. "Kelly didn't mention nobody else, even with Byrnes doing his worst. Either he's tougher 'n he looks, or that's all he knows. As for some shadowy money funding the whole operation, nothing we turned up points that way. Don't suppose we'll ever know for sure, but I got no reason to think we missed anything."

I sighed. Why couldn't anything ever tie up neatly, like it does in the yellow-back novels? "At least Mr. Roosevelt is safe."

"What about your bounty hunter friend?" Chapman asked. "She on the mend?"

"She must be," Thomas said, "because she's back at One-Eyed Johnny's as if it never happened. One would think three days in a coma would inspire her to look after her health a little more carefully, but apparently not."

"Hard to kick the bottle," Chapman said. "I know it better 'n most. Anyways, I oughta get going. Good day to you both."

As Chapman headed down the walk, he passed another visitor on his way up, and they stopped to greet each other. I glanced at Thomas and saw my surprise reflected in his eyes.

Our visitor was Theodore Roosevelt.

"Good morning, sir," Thomas said, shaking his hand. "What a pleasant surprise."

Mr. Roosevelt thumped Thomas's shoulder as if they were lifelong chums. "I'm sorry for dropping by unannounced," he said cheerfully, "but I'm bound for England tomorrow, and I'm in rather a hurry to get everything arranged."

"Not at all. Please, come in."

"I'm very sorry about the election, Mr. Roosevelt," I said.

He brushed it off like a consummate politician. "You're very kind, but truly, I cannot be disappointed at the result. I was defeated fair and square."

If I didn't quite believe him, I thought it was very well spoken.

"How can we help?" Thomas asked, gesturing for his guest to come through to the parlor.

"Forgive me, but I can't stay. I just wanted to reserve your calendars, both of you. I've a bit of business out west, if you're interested."

"Out west?" My heart skipped a beat. The farthest west I'd ever been was New Jersey.

"The Dakota Territory, at my ranch. Or rather, in the general vicinity thereof."

"What is the nature of the matter?" Thomas asked.

"That's just it, I'm afraid." Mr. Roosevelt's brow creased bemusedly. "I haven't the vaguest idea."

Thomas blinked. "I'm . . . sorry?"

"It's a very long story, and a strange one. I'm afraid there just isn't time. We'll talk when I'm back."

"It's not urgent, then?" I asked.

"Urgent enough," said Mr. Roosevelt, "but there's nothing to be done about it until spring. I just wanted to make sure you reserved the time."

"When would you like us?" I asked, already thinking about how I'd explain my absence to Mam.

"May, I should think, through perhaps to the end of June. What do you say?"

Thomas inclined his head. "We would be delighted."

"Excellent. I'll have the papers drawn up." Mr. Roosevelt donned his hat. "Needless to say, it will be dangerous. And the matter must be kept absolutely confidential."

"Well, sir," I said, "you know our motto. 'We never sleep, and we never tell tales.'"

Mr. Roosevelt gave an enigmatic smile and turned to go. "You might regret that second part, Miss Gallagher," he called over his shoulder. "Because I promise you, it will be a tale for the ages."

AUTHOR'S NOTE

The mayoral race of 1886 is widely regarded as one of the finest in New York history, contested by three outstanding candidates. (A fourth, William Wardwell of the Prohibition Party, was on the ballot, but never taken very seriously.) Even at the time, the exceptional caliber of the contenders was recognized. "A place whose citizens have their choice in voting for Mayor between three such interesting and accomplished men," declared *The Sun*, "is justified in thinking no small beer of itself." Abram Hewitt was a prominent businessman, Henry George a brilliant writer and gifted orator. Theodore Roosevelt, meanwhile, was "a painstaking historian, a spirited and indomitable politician, a mighty hunter, and [crucially] the handsomest man of the three." He was also a person of extraordinary charisma and energy, who instantly became the center of any room. Those who met him often commented on the effect of a mere handshake; in the words of biographer Edmund Morris, "a lightning moment of contact [was] enough to transmit the full voltage of his charm."[1]

Sadly for Roosevelt, even his preternatural charm couldn't deliver him a victory in the race of 1886. Though he received a rousing reception from Republicans gathered at Cooper Union on October 27, on the night of his twenty-eighth birthday, he privately harbored doubts about his chances. In the end, large numbers of wealthy Republicans ended up voting for the Democrats, a phenomenon resentfully dubbed "the brownstone defection" by *The New York Times*. The *Tribune* was even more blunt, laying Roosevelt's defeat at the door of "Republicans who were frightened into voting for [Hewitt] through fear of George." It was a humiliating loss for Roosevelt, but as historians Burrows and Wallace dryly observed, "he would be heard from again."[2]

The plot against Roosevelt's life featured in this story is pure fiction, though he was the target of an assassination attempt years later, in 1912, when he was shot in the chest outside a hotel in Milwaukee. The bullet passed through a thick wad of pages in Roosevelt's breast pocket—his speech, which probably saved his life. In classic TR style, he insisted on delivering his remarks before being taken to the hospital.

Nikola Tesla found himself between jobs in 1886, following his now-famous falling-out with Thomas Edison. Soon after, of course, he would become one of the most celebrated inventors of his day. His genius was rivaled only by his neuroses, which in-

---

1. Morris, Edmund, *The Rise of Theodore Roosevelt*, Random House, New York, 1979.

2. Burrows, Edwin G. and Mike Wallace; *Gotham: A History of New York City to 1898*, Oxford University Press, New York, 1999.

cluded a bizarre affection for pigeons, the compulsion to calcu-
late the cubic contents of his dinner, and an obsession with
numbers divisible by three. Tesla also claimed to have abnormally
acute senses, which often caused him great discomfort. He could
allegedly hear a watch ticking from three rooms away, and a thun-
derclap from 550 miles. At one point, he claimed, he had "the sense
of a bat and could detect the presence of an object at a distance of
twelve feet by a peculiar creepy sensation on the forehead." Even
so, he never hesitated to handle hundreds of thousands of volts of
electricity, even if it would occasionally cause his flesh and clothing to glow. Spectators were routinely dazzled. Take, for example, the awestruck report of one journalist in 1899, visiting Tesla's
lab with Mark Twain:

> Fancy yourself seated in a large, well-lighted room, with
> mountains of curious-looking machinery on all sides.
> A tall, thin young man walks up to you, and by merely
> snapping his fingers creates instantaneously a ball of
> leaping red flame, and holds it calmly in his hands. As
> you gaze you are surprised to see it does not burn his
> fingers. He lets it fall upon his clothing, on his hair,
> into your lap, and, finally, puts the ball of flame into a
> wooden box. You are amazed to see that nowhere does
> the flame leave the slightest trace, and you rub your eyes
> to make sure you are not asleep.

Tesla did not, to my knowledge, name the flame ball Scarlett, which seems a shame.

Small wonder Mark Twain found Tesla so fascinating, and
could often be found in his lab. I was unable to verify the date
of their first meeting, but it was probably sometime after 1886.

(Both men being notoriously apocryphal in their accounts, it's hard to be sure.) Mark Twain was intrigued by unexplained phenomena, especially the idea that minds could communicate with one another in what he termed *mental telegraphy*. Such was his interest that he joined the American Society for Psychical Research.

By 1886, Inspector Thomas F. Byrnes was a larger-than-life figure in the New York City Police Department, a man who seems to have been feared and respected in equal measure. Infamous for his brutal interrogation techniques, which he referred to as "the third degree," he was also known for his "rogues' gallery" (a term originally coined by Allan Pinkerton), a compilation of photos of known criminals, and the Mulberry Street Morning Parade, a precursor to the modern police lineup. Byrnes allegedly amassed a personal fortune of more than $350,000—impressive for a man whose annual salary was somewhere in the realm of $2,000 to $5,000 (sources differ). Rumors of corruption swirled around him for years, until eventually he was forced to resign by a reform-minded police commissioner, one Theodore Roosevelt.

The Noble and Holy Order of the Knights of Labor was at one point the largest and most important labor organization in the United States, boasting a membership of some 800,000 (of whom Henry George, writer and mayoral candidate, was one). Though the Knights were quick to distance themselves from anarchists in the aftermath of the Haymarket Affair, in which an unknown person threw a dynamite bomb at police, their reputation was forever tarnished. Whispers that the bombing was actually the work of the Pinkerton Agency were never substantiated, and the rumor was rejected by several high-profile anarchists, including Johann Most.

Rose's experience at Bellevue Hospital is loosely based on

the account of Nellie Bly, a reporter for the *New York World* who famously went undercover and had herself committed at the insane asylum on Blackwell's Island in 1887. Her harrowing reports in the *World* shocked readers nationwide, and are credited with spurring much-needed reforms at that institution. *Ten Days in a Mad-House,* a compilation of those stories, is available online.

Writing about the Gilded Age—and especially an election in which glaring inequality, corporate oligarchy, and the rise of populism were front and center—it's impossible not to see parallels with our current political climate. It took decades of progressive reforms to begin addressing the major challenges of the day, beginning with the breakup of industrial monopolies like J. P. Morgan's Northern Securities and John D. Rockefeller's Standard Oil.

The politician credited with leading that reformist charge was, of course, Theodore Roosevelt.

Calgary, Canada
April 2018

The New York Times
October 29, 1886

ROOSEVELT'S STEADY GAIN

The Good Effect of the Cooper Union Meeting

THE CERTAINTY OF HIS ELECTION BECOMING MORE AND MORE APPARENT AS HIS CANVASS GOES ON.

Neither the bustle and noise attending the dedication of the statue of Liberty nor the nasty weather that prevailed yesterday seemed in any way to interfere with the onward progress of Theodore Roosevelt toward the Mayor's office. Every day the certainty of his election grows more and more apparent, and the specious appeals and theorizings of Mr. Hewitt's friends, made with agonizing earnestness, are of no avail in stemming the tide which has set in so strongly in Mr. Roosevelt's favor.

The wonderfully enthusiastic meeting at the Cooper Institute on Wednesday evening had a very marked effect yesterday among business men, some of whom had been hesitating to see what their neighbors' opinions were concerning the drift of public sentiment as to which was, not the better of the two leading candidates, for there was and has been no question as to that, but the stronger of the two. Those who were in attendance knew it was a meeting whose hearty earnestness has not been excelled at any political meeting held in New-York in years.

A fine crayon portrait of Mr. Roosevelt, handsomely framed, was hung in the County Committee headquarters, at the Fifth-Avenue Hotel, yesterday. A large number of lithographs made from this portrait have been made for distribution throughout the city, several thousands having been sent out yesterday.

At 10 o'clock this morning merchants engaged in the butter, cheese, and egg trade will meet at the hotel to make arrangements for participating in the parade and business men's meeting to be held to-morrow afternoon. Colored voters throughout the city are doing some excellent work for Mr. Roosevelt. They are thoroughly organized in the Ninth, Thirteenth, and Eleventh Districts, and will see that all colored men who are registered cast their votes next Tuesday, and are not deprived of this right by any Democratic machinations.

Mr. Roosevelt will have a busy time to-day. After receiving all day at his headquarters in the Fifth-Avenue Hotel, he will make five speeches during the evening. Republican ratification and jollification meetings will also be held this evening in the First District, at which excellent speakers will be present; under the auspices of the Union-Square Roosevelt Club, and at No. 105 Clinton-place, where the independent voters of the district will have a grand rally and listen to a number of excellent speakers. The Executive Committees of the Down-town Roosevelt Club and the Dry Goods Roosevelt Club will have a meeting at No. 47 Broadway this afternoon.

Mr. Hewitt's literary bureau is still actively at work trying to give the public an idea that working-men find something or other in the Democratic ticket and its candidates to indorse. Last evening there was sent from that bureau to all the morning papers a report that a meeting had been held "by members of Knights of Labor assemblies and trade unions." The bureau also kindly sends out a set of resolutions adopted unanimously in which the order to parade is denounced as well as the candidacy of Mr. George. That this whole scheme is a very cheap trick on the part of the Democratic leaders is shown by their own report. The resolutions refer to General Master Workman Terence V. Powderly as "our Grand Master," a title which all Knights of Labor know does not belong to Mr. Powderly. Mr. Hewitt should put another and shrewder hand at the work of manufacturing bogus labor news, if possible one who knows something about labor organizations.

New-York Tribune
October 29, 1886

WORLD-LIGHTING LIBERTY

The Bartholdi Statue Unveiled

COMPLETION OF THE GREAT WORK ON BEDLOW'S ISLAND—THE PARADES AND CEREMONIES INTERFERED WITH BY RAIN AND FOG—A GREAT DAY FOR BARTHOLDI AND FOR THE TWO REPUBLICS—THE LAND PARADE SUCCESSFUL IN SPITE OF OBSTACLES—VESSELS ON THE WATER LOST IN MIST—EXERCISES ON BEDLOW'S ISLAND—ADDRESSES BY SENATOR EVARTS AND MR. DEPEW—THE TORCH NOT LIGHTED

Only the luckless weather yesterday robbed New-York of one of those brilliant spectacles which come now and then with great national celebrations and leave a dazzling memory of pomp and circumstance for years to come behind them. As it was, the promises of clearing skies which the Signal Service men had tantalizingly sent out were broken one by one to the most patient hope, and the day dragged along from one ceremony to another in a disgusting mess of rain and fog, which lightened now to a misty drizzle or thickened afterward to a steady pour.

The huge land parade formed off Fifth Avenue in the wet and marched along the slippery, muddy streets with dripping ranks and ragged edges. The Presidential party and the French delegates stood shivering for hours on the unsheltered reviewing platform and looked drearily forward to the moment when the long procession would pass. The naval column in the North River was hid almost from the start in fog and mist. No traces of the great marine spectacle which a fair day had promised were to be seen from the Battery or the Brooklyn Bridge.

At the island itself a raw east wind swept the open ramparts of old Fort Wood and the soft drizzling rain fell in slanting sheets on the crowd huddled closely in the grand stand under the protecting shadow of the pedestal's foundations. Umbrellas and great coats were useless and the ceremonies were shortened unexpectedly, but, perhaps, to the relief of many, by a mistake of signals for the unveiling and the salute.

Yet in many ways the ceremonies of Bartholdi Day will always be memorable here. The land parade itself was 20,000 strong and though the rain fell incessantly on the slippery streets, the line showed scarcely a straggling or broken edge.

The crowds along the route, too, numbered hundreds of thousands, all filled with enthusiasm and reckless good will. Men and women pushed and trampled upon one another and the slushy mud was spattered right and left; yet good order was kept and fewer disturbances were reported to the police than on any other recent great celebration day.

Nothing, too, could quite overcome the impressiveness of the unveiling itself or the graceful flow of eloquence with which the splendid gift of the French people was finally turned over, after so many years of waiting, to the hands of the United States.

It was a great day for Bartholdi, who saw at last the fulfillment of that sculptor's fancy on which he has lavished so unselfishly the best ten years of his life. And if one may believe the poets and orators, or judge by the enthusiasm of the crowd, in distress and discomfort as it was when the stately figure of the huge, clear-lined, pure-faced Goddess was unveiled, it was a great day for Liberty, for America and for France.

Pearson's Magazine
May 1899

THE NEW WIZARD OF THE WEST

By Chauncy Montgomery M'Govern

AN INTERVIEW WITH TESLA, THE MODERN MIRACLE-WORKER, WHO IS HARNESSING THE RAYS OF THE SUN; HAS DISCOVERED WAYS OF TRANSMITTING POWER WITHOUT WIRES AND OF SEEING BY TELEPHONE; HAS INVENTED A MEANS OF EMPLOYING ELECTRICITY AS A FERTILISER; AND, FINALLY, IS ABLE TO MANU-FACTURE ARTIFICIAL DAYLIGHT.

Not to stagger on being shown through the laboratory of Nikola Tesla requires the possession of an uncommonly sturdy mind. No person can escape a feeling of giddiness when permitted to pass into this miracle-factory and contemplate for a moment the amazing feats which this young man can accomplish by the mere turning of a hand.

Fancy yourself seated in a large, well-lighted room, with mountains of curious-looking machinery on all sides. A tall, thin young man walks up to you, and by merely snapping his fingers creates instantaneously a ball of leaping red flame, and holds it calmly in his hands. As you gaze you are surprised to see it does not burn his fingers. He lets it fall upon his clothing, on his hair, into your lap, and, finally, puts the ball of flame into a wooden box. You are amazed to see that nowhere does the flame leave the slightest trace, and you rub your eyes to make sure you are not asleep.

The odd flame having been extinguished as miraculously as it appeared, the tall, thin young man next signals to his assistants to close up all the windows. When this has been done the room is as dark as a cave. A moment later you hear the young man say in the laboured accentuation of the foreigner: "Now, my friends, I will make for you some daylight." Quick as a flash the whole laboratory is filled with a strange light as beautiful as that of the moon, but as strong as that of old Sol. As you glance up at the closed shutters on each window, you see that each of them is as tight as a vice, and that no rays are coming through them. Cast your eyes wherever you will you can see no trace of the source of the odd light.

Scarcely have you begun to marvel when the light goes out by a touch on a button by the young man's hand. The room is in darkness again until the same laboured accentuation causes the reopening of all the shutters. Some animal is now brought out from a cage, it is tied to a platform, an electric current is applied to its body and in a second the animal is dead. The tall young man calls your attention to the fact that the indicator registers only one thousand volts, and the dead animal being removed, he jumps upon the platform himself, and his assistants apply the same current to the dismay of the spectators.

You feel a creeping sensation course up your back, and you see the indicator slowly mounting up to nine hundred, and then one thousand volts, and you involuntarily close your eyes, expecting the young man to fall dead before you the very next minute. But he does not budge. Quickly the indicator goes up, up, up, until presently it shows that ten thousand volts, then two million volts of electricity are pouring through the frame of the tall young man, who does not move a muscle.

At a sign, the current is stopped, the room is again made dark as night, and presently the visitor sees the sharply-defined black silhouette of the young man, with a beautiful halo of electricity in the background, formed by myriads of tongues of electric flame which are darting out from every quarter of the tall, thin frame.

To tell of these and a thousand other wonders that Tesla does in a trice gives only a faint conception of their effect on the visitor. To really appreciate them one must see, hear, and feel them in the flesh. It is a scientific treat of a lifetime, but it is a treat that few can enjoy, for the laboratory of Tesla is securely locked against everyone not provided with an introduction from a personal friend of the audacious wizard.

ABOUT THE AUTHOR

ERIN LINDSEY has lived and worked in dozens of countries around the world, but has only ever called two places home: her native city of Calgary and her adopted hometown of New York. In addition to the Rose Gallagher mysteries, she is the author of the Bloodbound series of fantasy novels from Ace. She divides her time between Calgary and Brooklyn with her husband and a pair of half-domesticated cats. Visit her online at erin-lindsey.com, facebook.com/ELTettensor, and twitter.com/ETettensor.